monsoonbooks

SINGAPORE SLING SHOT

New Zealand-based author Andrew Grant
to Singapore, where he has appeared on television and radio. A keen cook, pistol shooter and dedicated fisherman and hunter, he has trained in boxing and the martial arts. Grant has had a wide variety of occupations over the years, including being a professional hunter, bodyguard and merchant seaman. In 1993, following a long career in radio, where he won many prestigious awards for his radio commercials, he turned to writing full time. The author of twelve books, this is Grant's second Daniel Swann thriller set in Asia.

Other Daniel Swann thrillers by Andrew Grant

Death in the Kingdom

ANDREW
GRANT

SINGAPORE SLING SHOT

monsoon

monsoonbooks

Published in 2009
by Monsoon Books Pte Ltd
52 Telok Blangah Road, #03-05 Telok Blangah House
Singapore 098829
www.monsoonbooks.com.sg

ISBN:978-981-05-9225-7

This is a work of fiction. Some locations, many objects and all of the people depicted, with the exception of historical characters, are figments of the writer's imagination.

National Library Board Singapore Cataloguing in Publication Data
Grant, Andrew, 1956-
Singapore sling shot / Andrew Grant. – Singapore : Monsoon Books, 2009.
p. cm.
ISBN-13 : 978-981-05-9225-7

1. Murder – Fiction. 2. Singapore – Fiction. I. Title.

PR9639.4
828.9933 -- dc22 SLS2008013261

Printed in Singapore
12 11 10 09 1 2 3 4 5 6 7 8 9

Dedicated to Carol

When seasoned warriors face those less experienced, their greater experience will enable them to prevail and conquer, no matter that their numbers are less—providing they are true to their warrior code.

Tseu Teng

Prologue

Stanley Loh is running for his life. He is sixty-five years old. The desperate jump he made from the hotel patio into the surrounding jungle ended in a heavy landing. With a badly bruised hip, he bites back on his agony and scrambles through the tangled, thorny undergrowth to the beach road. Here he runs, but the injury, combined with his age and the onset of an asthma attack, is making movement extremely difficult for the fleeing man.

Loh lurches along the road in an ungainly, shambling, hobbling motion, trying to overcome the pain in his hip and to fight the giant burning fist that is gripping his chest. He is wheezing like a man being slowly strangled.

He looks back over his shoulder. Three men emerge from the shadows of the scaffolding that shrouds the front of the Silver Sands Hotel. They run out into the sunlight, pause, see their quarry two hundred metres away along the tram road and start after him.

The men are young, fit and armed. Just a few moments before they had been waving their guns at Loh. Now the weapons are hidden under their clothing, but their threat is just as real.

The trio begin to close in on their prey. Running like hounds chasing down an injured stag, they are gaining on Loh. Gasping with pain and struggling for breath, the injured man hobbles on.

Clutched in Stanley Loh's left hand is the object that the hunters desperately want. It is a small digital recorder, little more than a simple electronic toy. However, the value of what is contained on the device can be measured in billions of dollars. Its true significance is that the information captured in its digital heart will either establish the dominance, or the downfall, of the master of the hounds who are relentlessly running down their quarry.

1

The fleeing man had been duped into coming to the hotel alone, and for that he accepted he was totally to blame for what happened. He knew he should have expected a trap. The others, his business associates, were supposed to have been there for a group meeting. They weren't. He should have realised they had not come to the meeting. Their customary fleet of chauffeur-driven limousines had not been lined up in the hotel car park. Loh had missed the implication of their absence and he was now paying the price.

When he had driven in to the hotel car park there had been no vehicles parked but for a solitary dark-coloured panel van and the gold Bentley, the car he well knew belonged to Thomas Lu—the man who would have him killed.

Under renovation, the hotel had been deserted when Loh entered. Deserted but for Thomas Lu, his three henchmen and their guns.

Lu had offered Stanley Loh a deal, but it was the one deal that he could never accept. The deal was not his to make, and by not accepting it, he effectively signed his own death warrant.

Loh's refusal had been signalled by his desperate attempt to escape from Lu and his henchmen by crashing through a patio door and throwing himself into the jungle that pressed in around the hotel.

Now Loh was cut off from his car. Unlike his missing business associates, Loh had driven himself, and because of this, he had no chauffeur or bodyguard to come to his aid.

The Mercedes, which was still sitting in the hotel car park, had a Terbutaline inhaler in the glove compartment. His other inhaler, the one he habitually carried with him at all times, was in the briefcase he had abandoned in the hotel when he had taken flight.

Stanley Loh needed help, but more than that he needed to hide the recorder that he was still clutching in his left hand. What it contained was the one thing that could wreck Thomas Lu's grand plan.

The fleeing man knew full well that with him dead and the recorder safely in his hands, Lu would most assuredly win the billion-dollar game that was being played out.

It was mid-morning on this grey Singapore day. It was Wednesday, and it was raining. Siloso Beach to Loh's left was deserted, but as he ran down the tram road, he could see people ahead. They were above him, milling about on the concourse beyond the Delifrance café. A tour bus was offloading umbrella and camera-wielding tourists. These dazed human sheep were gathering in a loose group waiting to be marshalled by their tour guide.

Loh gasped his way up the steps and pushed through the crowd. The desperate man guessed the tourists were Taiwanese. Loh spoke both Hokkien and Mandarin and he knew he could ask them for help in a language they would understand. But what help could they offer? They were far from their homeland and would be confused by any such request from a panting, wheezing, limping stranger. This was neither their fight nor their flight. It was solely Stanley Loh's.

Loh stumbled on across the wide asphalt plaza. There were no taxis waiting and a red-line bus was just pulling away from the bus bay. There were people ahead and to Loh's right. Many were moving towards the aquarium complex, while several others boarded the tram for the Fort Siloso tour. Two hotel security staff were standing at the entrance to the driveway of the Rasa Sentosa Resort. Could he find shelter in the resort? Could he make it that far? Loh's breathing was becoming more and more difficult and his panic was building.

The Siloso tram was about to depart. It was only half-full. The driver looked at Loh as he boarded the small vehicle, unsure whether or not he was part of the pre-ticketed tour party already onboard. He turned towards the tour guide, seeking confirmation, but the guide was in conversation with one of her charges. The driver shrugged. They would sort out the ticket, or lack of it, later. He had a schedule to keep.

Loh slumped into a seat and the driver pulled away. The stricken man's breathing was worsening and several of the passengers were staring anxiously at him. Turning in his seat, Loh saw the three young men burst through the crowd of Taiwanese tourists who were still milling about beside their coach. The trio stopped running. They stood, eyes darting around the concourse as they tried to catch sight of their quarry. Loh hunched down into his seat, but he knew he was too late. He cursed silently, sobbing for breath. One of the gunmen was looking directly at him.

The tram wasn't moving fast, but it drew away as the three gunmen regrouped for a moment of quick conversation. One turned and raced back towards the beach while the other pair started to jog after the departing vehicle.

The tram paused for a moment at the pick-up point inside the fort gate and several more tourists boarded along with a fort guide. Loh sat trying to breathe, willing the driver to get them moving. Eventually the little tram pulled away again.

Loh watched as the two following gunmen passed the entrance to the resort. They stopped at the ticket kiosk. Because there were several other guides manning the pick-up station inside the main gate, the pair would need to buy tickets from the kiosk or risk a scene.

Stanley Loh's reasoning proved correct. He saw one of his pursuers reaching into a trouser pocket as the tram purred on up the driveway. He lost sight of the gunmen as the vehicle rounded a corner. The sound of martial music being pumped from the fort's sound systems filled the air.

Loh had been to Fort Siloso many times in the past; including a sponsorship function only a matter of weeks previously. Over the preceding decade and a half he had also been there with his children. He remembered the place well. Even as his breathing became more and more distressed, his panic, fuelled by the asthma's relentless attack more than the pursuit itself, was rising. He knew he had to work out a survival strategy. He had to hide the recorder and then contact his brother and tell him what was happening.

Loh reached for his cellphone as the tram passed the guardhouse into the fort proper. He would call his brother.

The Nokia was broken. The casing was split and the screen

blank. The stricken man cursed aloud as he pushed the ruined device into his pocket. When he'd jumped, the phone had been in its sheath on his belt at his right hip. It had taken much of the impact when he'd hit the ground. Now it is useless.

The tram reached the first plateau and pulled up in front of the long, two-level building that Loh knew held the souvenir shop on the ground floor and the surrender rooms above. Suddenly he had an idea where he could hide the recorder.

The stop at The QuarterMaster Store, as the souvenir shop was known, had been to pick up another guide. Now Loh stood up and brushed past the guide as she came aboard.

"Toilet," he managed to blurt out as he stepped down. The guide pointed down the slope to a building set below the plateau. Loh knew very well where the toilets were, but he had no intention of going in that direction. He waved the driver on.

The tram started off again, heading on up into the fort complex. Loh turned to look back the way he had come. The two remaining gunmen were jogging into view on the driveway below. They were almost at the guardhouse and they had seen their quarry. Like the hounds they were emulating, they increased their pace. There was no sound of baying; rather the sound of bugles and drums fill the air above the rasping of Stanley Loh's breath.

Loh started for the steps to the left of The QuarterMaster Store. These stairs he knew led to the surrender rooms. Gasping as his asthma continued to tighten its terrible grip on him, Stanley Loh staggered up the stairs. This was the exit from the surrender rooms. He didn't care. As he stumbled into the foyer, he hoped that there was no one in the nearest chamber.

The sliding door into the long surrender room stood open. Loh knew that this room was a replica of those used in WWII. Beyond it was a much smaller room where the Allies had surrendered to the Japanese signalling the fall of Singapore.

In the long room mannequins of uniformed soldiers and sailors stood against the walls. Seated at long tables on either side of the central walkway were figures of the surrendering Japanese and their Allied victors. Some were signing or studying the surrender documents, others were just sitting staring blankly at nothing.

The wax figures, although crude, created a powerful aura. But Loh wasn't interested in the historic significance of the tableaux laid out in front of him. There was no living person in this room other than himself. He could hear voices in the room beyond, above the sound of the recorded commentary.

He stumbled on, gasping like a broken steam engine. He was still clutching the tiny digital recorder in his left hand. The device was a little larger than a cigarette lighter. He stopped. Now he could see what he was looking for—the perfect hiding place. Loh moved forward, pressing against the wooden railing. He stretched desperately to reach his goal.

As he leaned across the railing to secrete the tiny silver device amongst the frozen figures of the tableaux, a buzzer sounded. He had broken an invisible sensor beam and triggered the alarm. Desperately, Stanley Loh stilled his gasping for a moment and by leaning as far as he could without falling over the thigh-high railing, he managed to slip the recorder into the hiding place he had selected.

Satisfied that the recorder couldn't be seen, at least by any casual observer, Loh withdrew and the buzzer immediately stopped sounding. But now he wanted the alarm to sound. He needed to summon help. His asthma attack would kill him if he didn't get aid, and soon. He also needed people around him as protection against Lu's thugs.

Loh collapsed to his knees and leaned against the railing, his arms dangling inside it. He had intentionally broken the invisible beam again and the buzzer sounded.

The guide escorting a party of tourists through the first of the surrender rooms came rushing into the long room in response to the reactivated buzzer alarm. She saw the gasping man sprawled across the railing.

"Sir?" the young girl called urgently. "Sir, are you all right?" The guide tentatively touched Loh's shoulder and he slowly turned, letting his arms fall to his sides. He had done it; hidden the recorder and gained the attention he so desperately needed.

"Asthma," he managed to gasp. "Doctor!" Stanley Loh was now

sitting on the floor, his back against the display's railing. The girl ran for the exit door to find a telephone in the shop below. As she left, the two pursuing gunmen entered the chamber. They stopped when they saw Stanley Loh sitting on the floor at the far end of the room. There were people gathering near the stricken man. The tour group had followed their guide through from the other room to see what had been causing the commotion.

One of the gunmen made a decision. He rushed towards Loh and squatted beside him. Loh, barely conscious now, felt the man's hands searching his pockets. To an observer it would have seemed that the man was perhaps a colleague of the stricken man and that he was searching for Loh's inhaler, because the distressed wheezing indicated that an asthma attack was in full flight. With a grunt of triumph, the gunman removed the cellphone from Loh's pocket. His momentary triumph turned into a snarl of frustration when he realised that he was holding a ruined cellphone and not the digital recorder. He dropped the remains of the Nokia onto Loh's thighs and stood.

Loh was conscious enough to see the cold, hateful look in the man's eyes. He knew that without the presence of the tourists, the gunman would be breaking his fingers or worse.

"I'm a doctor, let me see him!" The voice belonged to a tall, overweight European in long, voluminous khaki shorts. From his position on the floor Loh noticed, almost distractedly, that the man's legs were fat, white and very hairy. The man knelt beside Loh. There was a wide-brimmed hat and a startlingly red, bushy moustache. The face was sunburnt but the eyes, behind their rimless glasses, were kind. "Asthma attack?"

Loh nodded. The accent he recognised as Australian. The gunman, still standing nearby, reluctantly moved away.

"No inhaler on you?"

The stricken man managed to shake his head.

"Fortunately, or rather unfortunately, my wife is asthmatic," the doctor said. He held out a large hand and the woman standing behind him, plump and bleached-blonde, also wearing baggy shorts, rummaged in her large shoulder bag. She found an object and put it into the doctor's hand.

"Terbutaline, is this what you take?" The doctor held the puffer for his newest patient to see. Loh nodded and reached for the inhaler. He took it from the doctor's palm and gratefully sucked the life-saving drug into his lungs. He wanted more, but the doctor gently took the inhaler back. "No, that will allow you to get to hospital. Technically what I've just done is illegal," he said as he straightened. "However, sometimes we need to break the law to save lives."

"Thank you," Loh said. As the doctor stood, he could see that the gunman who'd searched him had withdrawn only as far as the end of the room. There he was standing with his accomplice, waiting, watching. The guide who had run downstairs to call for help pushed past them and came rushing back to where Loh was sitting.

"The ambulance is on its way," she said.

Stanley Loh nodded his thanks and closed his eyes. Even if he had the energy to move, he couldn't retrieve the recorder with all the people present, particularly Lu's henchmen. He would go to hospital and get control of his asthma. Later he could arrange to return to collect it and present it to his associates. Before that, however, he would call his brother in Bangkok from the hospital and tell him everything that had taken place. Stanley Loh was his brother's emissary in Singapore. He was the smiling public face for a man who preferred to remain in the shadows.

Standing on the terrace outside The QuarterMaster Store, Lu's gunmen, along with a handful of tourists and fort staff, watched as the ambulance attendants loaded Loh into their vehicle. A few seconds later, as it roared away under flashing sirens and lights, the pair made their way back to the larger of the surrender rooms. They knew the recorder was hidden somewhere in the long room and they intended to retrieve it if they could.

Luck was against them. The constant stream of visitors through the surrender rooms didn't allow the gunmen to do anything other than stand helplessly behind the barriers and vainly try to guess where the recorder might be hidden. To find it, they knew they would have to get into the display area and rummage through it, a section at a time.

Eventually, the guides started to become suspicious of the pair's continued presence. Lu's two thugs left the fort. One kept watch at the main entrance while the other returned to the hotel to face the wrath of their master.

2

In Singapore General Hospital, Stanley Loh was given sedatives and steroids which gradually got his asthma under control. Despite the admonishment from the attending physician, he managed to get a telephone brought to his bed. He made the call to his brother, but encountered only the computerised voice of the answer service. Loh quickly detailed everything that had happened.

At a few minutes to four that afternoon, Stanley Loh left Singapore General Hospital by taxi. Still under the influence of strong sedatives, he was not tempted to return to Sentosa to attempt to retrieve his car. He would have someone do that for him.

On the ride back to his home on Goodwood Hill, Loh went over the events of the day and those leading up to it. The one fact that kept coming back to him, and the one he silently cursed himself for, was that he knew he should have seen it coming. The final attempt at bribery and the attempt on his life. Perhaps if Thomas Lu had not seen the recording device, he may have managed to stall his answer and perhaps even walk free from the hotel. However, once Lu had seen the recorder, knowing full well what was on it, there was no way that he, Stanley Loh, would be able to leave the deserted hotel alive—other than by doing what he had done and thrown himself off the patio.

At the ornate iron gate leading into his house, Loh paid the cab driver, giving him a generous tip. As the taxi pulled away, he fumbled to key in the gate's digital combination. Normally, when he was in one of his three cars, a remote sensor opened the gate as the vehicle approached it.

The van was parked thirty metres down the road. The vehicle was dark in colour and almost invisible in the shade of the late afternoon sun and the dense jungle fringe.

Whether it was the sedatives still at work in his system, combined with his distraction at trying to recall his gate combination, or not, Stanley Loh did not register the alien vehicle. He did not recognise it as the same van that had been parked in the Silver Sands Hotel car park.

On legs that were still a little unsteady, and with the grinding pain in his right hip, dulled only slightly by the painkillers he had been given, Stanley Loh walked through the double gate. The heavy metal leaves automatically clanged shut behind him as he started down the driveway.

The wide asphalt vehicle access curved away down the gentle slope to the four-car garage set between the house and the servant's quarters beyond. Rather than follow the driveway, Loh chose the more direct route. He started down the path that ran through the beautifully tended shrubs and flowers of the formal garden.

He was part way down the concrete path when he saw the boot lying in a bed of flowers. Loh frowned. The boot was made of green rubber. It was the sort of boot that his gardener Cheah Kah Hin usually wore. Moving further down the pathway, he then saw Cheah. The old man, with one foot bare and one wearing a green rubber boot, was lying on his back behind a small hedge.

Loh's first thought was that perhaps his gardener had succumbed to a heart attack. But as he stooped stiffly over the body, he saw a trickle of blood that had escaped from the black hole between the old man's eyes. He knew this had been no heart attack.

"Of course it's not a heart attack," Loh snarled to himself as he desperately tried to shake off the drug-induced fog he had been wallowing in. "My family!" He said aloud as he started towards the house at a run. His tired and painful limbs were uncoordinated from the strong sedatives and further unbalanced by the pure terror that had begun to well up inside him.

Loh was almost at the steps leading to the patio when he heard a noise. It was not something he could identify. There were four distinct sounds, spaced a fraction of a second apart. They were loud but at the same time they were muffled and indistinct. Loh shook his head in denial. No matter what caused the unfamiliar noise, he knew he must see to his family.

Stanley Loh crossed the patio and pressed his face against the glass of the French doors. He shaded the window with his hand so he could see into the room beyond. Helen, his wife, was sitting on one of the couches. Beside her was Arthur, their son, and next to Arthur sat Amy, their daughter. All three of them had their mouths covered by shiny silver tape. Their hands and feet were also taped.

There was a noise to Loh's left. A man was coming onto the terrace walking from the direction of the staff bungalow. This was one of the pair from the surrender room. This was the man who had searched him. The man with the cold eyes!

The gunman was carrying an automatic pistol and attached to the barrel was a long fat tube. Stanley Loh had seen similar guns in dozens of movies. Drugged state or not, he knew its purpose and he knew now what had caused the muffled sounds he had just heard. Along with Cheah, the gardener, there were four other staff living on the estate. They were, in all probability, dead, Loh knew this without a doubt. To kill one or five, it made no difference to men like this.

The gunman saw Loh standing at the French doors. He smiled and raised his gun as the door opened. Stanley Loh had been expected.

The man in the doorway was Thomas Lu.

Tall for a Singaporean, Lu was also skeletally thin. As always, including when he and Loh had met just hours before, he was dressed in his uniform, comprising a sober black suit with a crisp white shirt and a dark tie. With his artificially darkened hair worn overlong at the back, and with his high cheekbones, Lu, who at all times kept his eyes hidden behind dark-tinted glasses, was known in Singapore business circles as The Undertaker. He had a reputation for sheer ruthlessness, but until today that ruthlessness had been more by reputation than reality to Stanley Loh. Now he was about to live or die by that reality.

"So pleased you could drop in, Stanley," Lu said as he stepped aside to allow his gunman to usher Loh into his own home. The eyes of the three people most dear to Stanley Loh were wide and totally terrified. The eyes silently implored him to save them. But Loh knew he would die here with them. He had no doubt that would be the way it was going to happen.

"Now, Stanley, you know what I need. Tell me where to find it and you and your family can live happily ever after." Lu smiled as he spoke. However, the smile carried no warmth whatsoever. Loh knew that the eyes behind the dark glasses were as cold as the ice that was sliding down his spine.

What Thomas Lu didn't know was that Loh, having discovered the corpse of his gardener and heard the sounds of the other members of his staff being killed, knew that no matter what, he and his family would be killed. There was simply no way that Lu could let them live. Not now. The stakes were simply too big and blood had already been spilt.

Loh knew he had one chance and one chance only to save his family. The gunman who had escorted him into the room was standing to his right, his weapon pointed at his captive's belly. Lu was also holding an automatic loosely in his right hand. Its muzzle was directed at the richly polished parquet floor. There was a second gunman standing at the far end of the couch on which the Loh family were sitting. This man's automatic was pointed at Helen.

"I ..." Loh stuttered. He swayed unsteadily on his feet, acting now. "I'll tell you, please, just don't hurt them." Lu smiled in response as he watched the seemingly dazed and stricken man cave in. The Undertaker knew he had won and began to gloat.

The gunman nearest Loh relaxed slightly; the old man swaying in front of him was finished. The muzzle of his gun drifted away from its target.

The drugs in Stanley Loh's system had been washed away by the surge of adrenaline that now coursed through him. Seeing his family sitting there awaiting their inevitable execution had given him a strength far beyond his physical limits.

In his youth Loh had trained in kung fu. Now, as he staggered again, seemingly holding out a hand for support, he was the very picture of a man in great distress. The nearest gunman put out a hand to steady the stricken man. As he did so, Loh suddenly stepped into him. The hard heel of his left shoe ground into the gunman's instep as the sword edge of his left hand connected with the man's nose. Simultaneously, Loh's right hand tore the gun from the man's loosened grip.

Unfortunately, Stanley Loh was unfamiliar with firearms. He fumbled with the weapon, almost dropping it. The gunman standing at the end of the couch, however, was very familiar with the weapon he held. He switched his aim from Helen Loh to her husband's head.

The last thing Stanley Loh heard before eternal blackness claimed him was the sound of Thomas Lu screaming "No!"

3

"Daniel, I need you."

"Where and when?"

"Singapore, as soon as you can get there."

"Tomorrow morning."

"Use another identity. What's good?"

I had to think for a moment. I have a near photographic memory, which is a blessing at times and a curse at others, especially in the dark of a sleepless night when certain images come to haunt me.

"Edward Davidson, Australian. Old Ed hasn't seen the light of day for a year or two."

"I'm in Bangkok. It'll take me two days to get there. Be a tourist. There'll be a reservation at the Carlton under Davidson. Smoking or non-smoking?"

"Smoking."

"Still killing yourself by degrees, my old friend?"

"Yeah, I guess."

"Do the innocent tourist thing. Get a pair of those stupid shorts, a flowery shirt, a camera and a hat."

"Fucking thanks."

"Just don't draw any attention to yourself."

"Dressed like that people will think I'm Jo Jo the fucking clown," I grumbled. Sami almost chuckled.

"I'll see you in a day or so. By the way, get tomorrow's *Straits Times* and everything will become clear. Stanley Loh was my half-brother. Ciao!"

"Ciao!" I responded as the phone went dead.

You're probably wondering why I didn't ask Sami what it was all about. That's the thing in our relationship. Like the musketeers,

Sami Somsak and I are there for each other. We always have been and always will be. He needed me and that was all I needed to know. I put my bourbon glass down on the bedside cabinet and lay back against my pillows.

"Was that bad news, Daniel?"

The speaker is the beautiful Mai Ling. She has shared my bed off and on for the past two weeks. She is propped up on one elbow looking across at me with genuine concern in her eyes. Mai is a very genuine woman. That much I do know.

"I'm not sure," and I honestly wasn't. Was it bad news that my old friend needed me? Suddenly, for the first time in what seemed like weeks, months even, my brain was as clear as ice. It was a few minutes past one in the morning. Mai and I had enjoyed an evening of pubbing and a long romp in my ruined bed. Now it was time for another sort of action.

"I have to get ready to leave," I told her as I got out of bed and headed for the shower, leaving one very beautiful and slightly bewildered lady staring after me.

As I showered I wondered what had happened to Sami's half-brother. The half thing was just that, unimportant. Brother was the power word. The different name didn't phase me. I knew Sami's heritage. He was a combination of Chinese, Japanese and Thai and I knew he had relatives all over Asia. Stanley Loh was most obviously one of Sami's Chinese half-brothers. Sami's mother, Mary Song, was a Chinese-Thai, his father a Japanese officer. There had been no marriage. His mother had been one of the unfortunate comfort women put into sexual slavery by the Japanese. Fortunately, perhaps, Sami's father had become Mary Song's exclusive patron. He was executed after the war. Mary then married Chinese businessman Martin Loh, and had several more children by him.

So what had befallen Stanley Loh? No doubt I could dial up CNN or Asia News or go online to find out, but I wouldn't do that. I'd pick up *The Straits Times* when I got on the plane. I had no doubt that he had met a nasty end. Sami wouldn't have called me unless he wanted to use my particular skill set.

The thing is, as a nanny or a shrink I'm useless. Sami knows that only too well. He also knows that I can offer him only two things: my friendship and what is perhaps my singular talent. That talent is not particularly marketable in the world at large, however in the world Sami and I spent many years living in, and perhaps the world Sami still lives in, my skills are a currency in themselves.

If I had a CV, it would probably dwell on the fact that I have the unique ability to find people and kill them. I am a hunter. I'm trained to hunt people to the death, and that being the case, Sami probably wants me to kill someone. So be it!

Out of the shower, I stood dripping on the plush carpet as I used my laptop to book a flight to Singapore. Mai Ling was dressing. She knew a cue when it came her way, even when it was unspoken. I gave her cab money and made a promise that I'd call when I got back. I probably wouldn't call, and she probably wouldn't expect it. Our words were just farewell smoke. There are plenty of girls like Mai around Hong Kong, and variety, they say, is the 'spice of life'. Cynical? Yes, I am a cynic and that's, in part, why I am still alive. I doubt anything and everything. In my world there are no such things as coincidence and luck, good or bad. It just is or it isn't.

Maybe I won't survive Singapore. Of course, if my old friend and enemy Tuk Tuk Song dies in the meantime I may return to Thailand instead, and I may not ever come back to Hong Kong.

It is 02:30. My flight to Singapore is the early 07:10. Cathay bus. I try to find tourist clothes but my wardrobe doesn't extend that far. I'll shop when I hit town. It's about a four-hour flight on a good day, so I'll have plenty of time. I selected my Ed Davidson passport from the twenty or so in my under-floor safe. There is a current Amex in the same name. I add a back-up passport and a few thousand US dollars in cash and pack a small bag. Unfortunately I will be leaving my favourite hardware behind. My Walther P99 stays in the safe along with the several other weapons stored there. They included the .380 Beretta I took from Sir Bernard Sinclair after I killed him. Ah, the memories!

I got dressed and made coffee. No more alcohol, at least until I'd read the newspaper. I hadn't done much of anything physical for almost four months and it showed. I knew I was seriously out of shape and quite probably I was going to regret that. The life of the rich and indolent unfortunately overtook me in the aftermath of the Thai incident. Incident is a pretty ordinary word to describe a most extraordinary situation, I suppose, however it will do for now.

At 05:15. I was in a cab on my way to Chek Lap Kok Airport. Oh, by the way, my name is Daniel Swann. Pleased to meet you!

4

FAMILY AND STAFF EXECUTED,
SINGAPORE IN SHOCK

Singapore is in shock following the discovery late yesterday of nine bodies in the luxury Goodwood Hill residence of Singapore business entrepreneur Stanley Loh. Initial police reports indicate that all nine victims had been shot execution-style.

The dead have been formally identified as: Stanley Loh, 65, his wife Helen, 60, son Arthur, 27, daughter Amy, 25. Also found dead at the Loh's exclusive Goodwood Hill residence were staff members, identified as: Cheah Kah Hin, 78, Teoh Sui Lan, 77, Mary Yap, 47, her daughter Emily Yap, 26, and Michael Yee, 29.

The police have released no further details, but are appealing for information from the general public. Mr Loh was one of the principals behind the Intella Island Development, the proposed creation of a twelve-hectare artificial island to be constructed off Marina Bay. The US$6-billion development has been hailed as the most significant development of its kind ever seen in Singapore.

"Fuck!" I muttered laying the paper down. The stewardess was hovering. She pretended she hadn't heard me swear. She instead asked me if I wanted a drink. I wanted one, but it was 09:30 and judging from what I'd just read, I was going to need to keep a clear head. I declined and ordered breakfast instead. I'd have gone first class on this flight if I'd had the option, but there was no availability, so here

I was slumming it in business. My how times have changed. Once it was steerage. Now here I was complaining because I didn't have the option of first class. At least I had salmon with eggs Benedict. Not a bad breakfast at all! Thank you, Sir Bernard!

At Changi, I cleared the formalities and grabbed a cab for the Carlton. I've been to Singapore many times over the years, so it holds few mysteries for me. What I had to watch out for was that I'd rarely been there as Daniel Swann. Singapore immigration probably had a dozen versions of me on record, so it was important I do nothing to cause the authorities to want to have a closer look at me. The passport, incidentally, was a real one. It was just that Ed Davidson wasn't.

Compliments of The Firm, I had departed with a whole bunch of genuine identities, most of them not recorded on any official file. I can thank my former boss, the crafty Sir Bernard Sinclair, for that. He never let his left hand know what the right was doing and cunning was his middle name. In the end his own deviousness worked to my advantage and very much to his disadvantage and, ultimately, his messy death. Being a turncoat spymaster can be a tricky occupation at times, it seems.

I'd actually stayed at the Carlton in one of my many incarnations on a previous visit. The hotel is handy to everything and not too ostentatious. It's the sort of place that has a lot of tourists going through it rather than business people. From my observations, those on business with a company credit card on tap are inclined to go a little more upmarket. Whatever, the place suited me just fine.

No one greeted me by any name I had used previously. That was a positive start at least. My reservation was in the name of Edward Davidson of Perth. So Ed Davidson, Australian tourist, I was. For the moment at least.

Sami hadn't gone overboard on the accommodations. The room was large and comfortable. There was a sizeable bathroom. A bottle of JD was sitting on a side table awaiting me. There was also a small package wrapped in plain brown paper. The name Mr E Davidson was on the label. I tipped the porter after he did the usual flutter around. When he left I slipped the door security latch across and broke the seal on the bottle of bourbon.

It was 13.30 and the sun was definitely over the yardarm. I opened the package and found a pre-paid phone and a thick wad of big Singapore bills. There was a plain white card with a number on it. The number had a prefix of 66 2. Bangkok. I flicked the phone on and it found SingTel in seconds. I tapped out the number on the card. I only had a few seconds to wait.

"Daniel!"

"Daniel in da' house," I replied with my best Ali G impression. Sami managed a chuckle. "I read it," I added. "Some heavy shit going down."

"That's an understatement," Sami replied grimly. "In a nutshell, Stanley was taken out because he refused a deal regarding his share of the Intella Island development. My share, Daniel," Sami added bitterly. "I'll explain in full when I get there. In the meantime play at being a tourist. I have to go. I'll call you later and tell you what I need you to do. And thanks, old friend!"

"No need," I replied. We cut the connection at the same instant.

Intella Island was the talk of Asia. It was the development of the century, according to the various business publications I had come across.

The Intella Island project frequently appeared on Asian current affairs and news programmes with an elaborate and very realistic large-scale model as the main image. There were 3-D graphic presentations on a dedicated website and artist's impressions of the finished development had been all over the media for the past few months.

I figured that if Stanley Loh had been involved in Intella, that most probably meant Sami was as well. By the way, the name Intella derives from Intelligent Island. The whole thing was to be run by a giant super-computer, it seemed. Anyway, Stanley Loh was no longer in the loop, but maybe Sami was. Time would tell that story. In the meantime I needed tourist clothes and a camera, so I went shopping.

Downtown Singapore is easy walking. I strolled off up Bras Basah and Orchard Road towards Somerset and zeroed in on Centrepoint. I'd been there several times in the past and I knew it was tourist central with everything under one roof. Hey, I was a tourist after all.

First I hit Robinsons, which made most of its weekly wage bill off me. Then I found a camera outlet and bought a compact Sony digital. It had more pixels than I thought possible. I was paying cash for everything, eliminating any paper trail, at least until I wanted one.

The major problem about doing anything in Singapore is the constant CCTV surveillance. There are cameras everywhere and that was something I was going to have to give some thought to when it came time to doing whatever it was Sami had brought me here for.

Carrying several bags, I left Centrepoint and contemplated grabbing a cab. The lure of beer and food was, however, stronger than the desire to go back to the hotel just yet. I knew there was a row of bars and restaurants behind the complex, so I cut back and found Cuppage Terrace. Many of the restaurants were closed but there was a small pub at one end. The Cable Car, the signage said. It suited me fine. It was virtually deserted at this early hour. I sat outside and lit what was one of my first cigarettes of the day. I almost felt proud of myself.

The Tiger beer was cold and the Chinese restaurant next door did bar service. It was 15:50; the day that had started early several hundred kilometres away was still young. With a cold beer in hand and a full stomach, I decided to loiter awhile.

I was on my third glass when my new cellphone rang. It could only be one person.

"Sami?"

"Daniel. I'll be flying in late morning, day after tomorrow. I have to attend family business and then we can meet up. I'll call when I'm done. Okay?"

"Sure! Where are you staying?" I asked, thinking he also might book in to the Carlton.

"I've got an apartment in Cairnhill. Under any other circumstances I'd have you stay there but we need to keep some distance between us. I'll explain it all when we catch up." Sami sounded tired. I could hear him take a sip of something. He didn't drink alcohol, not even under extreme stress.

"You okay?"

"I'm okay, Daniel, thanks," he replied. "There will be a woman asking for you at the desk at half nine in the morning. Her name is Simone. She's your cover. She doesn't know the finer points of what we do, so don't tell her too much at this stage."

"Okay. So what exactly do you want me to do?"

"Go to Sentosa with Simone. Camera and all! Visit the fort and spend some time in the Japanese surrender room. Get to know the room well because you'll be going back. And watch for watchers because they'll be there. I'll call again when I work out my timing."

"Okay." I had no idea what the hell was going on, but I trusted Sami with my life, so I went with the flow.

"Enjoy your tour of the fort." Sami paused. "By the way, Simone used to work for Stanley. She'll play an airhead wife. She isn't an airhead."

"I'm pleased about that." I didn't fancy spending too much time with some dumb bimbo. Life's too short.

"Don't mention the significance of the surrender room."

"I don't know the significance of the fucking thing."

"You will. Take plenty of photographs, access, alarms, all of it. You did get a camera?"

"Sami!"

"Sorry. Of course you did. Do read the manual," he added with a strained chuckle, "and look at ways of getting in and out of the fort in the dark. I can tell you that Stanley was chased into the fort and almost died of an asthma attack. He hid something in the Japanese surrender room. It is something of vital importance. Afterwards he made it to hospital. He called me from there and got my cell secretary. The men hunting him went to his home and waited for him to show up. The rest you know. I must go. Take care!"

"Sami, what did he hide?"

I was too slow. Sami had broken the connection and was gone. I snorted. That was his way. I hadn't coined the name The Onion

Man for him for nothing. No matter what, he had given me enough information to begin my game. The rest would follow when he was ready.

I put the cell back into my jacket, lit a Marlboro and pondered those last words and Sami's momentary slip-up over the camera. It wasn't like him to doubt I'd do exactly as he asked. He knew me better than that. However, obviously there was a lot going on and he was running to keep up. No doubt the "family business" he would have to tend to on landing would include arrangements for the funeral for his brother's family and the others. That was enough to rattle anyone's cage.

Sami Somsak is one of the strongest people I know mentally, and the most enigmatic. I gave him the nickname The Onion Man many years ago. Basically, it was one way for me to acknowledge and explain the incredible complexity and multi-layered personality of my friend. To say Sami was deep was like saying that molten lava was warm. I finished my cigarette and my musing, had another swallow of beer and decided to check out the camera, just as Sami had suggested.

I fished the package containing the Sony out from amongst my shopping and spent the remainder of my pint and another figuring out how to work it. It was really dead easy. The camera was compact, but it had a 5X lens. I'd bought a one-gigabyte card. According to the brochure, I could shoot several thousand shots set on low to medium resolution with it. I set the dial up for five megapixels. That gave me several hundred images that could be pumped up large enough to see relatively fine detail as required.

Sami hadn't told me specifically what to photograph beyond the alarm system and general background. That being the case, I would simply concentrate on whatever was in the room in question, taking in any obvious security features and anything else I could identify. Outside I'd just do tourist stuff. I'd pose with my beautiful ersatz wife all over the place and photograph her with lots of background.

How did I know that Simone, my wife to be, would be beautiful? Well, Sami does beautiful with his women and I guess the same gene would have been at work in his half-brother. I sure hoped so.

The pub was filling up as I left. It would have been pleasant to have stayed and met up with a few of the locals, but I was on a mission and a hangover tomorrow was not factored into my plans. I found a cab a few metres down the street and headed back to the Carlton. Okay, it isn't far to walk, but I was loaded like a pack mule.

5

Simone DeLue was beautiful, just as I had anticipated and hoped she would be. Stanley and Sami definitely shared that same chromosome relating to good-looking women. Or at least they had done so. That's the thing about death. It takes a while for the brain to get to grips with the tenses.

When I came down from my room, she was waiting in the lounge off the main reception area. Like me, she was wearing long shorts. Hers did not look at all stupid on her. I wasn't sure if my shorts looked as stupid as I felt they did. I was, however, thankful that my months of indolence back in Hong Kong had included sitting or lying, albeit generally in a semi-comatose state, on my terrace or by the condo's pool. Therefore I had managed to maintain a decent tan that at least made my damn shorts bearable. There is nothing worse in my book than seeing lily-white, hairy sticks of spaghetti poking out of a pair of voluminous shorts. It's especially pathetic when the hairy spaghetti sticks end in what appear to be enormous oversized sneakers or boots. All an illusion, of course, because of the spaghetti legs combined with normal-sized feet. That always reminds me of Minnie Mouse cartoons or of Spike Milligan's drawings.

Simone's tan was the golden tan of the fair skinned, the colour of honey, while her hair was straw gold. There had to be some Scandinavian in her genetic mix. She was tall and looked very athletic. Her eyes, which tracked me as I came towards her, were clear and blue and very much alive. Sami had obviously described me, but the shorts were probably the giveaway.

In addition to the stupid shorts, both of us had on polo shirts; hers was lime green, mine was light blue. We were the damned Bobbsey Twins!

My outfit was completed by a wide-billed baseball cap bearing a BMW logo. It had been the least offensive of those I had been looking at. My striking companion didn't have a hat on. With her mass of blonde curls tied back by a green ribbon that wasn't an accidental match to her shirt, she didn't need any sun protection. We were both wearing dark glasses. Mine were on my hat, hers pushed into her hair.

I noticed that Simone's Nike trainers were not brand new. They'd seen some use. Judging by how trim her long body looked, she was into the gym or was a runner which, of course, probably accounted for the shoes. My own swooshes were straight out of the box. My usual footwear, my faithful boots, were in my wardrobe. Cowboy boots and shorts do not a match make. Not even for a hokum Aussie tourist.

Simone carried a camera slung over one shoulder and a leather bag over the other. I had the Sony in its case clipped to my belt. I'd added a sleeveless khaki vest over my shirt. My wallet, cigarettes and sundry other bits and pieces were all stowed in its many pockets. The vest was practical and, of course, it is just the sort of thing tourists like me seem to wear, especially in the tropics.

We made a show of greeting, and to a casual observer we were old friends or separated spouses meeting up. There were kisses and hugs. I must admit that I found it all most pleasant. Arm in arm we headed out front to snare a taxi.

Safely ensconced in the back of a blue Comfort cab en route to VivoCity and the Sentosa train, we dropped the charade momentarily.

"I feel like a right idiot," I said.

"You look like a typical tourist," came the reply. Simone's English was perfect with just the bare trace of an accent. Dutch or South African, I couldn't quite be sure. "Mr Somsak said you'd hate this bit." She was smiling. It was a nice smile.

"Yeah," I muttered. "He knows me too well. So, what's on the agenda?"

"We'll have breakfast at Vivo and get the monorail across to the island. No point in us going over there too early. Things don't open until ten or so."

"You've been there a lot?"

"Two kids. It's Singapore's playground," she replied. The faint, flat touch of bitterness in her voice belied her smile. "When it's the weekend or school holidays and the kids are restless and you're trapped in an apartment block and you're not filthy rich, you soon learn to love and hate the place."

The obvious questions reared their heads. Was she married? How long had she been here, etc, etc? I bit them back. This was a one-day gig. The less I knew the better, in all probability. She had other ideas.

"Sorry," she replied. "I'm divorced, two kids, girl, eleven, and a boy thirteen. I work for Stanley's company, administration, nothing more. I know the company is actually owned by Mr Somsak." Simone paused momentarily. "I have been in meetings with Mr Somsak and Stanley, so I know how things are. Were," she corrected herself and pushed away the obviously less-than-pleasant thought that momentarily clouded her expression. "This is a welcome change," she said, changing gear and putting on a patently false happy face. "I get the chance to play-act."

"As payment for your performance I'll be buying the best lunch we can find," I added, "following an absolutely disgustingly rich and unhealthy breakfast."

"Sounds good." This time Simone DeLue smiled as if she meant it. Maybe, work aside, this would be a nice day all round. And hey, my mind was definitely above my belt on this one, and while that's not a first, it's a pleasant change of pace for me. I was here to save Sami's arse, not get laid, pleasant as it would no doubt have been with my companion of the moment.

We had coffee and pastries on the balcony of a café at VivoCity. The view was of the busy harbour basin towards Sentosa. The amount of building work going on across that short stretch of water completely astounded me. Simone told me that a casino and God only knows what else was being built over there.

"How things have changed."

"How so?" Simone wanted to know.

"Not so long ago gambling was an absolute no-no here. Changing times, I suppose. The powers that be have decided to capitalise on the gambling revenue. Easy money for the coffers."

"I guess," she agreed as we stood and prepared to go to the fantasy land across the water.

Now I'd been to Sentosa once a few years before when I'd been based in Bangkok. It hadn't been a fun trip. I'd had to give one of her Majesty's flunkies a severe spanking for an indiscretion involving some missing embassy funds. He had fled Bangkok and holed up in a hotel on Sentosa island. He wasn't particularly bright and we'd tracked him down within days. I'd managed to retrieve the bulk of the funds and, following orders, I engineered a slight accident that put him in hospital for several months. I didn't enjoy what I had been instructed to do, so my one and only visit to Singapore's fun island hadn't been pleasurable in the slightest. The things we do, huh? Or rather the things I did for Queen and country in my other life. That life was now over.

The monorail to Sentosa took about thirty seconds. Well, it seemed that quick. In reality it was probably a three-minute ride from land to land and another three minutes to the first stop as we rumbled over the massive construction work going on below us.

Simone led the way as we left the unit and made our way downstairs at the first station. There had been only a few passengers on the train with us. Most of them were young people who looked as if they had dragged themselves out of their beds and were heading to their jobs on the island.

We swiped our tickets and went sightseeing. Above us was the peculiar Merlion symbol Singapore has adopted as its mascot: lion's head, mermaid or merman's body! I knew from my time here all those years ago that the tower served as the base for the spectacular light and fountain show that used to run nightly on the island. That was before they tore everything up to build the casino and waterworld. I guessed the lightshow or something like it would be reactivated as part of the new-look Sentosa in time. I just hoped they wouldn't go and build another fucking Disneyland on the island.

There was a flower show being held on Sentosa this day. Huge, elaborate displays were set up all around the terraces beside the Merlion. The people looking after the dozens of displays were watering them and tweaking them, no doubt in preparation for being swamped later in the day by hoards of visitors. Simone and I played the tourist card to the hilt. We posed for photographs and found that at every display we stopped at, someone would insist on taking photographs of us as a couple, and on both of our cameras.

It took an age before we finished winding our way up the pathways, through the gardens to the escalator that then carried us to the wide lookout plateau where the cable car from the mainland was anchored. The revolving Sky Tower and various other attractions were scattered about the large terrace. Some Indian guy with a yellow python was busy trying to drape his friend over a group of squealing female Japanese tourists. There were several of those king-size pay-as-you-go binoculars mounted by the edge of the plateau. I decided to commandeer one of those later.

"Refreshments," I said as we reached the bar near the base of the Sky Tower. I waved to the barman that we were interested and guided Simone down the few steps to the large wooden deck below. This was the perfect place to sit and check out both the earthworks below and the city across the harbour. I went to the railing and leaned on it, taking in the view just as Joe Tourist would do. In fact, I was actually Dan the Survivor checking out the lie of the land. My life could very well depend on that at some time in the very near future.

Sami wanted me to retrieve something from the surrender room at the fort. That much I knew. Prior to doing that I needed to obtain all the information I could about the fort and the island. Information harvesting is an agent's—or should I say former agent's—stock-in-trade. As I stood there, Simone leaned into my shoulder, pointing and chattering. She was right into her role as the blonde, ditzy wife. While she talked, I grunted replies of a sort and analysed what I was seeing.

Beyond the bridge linking Sentosa to the mainland was an island filled with containers. It technically wasn't an island any more because it was firmly attached to the mainland by a multi-lane umbilical cord.

In addition to a mass of docked ships and containers there were what I guessed to be banks of offices or maybe condominiums on the island. What a combination! Imagine living right next door to one of the world's busiest container ports. Singapore sure needed more land and I guessed what Sami and his guys were doing via the Intella development was providing that; after a fashion anyway.

A wide channel separated the island from the massive container port on the mainland shore. This fenced compound was dozens of containers deep and it stretched for kilometres from the Sentosa Bridge off into the distance. Huge fixed hoists and enormous blue-grey straddle carriers were working. The portside cranes were playing Pass the Parcel with containers, handing them on to the big straddle carriers that carried the boxes back from the dockside and stacked them into the rows that stretched back towards the city. Smaller yellow carriers scuttled around all over the place like huge, mechanical ants. These guys were repositioning containers and loading truck and tractor trailer units.

The whole operation of the container port seemed to me to be some sort of mechanised dance. Someone, somewhere was choreographing this insane two-step—or was it a foxtrot? Hell, I don't know. Dançing isn't my thing.

"It's quite incredible, isn't it?" Simone had dropped the ditzy act for the moment.

"Absolutely," I agreed. A waitress was hovering behind us. I ordered a beer, Simone an orange juice.

"Too early for alcohol?"

"Don't drink," came the reply as we went and sat at a table. "My husband did, and that was part of the problem."

There was no real reply to that one. I fired up my camera and flicked back over the images it had harvested to date. I sent most of them into the delete bin. I did keep a couple of good shots of my companion and one of she and I together standing in front of an enormous floral butterfly. Whether I was playing tourist or just keeping a snap or two of this very pretty woman for my own purposes, I had no idea. Sometimes the line between reality and fantasy can get a bit blurred with me.

The drinks came. Part of me wanted to feel a little ashamed of the pre-lunch beer while my companion abstained. The animal inside me, however, just laughed and told me to drink up. I did. There is nothing quite like a cold beer when the humidity is about ninety-eight percent. I knew my shirt was going to take a big sweat hit and I didn't care. I was Ed the Tourist from Perth and tourists sweat in Asia. Actually, given the climatic similarity between Singapore and Hong Kong, I was used to the heat and humidity, and short of getting physical, a big cold beer was the easiest way to work up a convincing sweat. Therefore I could justify the brew. Not that I really had to justify it, of course.

Simone and I sat and drank our respective drinks. There was no one sitting within earshot, so we dropped the corny dialogue for the moment and let ourselves sit and talk like real people. It was a pleasant interlude. I debated a second beer but decided against it. I'd received a Sentosa map with my monorail ticket. It showed the island enlarged. So, just as all tourists do, I spread the map on the table and looked it over. Incidentally, the container island was called Pulau Brani.

Sentosa island is shaped vaguely like a pizza slice. The wide end is basically to the east, the pointy end to the west. Fort Siloso is at the pointy end. There are golf courses and resorts and all sorts of things happening at the thick end. In the middle we have the bridge and the core of Singapore's playpen. As the island narrows, the protected beaches on the seaward side become features. There are hotels scattered about, especially along the beachfront. A big resort complex labelled the Shangri-La Rasa Sentosa Resort is at the narrow neck of the island. It sits on one side, the aquarium complex on the other. Beyond the aquarium and resort there is Fort Siloso.

I don't know the history of the fort other than that when the Japanese invaded Singapore, they cleverly didn't come in by sea and face the guns of the fort. They snuck in the back door, and unfortunately for everyone in Singapore, the fort's guns were all pointing the wrong way!

So the Japs took the island and Fort Siloso became an infamous prisoner-of-war camp. In the years since the war, the place has become a war museum, and that was where we were heading. I silently promised to read up on it one day but today was not that day.

Before we headed on to the fort, I decided we'd take a ride up in the Sky Tower. The map I had was just a simple schematic. I wanted to see the reality and the tower, at some hundred plus metres high, had to be the perfect vantage point. Carlsberg, one of my favourite beers, had naming rights.

I bought tickets for the both of us and we were ushered into a circular observation cabin. We settled on the bench seat that runs right around the inside wall of the cabin and we were away. As the tower rose, it rotated and Singapore and Sentosa were laid out below us. I used the camera and shot a 360-degree panoramic when we hit the top. The map of the island, I decided, was actually reasonably accurate. I could see that behind the resort there was quite a sizeable patch of jungle that pushes back along the seaward face of Siloso Point. The fort itself occupies the crest of the ridge and runs back down the harbourside.

After the short ride, we ignored the other attractions on the terrace. Simone took the lead and guided me across the terrace and down along a pathway into the trees. "The Dragon Trail," she explained. "When they were younger the kids used to love this," she said as we walked down through the dappled green tunnel. There were pieces of sculpture scattered around, skeletal bits of a prehistoric monster. "Imagination is a wonderful thing," she added. "They used to come up with all sorts of things, stories and games based on what they saw or imagined in here. The innocence of children is so refreshing," she added rather wistfully.

"Innocence is wasted on the young," I replied cynically, well aware I'd just mangled a cliché or whatever. Simone turned to look at me.

"That's rather a cruel thing to say."

"I guess it is. Being innocent did shit for me when I was a kid. I'd love a big dose of it now."

"Now you just sound bitter."

"Sorry. Let's go back to being Mavis and Ed out of—where the hell are we from again?"

"Perth!"

"That'll do, cobber," I said in my best attempt at an Australian accent. "So what's a nice sheila like you doing in a shithole like this?"

Simone started chuckling. It was a nice sound. I forced myself to lighten up. Thinking about my childhood gets me down sometimes. Oh hell, let's be honest: it gets me down every time.

We emerged from the jungle trail onto a roadway. There was a beach ahead of us. A long, wide expanse of white sand and palms stretched away in both directions. Siloso Beach the island map labelled it. An electric tram loaded with people honked us out of the way and slid past. There were people all over the sands, family groups, youngsters and huddled young lovers. Some were playing ball games, some picnicking under the palms. In the sheltered waters between the shore and the very artificial islands there were people swimming and playing in canoes and on floats.

Kiosks selling beach kit, soft drinks and food were scattered along the edge of the sand. There were pavilions and play areas, changing rooms and toilets and all the usual seaside stuff. It was a really well set out playground and there were plenty of people around on this sunny Singapore day.

"School holidays," Simone said, guessing what I was thinking. "Singapore is very well organised, as you will probably no doubt know." There was no hint of anything in her voice. "It's a great place to bring up kids."

I glanced at her. An open face looked back at me, but I could read her eyes. They said, "Great place for kids, shitty place for adults like me. Young, attractive, bored, divorced and tied to the place."

I knew without a doubt that if I suggested that we might work at breaking her cycle of boredom for an hour or two before she returned to her kids that she'd be more than willing. I'm not that damn arrogant to suggest that I look like God's gift to women and that they swoon over me. I just have the ability to read people and I was reading her, and that was exactly why I wasn't going to even attempt to go that route. To do so would be a cheap shot and a quick fix, and in the end it wouldn't do anyone much good. I'd just have done my male whore thing again and she'd be back where she started and the despair she felt would just have a fresh sprinkling of broken glass to grind into her soul. Shit, why such deep thoughts? Lighten up, arsehole, I thought.

Now we were climbing steps. There was a Delifrance café to our right. Was it time for lunch? I glanced at my watch. It was a few minutes after midday.

"Lunch?"

"Sure."

Then I focussed on the towering white façade of the Rasa Resort. Now that had to be the place to find an absolutely over-the-top lunch.

"There," I suggested, pointing.

"Why not?"

"Rasa Resort it is."

6

It may seem that since we set out, Simone and I had done nothing but breakfast, morning tea and now lunch. True, we had, and that is exactly what tourists do. This part of staying in character came easily to me. At the hotel we lunched outside above the pool shaded by huge umbrellas. I'd promised my companion the best lunch money could buy and if it wasn't the best, it sure came close. I'm a seafood nut and when there is lobster on the menu I'm a sucker for it. Simone, it appeared, also had a thing for the regal crustacean.

"Way out of my budget," she confided in me. "Last time I had it was years ago."

"Sami's paying," I replied. "You can have two if you want."

"That would be pure greed."

"So?'

We both laughed. Hey, my dark thoughts had vanished. I was actually enjoying this little interlude. It was almost like a real date. The sort of thing normal people got to do.

When the lobster arrived, Simone did something that struck me as rather strange. She carefully arranged a salad leaf over her lobster's head. When I asked why, she gave me a sheepish grin.

"I don't like making eye contact with my food," she replied.

I had to laugh, and despite my crustacean's black beady stare, I left it unblinkered. We did our two magnificent specimens true justice. I'd matched my beast with a New Zealand sauvignon blanc. Simone stayed with iced water with a touch of lime.

After coffee, I settled the tab which represented a king's ransom, of course, but that was to be expected. I used the card that matched my passport. Now I wanted a paper trail. Mr Ed from Perth was definitely in town!

It was 14:15 when we walked down the hotel driveway and hung a left turn to present ourselves at the ticket kiosk for the fort. A few metres up the hill were the fort gates and immediately beyond that a long covered shelter. Here eager youngsters in uniform stamped our tickets. Schoolkids probably. They were all smiles and helpful, youthful bubbling enthusiasm. There is a tram, they told us. Would we wait? No thanks, we wouldn't!

Simone and I set off up the driveway. It wasn't particularly steep and, full belly or not, the walking was easy. We stopped to coo and take photos. The two-tone brown bus purred down the hill past us, and the driver gave us a wave and a smile as he went past. We reciprocated. Everyone had a smile here, it seemed, even me. Sentosa, the island of smiles! That could be the place's new marketing slogan.

As we walked up the driveway, the harbour was below us and to our right. A metal fence was erected below the driveway, no doubt to keep non-paying guests from coming up from the sea through the small fringe of jungle and crashing the Siloso party.

On the right side of the road was a blockhouse, which I guessed was the true entrance to the fort proper. On the left was what must have been the original guardhouse. I could see mannequins dressed in the uniforms of a previous century on display inside.

We arrived on a wide terrace to find a quartet of sizeable pieces of heavy ordinance positioned there. The long barrels of the guns pointed across the harbour towards the city. At least this time round the artillery was positioned the right way, albeit a few decades too late.

There was a long two-storey building to the left. Downstairs was a souvenir shop. The signs identified it as The QuarterMaster Store. Upstairs, according to the brochure I had been given with my ticket, were the surrender rooms.

"Watch for watchers," I breathed to Simone as we stood shoulder to shoulder taking it all in. The roadway carried on up the hill, past a battery of short fat mortars before turning in a switchback and cutting back to the left. There were several buildings up there with their entrances facing towards us. The rest of these various structures appeared to be buried into the ridge behind.

Drums and bugles were sounding loudly in the still, sticky air. The fort's sound system was not going to let us off easy. There didn't appear to be anyone paying any attention to us that I could see. There was a small group of tourists above us on the roadway along the side of the ridge. They had a guide in attendance. There were also one or two other people in view, some walking along pathways in the trees behind The QuarterMaster Store. I couldn't make out anyone obviously standing or sitting staring at us, or anyone else for that matter. That, of course, didn't mean there was no one in the bushes or at the windows of any of the buildings and various structures scattered on the side of the hill.

Then I realised that indeed there were two sets of eyes on us. Two girls standing outside the souvenir shop were looking our way. They were fort guides and they were obviously waiting to offer us their services when we came into range.

"Let's get guided up and do the full nine yards," I said to Simone. She agreed cheerfully, jolly tourist wife that she was. She, of course, had no idea that I was going to be very focussed on one specific part of the complex when we eventually got to it.

We advanced on the waiting guides, purchased bottled water and set out to explore Fort Siloso in the company of a pretty young lady.

Our guide was Wenn. She was nineteen years old and a student. This was a part-time job for her. She was enthusiastic and informative. She had learned her lessons well. I doubted I was going to have to read up on the history of the fort. I just had to log her words into my memory banks.

Our enthusiastic young guide was intent on showing us around the entire fort complex. I knew that would take forever. I wanted to get to the surrender rooms. I explained we had limited time and asked for the quick tour. Wenn agreed and decided to start us at the very bottom, and it was down there that I found an excuse to loiter. I lit a cigarette while Simone distracted our guide with girlie conversation.

We were at the lowest point in the fort complex. The sign said we were at the Fire Direction Tower at Siloso Point. The channel between the island and the small promontory on the mainland was maybe only a couple of hundred metres wide. It may have been more. Distance across water can be tricky to judge, but no matter the exact meterage, it wasn't far at all.

"Look at ways of getting in and out of the fort at night," Sami had said. Swimming across the channel was a possibility, however I had no doubt that there was a serious tidal rip through this narrow stretch of water.

Standing in front of the small artillery piece mounted below the fire tower, I looked down the steep, tree-covered cliff towards the water. Below I could make out a building painted in shades of green, situated at water level. It was either a supply landing area or a water-level observation post in the form of a blockhouse or bunker. That being the case there had to be a way down to it.

Stepping a couple of paces to my right, I saw the ladder. It was one of those ones that had circular frames set at intervals down it to stop clumsy oafs falling off. Like the building below, it had originally been painted green, now it was mostly rust-coloured, however it looked strong enough to hold me. The only problem was the metal plate padlocked over the top where the ladder met the railing at the edge of the terrace. I figured that it would be easy enough to swing around the plate and get up to where I was standing. So now I had one possible means of getting myself into the fort through the back door.

Our guide was looking slightly nervous. Simone's attempts at distraction had worked to a point, but Wenn obviously took her guide role very seriously. Was I planning to jump? I could see that thought plainly reflected on her pretty face. If I did jump here it was broken limb territory only. I made a show of stubbing out my cigarette and joined them.

Now we had come down to the fire tower via a long open-topped tunnel, if you can call it a tunnel. It was more a very deep concrete trench with a mesh grill across the top. Going back, Wenn led us up a whole bunch of steps. We emerged on the hill above the control tower. Jungle fringed in on both sides of the long grassed spur that ran back into the fort complex. This would be the perfect place for a watcher to hide both from fort staff and the public. There was an old guy using a rake further along the spur towards the buildings. Beyond him the roadway curved on upward to more buildings, Fort Siloso Square my fort leaflet said. A few people were getting off the busy little tram up beyond that. Apart from these folks, there was no one else to be seen.

I didn't even try to spot anyone in the bush. Instead, I adjusted the pixel level on my camera to full out and took shots across the harbour. Then I made a show of posing the laughing Simone and Wenn close together and photographed them both with the water as a backdrop and with the road and fort buildings behind them. I used the widest lens setting so that I could obtain shots down both fringes of jungle. Maybe later, using a computer and the ten-plus megapixel images, we could pump things up and see if we could spot someone hiding amongst the foliage.

I continued to pose the girls and take photos as we meandered on through the various displays with their commentaries and that damned music. If it had really been as noisy back then, I think I would have preferred being in battle.

Eventually, having explored right up to the high point of the fort complex, we made our way down the wooden boardwalk to The QuarterMaster Store. Here I thanked our young guide for the tour and told her we would take in the surrender rooms by ourselves.

Access to the second level of the building was via stairs at either end. I led us to the right. An invalid lift was in operation. An elderly European man in a wheelchair was coming down. We waited while he was off-loaded by a guide and a middle-aged female companion. Perhaps a daughter! From the man's comments, I deduced he had been a prisoner here during the war. This must have been a bittersweet return for him. I just hoped his nightmares didn't come back to haunt him because of it. This place had been a living hell for so many—I'd learnt that for a fact this day.

I led Simone up the broad stairs to the double doors. I noted that there was a standard deadbolt fitted as I opened one wing of the door, ushering my twittering other half inside.

Alarm panel, smoke alarm and what I presumed were air-conditioner controls were to the right of the door, along with a fire extinguisher fixed to the wall. Large display boards and photographs covered the rest of the walls. To the front left were figures, wax figures. Gloating Japanese military in their green-brown uniforms, some sitting, others standing, looking down at four forlorn-looking Allied officers dressed in pale tropical kit. One of these officers was looking over his shoulder at me as if registering the intrusion.

A recorded voice began its recitation. Simone and I were the only people in this first room. The captions indicated that the tableaux represented the moment the Allies surrendered Singapore to the Japanese.

I used my camera. I posed with Simone in various spots and managed to capture virtually every inch of the room. I know Sami said I should focus on the Japanese surrender room, but if I was coming back here, I needed to know if there were any hidden mantraps. There didn't seem to be any cameras in operation, not visible ones anyway. If I was on camera, I wanted to appear simply as an over-enthusiastic tourist, so I babbled nonsense as I posed and reposed Simone.

The door behind us opened and a loud group of Europeans erupted into the room. I took Simone by the arm and we moved on.

The second of the surrender rooms was a long room and we were the only living bodies in it. There was just the two of us amongst a couple of dozen wax mannequins. We stood at the entrance and I used my camera to grab a quick panoramic sequence. There was no telling if the people behind us were about to come charging in. They gave the appearance of being the sort of tourists who do five continents in three hours or less.

There were long tables on each side of the room and a pedestrian corridor down the middle. A low wooden railing on either side defined the boundary. I noted that there was an empty chair at the head of the table to my immediate right. A battered leather briefcase lay on the table in front of the empty seat. A long row of seated, uniformed Japanese and Allied military types stretched into near infinity. A naval officer in white was standing between the table and the pedestrian way on my right. There was a support pillar beside him and there was a transparent screen protecting his back from any groping hands, I presumed.

The other side of the room was almost a mirror image, except in this case the standing figure in front of the table was dressed in khaki. He also had a screen protecting his back. There didn't appear to be any cameras in this room either but I wasn't betting they weren't there. I'd check the images later. I was, however, prepared to bet there was some sort of proximity alarm system to prevent anyone looting anything from the display. It was probably just an infrared beam, like the others I'd seen placed around the various displays we'd just looked at.

So in case there was a keyhole camera or two at work, I again posed Simone strategically and took a whole bunch of shots. When the boisterous crowd from next door came in, it was time for us to bail out.

"Aquarium," Simone said as we walked down the fort access road. I would have gladly settled for a drink, but yes, we were still in tourist mode and the aquarium was next on the agenda.

Before the entrance into the aquarium itself was a pool divided by a bridge. One side contained fishes of the finned variety. The other side of the pool had turtles and goldfish in it. Huge turtles, enormous things. We stopped for a moment to watch them. Very occasionally they stuck their heads up out of the water to breathe.

"Such old faces," Simone commented, and I guess she was right. These things live to a great old age. Suddenly she squealed, grabbed my arm and pointed into the shadows at the far side of the pool.

There, at the bottom of the pool, was a body. It was black and almost lost in the shadows cast by the bridge leading into the aquarium. But it wasn't a dead body. It was very much alive. A plume of bubbles exploded to the surface. It was a diver in a wetsuit using what seemed like a giant pool vacuum cleaner.

"Housework," I said to Simone, who breathed a huge sigh of relief. The mechanism of the pool cleaner was across the pool. It sat humming and spluttering as the diver worked. Some of the turtles were interested in the diver and his activities. He frequently had to push them away as he worked. None of them seemed to be trying to bite him; rather they were just bumping him with their shells. Given their size, some of these big bruisers would have had quite an impact.

Even so, the guy just kept on cleaning.

We took the aquarium tour. I didn't particularly enjoy it. After my time spent crawling through a wrecked submarine on the bottom of the Andaman Sea, I wasn't as nearly as impressed as Simone was by the display, as good as it was. The sharks especially left me cold. I still had the vision of a giant Tiger shark steaming out of the blackness into the light from an underwater scooter's headlamp, and racing away with a diver clenched in its huge jaws. Believe me when I say that is the stuff of nightmares.

"Let's go get a drink," I said as we emerged from the aquarium back into the sunlight. I felt a big cold shiver run down my spine and I momentarily forgot my companion of the moment was teetotal. Sharks can do that to one.

"Let's," came the reply.

By mutual agreement, we ended up back at the Sky Tower bar on the Imbiah plateau. It was 16:20. A huge chunk of the day had been spent touring the fort and aquarium. Simone had orange juice and ice while I damaged a pint of the sponsor's brew.

"Did you get whatever it was you were after up at the fort?"

"I have absolutely no idea. I was flying blind," I replied. "Sami wanted me to get an overview and see if I could spot any watchers. I got the former but didn't see the latter."

"Are you a spy?"

The question came so totally out of the blue that I must have registered more than a little surprise. I shook my head and tried to laugh it away.

"Whatever gave you that idea?"

Simone looked at me thoughtfully, her head cocked a little to one side. It was a good look.

"I accidentally heard Mr Somsak talking to Stanley about his friend Daniel. He said that his friend—you—had consigned his boss to hell and no longer worked for the British Government. He said he hoped that you would come work with him."

"It is most unlike Sami to let someone overhear him," I replied, taking a gulp of beer while I searched for a response.

"I was in my office next to Stanley's. The intercom suddenly came on. I couldn't help hearing what he said. Stanley had put his briefcase on his desk and it had jammed the talk button on the console down. I immediately went through and told him, of course."

"Of course," I replied, matching her grin for grin. I do believe she would have done just that. "So how come you call Stanley by his first name and Sami, Mr Somsak?" I was trying to move the conversation away from where it had been heading.

"I worked for Stanley for five years. He told me the first morning to call him that. I've only ever seen Mr Somsak a dozen times. He never asked me to call him by his Christian name."

"Call him Sami," I replied. "Everyone does."

"Maybe," Simone countered. Then she fixed her big blue eyes on mine. She hadn't forgotten her original question, despite my rather feeble attempt to distract her. "I think you are a spy or a secret agent, or you were one."

"Imagination and the wrong end of the stick, my good lady. I'm a security consultant, nothing more, nothing less." I learned a long time ago that if you're going to lie, stay within earshot of the truth. It's easier that way. I finished my Carlsberg and waved the waitress over. I could have decided that the day was done and found a cab or grabbed the cable car across to the mainland, but that would have indicated she had been right and anyway, I was enjoying her company so why rush things?

"Is seduction on your agenda?"

For probably the first time in my life, I was absolutely speechless. Simone lowered her glass. Her big blue eyes stayed locked on mine. They were like blue laser beams.

"I'm just asking because, if it is, I'll need to organise my sitter for my children."

"Would you like it to be on the agenda?" I asked. My throat was dry despite having just bathed it in Mr Carlsberg's best lager.

"Very much indeed. I don't have a boyfriend and casual sex is not my thing, even if the opportunity arises. We have people in common, so that makes us definitely not casual, and anyway, it appears we are man and wife." Simone held up her left hand. On her ring finger was a gold band. I hadn't noticed it before. When she played a role, she certainly played it for real.

"So we are," I replied. All of my earlier thoughts about being Mr Virtuous went right out the window. Hell, I was helping a lady in distress, or something.

The waitress arrived as Simone flipped open her cellphone to call her sitter. I forewent another beer and called for the bill. I paid for our drinks and we went in search of a taxi.

7

Being the imperfect gentleman I am, all I will say about the night I spent with the beautiful Simone DeLue is that it was spectacular. She admitted at some stage that she hadn't had sex for more than a year. It showed. Her enthusiasm bordered on the psychotic. Eventually things calmed down and moved on from her lonely, animal lust to another place. Later still, mutually exhausted, we ended up in the huge spa bathtub.

Room service delivered a bottle of Moet and glasses. Yes, Simone drank some of it. Not much to be sure, but lying there amongst the bubbles she let the yeasty golden velvet of the champagne tickle her senses.

Simone DeLue left my room very, very, late. Or was that very early? The phraseology always confuses me. Whatever, it was 03:30 when we said goodnight.

"Will I see you again?"

"I hope so, but no promises."

"I hope so too. Take care, Mr Spy!"

With that she was gone without a backward look. I closed the door and locked it. How different this night had been from my escapades of the past few months. Sex for sex's sake, especially when you're an addict like I am, is a totally empty experience, beyond the physical at least. This had been good sex. It had meaning of sorts. We had connected throughout the day. Dare I say it? We'd had genuine fun as we'd play-acted our roles as Mr and Mrs Ed from Perth. Big kids, I guess, but it had been fun none the less, and fun is something I haven't experienced much over the years. It was another day when I didn't have to kill anyone, and that can't be bad.

But as for the sex Simone and I had just shared, that had been quite wonderful. The thing is that, since quitting Thailand, sex for me had been bar, pick-up, home and bed. Several girls had been on a repeat loop but after a couple of weeks I moved on. Variety is supposedly the spice of life. How about we replace that cliché with another claim. How about "Variety is the flat grey sludge of boring repetition"?

On her way home by cab, Simone DeLue was smiling to herself. She was exhausted, sore and happy. She'd had no intention of inviting Daniel to seduce her. That had never been in her plans. She'd imagined a day out play-acting. She'd anticipated some nice food and a few laughs and that would have been that. A pleasant day away from her normal routine.

In fact, she admitted to herself at one point during the day that she hadn't really been sure she even liked the man she was with. However, somewhere along the way her perception of him had changed.

In her book, physically Daniel Swann was every woman's dream, or at least he was very close. He was good looking in a rugged sort of way. He had a great body and he knew how to use it. However it was the little things that made her really connect with him.

Throughout the day she'd had glimpses beyond that hard, almost callous exterior he presented and she knew there was a lot more to Daniel Swann than he was prepared to show the world.

She had seen immediately that he was smart and humorous, but she had felt that there was a very real sense of vulnerability about him. She had gone in search of it and in doing so she had experienced both the toughness and the gentleness of this man who she so much wanted to see more of.

"My spy," she murmured as she stepped into the elevator at her Toa Payoh apartment block. She was still smiling when she eventually found sleep.

After a long lie-in I had a shower that probably drained the hotel's hot water system dry. A room service breakfast followed and then it was time for me to get serious. I had my Toshiba with me. I connected the camera to the laptop and started sifting through the hundred or so images I'd taken at Siloso. I saved a couple of good shots of Simone into a separate folder. I don't think there was one bad of her in the bunch, but these particular ones were very good and the romantic in me decided they were keepers.

Once I'd done that I started to analyse the remaining images and see if I could spot the surveillance types Sami thought would be somewhere around the fort. Now, I've got a jungle fighter's senses when it comes to watchers and the watched. I hadn't felt the burn of eyes on me throughout the hours we had spent either in the fort complex or on Sentosa itself.

I pulled up the images I'd taken on the spur above the watchtower and started to examine the bush edge, winding the magnification to maximum. Leaf by leaf, I quartered the jungle. It was taking me forever, but breaking down camouflage patterns and seeing the reality behind them is an art form. I switched the colour images to monotone and looked for human outlines, a head, an arm, a hand. If I had been colour blind it would have been easier. Conventional camouflage can often be completely useless against an observer with that condition. I didn't have that luxury or handicap, I just had to do it the hard way.

I was starting to think this was all a waste of time when I finally saw something. I had a fresh image onscreen and was still in colour mode when something caught my eye. It was tiny, black and shining against the green haze of the jungle background!

Looking along the right hand, or ocean side of the spur, there was an indentation in the jungle edge and situated in the small clearing was a tower, radio, cellphone or something. Its function didn't matter. What did matter was the fact that on a cross spar of the tower's skeleton frame, about ten feet above the ground, someone had mounted a small camera.

Now, without a bunch of megapixels and a trained eye, the camera, which was held in position with a strip of wide grey tape of about the same colour as the metal of the tower itself, probably wouldn't have been seen. Certainly not at a glance! What gave it away was the small, dark circle of the lens. The lens wasn't large. It was no bigger than a Singapore one-dollar coin, but it was black and there was a spark of reflected light on it. It was probably that spark that had caught my eye in the first place.

The camera, which I presumed had a wide-angle lens, was positioned so it was looking along the spur towards where I had been standing to take my photo. I was prepared to bet there was another pointing the other way looking down towards The QuarterMaster Store and the surrender rooms.

I looked for a telltale bulge on the corresponding crossbeam on the opposite side of the tower framework. Obviously I wasn't about to see a lens from this angle, purely because it would be pointing in the other direction. And yes, there was a grey bump on the straight edge of the beam on the far side. Camera number two.

"Clever!" I muttered, lighting a Marlboro. I was perhaps rewarding myself for being an eagle-eyed genius, or lucky bugger. But yes, the camera option was clever. By using the technology they—whoever they were—could mount a continuous watch while staying out of sight.

The cameras, of course, didn't mean there was no one in the jungle itself. Perhaps there was even a Japanese death squad left over from the war bivouacked in the seemingly dense bush waiting to come out and take Singapore for a second time. Whatever, Sami had been right with his call so far.

Cameras of the type that were set up on the tower were not standard CCTV. These were small mil-spec devices. Expensive and cutting-edge technology. They were the sort of thing I'd seen the US Special Forces guys using what now seemed like years ago in the jungle in the Thai highlands. With long-life batteries and remote sender devices, they could remain *in situ* for long periods of time and still function. They also operated in extreme low-light conditions. I had to figure that if the unknown watchers had two cameras set up, they probably had a whole bunch more.

I checked all the other images I'd taken to try and spot any other cameras. I looked at all the hard sites like railings, posts and buildings. Even the artillery pieces and the big stand-alone trees that dotted the hillside above The QuarterMaster Store. I had one possible hit.

Behind the store on the steep hillside there was an outdoor

display showing how heavy cannon barrels were hoisted up the slope to the top of the fort. Beyond that there was an object sitting in the crook of a tree branch. This was little more than just another bulge where possibly one should not be. It was green and brown and matched the colour of the tree. However, the green lump had a circular black centre. Under maximum magnification, the pixels onscreen were almost the size of bricks and they all but destroyed the image, but I was prepared to bet that, yes, it was a camera. If I was right, positioned where it was it would cover the back of The QuarterMaster Store building and any approaches up the roadway from the main gate below.

With a transmitting range of several kilometres, our adversary's screen-watchers could be in the jungle, in a vehicle parked somewhere on the island or even sitting in the harbour basin in a launch. They could even be across the harbour in an apartment for that matter. However, I figured that wherever they were, they would have people within easy reach of the surrender rooms and whatever Stanley Loh had secreted there.

The watchers had one big advantage. Because the fort is situated at the narrow end of the island, anyone attempting to leave and reach the train, bus, car, cab or whatever had to pass through the concourse outside the aquarium. I was sure that the guys using the cameras had people stationed right there to intercept their target if anyone made the pick-up and tried to get away.

I switched to the images of the two surrender rooms. I'd photographed the panels to the right of the door over a smiling Simone's shoulder. There were five boxes in all. One was a black-fronted keyed unit, below that a standard digital alarm box. To the right a small keyed box, a faceless panel, possibly hiding fuses. There was a red box below that, a fire alarm control box, I had to assume.

I was figuring there was a general sensor movement system for the entire floor as a whole. That theory matched the sensors I'd spotted. The second alarm system was probably the infrared trip alarm around the displays. Fire alarm and fuse box aside, the remaining two boxes probably related to the air conditioning and the lights. Short of actually getting right up close and personal with them that was my best guess.

I skipped through the images in the Allied surrender room and started in-depth in the Japanese room, looking at everything in high resolution. As with my study of the exterior shots, it took time. I ordered a pot of coffee and a sandwich and smoked my way through half a pack of cigarettes before I finished.

Whatever Stanley had hidden in the room, I didn't find it on my image search. All I found were a lot of waxy faces of various shades of the rainbow attached to stiff mannequins dressed in the ill-fitting uniforms of a dozen countries and services. Apart from the glazed-over eyes, nothing leapt out at me and said, "This is it!"

It was after midday when I finally shut down the computer. My own eyes were glazed and red from the strain of trying to rearrange millions of pixels into some sort of meaningful order. I stood at the suite window and watched the world roll by below. The day outside looked like another very warm one. Was there really anything else here?

I decided on a swim. When I got outside, yes, it was hot, but for a change the humidity wasn't pushing the high nineties. I went poolside for a couple of hours. The pool was virtually deserted but for a young Japanese couple with a pair of toddlers. I swam and dozed on a lounger in the shade. I ordered a sandwich and a solitary beer and that was it. I was tired. Tired from the brain draining, eye-sucking exercise on the computer, and physically tired from my bout with Simone.

I was sound asleep when my cellphone woke me. Sami had completed the funeral arrangements for Stanley, the family and his people. The bodies had been released to the undertakers. Now it was time for he and I to get together and have that long-overdue talk.

I returned to my room to shower and dress. Ed from Perth wasn't going out this evening, Daniel Swann was. There would be a car waiting down the street. I would be spirited into a car park basement. All the usual secret squirrel stuff. However, if it meant the chance to see my old friend and help him fight this, his latest war, just one of the many we had fought together, so be it. I was in!

8

I've seen sophisticated models of various proposed developments before, but never one quite like the one that was set out in the office that Sami Somsak occupied. What had formally been Stanley's domain was situated on the fifteenth floor of a building on Scotts Road just a hundred metres up from Orchard.

I'd seen the images of the Intella Island model in the newspapers and on television, but nothing had prepared me for the scale of the thing. It was massive! There was a fringe of buildings surrounding Marina Bay. A long wide bridge with four huge towers set along its length pushed out from the city. The bridge had three lanes going in each direction and between the separated bridge spans were two rail lines extending from Marina MRT to the island. The towers on the bridge structure were tall, very tall. They straddled the road and rail access, their feet plunging into the blue plaster water.

The bridge terminated inside the massive Intella Island rather than on it. The island itself was octagonal in shape. Scale was difficult for me to judge but it was huge, dwarfing two ocean liners moored on the seaward side. Tall buildings, many with helicopter landing pads on their roofs, dominated, but at the heart of the island was an open expanse, a large park. Streets bisected the buildings in neat grid patterns. I could make out models of tiny pedestrians and tram-like coaches. There were no cars in sight other than on the bridge.

"Impressive isn't it," Sami said, coming to stand beside me. "Twelve hectares of man-made island. On the upper level, parks and sunlight and offices, hotels, apartments plus a casino, of course," he added without a hint of irony. "We estimate habitation for perhaps a quarter of a million people in these thirty acres, and in the apartment towers and hotels on the bridge itself."

Thirty acres made sense to me while hectares didn't. A quarter of a million people living on the island, now that was impressive, and I said so. Sami nodded. "To Singapore that is valuable space and it will be even more so because in effect, we are multiplying that thirty acres three times."

"How the hell will you do that?"

Sami laughed. He pressed a button on a console on the side of the display and from somewhere below the model there was a click and a whirr. The entire top layer of the island model rose in the air on telescopic supports and moved a metre and a half towards the high ceiling.

Below the upper level, where the park and the buildings had been, was a whole other infrastructure. There were long arcades and malls. There were gymnasiums and retail shops, supermarkets and cinemas plus an MRT terminal. There were tram stops and the end of the bridge was here, one level down from the surface. The whole thing was a mind-boggling to me. There were dozens of other services and facilities mapped out and I was having trouble taking it all in at once.

"A whole other world," Sami said, "and there's more." There was another click and the sound of electrics at work and the level I was looking at was whisked away skywards after the other. Now I was looking at cars, little models of cars, hundreds perhaps thousands of them. This new level was a giant car park. The support columns and foundations of the buildings above separated dozens of car-parking areas. It was like looking down on the compartments of a giant beehive. Access roads, like veins, led to arteries which in turn led into a huge concourse that fed up and onto the entrance and exits to the bridge.

"Car parking for ten thousand vehicles on two levels," Sami said. "No vehicles on the streets above but for electric trams and, of course, the Grand Prix racers and other events."

"You what?"

"Using the bridge, the roads around Marina Bay and the island, we envisage the world's most unique Grand Prix circuit. We can dock eight of the world's largest luxury liners at one time and provide a racing circuit that can be as long as twelve kilometres with possibly the best spectator viewing of any." He paused. "Those are just some of the many little innovations that have been designed into the project. Under the car parks we have a desalination plant and a fresh water storage reservoir the size of the island that goes right to the sea floor. Fresh water, of course, floats on salt water, so the sea itself will provide the actual base for the water storage area.

"Bloody hell!

"Yes, Daniel. The plan is that the consortium will build the island structure and the bridge itself sans buildings. The government will build the MRT and other investors will build everything else. We will be the landlords and, of course, our rents and profit-share arrangements will be worth many billions a year. This is my retirement fund."

"What the hell are you going to build it out of?"

"Steel and concrete, Daniel, in huge quantities. A massive collection of steel casements driven into the sea floor and drained. This will gradually create what amounts to a dry hole in the sea. When the lower level is sealed and filled with water it will add to the structural strength of the whole and everything else will be built around and over it, layer upon layer like a wedding cake. You could consider, in construction terms that it is rather like a giant oil rig." Sami was like a kid now. His enthusiasm was almost contagious. I don't think for many years, if ever, I have seen him so animated.

"Yes, Daniel. Five years, six billion dollars and that's just the groundwork. And that brings us to the present and the man who killed Stanley." The smile vanished. Now it was to the business in hand. The transition was instantaneous. Another layer of Sami Somsak had been revealed and just as quickly hidden again. I wondered if I would ever have a glimpse of that Sami again.

"The man who wanted Stanley's share of the pie, which in effect was my share, is Thomas Lu."

"Who is he?"

"A nasty character. Singapore born. Mixed ancestry. Made a great deal of money through some particularly dubious means." Sami looked at me with a half smile. This was potentially the pot calling the kettle black. He moved towards his desk, leaving much of the model of Intella Island suspended in the air behind him. The island was obviously on hold in more ways than one until other business had been dealt with.

Sami sat behind the desk while I took a chair to one side. Sami flicked a button on his laptop and turned it so I could see the screen. There was a street shot that had been taken of a man coming down a flight of broad steps. There were other people in the shot but the man in the centre of the screen was so distinctive he would have stood out in a crowded wide-angle shot. Lu was a tall, thin Chinese man with a mass of straight black hair worn thick at the back, mullet-style. He was wearing dark glasses and a dark suit. The mouth was thin-lipped, cruel even. I'd have put his age to be late fifties, early sixties, but at first glance he appeared younger.

Thomas Lu's mouth was open, frozen in mid-speak. He was perhaps abusing whoever was on the other end of the camera. His expression didn't indicate he was at all pleased with the intrusion. "Newspaper shot. He'd just lost a court case," Sami offered by way of explanation. "He's notoriously publicity-shy."

"You're certain it was him?"

"Absolutely. Stanley called me from hospital and left a message on my cell service. I was out on the Gulf and didn't receive the call."

Sami sounded bitter. I knew he'd been on board his massive floating drug laboratory where, because of the extreme danger of causing an explosion, all cellphones were banned. That being the case he'd missed the opportunity to take Stanley's call and perhaps save his half-brother's life.

"If I'd answered the call I could have provided him with protection."

"You didn't," I responded bluntly, "and it probably wouldn't have made any difference. I bet that Lu was already at Stanley's house and had his family. They were dead whichever way it went."

"Maybe."

Sami didn't sound convinced. I didn't know the exact timing of events, but I guessed that with murder on his mind, Lu had made a beeline for the house on Goodwood Hill even before Stanley had been well enough to make the call to Sami. Who knows.

"So exactly what happened on the island?"

"Stanley went to a meeting Lu had arranged. He was told the other members of the Intella Island syndicate were going to be there. It wasn't their usual venue, but Stanley didn't get suspicious, which was his first mistake perhaps." Sami shook his head, whether at his dead half-brother's moment of misjudgement or his own inability to have helped him.

"So when Stanley got to the hotel, which incidentally Thomas Lu owns, the place was deserted but for Lu and his crew. Stanley is"—Sami corrected himself again with hardly a pause—"was no fool. Lu had already offered to buy out his, or should I say my, share of the development. When Stanley saw that the others weren't there, he knew Lu was going to play hardball." Sami took another sip of water. I ignored the bourbon in front of me. I had a feeling that I was going to need to get sharp and stay sharp for whatever was to come.

"Stanley always carried a digital recorder into his meetings as insurance. It's a small device and he kept it hidden. No one knew he had it on him. In his message he told me he knew after Lu's first approach that he needed to get hard evidence if the partners were to be convinced Lu was pulling a stunt. Without evidence, it was simply his word against Lu's and Lu has cronies in the syndicate who would stand by him."

"Back the truck up. What stunt? What was Lu trying to achieve other than a buyout? That's just business, isn't it?"

Sami nodded. He looked tired and the oldest I had ever seen him. Sami Somsak is close to seventy. Normally he looks like a fresh-faced fifty-year-old. Now he looked his age. Grief and guilt combined are hard masters. I knew that from my own experiences.

"Sorry, I forget you weren't fully in the loop." Sami took a sip of Evian. I continued to leave the bourbon alone and waited while my friend gathered his thoughts.

"You're right, of course. Offering to buy out a partner is just business, but in reality here's how it stacks up. There are six partners in the Intella partnership. Each of us is in for US$1 billion." The vast amount of money should have caused some reaction in me, but I didn't say a word. Big numbers and Sami Somsak go hand in hand.

"We have all put a quarter of that into a trust fund, the balance to be paid incrementally as the project proceeds. Some months ago Lu was rumoured to be having financial difficulties and was struggling to raise the capital for his deposit. Suddenly, without warning, he made an approach to Stanley to buy out Stanley's share for a very hefty profit." Sami paused and stared into space for a moment, watching a war bird slash across the horizon, heading east. "I guess Lu figured that of all the partners, Stanley, the quiet one, was the soft target."

"Lu obviously doesn't know about your connection to Stanley!" I said, stating it as a fact not a question, knowing that if that connection had been common knowledge, no one in their right mind would have messed with Stanley.

"They didn't know. Very few people do and they are all pledged to silence." Sami gave a tired smile. We both knew the penalty for breaking that silence. Loyalty was everything with my friend. To betray his trust was to ensure very quick and terrible retribution. "If Lu had known about the connection, he would have most certainly stayed away from Stanley. Again, Daniel, that was my fault."

"It's not your fucking fault," I snapped. "Shit happens, Sami. For God's sake, you of all people know that for a fact."

"Yeah," he admitted, rubbing a hand over his face. "You are, of course, right, old friend. Shit happens!"

"So where did Lu score the cash? I mean if he tried to buy Stanley out, he found big bucks somewhere?"

"A South American drug cartel, Colombians," Sami replied. He reached out and tapped the keyboard on his laptop once more. There were three men in the full-screen coloured shot. They were a heavyset trio of Spanish extraction and all bore similar features that the inevitable dark glasses couldn't hide. They were brothers or a father and siblings. Their ages ranged from maybe mid-thirties to perhaps early sixties. The elder man had a badly pockmarked face, the middle one sported a vivid scar across his forehead. The younger of the three didn't bear any obvious scars but dark glasses or not, I could sense mad eyes staring out at the camera.

"Before you ask how I know, I have someone in Lu's camp,"

Sami said in answer to my unasked question. "These gentlemen are the Mendez brothers out of Bogota. Carlo, the oldest, Marco, the middle one and Raymond. The Americans have been hitting them hard and they haven't been able to launder their billions north of Panama. They're choking on their profits and looking for investments that the Feds can't touch."

"So Lu goes to them with a proposition and suddenly they see a big juicy pie sitting there half way around the world and they want a slice or two?" I was guessing, of course, but I figured it would be close to the mark. Sami nodded.

"They want it all, and the way they play, they'd get it in the end if they manage to secure a foothold. We don't need Lu or his money and we certainly don't want theirs. There are plenty of other investors who want in; Intella Island is the hottest property in Asia and that's not simply media hype. Lu only got invited into the syndicate because of his history with several of the others. At the end Stanley, bless his soul, knew that if he could give the others hard evidence on what Lu was planning, Lu was out and Intella was safe from the South Americans."

"So Stanley records the offer Lu makes. He refuses and Lu tries to kill him."

"Yes, in a nutshell. Obviously the Colombians are leaning on him really heavily. According to Stanley, he is terrified of them and sweating on it. They agreed to make up Lu's shortfall on the condition he got them a full share of the action. The rest you know. Lu unfortunately saw the recorder. Stanley managed to escape, but he is—" Sami paused and blinked—"He was a chronic asthmatic. He made it to the fort and into the Japanese surrender room and hid the recorder before he collapsed."

The picture suddenly became crystal clear. Sami wanted me to collect the recorder from wherever Stanley had hidden it. Then when he presented the syndicate with the evidence contained on the device, Sami would have Lu thrown out of Intella, taking his South American money with him. I had no doubt that after he'd destroyed the man financially, Sami would then cause Thomas Lu to cease to exist. That was, of course, if the Colombians didn't get to him first. Those guys have a reputation for violence second to none.

"Why do you need me to get the recorder? Jo would go in for you and he's probably in better shape than me." I was referring to Jo Ankar. If I was Sami's left-hand man and friend, Jo, a former Thai Special Forces Major, was his right hand and his brother in all but blood.

"Jo is away on other business," Sami replied smoothly. He was wearing his inscrutable face now and I couldn't tell if he was lying or not. "But I need you back at my side, Daniel," he added. "Hong Kong is not doing you any good. Will you do it?"

"Of course I will."

9

I don't like funerals, but I was fortunate in that this time I didn't have to attend the huge service for Stanley's family and his faithful retainers. Sami wanted me to be the invisible man. We were not to be seen together in public and all communication was to be via the pre-paid cellphone.

So once again I was to play Ed the Tourist from Perth. Tomorrow, when the dead were buried, we would formulate the plan to retrieve Stanley's recorder. Sami hadn't yet told me exactly where it was in the surrender room. Maybe he hadn't wanted me strolling in and lifting it.

I decided to trust his judgement on this. The reality of it all is that we were in one of the most law-abiding, buttoned-up, safe, self-regulating corners on earth. People in Singapore notice things and they aren't slow about coming forward. If I lifted the recorder in daylight, setting off the alarms, I was as sure as hell going to get noticed and a camera, or series of cameras, somewhere were going to capture my image. I'd have a street life expectancy of minutes, perhaps an hour or two, before I was caught. If I was any or all parts of the Chinese-Malay-Indian mix, I might last half a day on the run. That being the reality, I knew it would be better to do my pick-up run at night and in disguise and hopefully avoid those eyes and the inevitable cameras.

Simone wasn't available to play tourist wife. She was at the funeral, as expected, so I did Ed from Perth as a solo act. I costumed up, including a broad-brimmed Akubra-type hat minus the dangling corks. Having schooled up with a guidebook, I headed for Changi Village. I had been there once in a previous life. I could have caught a bus, but playing the tourist for my character meant I didn't know the city or the MRT and bus system. I cabbed it to the village and made my way to the jetty and a bumboat.

My ultimate destination, thanks to the guidebook, was the island of Pulau Ubin, also known as Granite Island, a sort of national park just a few minutes off the mainland. The trip only took fifteen minutes. The boat had a dozen or so people on it and it cost peanuts for the ride.

The island turned out to be a pretty laid-back sort of place, if you discount the million or so fish farms moored along the shore. The village information office near the end of the jetty provided me with another schematic map. While not to scale it gave me an idea about what was more or less where.

The village had a few small stores, a seaside restaurant and a fetish for bicycles. For a couple of dollars you can rent a bike from any one of half a dozen outlets. It's a great way to get around and get yourself a sore arse in the process. I hate bicycles for just that reason.

I bought a couple of bottles of water and stowed them in my day bag. Then with my camera in hand, just like a regulation loopy, I set off to explore the island of Ubin. It was a few minutes to midday and it was both hot and humid. There was no cooling sea breeze to be found. Never mind, I wasn't there to sightsee, I needed some serious exercise.

A few of my fellow passengers from the bumboat had decided to take the cycle option. With a lot of whooping and hollering, half a dozen youngsters shot by me as I plodded on along the road, heading to what my map told me was Pekan Quarry. The map indicated camping areas and huts all over the place and five former quarry sites, now filled with water. The granite moles had been busy once upon a time.

The contrast between the relatively deserted Pulau Ubin and Singapore, the island and city, was quite remarkable. For at least fifteen minutes I saw no one, and then a van loaded with people and bags went past, no doubt heading for one of the camps or the island's sole resort.

I tired of the hard road surface and decided to explore the jungle. I feel more at home under the canopy, always have done. The bush scares some people, many people in fact, but to me it is like a homecoming of sorts. After all, I spent several years of my life in the jungle when based in Thailand with The Firm. Back then I frequently had Sami Somsak and Jo Ankar by my side as I spent much time doing what I did in Northern Thailand, Cambodia, Myanmar and Vietnam.

I found a narrow, barely formed track and followed it, moving deeper into the bush. Eventually I came to a house sitting in what had once been a clearing before the jungle started to reclaim it. The building was falling down. The windows were gone and the door had collapsed onto the porch that ran across the face of the structure. Abandoned rubber estates, the guidebook said. This was obviously one of them. Curious, I went inside.

It was as if the former residents had truly abandoned the place, leaving behind much of what they owned in the process. Perhaps this had been an alien invasion? There was furniture, crockery, cooking utensils, a wrecked bicycle, even an old television in a wooden console. Mouldering clothes were strewn everywhere. Beds had collapsed and bedding was rotting on the rusting springs.

What had caused the people to leave so suddenly without even taking their damn clothes? I'd seen similar in other places in other jungles. In many of those instances a rotting, bullet-ridden corpse or a pile of bleached bones indicated what had happened. Gang warfare, bandit raids, bad luck, they all caused chaos and death, particularly in places where the only law was the gun, and drugs were the local currency. But here in peaceful Singapore?

Whatever the reason for the sudden exodus of the people from the house, I moved on. I came across several others in an equally deserted and dilapidated state as I followed the pathway deeper into the jungle. I didn't bother going inside to examine any of the other former homes. My curiosity is finite and the house I had already gone through reminded me of other times and other ruins. Those memories weren't any I wanted to dredge back up or dwell on.

I pushed on into the jungle and the track began to climb up what

I guessed was a hill in these parts. I was focussing better now as I slowly came back into jungle mode. Bird spiders as big as my hand hung on their webs strung between trees, patiently awaiting their prey. Most of these magnificent spiders are beautifully coloured. I'm not sure if that is to attract the birds or scare off predators. There are birds aplenty, so no doubt the arachnids live well.

I disturbed a wild pig feeding on a fallen coconut. The little porker scurried off into the undergrowth with a scolding squeal. Or perhaps it was a squeal of fright, I'm not sure which, not being an expert on pig talk.

I was sweating heavily. The excesses from several months were trying to find a way out of my body through my pores. I stopped and drank one of my bottles of water without taking it from my lips and then I set off again. I was really hammering my body. Okay, I know one day of exercise does not a fitness regime make, but a decent effort will do me some good. Won't it?

I arrived back at the village late in the afternoon, and I was completely knackered, a total sweatball. I'd covered a lot of kilometres, mostly in the bush. I'd seen just about all the wildlife the island had to offer, including a whole family group of little porkers. If I'd wanted to, I probably could have engineered a snare or even rugby tackled one. However, I suspected the local rangers would not take kindly to me slaughtering their wildlife. So even if I had vaguely contemplated a feed of wild pork, I now settled on the domesticated variety.

The restaurant on the waterfront served up a good pork curry that I accompanied with some deliciously cold beers before catching a bumboat back to Changi Jetty. There was a cursory bag check on arrival, which surprised me somewhat. I found a cab to take me back to the city. When I dropped into my seat, I promptly closed my eyes and teetered on the edge of an exhausted sleep. Ed the Tourist from Perth was completely buggered. The expedition into the wilds of Pulau Ubin had been a big undertaking. I decided that as soon as I was delivered back to the Carlton, I would submerge myself in a long hot bath with a cold lager close to hand.

Simone was waiting for me in the foyer lounge when I arrived. I revised my plan for the evening. She had arranged a sitter for her boys and tomorrow was Saturday. She didn't work Saturdays. Tomorrow she wanted me to meet the kids. That set alarm bells ringing way back in my brain. Whatever, I thought, we will have a picnic. In the meantime we have some time to ourselves.

10

"You drop me here, thirty metres off shore and I swim to the landing. From there it's up the ladder. I clamber around the steel plate at the top and into the observation post."

"Will you use the tunnel or take the ridge line?" The map Sami had spread on the desk was actually a large-scale satellite photograph and it showed Fort Siloso and the body of the island back to the bridge in great detail. Sami's finger was tracing the topside route. I shook my head.

"I'll use the tunnel. I want to delay getting caught on camera as long as possible. When I come out of it I'll be running. I'll have maybe five minutes tops to get into the surrender rooms, grab the recorder and get back in the water."

Sami nodded and dropped a key onto the table in front of me.

"For the door into the first surrender room," he said.

"How the hell did you get that?"

"Singapore's finest pickpocket managed to get an impression of it," he replied with a smile. Then he laid a small strip of paper beside the key. "The alarm code for the main alarm. Standard thirty-second delay, and before you ask, we planted our own mini-camera focussed on the keypad. We recorded one of the guides setting the alarm and locking the place down for the night."

"Smart," I responded, meaning it. "So, you've had people in and out of the place all along. Surely they could have lifted the recorder." I probably sounded a bit pissed off. I was beginning to feel as if I was being unnecessarily set up for this exercise.

"Too risky," Sami responded. "Yes, we've had people in and out, and so has Lu. My observers have picked a steady stream of loiterers in the surrender rooms. They rotate about fifteen people through there every couple of hours. They go away, change a shirt, put on dark glasses or whatever and come back in singles and pairs. They're using Lu's hotel, the Silver Sands, as their base. It's here." Sami indicated a building situated about a half kilometre away from the fort entrance down Siloso beach.

I did some calculations. If all of Lu's people were stationed there at night, I could stroll out of the Japanese surrender room and stop for a cigarette before I hit the water. Hell, I could probably even have a latte. I shook my head. I was dreaming. While most of Lu's thugs might be down the beach, I would put the big money on the fact that there would be half a dozen close to hand and they would be in radio contact with those monitoring the cameras. These guys were most likely in the hotel.

"We really have only one chance at this, Daniel, and that is why it has to be you. It's about a lot more than the money. This is about my half-brother and his family and the others. I want to bring Lu down, disgrace him, humiliate him and then crucify him, and that little recorder is the only thing that can do that. We have to do it right."

"Okay," I conceded, and he was right. Given any other building in any other location I'd have argued, but the unique location of the fort made getting away with the goods difficult enough, and having Lu's loiterers in the surrender rooms was the clincher. They were just waiting for someone to turn up and retrieve the recorder. There was no alternative. The pick-up had to be done when the place was deserted.

"So where the hell is the damn recorder?"

"In the right sleeve of this man here." Sami touched a button on his laptop and the face and upper body of a wax mannequin dressed in the uniform of a Japanese officer appeared. There was a wide, open-neck white shirt and gold braid on the right shoulder and also balancing off two bars of ribbons on the left. The dummy was wearing glasses, had a moustache and showed a lot of forehead. He was staring blankly down at a brown leather attaché case lying on the table in front of him. His waxen hands were resting on the table. I realised that I had taken several photographs of the same guy myself.

"Lieutenant-General T Numata, Chief of Staff, Southern Army," Sami said. The name appeared as white block letters painted on a wooden plaque sitting on the table beside the attaché case. The image flicked back to Numata's hands.

"Smart Stanley," I said. The poor guy had had the presence of mind to choose the arm that lay at a slight angle across the body. The sleeve opening was partially obscured by the hand itself.

"He pushed it as far up into the sleeve as he could reach," Sami said. The sleeve and hand came in for a close-up shot, filling the screen. There was no sign of the digital recorder. "The recorder is about the size of a cigarette lighter," Sami added. "Basically it's an MP3-type device that Stanley used as a personal note taker."

"So the plan is to hit the surrender room, disable the alarm, get the recorder and get into the water straight out front. What about the proximity alarm?"

"I don't think it will be an issue. One of my people triggered it. She accidentally dropped her camera over the railing. It appeared to be just a localised buzzer and sounded in the chambers themselves and The QuarterMaster Store below. It probably doesn't go onto a monitoring switchboard."

"You're right," I replied. "If I hit and run, it'll only sound for a few seconds while I'm groping our little waxwork and anyway, Lu's people will have already seen me on camera so they'll be moving. That being the case, what's a buzzer between friends?"

"Precisely. You grab the recorder, get out of the building and hit the water. We'll be waiting. A most simple plan!"

"Yeah," I agreed. "What could possibly go wrong?" I muttered dryly. Mentally my fingers were crossed. The great god Murphy and I were absolute enemies. The bastard had played his games with me too many times for me to ever think anything was going to go according to plan—ever!

"They must come for it. We know that Stanley made a very long telephone call from his hospital room. He told someone where he had planted that cursed recorder."

Thomas Lu was pacing the lounge of the Silver Sands' presidential suite. The room was virtually empty of furniture. The naked walls were stripped to bare plaster. The carpet was gone and only a layer of rubberised underlay muffled the sounds of the agitated man's movement.

There was a trestle table against one wall, and on the table sat four small television monitors. Two men sat watching the screens. Another man sat on a straight-backed chair to the left of the table. He wore a radio headset connected to the console that was positioned on the rung of a ladder that leaned against the wall beside him.

Thomas Lu was talking mainly to himself. He was a worried man, scared even. Nothing had gone as he had planned it. Stanley Loh had rejected the offer to sell. He had recorded the threats and the pleas that he, Thomas Lu, had made to the dead man. Now that damn recorder was a sword, a very big, sharp sword and it was hanging directly over his head.

Lu knew that whomever Stanley Loh had contacted from his hospital bed would come for the recorder and doubtless the evidence it contained would be used against him, to destroy or blackmail him.

Thomas Lu had been certain that with Loh's family held captive, he could have made the man talk and tell him where the recorder was hidden. Loh and his family would still have been killed, of course, but he would have played the lie long enough to have retrieved the recorder. As it was, Loh's final act of getting himself shot had foiled even that alternative. The man who killed Loh was dead a heartbeat after Loh's body hit the floor, killed by Lu in a fit of frustrated rage.

Now Thomas Lu stopped pacing. He went and stood at the suite's huge picture window. Below him lay Siloso Beach and beyond the breakwater islands was the grey ocean. As far as the eye could see there were ships of all sorts, all riding at anchor, waiting to enter the harbour and load or unload their cargo.

On board one of those ships Lu knew was a container that held two billion American dollars. One of those billions was for him. It was a combined finder's fee and the balance of what he needed to secure his full share in Intella. The other billion was for the share he promised he would secure for the Colombians.

The problem now was that Lu hadn't managed to secure that share from Stanley Loh to fulfil his end of the bargain, and unless he retrieved the recorder there was no guarantee he would have any shareholding whatsoever in the project himself, and certainly nothing for the South Americans. He needed that recorder and it's damning evidence.

"They must come," Lu whispered to his reflection in the window as dusk gathered outside. "They must come for it."

11

"Tonight we go!"

"Tonight it is," I replied. "Have you got the odds and sods I asked for?"

"Yes, no problem. At 19:30 get the MRT to Marina Bay. When you come above ground just walk straight down the pathway. There'll be a car waiting."

"Got that," I replied and we hung up. When the time came I would walk the couple of hundred metres from the hotel to City Hall MRT and grab the red line. Ed the Tourist mightn't be up with the play on the MRT but his alter ego always used it in the past in preference to a car. The MRT is the quick, painless alternative to Singapore's above-ground traffic and the system is easy to understand and use. In my wallet I had a travelcard from a previous visit and it still had a few dollars worth of travel on it.

"What should I do until evening? I asked myself. It was only a few minutes after ten in the morning. There was a long day stretching out ahead of me. I hate the pre-mission waiting around and always have. I guess it's the same as a professional sports person. You want game on just as soon as you can. Once the ball is kicked off, the nerves go and the training cuts in. I hoped that despite my being out of shape, my training and instincts would get me through what lay ahead. Not for the first time, I promised myself that I would not get so far out of shape ever again.

It wasn't as if I didn't still have muscles. There was muscle, not flab. I hadn't gone that far downhill, however my body felt heavy. My breathing, thanks to a constant diet of cigarettes, still wasn't what it ought to have been.

Too late to remedy that now!

So what do you do when you have time to kill and you can't, for the sake of your life, go hang out in a bar? Right, you go to the movies, which I did. I watched Sylvester Stallone save the world and just to rub it in, Bruce Willis did it all over again in *Die Hard 49* or something similar.

When I left the movie complex in the late afternoon, I had seen more men die in those four hours or so than had died in two world wars. The explosions were getting bigger and bigger and louder and louder. I wished then that I could have the pair of them, Stallone and Willis, in character and with live ammunition at my side that night. Not really, but sometimes it's depressing to be a mere mortal, even when you know that what you've just witnessed is pure Hollywood farce.

Back at the Carlton I ordered a light meal via room service. Pasta with fish, the perfect athlete's food. Not that I'm an athlete as such. It's just that if things didn't go to plan I could be swimming further or running longer and faster than anticipated, and maybe, just maybe, a little dietary help would make things easier for me. Christ, enough of the soliloquys!

Casting my uncertainties into the darkest corner of my brain, I finished my meal. Then I showered and dressed for the night to come.

It was only 18:30 when I left my room. I couldn't take it any more. I went for a quiet stroll just to try and keep the butterflies at bay. That's the thing. In my former job, anyone on the outside looking in saw a cool, calm and collected Daniel Swann about to go nonchalantly into battle. It might have seemed that way on the outside, but underneath it was always the same sheer hell. The stomach churning and the nerves wound as tight as guitar strings. The calm was and still is all an act. I sweat bullets at times like these.

Eventually, having strolled along the river, I found myself at Raffles Place at the appointed hour. I went down to the MRT and made the one-stop journey to Marina Bay. It was 19:35 when I came topside.

The Marina Bay MRT is set in parklands and there were few

people around at this time of evening. A hundred metres away I could see a light-coloured Mercedes parked on Station Road. I made my way towards it. I didn't recognise the man in the driver's seat, but Sami was in the back. No sooner was I in my seat than we are moving.

The boat was an ordinary-looking fishing trawler about fifty feet long. It was a far cry from the super-fast speedboats Sami uses out in the Gulf of Thailand. The plan here was simply to blend in with everything else afloat around Sentosa island and the inner basin. There were only four of us onboard: me, Sami, the skipper and a deckhand. I wasn't introduced and they didn't exhibit the slightest curiosity in what we were doing or my role in it. No doubt these were more of Sami's people. People used to doing exactly as they were told.

The outfit I changed into was a black skin suit. It wasn't a true wetsuit and it wasn't made of neoprene. This was a light, breathable space-age fabric that supposedly doesn't retain water but keeps the body heat in when in water and under extreme conditions. Under the suit I just had on a pair of briefs. There was no need for fins. I had rubberised dive socks on to protect my feet when I came ashore. There was a pair of trainers in the waterproof bag I'd be wearing when I hit the water. The sack also contained my communications headset, a flashlight and a nine-millimetre Browning Hi Power along with a shoulder holster. The Fairbairn Sykes clone I already had in a sheath on my belt.

I'd left my stiletto behind in Hong Kong, but the Fairbairn Sykes is as good a fighting knife as was ever made. As a final commando touch, I blacked out my face using greasy makeup. If I was caught on camera I didn't want the real me revealed. Plus, for creeping around in the dark, a black face is definitely *de rigueur*.

In the carry sack I also had a waterproof vinyl camera bag for the digital recorder. To drown the thing would not be desirable, especially given the cost in lives to date and the effort we were putting into recovering it.

We'd boarded the fishing boat at Tuas, on the far side of Jurong Island, the huge fuel refinery. Sentosa is only a few kilometres to the east. The night was a blaze of lights from the refinery and the tankers docked there or moored, waiting their turn to load or unload their precious cargo. The hulking sea monsters were everywhere. Each one was lit like a Christmas tree.

"All that energy being burned," Sami said as he came to stand beside me. "We are wasteful creatures."

"You're philosophical tonight," I replied, wondering what had brought this particular train of thought into play. Sami nodded.

"Wasted lives, Daniel. I can't help thinking of Stanley and how it all could have been avoided." He paused. "Now I'm asking you to risk your life in an attempt to right it. I'm not sure I should have done that."

"Stop the bull, Sami. I'm here and I'm doing it. I'm a friend and as you so convincingly put it to me, I'm the best man for the job."

"I know."

"Right, now I need to crap!" I looked around for anything resembling a toilet. Maybe I was going to have to hang my arse out over the stern? Instead, Sami pointed to a tiny, cupboard-sized door behind the trawler's bridge area. I crossed the deck and pulled the protesting hatch open.

The toilet was smaller than a damn wardrobe and the bowl had no seat. There was, however, a roll of paper hanging from a wire. The light didn't work, so in the end I left the door open—modesty has never been my strong point. My gut was water!

Ten minutes later we were approaching the narrow neck between Sentosa and the mainland. It was a few minutes to midnight.

"Labrador Park." Sami pointed to the mainland spur that was running into the sea opposite Fort Siloso. "There are the remains of another fort there." Sami leaned into the cockpit and said something to the man at the wheel. "Fort Pasir Panjang," he added when he turned back to me.

"Thanks for the history lesson," I muttered. My gut was still churning although there was now nothing in it. I was tense and Sami knew it.

"Just trying to distract you."

"I know. I just want to get moving."

"Any minute now." Sami ducked back into the cabin for more words with the skipper while I sucked in big gulps of air and settled the hood of my skin suit in place. I pulled on a pair of swim goggles and I was as ready as I was ever going to be. Let's get the game under way, I thought.

Apart from the reflected light of the city and ships on the water, Sentosa, from the angle we were approaching, gave nothing back. I could see a few dim lights down towards the neck and the construction lights where the new casino and other parts of the new complex were being built beside the bridge. From this angle, the island was just a dark mass.

The boat slowed. Sami came back out on deck.

"He'll nose us in a bit further. The tide is running out, so we'll go past the target and you can let it carry you back." As he spoke, he put on a pair of night-vision glasses. Sami hunched behind the cabin bulkhead to cut out as much light as he could from the cabin and the city behind us. I stood waiting as he scanned the island shoreline for a few seconds. Then he pointed.

"There!"

I squatted beside my friend and followed the line of his arm. I couldn't see anything but for the black silhouette of Sentosa framed against the glow of the hundreds of ships anchored beyond it. The boat was creeping closer to the island and finally I could see a faint line of phosphorescence where the water foamed on the rocks of the shore, but that was it.

"We're forty metres off the rocks," Sami said. He was still pointing, but now the direction he was indicating was several degrees back towards the boat's stern. I momentarily glimpsed a structure against the rocks and jungle. That was it. I had my point to aim for.

"Okay. I'm away."

"Good luck, Daniel. Watch your neck!"

"Always."

I took four big paces and levered myself off the low railing, throwing myself as far from the boat as possible to get clear of the propellers. I held my swim goggles in place with both hands as I landed feet first and sank.

The water was surprisingly cool. My momentum carried me under a metre or two and then I was drifting back towards the surface. I could feel the pull of the outgoing tide grabbing at me. It wasn't fierce, but things can be deceiving. When my head broke the surface of the water, I managed to quickly orientate myself and started swimming for the island, keeping the city lights behind me.

I began swimming breaststroke, but when I realised that I was drifting relentlessly towards the harbour entrance, I switched to the basic Australian crawl. I'm a strong swimmer, but because I'm out of condition I made hard work of what was a very short swim. I was still crabbing across the current when eventually my hands touched rock. I dropped my goggles, leaving them hanging around my neck as I started picking my way through the slick rocks and tangles of weed towards the shore.

My night vision was growing better. The lights from the oil refinery in the distance showed me a hard edge in silhouette away to my right. I made my way towards it and the darkness slowly gave up one secret at least. There was a ramp and landing stage with a small pillbox behind it. Beyond that again was a concrete pathway that pushed back into the dark under the cliff face.

I climbed up onto the landing. The concrete was covered with weed and the outgoing tide had left it as slick as ice, so I stayed on my hands and knees and crawled up the ramp until I got onto the dry surface. I looked back towards Sami's boat. Big mistake, of course, because in an instant the night vision I had been cultivating was blown away by the glare of a million city lights. I cursed, but I did make out Sami's boat as it continued on up towards the Sentosa bridge. The plan was that they would stooge around up that way until I could collect the recorder, then they would come back at a run. My head-mounted flashlight would guide them to me in the water. Simple plan.

Simple plan, my brain repeated as I turned back to the task in hand. I hate that phrase. I opened the waterproofed bag and firstly got into my shoulder harness. I'd checked the gun on the boat, but I checked it again. There were thirteen rounds in the magazine and one in the breech. If I need any more, I'd be out of luck. Singapore is not the place to start a gun battle and if my meagre supply of ammunition didn't do the job then so be it.

I pulled off my dive shoes and stowed them in the bag before getting into my sneakers and slipping on my gloves. The lightweight gloves were made from leather and a fire-resistant fabric. When I played soldier, spy or whatever, we called them "flash gloves". They are designed to withstand heat and protect your hands from minor blasts and the like. They were crucial now in order to keep my fingerprints and any DNA out of the picture.

The last pieces of my attire were my communicator and my headlamp. I would only use the light once I was in the building. I closed the sack and shrugged my way back into its straps. Now it was time to check in with Sami. The transmitter I had was a live mike model. Once it was turned on I could simply talk and it would transmit. No need for switches or buttons.

"I'm ashore and about to go climbing."

"Careful."

"Always." I moved past the blockhouse and started along the pathway that linked it to the fort. Trees cut out the stars and the smell of salt water mingled with the rich, earthy smell of rotting humus. Welcome to the jungle!

The ladder was badly rusted, as I had noted from above, but it appeared strong enough to hold me. I slowly started climbing, keeping my weight distributed to the sides rather than on the centre of the rungs. It wasn't high, as ladders go, but it was high enough. If it gave way, I was going to crash-land on the concrete below or, if I missed that, it was down onto the rocks beside the concrete slab.

A couple of times the rungs creaked alarmingly. One of the safety hoops was hanging drunkenly in space because one end had detached itself from the ladder. I managed to negotiate my way carefully around it. The sound of the offending piece of pipe falling would be heard clearly over and above the hiss and slap of the water by any watcher sitting above me in the dark.

Hazard number one overcome, I found myself at the plate that sealed off the ladder. I had figured from day one that getting past it would be easy enough, provided there was no one above sitting waiting for me. I hung there on the ladder and strained my ears, trying to separate the sounds of the water and constant hum of the city from the silence of the island. Of course there is no such thing as complete silence outside of a vacuum. What we call silence has many voices. There is the noisy silence of nature and then there is the unnatural silence of the hunter waiting for his prey. After many years in the bush, hunting and being hunted, I have developed the ability to recognise this silence. That ability has been the difference between life and death many times. Their death, my life!

Hanging there on the ladder with my senses on full alert, I gave silent thanks for my decision to go and play in the bush on Ubin. Those few hours reawakened instincts in me that had been seriously dulled by alcohol and bad living. They had almost been lost to me. Now they were back and I knew I was not alone.

12

The watcher was sitting on the edge of the gun platform. He was bored. This was the third night he had been there. He and the others had waited until the fort shut for the night and then they had quietly drifted into the complex to their assigned positions. Once there, they had to stay alert, not only for the expected attempt to recover the recording device they had been told was hidden somewhere in the surrender rooms, but also for the occasional ranger patrols. But they weren't there to stop anyone getting into the fort; they were in position to stop anyone leaving.

Wang Yoo's instructions had been to hide himself in cover, but after two fruitless nights sitting in the deep shadows, he moved out into the open. He was scared of snakes and out in the open he believed he would see a snake before it saw him.

Yoo wanted a cigarette, badly. Lu had ordered them not to smoke, not to do anything that would alert others to their presence. So far, Yoo had obeyed the directive. Now, tired, bored and hours from his bed, he decided that he would enjoy at least this one small pleasure. He knew that the boss would not be coming to the fort this or any other night, and he also knew that the others were all in their designated positions. They would not come roaming, so there was no one to tell on him off for his minor indiscretion.

Yoo shielded the flare of his cigarette lighter with his cupped hands and lit up, gratefully sucking the nicotine hit into his lungs. He doesn't see the shadow that moved away to his right. He didn't hear the sickening thud as his skull and a metal stanchion collided.

I had no qualms about laying the watching man out. There was a gun in a belt holster and a cellphone in his pocket. I think I probably hit him too hard. He was still alive, but no doubt his skull was fractured. Would anyone come to relieve him or was he there for the night? I had no way of knowing. I could have left him sitting there and slipped away, but what I didn't want was to have him come after me, or be there to intercept me if things went wrong and I had to return the way I'd come.

I tossed the gun, a Chinese copy of a Russian Markarov, seawards and followed it with the cellphone. There was no way this mid-thirties Chinese guy was going to be a threat to me, so I left him where he lay. Callous? Maybe, but this game was to the death and the death wasn't going to be mine.

I skirted the fire direction tower and paused where the tunnel leading back into the fort begins. Tunnel is a euphemism in this case. This is more like a very deep concrete trench with a steel mesh roof across the top. Various magazines and rooms open off it as it pushes up and back towards the heart of the fort.

Was there someone stationed in the tunnel or perhaps up above, where they could see down through the mesh roof? Anyone with night vision glasses would have a field day. I figured that there were none of those in operation over here. Otherwise why did the guy I'd just brained not have a pair? Rightly or wrongly I had to go with my gut instinct. I could have used a night scope myself right then, but they're cumbersome at best and they have some big disadvantages. Anyone flashing a high-intensity light beam or a laser into the system can fry your eyes—permanently.

I started up the tunnel, moving slowly, hugging the walls, senses tasting the night. Overhead a military jet blasted the night apart, destroying my hearing for the moment. As the aircraft's rumbling roar faded, something stirred in the night. A rat in one of the side rooms? A lizard maybe or even a snake? Whatever, my senses told me it wasn't human, so it was of no concern. I carried on climbing up towards the core of the fort.

The tower with the two cameras was above and to my right. I couldn't see it from down in the concrete trench, but I knew that once I emerged from the tunnel I would be in view and the alarm would sound. The thing was that until I had the recorder, Lu's thugs wouldn't try and stop me. That was my theory anyway. The alternative was that they would try and grab me and apply some very excruciatingly painful techniques to my body to try to get me to spill the device's location. I had to figure that they wouldn't have time to go that route, so they'd wait for me to get the MP3 or whatever Stanley's recorder actually was, then they'd jump me.

I was near the tunnel entrance. The trench was ramping up to ground level. The mesh was gone from above me. I stopped moving with my head just below the edge of the concrete wall. When I emerged it would be at a jog. I checked that the key to the door and the alarm code were in the zip pocket of my top.

I bellied forward a half metre. Now I was at the very edge of the tunnel but still below the level of the cameras. To my right were two buildings and ahead was the road leading on up towards Fort Siloso Square. There were several low-voltage lamps dotted about but no serious security lights. The glow from the city had lightened the gloom to a grey-on-grey tone. It was like looking out through a window on a dull day through a layer of thick gauze.

To my left the road curved down to The QuarterMaster Store. A long line of trench mortars was set above the road. Behind the squat, wide-mouthed guns a footpath ran across the face of the hill. Off this was the bridge that led to the top level of The QuarterMaster Store where the surrender rooms are situated.

In total I had about a hundred yards to travel. I estimated ten seconds to open the door. Twenty more to disable the alarm. A minute to get orientated and find Lieutenant-General T Numata's waxen image. Another thirty seconds and I would be on my way back to the water, hopefully well ahead of Lu's guys.

What is it about smokers? Okay, I'm a smoker, but there are times when you need to fight the urge, and this was definitely one of those times for me. However this was obviously not the right time for the man in the trees up ahead of me, just as it hadn't been for the one I'd taken out down at the fire control tower. I could see the ruby glow of the cigarette back in the trees. The goon wasn't bothering to shield it. This was just another idiot on Thomas Lu's payroll. The guy was possibly only seventy metres from the ramp into the surrender rooms. He could be at the door in a matter of a minute or less once I went in.

I lay motionless, trying to get a handle on this. I hadn't figured that Lu's men would be so close. Seventy metres is far too close for comfort. This guy would probably let me go in and then follow me, if not into the building, onto the bridge at least. There he would probably try to nail me coming back out. If Lu had one man hidden this close, how many more did he have staking the place out?

"Plan two," I whispered. The voice-activated headset sent my verbalised thought out to Sami.

"Say again."

"Just talking to myself," I replied. "Sami this is going to be fast and loud and dirty. Start back right now."

"Roger."

Sami was gone. I was alone and I was shit scared. This was not going to be pretty in anyone's book. I was going to be killing some guys and they were going to be trying to kill me. Problem was this wasn't the Thai or Cambodian jungle, this was Singapore. Guns and gun battles, especially those resulting in death, were not going to amuse the powers that be, and that most assuredly was a fact.

"Fuck it. Let's do it!"

I get to my feet and started for The QuarterMaster Store. My jog became a sprint as I raced down the pathway behind the mortars and crossed the bridge, fishing the key to the door out of my pocket as I went. I could sense rather than see movement in the shadows on the hillside above me. I was tempted to hit the landing, go down the steps to the lower level, wait for this clown and take him out before I opened the door, but there would be others coming. Speed was my friend, my only fucking friend right at that moment.

There was a dim light on the landing, but I snapped on my headlamp as I reach the door. The key went in easily enough but it wouldn't turn. I applied more pressure, praying that it wouldn't break. Finally, the lock snapped back and I was in. I was moving as quickly as I could. The beam from my headlamp sliced through the pitch-blackness inside the windowless room. I ignored the alarm completely. It didn't matter if it was activated. In fact that might work in my favour, I thought.

The beam from my lamp picked up the faces of the men sitting and standing around the table. This, the tableaux in the first room, unnerved me for a second. The face of the one seated figure was looking directly at me. In the light of day he was realistic enough but in the lamplight he looked as if he was about to ask me what the hell I was doing there.

I went through into the second room at a jog. The narrow beam of my headlamp cut a swathe through the blackness but it didn't reach to the far end of this the longer room. The standing and seated figures down there faded into shadows. But I wasn't looking for my target down there.

Numata was the first seated figure to my right. I stepped over the railing and the proximity alarm sounded. It was an annoyingly high-pitched buzzer, as these things tend to be. I reach across the table for Numata's right sleeve and start groping for the digital recorder.

At first it seemed that the sleeve was empty and then, just as the main alarm started its banshee screaming, I found it. Small, metallic and worth billions of dollars. I pocketed the note taker and zipped my pocket closed as the beam from a flashlight flared back in the room beyond. The man on the hill was coming in after me. I figured he'd wait outside. Damn!

I debated sprinting to the exit door at the far end, but no time. Instead I killed my light. I was about to go around the table and crouch behind Numata's figure when I had a brainstorm. The empty seat at the head of the table, it was right beside me. Head? I was wearing a hood. There was an Indian soldier wearing a beret standing behind the chair. I yanked the beret off his head and I fell into the chair, pulling the Browning from my shoulder holster as I did so. I pulled the headlamp off my head and let my communicator fall down my chest as I pulled the beret on. Hopefully, having my face blacked out I'd look like an African officer. Whatever, I needed to buy a moment of time.

I froze as the light came probing into the room. I was facing away from the doorway, which was slightly behind my left shoulder. The man with the flashlight was no doubt pressed against the side of the entrance. My survival in the first instance depended on whether he was on the left or right side.

The light beam started down the left wall and swept the long room moving left to right. He was against the near side and that meant he wouldn't have the angle to see me unless he stepped right into the room. If he'd been on the other wall, he would have swept my side first.

The light just touched my shoulder and swept back the other way. I sensed Mr Smoker had moved into the room. Then I could see him out of the corner of my eye. The beam swung back. He was slightly in front of me now. My impression of a waxwork had worked, it seemed. The guy with the light was probably looking for a standing, crouching or prone figure, not one seated at the head of the table, obviously part of the display.

The alarm siren was shrieking and the buzzer too. It was nerve-shredding pandemonium in the surrender room and no doubt for a hundred metres in every direction outside. I figured the rangers and cops and everyone in Singapore would be heading this way soon to see what was going on. The guy with the light continued moving forward. The gun in his right hand reflected the light from the flashlight held in his left. He advanced further into the room, pushing the gun and light ahead of his body. Then he crouched and began sweeping the light under and behind the tables, trying to find a living being amongst the ghosts. I stayed motionless for the moment, but it was time to be going. I didn't want to be there when another of Lu's little helpers came in.

Chow Lee's heart was pounding, his ears ringing from the screaming alarms. He was sweating, close to panic. The Fang Triad gang member was not comfortable using a gun. The automatic in his hand felt unnatural. He preferred a hatchet or a knife. However, the man he had tracked into this place had a gun. Where was he? Where was the shadow he was hunting?

Lee pressed against the wall at the entrance to the Japanese surrender room and passed the beam of his flashlight down the long room. He had never been in there before. The figures standing and seated seemed so lifelike. The muzzle of Lee's gun jerked from one side to another.

Lee took a deep breath to try and steady himself. The sounds of the alarms and his adrenaline overload had left his nerves raw. He moved the flashlight beam to his right. There were more figures. A tall one in white stood leaning over a table. The muzzle of the gun jerked. Lee almost fired but he restrained himself, and the cone of light moved on. There was a figure seated at the head of the table immediately to his front right. This motionless figure was dressed in black, just another dummy. Lee stepped further into the room, his searching beam moving on again probing.

He crouched, stabbing his light under the long tables. Again he started on his left before he brought the light back to the right. He was searching for a crouching man hidden behind the seated figures. Had the man he was seeking already left the room through the exit door?

Lee's light probed further. He was half-turned now as the light moved down the room, probing the shadows under the table. Then the beam touched the feet of the seated figure at the head of the table and it stopped. Instead of plain shoes or military boots, this figure was wearing Nike sneakers. New-looking sneakers!

Black! There were uniforms of all colours on the dummies in this place, but no other one was wearing black. The man he had followed into this place had been wearing black!

Chow Lee's gun pointed away from the light beam. He tried to swivel on his knees, turning to bring the gun in line, but he was too slow. There were two flashes. He felt both of the bullets that killed him.

My two shots hit the man with the flashlight in the chest. The flashlight spun to the floor. I saw the shocked expression on the gunman's face as the light beam hit him and rolled away.

I stood and stepped over the railing. There was no way I was going to waste a second and check whether Mr Smoker was dead. I didn't care. The fact he was not shooting in my direction was all that mattered.

My head was splitting from the sound of the alarms. I needed to get the hell out of there and into the water just as fast as I could. The two guys coming in through the outer door, however, seemed to have other ideas.

13

"What is happening? Have they got him?"

"I can't tell, Mr Lu," the man on the radio responded. "They are not talking to me."

"Call them!"

"Yes, Mr Lu." The operator opened a channel and a ragged burst of gunfire filled the room through the radio's small speaker. The gunfire gave way to the wailing of the siren. There was no more gunfire, nothing other than the screaming alarm. The operator called out names, but he received no reply. "They are not answering, Mr Lu."

"Send the others."

"They are already on their way."

Thomas Lu sank heavily down onto a chair. It was supposed to have been so simple.

"What's happening?"

The thing about gunfights, particularly in the dark, is that they generally involve a lot of chaos, and this is exactly what happened at this moment in time.

The two men came in through the double door shoulder to shoulder. Big mistake! They were silhouetted against the glare of the Singapore night sky, while I was in the almost total darkness of a windowless room.

I was lying flat on the floor and the beam of the flashlight one of the newcomers was waving about passed by above me. There was a shout and shots, but they were not fired at me. The light was focussed on the surrender tableaux away to my left. The realism of the wax figure sitting with his head turned in the direction of the intruders had startled the newcomers. The unfortunate dummy now had no head.

This momentary distraction allowed me to get away five rounds in rapid succession. It wasn't fancy, but at a range of less than ten feet it was very effective. I covered the man on the left and fired twice, then I swung the gun onto the other man, the one with the torch, and fired three more. The last round was unintentional, but things like that happen in combat, especially with an unfamiliar weapon.

The sound of my shots barely registered above that of the alarm. The newcomers were down. I then had seven rounds left in my automatic before the Browning became as useful as a doorstop.

Again I didn't stop to check on the fallen men or grab another weapon. I vaulted them and hit the landing rolling, my gun looking for a target. There were none there. No more bad guys waited on the landing or the bridge. The sky was blazing with stars and the moon was like a giant icy spotlight vying with the lights of Singapore for attention.

"Oh great," I muttered as I started down the wide stairs. Just when I needed the cover of maximum darkness, the universe took over. I just had to get across the terrace, down the ramp, past the toilets and the lower terrace, and into the water. Easy, huh?

"Are you okay? We heard the alarms and shots?"

"I'm okay. I have it. Going for the water now."

"Negative, Daniel. There's a Police Coast Guard boat heading straight for the fort. They'll be there before we are. Go for your entry point."

"Okay." I started to run for the ridge, but Sami came back to me immediately.

"Abort that. There's another launch coming in from the channel. We're going to have to bug out. Can you make the sea beyond Siloso Beach and we'll go round?"

"Roger that," I replied. I had to get out of the fort. I started down the roadway, keeping close to the wall on the right, hugging the shadows.

The black outfit I was wearing and my blacked-out face were hopefully doing their job. I was just another shadow, albeit a fast moving one.

There were police sirens, a lot of them, and they were getting louder. Then below me, around the curve of the driveway, I could see figures coming up towards the fort. The moonlight was glinting off the guns they held ready in their hands. These most definitely were not the good guys. I was still in the shadows and I didn't think they'd seen me. I knew they would in a few seconds unless I got the hell out of there. There was only one place to go: up!

I scrambled up the steep grassy bank to my right. It bordered the driveway for half its length. There was a narrow flat terrace on top with a wide drain running down the centre. I figured that I'd have at least some cover if I needed it. I was ten or fifteen feet above the road. There had been no shouts or shots, so I had to believe they hadn't seen me.

I stopped and knelt in cover at the edge of the jungle fringe. I needed to protect Stanley's recorder if I had to hit the water again. I pulled off the backpack and put the device into the waterproof vinyl camera bag I'd earmarked for it. I zipped the bag into my pocket. It was possible I might have to ditch the backpack at some stage.

I stayed where I was and continued playing at being a shadow as the half dozen guys who were sprinting up the road pounded by below me.

The moment they were gone I started away again, keeping as low as I could, slipping into the straps of the backpack as I went. Ideally, I thought I should ditch it, but I wasn't about to leave any evidence of my presence anywhere near Fort Siloso if I could help it.

I paused at the end of the terrace. There were lights at the hotel gate down and around the corner to my right and there were lights around the aquarium buildings and the concourse itself. There didn't appear to be anyone playing sentry near the vehicle barrier or the fort ticket office, but who could tell. I had to take a chance. In the first instance, I didn't want Lu's men to get me and, in the second, I couldn't let the police catch me in the fort.

I slithered down the grassy bank to the road and started towards the shelter of the aquarium complex. I figured I could move under cover as far as the covered bus shelter and then sprint across the concourse to the beach. There I'd swim out to the nearest island, go over that and drop into the water on the far side. I was not prepared to try and negotiate the nets strung between any of the four islands in the dark.

I made it across the road and had just stepped into the aquarium grounds when the first police car came howling around the corner beyond the bus shelter with its full sound and light show going. I threw myself flat behind some shrubs as the car swept on towards the vehicle barrier at the fort gate. Doubtless the driver hadn't expected the barrier to be down because there was a screech of brakes. The car came to a tyre-smoking halt.

As the three or four police in the vehicle got out of the car and descended on the barrier, I crawled on hands and knees towards the cover of the aquarium buildings. A second police cruiser arrived in equally dramatic fashion. This one had a spotlight in operation and its powerful beam started sweeping the aquarium grounds. The white scythe came towards me and I was caught with no cover.

No cover, that is, unless you count a pool filled with bloody great turtles. There was no alternative, so I vaulted into the water as the white beam from the spotlight swept by above me. The sound of my clumsy entrance into the pool hopefully was drowned out by the sound of cars and sirens.

Now, I don't know a hell of a lot about turtles, but from what I'd seen of these huge guys on my reconnaissance run, they had beak-like mouths. I was in water that was almost chest high. I felt a boulder move under my feet and something slammed into my hip. I needed to tuck myself away in cover with all my bits hugged in tight and hope that these big guys didn't get hungry for human flesh or that the guy with the spotlight didn't get creative.

At one end of the pool was a pedestrian bridge. I half-swam and half-waded to it and ducked under. The bridge was quite wide and that gave me the room to get well under and out of sight. Turtles were nudging me. One came right up to me and surfaced. We looked at each other eyeball to eyeball in the half-light before he turned and swam away. I'm not sure if these guys are nocturnal or not, or if my sudden entry into their world just woke them up. Whatever, they were agitated. So far, although I had been pushed and nudged, I hadn't been bitten. Long may the status quo remain, I thought.

There was a mesh under the bridge that cut the turtle pool off from the neighbouring pool or, I guessed, the other half of the same pool. If I could make it into the second pool, I could maybe get beyond the aquarium complex and into the cover of the trees.

I tried the mesh but it was heavy gauge and I didn't have the tools necessary to cut it, so option number one was not available. I decided that I just had to tough it out where I was for the moment and pray the police didn't get interested in the turtle pool.

There were more police vehicles arriving and, suddenly, one, and then two flashlights were playing on the water of the pool. Another joined it. I hunched low and turn my head away from the lights. Because I was deep under the bridge, I hoped that the light would bounce off the water surface and be reflected away and not penetrate the water. I could hear the cops talking. One suggested that no one in their right mind would be in the water with the turtles. Maybe he was right!

The cops' discussion was suddenly interrupted by the sound of gunfire. Several weapons were in action back at the fort. There were shouts from the direction of the fort gate. The trio with the flashlights ran off. The turtle pool hopefully was now forgotten. This surely was my chance to get out of there.

I slipped out from under the bridge and gingerly levered myself out of the water. There were at least eight or nine police vehicles clustered on the roadway leading up to the fort. A senior officer was addressing a heavily armed squad. Other officers were under cover behind vehicles and stoneworks, pointing a variety of weapons up the fort driveway. Shots were still sounding from up above. A police helicopter was working a big light above the fort itself. Attention, it seemed, was all focused back up that way and that suited me just fine.

As I ran along the covered walkway to the bus pickup point, yet another police car came roaring down the road. I took cover behind a large standing refrigerator and waited while it passed. I could have done with some light refreshments, but the door on the drinks chiller was chained and padlocked shut. I moved on as the latest squad car screeched to a halt beside the others.

This was the moment! Keeping low, I sprinted across the broad concourse. There were no shouts or shots and I was down the wooden terraces onto the sand. Here I took shelter behind a bar kiosk while I got my bearings.

"Sami?"

"I hear you, Daniel. Have you got a plan C?"

"Why?"

"There are two police launches patrolling the sea side and another chopper heading that way. We're having to move out."

"Shit!"

"Yeah."

"I'll go bush and work out a plan."

'I'll try and come up with something."

"Please do. My arse is feeling more than a little exposed over here," I replied, and I really did feel like a little boy lost. Right at that moment in time I was not feeling confident of anything. The only thing I did know was that I had to get the hell away from the fort. The gunfire had stopped but there were more police sirens in the air as well as the sound of approaching choppers, a whole bunch of them. It was time to move, but God only knew where and how.

With Simone, I'd walked the beach promenade past the hotels, including the one I knew to be Lu's. That was obviously where the second wave of his gunmen had hailed from. It was now almost 01:30, the Rasa resort still had lights blazing. I was sure their guests were wondering what the hell was happening. Some of them would no doubt be thinking WW2 was being reprised.

I could see that some of the beachside bars back towards the middle of the island appeared to still be open. Or at least they had lights on. Not that that would be any help to me, especially dressed as I was. I left my temporary sanctuary and started along the beach away from the fort. I stayed off the tram road for the moment, and then a chopper came sweeping in from behind the Rasa Sentosa Resort. The million-candlepower spotlight was turning the night into day along the beach. In seconds it would catch me if I didn't move, and fast.

I ran for the jungle fringing the beach road. I knew that one of the entrances to the nature walk started close to where I was heading. If I hadn't already overshot it, I might just get into the cover of the bush.

The entrance to the trail was right in front of me. I threw myself into it and rolled into the undergrowth. I lay there head down, making like a shadow as for a moment night turned into day all around me. The chopper thudded on by and was gone, at least for a while. I imagined that any young lovers having a late-night grope out on the beach were going to get a real shock this night.

On the trail, I started to climb quickly. Height is an advantage in virtually any situation. I needed to get off the island tonight because I had no doubt that there would be police and troops scouring every centimetre of Sentosa come dawn.

I turned on my headlamp and screwed it right down to the dimmest beam possible. The track forked. One pathway, the one I'd come down with Simone, curved away to my left. However, there was an old overgrown trail going away to the right, along the side of the hill. My only way off the island was either over the bridge or by swimming. The bridge was my first option. The old trail at least led in the right direction.

"Are you still okay?" It was Sami in my ear. I answered in the affirmative as I threaded my way along the defunct pathway. The jungle was reclaiming it and in a year or so it would be gone. For now it was the equivalent of a three-lane highway for an old jungle fighter like me. Another chopper roared by overhead. Even under the cover of the trees, I shielded my lamp, dim as it was. If the machines flying above the island didn't have heat-sensitive kit fitted, I had to believe that others with that technology mounted on them would soon be here. I pushed on as quickly as I could. I climbed a small ridge and one pace beyond that was a wide concrete pathway.

"The Luge," my memory yelled at me. I now knew exactly where I was. Then an idea hit me with the force of a snowball in the face. Would it work? I started jogging down the Luge runway. The Beach Station wasn't far away. The trains wouldn't be running at 02:00 in the morning and anyway, even if they had been, they would be the first things the cops covered. My idea was a desperate one, but then I was a desperate man. My options were running out with every passing minute. Another chopper swept overhead, forcing me to duck back into the bush for a moment.

The Beach Station, last stop on the short Sentosa railway, was deserted, as you'd expect at this time of night. I had to assume that there were security CCTV cameras in the station itself, so I avoided it. I skirted the station building and finally found what I needed. There was a concrete abutment, one that with luck I could scramble up onto. Once there it would give me access to what just may be my way out of there.

It took a running jump and a lot of upper-body work, but I made it onto the wall. The next stunt I was going to pull would see whether I lived or I died in a ball of sparks and the smell of barbecued flesh.

14

"They have all failed!" Thomas Lu was sitting in a darkened suite of the Silver Sands Hotel, unaware that the man carrying the very thing he most sought had just minutes before run past the hotel. There were three men in the room with Lu. Two were manning the monitors for the hidden cameras. The third was the man on radio receiver.

The image of a shadowy figure running across the bridge connecting the surrender rooms to the pathway was frozen in mid-stride on one of the monitors. Even on maximum magnification there was nothing to identify the man. His face was obscured by greasepaint, a hood and a communications set. There was a gun holstered under his left arm.

"Between them, this man and the police have killed six of my men. The police have the others."

The men sitting with Lu nodded but said nothing. They knew all this. The police had five men in custody and another was on his way to hospital with a broken skull. The man on the radio was monitoring the police radio frequency.

"Who is he? Who is he working for?" Lu stood and walked to the window. The men in police custody wouldn't talk. They were members of a Mainland Chinese triad. Lu paid the gang a lot of money to use their people to augment his own as required. They knew little and they valued their lives and the rewards that their silence would buy them.

The recorder was gone. The police were searching Sentosa for more of Lu's men. They didn't know about the outsider. They assumed that, for whatever reason, a group of Chinese gangsters had decided to use Sentosa island, specifically Fort Siloso, as the site for a gun battle. They had sealed off the island and would conduct a ground search of every inch of it when daylight arrived.

The railing attached to the side of the concrete train track wasn't electrified, which was just as well, considering I was hanging from it with both hands. I breathed a sigh of relief as I hauled myself up. I stood unsteadily on the nearest of the two wide concrete tracks that supported the trams. Obviously, when the Sentosa train stops running for the night, the current is turned off. I needed lucky breaks like that. It was that sort of logic that had caused me to attempt this stunt in the first place. Now I was standing on the concrete strip ready to take the next step.

The plan, such as it was, couldn't be simpler. The concrete tracks that the trains run on were wide, almost a couple of feet across (in old speak), and the tops were flat. They were also above the eye line of most people on the ground. Humans are good at looking down and straight ahead, but they don't naturally look up, at least not without cause, and that's a fact I was hoping would be proven true about now.

I took my first tentative steps and got my balance. Then I started to jog, slowly at first, but I got faster as my confidence increased. As I crossed above a road, another police car raced by underneath. I kept jogging until a sweeping chopper started to run an intercept course with the train track. I was close to the Merlion tower by then and I figured the pilot would have to stay well clear of that. There are all sorts of towers and aerials on the island, including the Sky Tower plus the cable car wires. The pilots would be most concerned with staying out of trouble. That at least would work to my advantage. I hoped.

I dropped back down onto the electric railing and squatted there, keeping as low as I could. I used one hand on the top strip to balance myself and prayed that one black glove against the white concrete wasn't going to give me away. It didn't. The chopper swept on above me and banked away over the water of the inner harbour, preparing to come back. I stayed where I was for the moment and waited for him to set his course. This time he ran a line a hundred metres away from me between the shore and monorail lines. I scrambled back onto the concrete track and started running again.

I passed through the deserted Imbiah Station and on towards the bridge. The lights of the construction sites glared up at me. With these intense lights, plus the city lights and the moon, it was like a gloomy day rather than the dead of night. I had no choice but to run on. If I couldn't get off the island before dawn I was in big trouble.

Twice, more choppers caused me to stop and hunch down, balancing on the electrical railing, but I was now beyond the construction area and just starting out over the water. It was maybe ten metres down to the tide. A long way to drop.

I guess that to think the police wouldn't have sealed the bridge was naïve in the extreme. Of course they had sealed the bridge. I could see the lights of a dozen squad cars flashing like a Christmas parade across the water between VivoCity and the St James' Power Station. What was my plan beyond this point? I didn't have a plan. I took time out after the next chopper pass to try Sami again.

The fishing boat had been stopped by a police launch. Sami had ditched the night-vision glasses and everything else even slightly incriminating. He had, however, hidden the communicator in the hold. There was a substantial cargo of fish aboard and he was playing the role of a deck hand. Genuine papers were examined and after a quick five-minute rumble, the boat was allowed to sail on. They had no choice but to head back for Tuas. The police boats had totally blockaded Sentosa. I was well and truly on my own.

It was 03:45 and another chopper was coming from the Siloso end of the island. I was part way across the main channel. If I chose to go on and maybe get in the water and swim towards VivoCity, I could get out again over there. Then I had to avoid the police and get to safety. Or should I drop into the water now and swim into the madness of the container complex?

That particular decision made itself with the appearance of another chopper coming from the direction of Changi. Is this the one that will inevitably be geared with infrared and all the high-tech gear? Whatever, I was now going to be sandwiched between the twin spotlights, one coming from each direction. There was simply no place left to hide but in the water below.

It was a long way down, but I didn't have a choice. I crossed my arms, and put my hands over my head to keep it and my communicator and headlight from being blown off on impact. For a moment I said a prayer of sorts. I'd dropped from Sea Kings in training but this was the highest I'd ever done it. Hell, it was a long way down. I stepped off the rail.

15

They say hitting the water from a great height is like landing on concrete. Well, the water sure as hell felt like concrete. The straps of the small pack on my back gouged into my armpits. Down I went, and down, and further down. I swear I felt the bottom for a second and then I was coming back up, slowly, so slowly. The lights from the choppers blazed down at me as they crossed overhead. All I could see in that instant was murky water, metres of it above me. I cursed the fact that I had succumbed to the smoking bug again and my lung capacity had suffered accordingly.

My assent seemed so slow that I was starting to panic. As a trained diver, I know there's plenty of air in the lungs. The real danger, of course, is giving in to the overwhelming desire to drag air into your burning lungs. Water, of course, is no substitute for oxygen for most of us. For the last metre or two, I was fighting that desperate urge.

Eventually I got to the surface and gulp air in I did—big time! There was a rip and it was carrying me under the bridge towards Pulau Brani. The tide, it seemed, had turned. That was good, I think. I kicked a little and angled to the left. I wanted to get out of there as soon as possible and figure out what the hell I was going to do next. That's the trouble with this sort of stunt, you have to make it up as you go along. Because of what I was wearing, I couldn't blend in with any crowd, even if I could find one to hide amongst. My change of clothes was on the damn fishing boat with Sami. I figured I might pass for a jogger wearing one of those new one-piece running outfits, but that was about it. The face paint wasn't going to help convince anyone I was just out for a run.

Cutting across the current was tiring. I swam breaststroke, keeping as low in the water as I could. The ambient light plus the glare from the searching choppers turned the water an oily black. Hopefully my head with the black hood over it was lost to anyone looking in my direction.

I was in a small basin. The bridge offshoot that connected Pulau Brani to the Sentosa Bridge was above me. Concrete channelling connected the mainstream to the basin beyond. The basin was lined with docked container ships on both sides. If I wanted to get to the mainland, I was going to have to cross that piece of water. The tide was now drawing me into one of the concrete channels. I went with it. Above, on the access road, I could hear heavy trucks on the move. The container port never slept and that was both good and bad for me.

The moment I was beyond the bridge, I started kicking for the stern of the ship moored closest to me. It was only thirty metres away to my right. I wanted to get into some sort of cover. I was feeling exhausted and I was getting cold.

The slab side of the container boat towered above me. I rested for a moment, clinging to the top of the rudder, then I moved on. The wharf at this point sat up on concrete piles. I swam under into the pitch-blackness. Only when I was five or six metres in did I turn on my headlamp. Ahead of me there were rocks, covered in waterborne debris. The rocks and the crap covering them climbed to the low concrete ceiling. At least there was room enough for me to get most of me out of the water.

Knee deep in the foul, oily tide, I could stand upright, my head just a centimetre or two from the concrete above. The first thing I did was start dissembling the Browning. If I were taken by the police I didn't want it on me, and the last thing I wanted to do was shoot an innocent Singapore cop. I thumbed the rounds out of the magazine and flicked them away. The magazine went in another direction, as did the shoulder rig. The barrel, body and slide I would drop as I swam.

I tried calling Sami, but under a metre or two of concrete, the signal wasn't going anywhere, even if he were still in range. I wasn't prepared to risk the cellphone yet. It was in a sealed bag in my pack. I didn't want to drown it. Standing there, shivering, I knew I had to be moving or I was going to be a candidate for hypothermia. I debated what to do with the knife. In the end I pulled the sheath off my belt and put it into the pack. My biggest dangers now were the cold and armed police and probably a mass of heavy machinery if I made it across the water to the other side.

I waded back out until the water was chest deep, then I started swimming again. This time, I stayed under the edge of the wharf and swam parallel to it, keeping the hull of the ship and the wharf's support pillars between the harbour and me. I swam past one vessel and then another. They were docked close, nose to tail. Inner harbour space was obviously at a premium.

I lobbed the remaining parts of the automatic away from me at intervals. I was now at a section of dock where there was nothing moored, but there were vessels in the harbour both coming and going. I could see across the two or three hundred metres of water to the far shore.

Across the channel there were ships lined up as far as I could see from my low vantage point. There were some gaps along the face of the wharf, but not many. A container ship was leaving, being manoeuvred into the middle of the harbour by a pair of busy tugs. However, there were at least two other vessels I could see waiting to dock. Christ, I was going to have to try and swim across with all that fucking traffic on the move.

A police patrol boat was moving along the far shore, a spotlight playing on the water. Were they looking for me or was it a normal patrol? Only they knew. Somehow, I was going to have to get across this busy piece of water, but once I'd done that, where the hell would I head to?

The communicator stuttered in my ear.

"Daniel?" The voice was faint.

"I can just hear you, Sami."

"We're driving back to the city. Where are you?"

"In the container basin between Brani and the mainland."

"Well done."

"Maybe; I've got to get across and through the container park and then what?"

"We'll stay in the area. Call when you can."

"Roger," I responded. Putting first things first, I would get across to the other side and worry about what came next when I got there. The police boat had gone to the bridge and vanished from my limited line of vision. I guessed its beat would bring it back down my way. I would let it go past and then start for the far side. While I waited for the launch to arrive, my attention was drawn to the skyline across the water. There were several tall blocks of flats beyond the container farm. That gave me an aiming point, both while I swam and as a possible destination when I got across.

The searchlight on the police launch came stabbing beyond the bow of the ship to my left. I eased back into the dark and put a pillar between the boat and me. The light flared off the water as it probed the shadows under the wharf and was gone. The boat's idling motor was barely audible over the other sounds of the port.

When the launch was gone, I started for the lights on the hill. My watch told me it was 04:35. Dawn was not a long way off and unless I found shelter and a change of clothes before then, I was going to get caught.

"The money has arrived in Singapore. You have made the necessary arrangements?"

"Yes," Thomas Lu lied. He had no intention of telling Carlos Mendez that Stanley Loh's death hadn't handed them the large chunk of the Intella pie they so badly wanted.

"Good," Mendez responded. "Raymond is flying in tomorrow. He is staying at a hotel called The Fullerton and he will contact you when he lands."

Thomas Lu felt his blood run cold. Raymond Mendez was the youngest of the brothers, and arguably the craziest. In his brief time in Bogota, Lu had learned to fear him. In a warehouse owned by the brothers he had seen the aftermath of a session where Raymond Mendez had tortured and later dismembered a police informant with a chainsaw. Mendez apparently had been laughing the whole time he was wielding the saw.

At the time, Lu knew he had been shown the macabre scene

as a warning of what would happen if he had any thoughts about double-crossing the brothers. Now, the fact that the Mendez cartel had sent Raymond to look after their Singapore business interests did not bode well for Thomas Lu.

"Did you hear what I said?"

"Yes, Carlos, Raymond is arriving tomorrow and staying at The Fullerton." For a moment the absurdity of a psychopathic low-life like Raymond Mendez staying in one of Singapore's grandest hotels caused Thomas Lu to stifle a laugh of sorts. "I will look forward to seeing him." That was Lu's second lie but Carlos Mendez showed no sign of detecting it.

"Good," Mendez purred. "I hope everything goes smoothly."

The not-so-subtle threat wasn't lost on Lu.

"I'm sure it will," he responded.

"And the arrangements for processing the money?"

"They are all in place."

These arrangements meant that when the money was delivered to Lu, he would then use an intricate combination of ghost companies and a dozen other financial devices to launder it over time and channel it into the Intella coffers as required.

"It will be good doing business with you," Carlos Mendez said. "I will come to Singapore and we will celebrate in style when the business is done."

"I look forward to that," Thomas Lu lied yet again as the line went dead. He hung up the telephone and sat, his pale face positively ashen. Lu had returned to his luxurious Nassim Hill Road penthouse only an hour previously while the hunt for any remaining gunmen continued on Sentosa. He had been delayed for only a few minutes at the roadblock on the bridge while his car was searched.

Now, sitting upright in his thickly padded leather executive chair, Lu's eyes didn't register the trappings of his wealth. They couldn't see beyond the bloody image of Raymond Mendez's dismembered victim. Raymond's unfortunate victim's hands and feet lay scattered, along with legs severed at the knee and thigh, arms at the wrist and shoulder. The man's genitals had been taken first and apparently stuffed in his mouth while he was still alive. The torso, bearing deep saw cuts, lay in a pool containing litres of blood. Raymond had used the severed head as a football, reputedly laughing as he kicked it around the warehouse, all the time shouting, "I am Maradona, I am the greatest."

Thomas Lu shuddered. The whole slaughter house scene had come straight from the archives of hell itself. While Lu himself was a cold-blooded killer, Raymond Mendez was a complete and utter sadistic maniac.

"What am I going to do?" Lu whispered. He now had no access to Stanley Loh's Intella development share. Every one of the partners had received, by special delivery, a letter from Loh's solicitors indicating that control of their deceased client's shareholding in the development had reverted to Stanley's brother and business partner. The letter didn't indicate who that person was, saying at the earliest opportunity a meeting of all the parties should be convened and at the meeting, their new partner would be revealed. The letter suggested a meeting on Friday night. That was two nights away. Thomas Lu had two days to find the recorder or track down the unknown business partner.

Lu had absolutely no idea that Stanley Loh had a brother, especially one he had been in partnership with. Who was the brother, and how could he, Thomas Lu, find him and persuade him to sell before the meeting? Did the brother have the digital recorder? Had it been his people in the battle at the fort? Lu had people desperately trying to find the identity of the brother.

Lu stood and went to the bar. He seldom drank, but now he poured himself a large tumbler of Chivas. He gulped at his drink, leaning against the bar for support. At the sound of the telephone he started, slopping the liquid. He slammed his glass down and crossed to his desk, shaking the whisky off his hand as he reached for the receiver of the ornate, old-style telephone.

"Yes?"

Thomas Lu listened to the person at the other end of the line in silence. If his face had been ashen before, now his complexion was a sickly grey. Lu's eyes, unprotected by the dark glasses he habitually wore, bulged in his head. He blinked several times and hung up the phone without a word.

"Sami Somsak," Lu whispered. For a moment he swayed like a drunk. He had to grab the edge of the desk for support.

"Of all the people," he whispered, "of all the people in the fucking world, it had to be him."

16

It took me twenty long minutes to swim from one side of the harbour to the other. Apart from almost being run down by a tugboat and having to dive to avoid the light from a patrolling chopper, I made it. I was cold and felt sick from exhaustion and the fact I had swallowed half of the foul water in the bloody harbour basin. My limbs were like lead. I was under the wharf, standing up to my waist in water. On the other side I had swum past several ladders as I made my way across the face of the wharf. These were just steel rungs set in the concrete pillars. There had to be similar ones on this side.

I vomited up bile and bilge water. Christ, I was cold and I was shaking. I was very close to hypothermia. I pushed back into the water and made my way along the wharf face; the cliff-like hull of another giant container ship was on my right side. Far above, I could see the blazing lights of the container cranes working.

I came to a ladder and without hesitation, I started climbing. There were only a dozen rungs and as soon as I was high enough to see over the edge of the dock, I stopped.

The place was insane. There were lights everywhere and shadows that flickered and vanished as the huge container mechanisms worked. There were straddle carriers of all sizes and there were trucks of all sorts, some with trailers. This was the world of boxes: giant rectangular boxes in every recognisable colour. The whole world in a box, I thought, as my mind started to go off on a tangent of its own. Fatigue was crushing me. I dragged myself back to the task in hand.

My next problem was how to get from the edge of the wharf, across a wide open concrete apron, and into the cover offered by the alleyways created by the stacks of containers. The answer wasn't that long in coming, as it turned out. A blue-and-white Toyota utility with a flashing red light in the centre of its roof appeared away to my right. It was travelling slowly along the wharf in my direction. There were two men in it, one driving, the other leaning out the passenger window looking at the ground. My first instinct was that this was some sort of inspection. The utility was moving slowly.

I went down another rung and waited. I could see the reflected red light from the utility bouncing back from the flank of the ship above me.

I waited until I figured it was past me and then I eased back up the ladder. The utility was ten metres away and moving on at that same pace. I glanced back the way it had come and saw no one, just the endless stacks of containers and the giant machines that moved them.

I climbed the last rungs and slipped over the edge of the wharf. I didn't hesitate now. I ran for the shelter of the nearest containers. No doubt there were CCTV cameras here and guards, armed guards, but I was going to rely on speed and what shadow I could find to remain invisible.

The alley I ran into stretched for a hundred metres, pushing deep into the heart of the container jungle. It was a metre and a half wide. Narrower bisecting alleyways ran off it parallel to the wharf at intervals. I looked up and the containers stacked eight or nine high almost created a reverse vertigo effect.

I crossed two intersections and almost didn't make it across the third. I barely managed to duck back and avoid the wheels of the big straddle carrier that crossed the alleyway in front of me. It was moving from left to right. I waited until the rear wheels passed in front of me, then ran on. From that moment on, I paused at each intersection to check for any more of the huge machines. My fixation on the dangers of cross traffic, however, was almost my undoing. What I hadn't figured on was the absolutely enormous straddle carrier that used the alleyway I was running down. I heard it before I turned and saw it coming after me. The wheels on this monster virtually filled the gap between the rows of containers. I sprinted to the next corner and ducked around it. I figured with Goliath coming this way, the little guys would keep out of his way.

I was right, sort of. The big guy rolled by and I was congratulating myself on being a clever bastard when another of the smaller carriers came hunting for me. I ducked back to what had become my superhighway and let the green thing roll on past. Goliath was at a standstill fifty metres away stacking containers or whatever was going on up there. I jogged on towards it. When he came back, I would carry on. In the meantime, while I waited for him to move and watched for the side traffic, I tried Sami again. This time the signal was good.

"I'm across the water in the middle of the container farm. I'm aiming for those blocks of flats on the skyline."

"We're not far away. Let me find out what they are and I'll get back to you."

Goliath was on the move, heading back my way. I checked out the next side alley for little brother and got out of the way. The huge tyres rolled past me and the way forward was clear again. I started off once more. I could see the end of the containers ahead of me. There was a road or roads, and trucks were rolling across the face of the container alleyway.

"Spottiswood Park is what you can see. The railway station is between you and it. There is a road on the park side of the lines. We'll wait for you there."

"Affirmative," I replied and carried on. I no longer felt hypothermic. My suit was almost dry and the activity had warmed me up again. I just felt completely shagged and that tiredness almost caused me to step under the wheels of yet another of the smaller straddle carriers. Small, in this case, was a relative term. The little guys were still enormous, it's just that when compared to Goliath, they seemed much smaller.

Whatever, I was close to the end of the alleyway when the green machine came zipping out of a side alley. I stumbled and almost fell under its rear wheels as it charged on by.

At the end of the rows of containers at last, I huddled in the shadows and tried to take it all in. There was a wide strip of concrete that ran off in both directions. Vehicles were moving on it. To my left was what appeared to be an office complex. There was an access gate complete with gatehouse to my right. The gatehouse was occupied. I could see just one man inside.

As I watched, a utility, maybe the same one I had seen earlier, rolled up to the gate and stopped. The gate man came out, exchanged words with the men in the truck, then, laughing at something one of the occupants had obviously said to him, went back into his office to open the gate. The utility drove off, turning onto the highway beyond as the electronic gate swung shut. I couldn't figure out if the road outside was part of the container complex or of the outside world. There didn't appear to be any other traffic on it but for the departing Toyota. It was almost 05:00. Perhaps, if it were a regular highway, then this morning at least Singapore was a late riser.

So, should I try and climb what I figured was the perimeter fence, which was at least four metres tall and had the standard angled top covered with razor wire? Or should I go out through the gate? There would probably be alarm sensors on the wire. Maybe it was electrified as well. As I pondered, my answer came in the form of a truck and trailer unit.

There was a container on both the truck deck and the trailer. The driver turned in towards the gatehouse. Now I could see there were cameras covering the gate and, yes, they were angled along the fences. I was going to be on video and if there actually was an eagle-eyed soul watching a monitor somewhere, I was going to be seen. Again it was a calculated risk. Watching monitors is a pain and generally those charged with doing so get bored shitless and find other distractions. If the monitor for the cameras I could see was in the gatehouse, then the newly arrived truck was probably distracting the man inside. I hoped that was true in this case.

The truck driver went to the gatehouse carrying a clipboard. It was my time to go. I stood and crouched like a half-folded pocket knife, then sprinted for the trailer unit. I didn't hesitate, but slid under it. There were enough cross members under there to hang on to. I lay on the concrete panting and waited, praying there were no alarm bells going off somewhere.

There was the sound of a vehicle door being slammed. I grabbed for handholds and hooked my feet up out of the way and waited. The trailer lurched, the truck's engine revved and I was on my way out of the container farm. At least I hoped so.

The truck rolled through the gate and started to turn to the left. As the trailer started the turn, I dropped off and lay flat while the rig roared off. Now, lying on a road of any sort is not a particularly desirable pastime, so as soon as the trailer was gone, I got to my feet. There was no traffic at all on this stretch of road but for the rapidly vanishing truck. Was I outside the damned container complex or not?

An alarm klaxon was sounding from inside the container farm. Then a siren joined in. Had they seen me or was something else going on in there? I could see the flashing lights of a security vehicle racing along the internal road towards the gatehouse. Had someone in a control centre belatedly reported seeing an intruder? Whatever, I had to get as far away from here as quickly as possible. Hell, that had been my entire life for the last few hours. Get away from the fort, get away from Sentosa, and get away from the fucking container farm. Part of me had had enough of running. I wanted to go to sleep.

I sprinted across the road and there was another fence, but this time there wasn't any razor wire and it was only a couple of metres high. I climbed over it easily enough and dropped down a low bank.

In front of me was a wide multi-lane road and there were vehicles, not a lot, but it appeared Singapore was indeed waking up and on the move. I was standing on a wide kerb. There was no footpath. A pedestrian here was going to draw unwanted attention, especially one dressed as I was. I waited until the road immediately in front of me was clear and sprinted across.

It was starting to get light. The sirens and alarms were still sounding. A police car came speeding down the highway I had just crossed. Were they after me? I still didn't know.

There was another fence ahead of me. Man, was I getting sick of fences. Again, this wasn't a particularly serious one. I climbed it and realised that I was at the railway lines. I crossed them and, yes, damn it, there was yet another fence.

"We see you, Daniel."

"I need a drink and a smoke and a long fucking sleep," I replied, scrambling over what I hoped was the final hurdle. But it wasn't. There was a road of sorts beside the railway line and beyond that I could see Sami's Mercedes. The lights flicked on and off.

The last fence had either fallen down in part or someone had driven through it; plastic strip filled the gap. I didn't have to climb. I simply stepped over the tape. Sami's driver was holding the back door of the Mercedes open. I fell inside and the door closed behind me.

"I'm fucked!"

"Well done, Daniel. That really was something."

"Tell me about it!" I pulled off my gloves and dropped them onto the floor at my feet. My hands were wrinkled and soft from too much water. I fished the vinyl pouch out of my zip pocket and passed it across to Sami who was sitting in the front passenger seat. Then I spread out across the back seat, closed my eyes and went to sleep as the car moved off.

17

It was mid-morning by the time I woke. The rear windows of the Mercedes were open. Someone had taken my sneakers off and removed the headlamp, communications unit and hood and put a cushion under my head. There was a rug covering me, and that was probably what woke me. I was cooking.

I was in an underground car park. The place appeared to be full of vehicles. A man sitting on a chair against the wall by the front of the car stood and came towards me as I pushed the rug aside and sat up. The door opened. It was K. His full name was unpronounceable, so years ago he'd switched to just using the initial K. He was one of Jo's former squad guys. Like Jo, he had spent more than a year and a half in the UK at Stirling Lines with 22 SAS. He was tough, highly trained and well-educated and spoke English fluently. We'd worked together on several occasions back in the good old days.

"Good day, Dan. Long time, no see." K gave me a handshake and a grin. "Sami said for you to please come up to his office when you woke up."

"Sure," I agreed. K held out a packet of wipes.

"Maybe you'd like to remove your makeup first."

I glanced at my face in the driver's mirror. I looked like a refugee from a black-and-white minstrel show. The chemically treated wipes lifted the greasepaint off easily enough. When I'd finished, K passed me a pair of sneakers, new ones. Sami had thought of everything.

I put the shoes on and got out of the car. Now my minder handed me a coat, a classic trenchcoat. I had to chuckle. If Simone were to see me in this, she would crack up. Her guess that I was some sort of spy would have been totally vindicated. I slipped into the coat while K closed the windows and locked the Mercedes. He led the way to the elevator. He obviously had instructions to get me out of public view as quickly as possible. In the lift he produced a key, put it in the panel and sent us skyward.

Simone was at her desk this time round. She gave me a smile.

"Mr Davidson, how nice to see you again. I like the coat!"

For a moment I stared blankly at her and then I remembered my assumed identity. I was obviously still punch-drunk.

"Just borrowed," I replied, "and it's good to see you, Mavis."

Simone chuckled at that. "Perhaps I'll see you later. Mr Somsak is expecting you."

K was waiting at the door to the inner office. He opened it and I went through. Sami was sitting at the desk. The huge model of the island was gone. Sami stood and came to embrace me, clapping me on the back as he did so.

"Thank you again, my friend. It's all there." He indicated the tiny digital recorder sitting on the desk. "We have Lu pleading with Stanley to sell. He talks of his partners. He's truly terrified of the Mendez brothers. When Stanley point-blank refuses to sell, the pleas turn to bribes and finally threats."

Sami went back to his seat behind the desk while I took a guest chair.

"Do you want to hear it?"

I shook my head. I didn't need to hear it. As long as it was what Sami needed to bring Thomas Lu down, that was fine by me. "What comes next? By the way, the office looks bare." I nodded at the space where the model had been.

"It's gone on public display to whet the appetite of the good people of Singapore. There is going to be a tremendous investment opportunity for everybody when the basic structure is completed." Sami chuckled. "We want to encourage them to dig deep. As to what comes next, there is an investor's meeting scheduled for Friday night. Everyone but Thomas Lu has responded that they will attend."

"Are you holding it here?"

Sami shook his head. "The consortium has a registered office at the Quillian Tower. That's the big one beside Marina Bay. Their meetings are always held there. I will be making a grand entrance."

"So they don't know you're involved yet?"

"I doubt it. I'm the mysterious brother."

"Lu must be shitting bricks!"

"I certainly hope so," Sami replied grimly, "I most assuredly hope so."

"What's the news on last night's events?"

"Gun battle at Fort Siloso is the headline. Suggestions are that rival gangs met at the fort and a shootout ensued over drugs. Three found dead, one seriously injured in the original skirmish and three shot dead and several others injured and arrested by police." Sami gave me a grin. "Am I right in assuming the first three were yours."

"And a guy with a busted head. It was a hectic night. The OK Corral had nothing on it."

"How are you feeling?"

"Absolutely exhausted. I think I'll go back to the hotel and sleep for a week."

"Your clothes are in the bathroom along with your pack. There's a shower in there if you want to use it."

I did want to use all of the facilities in the late Stanley Loh's bathroom. Showered and dressed, I collected my bits and pieces from the pack, then bundled the one-piece suit and put it back into the sack. I carried the rubber sack back into the office and dropped it onto a chair.

"I think you had better make that all go away. I dumped the gun in bits on my swim. There'll be images of me on CCTV somewhere, but hopefully with the hood, the greasepaint and a bunch of stuff hanging off my face they won't get much to go on."

"I think the cops are convinced it was a gang scrap. I don't think they're looking for the Lone Ranger," Sami replied. "By the way, I do have an idea on how to make that grand entrance for the meeting. I want you at my side when I do."

"Sure."

"Marina Bay MRT at 20:00 Friday. Look dangerous, something which comes naturally to you, of course."

"Oh shucks," I said, doing my best to sound like James Stewart. "You're just trying to butter me up."

Sami chuckled. "Yeah. We'll be armed. I have no reason on earth to trust Lu to either be there or be there without a bunch of thugs in tow."

"Watch your back between now and then," I warned. "If he's got people in the know, he might have already found out you're the new partner and he might try and take you out as well."

"Jo's flying in this evening and I've got my back well covered." Sami nodded to K, who was standing by the door. The former Thai Special Forces man nodded back. "You know me, Daniel."

"That's debatable," I said as I stood, grinning to show I was joking—not!

"K will have Edward take you back to your hotel. Sleep well, my friend."

As before, K led me out of the office. Simone smiled up at me. She really was a most attractive woman.

"Going so soon, Mr Davidson?"

"Indeed, Mavis." I signalled to her the thumb and little finger telephone symbol, screening it from K with my body. Simone gave an almost imperceptible nod. "Take care," I added as I followed K into the elevator.

Edward was waiting by the car.

Twenty minutes later, I was stretched out on the bed in my room. As is often the case when you're totally exhausted, trying to catch sleep is like trying to catch a handful of smoke. I turned on the television. Local news was playing the gun battle at Fort Siloso to death. I went to sleep.

18

"Thomas, my friend, it is so good to see you again."

"And you, Raymond," Lu lied. He was good at lying, but for the past day he had been lying to the Mendez family and that was not a good thing.

The pair of them were meeting in the magnificent foyer of The Fullerton. Raymond Mendez had wanted the Presidential Suite, but it was occupied. Reluctantly, he had had to settle for a lesser one. So far he had managed to control his temper, barely, but inside he was seething and Thomas Lu could sense it.

"The cargo has landed," Mendez said. "It will be delivered to the warehouse you specified in the morning. Now I think we should go and have dinner and experience a little of Singapore's night life."

Thomas Lu did not want to spend another second in the company of Raymond Mendez, but there was nothing he could do but agree with the man. To refuse could trigger the psychopath into a bloody rage. Lu had reservations at The Club, the newest and supposedly best restaurant in the city, one that Lu had not yet experienced himself. According to the considerable publicity the Cross Street establishment had garnered in the weeks it had been open, the imported chef had cooked with Ramsay and earned several Michelin stars of his own. It had taken considerable coercion and several thousand dollars to secure a private dining room at such short notice.

Lu's chauffeur was waiting beside the gold Bentley when the pair emerged from the hotel. Mendez nodded appreciatively at the car.

"Very nice, Thomas. I have been meaning to get one myself."

Thomas Lu grunted noncommittally in response as the men seated themselves in the vehicle's spacious rear. Despite his fear of the younger Mendez brother, Lu was even more scared of Sami Somsak.

The Thai was a legend to many in the region, a larger-than-life character reputed to be a guerrilla fighter, bandit, drug lord, pirate, cold-blooded killer or a combination of all, according to whomever was telling the story. Lu had never met the man, but he knew people who had, and people who had incurred his wrath lived to regret it. Again, according to local legend, many others had incurred Somsak's displeasure and had not lived to regret it.

"Will there be girls at dinner?"

Thomas Lu nodded. He knew that in addition to his sadistic traits, Mendez was sexually insatiable. The Mendez brothers had entertained Lu several times while he was in Bogota, and on more than one of those occasions he had witnessed Raymond's appetite for sex first hand. The man's sadistic side had been evident there as well. He was notoriously rough with those women who were unfortunate enough to end up in his clutches.

The "girls" Lu had engaged for the evening were escorts. He had warned the madam who was supplying them about Raymond Mendez's tastes and she had promised to send girls with a masochistic bent, girls who would do virtually anything if the money were right. Thomas Lu was prepared to pay the fee. He needed to keep Mendez out of trouble and maintain as low a profile as possible. It was a big task; however, the last thing he wanted was for Mendez to brutalise a woman and end up in court.

Lu knew there was no way that he could discuss this with the man without Mendez reacting the only way he knew how.

There is no reasoning with a maniac, Thomas Lu thought as they glided onto Fullerton Road.

I awoke late in the afternoon and when I went to use the bathroom, I found that every bone and every tiny muscle in my body was screaming at me. I filled the bathtub with water as hot as I could bear and climbed in, a hefty glass of bourbon in hand. I turned the spa jets on full and lay in the tub absolutely cooking. Now I replayed the events of the night. I ran the mental spool through from beginning to end, analysing it with the eye of the professional I had once been.

I concluded that I had been hellishly lucky to get away with things. Lu's thugs had outgunned me and the cops had come so close to catching me. Running along the train line had been a brainwave but the jump from the bridge into the water had almost got me, and the swim, combined with the madness in the container farm, should have taken me out of the game, given my level of non-fitness.

"Here's to a very lucky lad," I muttered, raising my glass in a toast to myself.

Later I got even luckier. Simone arrived. We dined in the hotel and afterwards she gave me a massage. Before the massage segued into a lovemaking session, she dealt expertly with my remaining aches and pains. It appeared she had trained as a massage therapist in her younger days. She hadn't forgotten her technique.

Because she had a sleep-in sitter minding her children, Simone spent the night. She had brought a change of clothes for work. We had a room-service breakfast and then I kissed her farewell as she left. Standing at the door watching her go, I couldn't help think this was almost a classic scene of domesticity. I stood at my door and watched her until she entered the lift.

"Damn," I muttered. Was I in danger of taking this thing to another level?

It was only 08:35 and I was already at a loose end. Killing time comes hard for me. I don't play golf or tennis. I don't do bus tours or shopping. Recreational sex is, of course, a great way to pass time, but I'd had my share of that for the moment. A pub-crawl was out because I had my date with Sami that evening and sobriety was most probably a prerequisite. I thought about another session on Ubin. I'd enjoyed getting back into the bush, and walking was one thing I did do well.

Whatever I was planning never got beyond that because my cellphone rang.

"Dan, Sami's in hospital." The voice at the other end was speaking Thai.

"Jo?"

"Yeah, Dan." Jo reverted to English. "I got in last night. Sami was coming out to meet me. He's okay, shaken and stirred and a broken arm. They're running tests."

"How?"

"Truck hit his car on the East Coast Parkway. Edward, his driver, was killed. The truck driver ran. The truck was stolen."

"Lu?"

"Sami thinks so. He told me to tell you that tonight is off. He's rescheduling the meeting for Monday."

"Okay. I'll come and see him."

"Negative. He wants you to stay off the radar. Lu's people will be watching the hospital, the offices and, no doubt, the apartment."

"How did Lu find out Sami was the new partner?" I voiced the thought aloud. Jo picked it up.

"I don't know exactly, but Sami used Stanley's offices and his car and the apartment."

"I thought Sami owned the apartment?"

"He does, but he's never even stayed there until now. He used to stay at Stanley's home. Stanley used the apartment as a getaway, a sometime love nest. He wasn't an angel, Dan."

"Naughty Stanley," I muttered.

"Whatever, Dan, either Lu had the Intel or he had people watching and put two and three together. No matter now, but Sami had a close shave."

"Mr Lu had better watch his arse."

"Oh yes." Jo's voice was flat with promise. "I'll be in touch if anything changes, my friend." With that, he was gone. I dropped the phone onto the bed. With Jo at his side, Sami was safe. I had total faith in Jo Ankar. He was probably the best Special Ops guy I had ever worked with. To get through him, Lu was going to have to use a very big tank.

Thomas Lu was in a foul mood. The attempt on Sami Somsak's life had failed. He knew that the Thai must be in possession of the cursed voice recorder, and that he would no doubt be planning to produce it at the scheduled meeting of the consortium. By killing Somsak, he could have prevented that happening. Now he had to stall the meeting and attempt once again to have the man removed. This time however, Sami Somsak would be well and truly alerted. He had no illusions that Somsak didn't know who was behind the attempt on his life.

Lu used his cellphone. It was answered in seconds.

"Your information was correct, but as you know, the attempt on his life failed. Please keep me informed as to his movements. Call me any time. Thank you." Thomas Lu closed the phone. Somsak wasn't his only concern at the moment.

Raymond Mendez had badly hurt one of the pair of escorts he had selected for his entertainment. The girl had lost several teeth and suffered other injuries. The second girl had fled Mendez's suite intact but naked and terrified, and she had raised the alarm. The cost of dental surgery aside, the settlement to keep the police out of the picture amounted to fifty thousand dollars.

Mendez had been evicted from his hotel suite and had moved to the Shangri La. Now Lu was on his way from his Nassim Hill penthouse to pick the man up. They were going to the warehouse in Jurong to await the container from Buenaventura.

Lu knew that the failed attempt on Somsak had put his own life in a danger as great, if not greater, than that threatened by the Mendez brothers.

"What can I do?" Lu whispered. The partition between the driver's compartment and the rear of the limousine was closed. The words were directed at his faint reflection in the bullet-proof glass.

The question went unanswered for the five minutes it took to drive to Orange Grove Road. Raymond Mendez was waiting as the Bentley pulled up at the grand entrance. The Sikh doorman came forward to open the limousine's rear door but Mendez brushed past the man, opened the door himself and threw himself into the car. He was scowling.

"Let's go," he ordered brusquely.

As scared of Mendez as he was, Lu bristled. This was his car. This was his town. He was about to reprimand his unwelcome guest when he had an idea. It was a moment of epiphany. The answer to all his problems. He smiled. Raymond Mendez turned to stare at him, his scowl turning into an expression of confusion.

"What's so fucking funny?"

"I have just had an idea," Lu replied.

"About what?"

"Just the solution to a personal problem. Drive on!" Lu said into the intercom and the Bentley purred away from the front of the hotel.

"I am going to sue The Fullerton. The pigs! I was a guest and they treated me like shit!"

"You did hurt the girl badly."

"She was a whore. Whores are there to be hurt. I was a guest. I'm going to make them pay."

"As you wish. In the meantime, let us go and collect this most valuable cargo," Lu said. Now that the idea had fully germinated, he was desperately trying not to giggle. The solution was so simple and it would be so very, very effective.

19

I had Friday and the whole weekend in front of me, and I had an idea. I rang Simone and explained what I'd planned, asking if she could join me. She agreed. She also eventually agreed, when I pressed her, to let me pay for her children's sitter to spend the entire weekend with the children. I would add enough to the fee to ensure that the sitter could take the kids wherever they wanted to go on the island and do whatever they wanted.

Simone left the office early and cabbed home to organise her kids, clothes and the sitter. One thing about being a tourist is that you can get away with acting like a total jerk. You're in a strange country, no one knows you, you can be totally obnoxious, and as long as no one gets pissed off enough to shoot you, you'll live to travel on.

As a result of my ten minutes on the telephone, at precisely 17:35 the Bell Jet Ranger hauled us off the ground heading towards Bintan. Simone was as excited as a kid. She had never flown in a helicopter before and in fact had only ever flown a couple of times in her life. To me, helicopters are like motorbikes: great for getting you places and that's about it. I've just done too many hours in them, generally in marginal conditions and often with people shooting at me. Whatever, it was the perfect way to get from Singapore to Bintan in a hurry.

We landed on the golf course at the Banyan Tree Resort. There was a golf cart and a driver waiting. The formalities consisted of registering and filling out an Indonesian visa form. They were over in a matter of minutes and we were shown to our villa.

"This is absolutely perfect!" Simone said as she stood gazing down to the ocean below, and it was perfect. There was a spa set in the deck outside the bedroom and as the sun went down we climbed in. Simone put aside her wowser persona and joined me in demolishing a bottle of Tattinger. It was beautiful, sitting there in the flickering candlelight sipping champagne with a stunning woman beside me.

The wait for the container was agonising from Thomas Lu's viewpoint. His attempts to placate or even converse with Raymond Mendez were futile. The psychopath's brain was operating in a way that Lu could not comprehend. Mendez was going to find the whore and kill her for complaining. He was going to sue The Fullerton. He was going to do this! He was going to do that! Mendez was raving. He stalked the floor of the deserted warehouse like a caged cat while Lu sat on a packing case and watched.

Thomas Lu had ordered his chauffeur to return to the city. The driver was on a mission. Lu lit a cigarette and waited. Mendez had his cellphone out and was shouting into it. It appeared he was speaking to his elder brother, Carlos. Lu smiled through the cigarette smoke. The solution to all his problems was almost to hand.

An air horn sounded outside. Mendez, who was nearest the pedestrian door, hurried to open it and step outside. Thomas Lu followed. The Isuzu side loader idling in front of the vehicle entrance held a single shipping container on its flatbed trailer.

Five minutes later the container had been deposited in the centre of the warehouse. As the truck left, Lu's Bentley slid silently into the warehouse followed by a plain black Lexus. Thomas Lu pressed a button on the door-control console to start the huge roller door closing. He turned back to the interior of the warehouse. Raymond Mendez was opening the container.

The Bentley parked and the chauffeur stayed inside. However the front doors of the Lexus opened and two men got out. These men were Chinese. They were dressed in casual clothes, but there was nothing casual about the silenced automatic one of them carried in his right hand.

Without a word, the pair advanced on the shipping container.

Raymond Mendez sensed their approach. He turned. The look of anticipation on his face turned to one of shock as he realised what was about to happen.

"No!" he yelled. He looked beyond the gunman to where Thomas

Lu was standing. "Thomas, what are you doing?"

"Ridding the world of a piece of shit!"

"My brothers will ..."

What Raymond Mendez's brothers would or would not do stayed with the younger Mendez. The single shot that killed him hit him precisely between his eyes. The low-calibre round didn't exit his skull, and the entry wound was little more than a small dark dot on the falling man's forehead.

Five minutes after Raymond Mendez died, Thomas Lu was standing in the shipping container. Opened in front of him was a large bale of hemp and plastic that was almost exactly two metres square. The wires that had held it closed had been cut. The thick hemp and multiple layers of plastic and paper at the top of the bale had been sliced open and pulled back to reveal tightly packed bound bundles of bank notes: US dollars, millions upon millions of them. Behind the first bale sat another, and another and another. Four bales, each filled with large-denomination American dollar notes.

"Two billion dollars," Thomas Lu breathed, "and now it is all mine."

Lu took a bundle of bank notes and stepped out of the container.

The body of Raymond Mendez was now gone, as was the Lexus and the men who had arrived in it.

"Now we will have our share and more besides," Lu said as he broke the binding tape and fanned the bundle of notes in his hands.

"And we will see the last of you, Sami Somsak."

20

They say all good things must come to an end. I guess that's so. All I know is that on the flight back from Bintan, I didn't want my weekend to end. How many years had it been since I actually had a weekend that wasn't dominated by pure lust but by something else? Whatever was happening between Simone and me was something that was new to me.

I mean, I'm not naïve, far from it. I married my former wife, the beautiful and brilliant Sylvia Dixon, when we were both caught up in an absolutely out-of-control whirlwind of sexual lightning. Sylvia and I were total sexual dynamite together, and unfortunately, on my part at least, that was our relationship, our marriage. In due course, my inability to keep my hands off other women spelt the end of our marriage.

With Simone there was wonderful sex, but there was more. She too was smart and beautiful and more, much more besides. Maybe because I'd aged a few years since I'd been married to Sylvia, I was becoming a normal human being for the first time. The futility of just screwing about in Hong Kong for the past few months had finally sunk in. It had been selfish and futile and puerile. I'd been like a randy hound chasing bitches in heat. It was nothing but empty sex.

"A penny or two for them?" Simone had turned away from the spectacular view as we approached Singapore, flying over the hundreds of ships at anchor below us. Ahead was Sentosa. She was smiling at me.

"Just thinking," I replied, giving her a grin. I wasn't ready to confide certain thoughts to her. Not yet!

As we came across Sentosa, I peered down towards the concourse where the fort road, aquarium and resort entrances collided with

Siloso Beach. No police vehicles this time round. We buzzed over the twin spans of the monorail bridge and now, when I saw just how far I had dropped into the water that night, I winced. I'd been damn lucky to survive that in reality. Jumping out of a Sea King hovering at ten metres in a training situation is one thing. Jumping off a bridge into unknown waters is entirely another. When I'd thought I'd felt the bottom under my feet, I probably had.

We wound down on the helipad at Changi and did the customs and immigration thing and were in a cab back to the city within half an hour. Simone suggested I go up to her apartment. I begged off for the moment. I said farewell to her with an almost chaste kiss and as the cab pulled away, she waved me out of sight. Damn! Things were moving too fast and I was powerless to stop this roller-coaster ride. Did I want to stop it?

Back at the hotel, I phoned Sami. He was okay. A broken bone in his left wrist and a few bruises were the sum total of the physical damage. However, he was very, very intensely dedicated to Thomas Lu's impending demise, both as a partner in Intella and in a physical sense. The bad news was that tomorrow night was out. Lu had asked that the meeting be convened to the Friday night and the other players had agreed.

"Why is he postponing the inevitable?" Sami asked. "He's up to something, Daniel. Another attempt on me perhaps?"

"Probably. Why don't you just copy what's on Stanley's recorder and send it to each member of the consortium. That would do it."

"I want to physically establish my place with them. A grand entrance, Daniel. That is what they expect. Then I want to play the recording and for them to see Lu for what he is. I want to break him in front of his peers. That is Stanley's revenge."

"Okay. I can understand that," I conceded.

"I have had it copied and those copies are there in case Lu does get to me. Whatever happens, he is going to be thrown out of the syndicate and ruined in business."

"Have you got a copy for the cops?"

"That's not the way I work, Daniel. When he is ruined, Lu will die, if not at my hands then Jo's, and if not Jo, then K will do it. If not K, can I count on you?"

"Of course. But he's not going to get to you."

"Not now," he said. "No, not now, Daniel, and I'm coming back at him hopefully in a manner he doesn't expect."

"How so?"

"We're going to find where he's hidden the money."

"That is a big ask, my friend." And it was a big ask. Small as it might be in mass, Singapore probably has as many warehouses and factories as people. There were probably millions of places to hide just about anything you wanted to.

"Perhaps not," Sami said with a smile. "I have many friends here in Singapore, a lot of them in official circles. As we speak, we are mapping Lu's movements in the days since Stanley's death."

"How the hell can you do that?" I wanted to know. "You think he's going to trace his movements on a nice big street map and give it to you?

Sami laughed at that.

"That's not as far fetched as you might think, actually. Thankfully, we have some very powerful computers at our disposal," Sami responded. "Digital CCTV vehicle footage with number plate recognition technology is being processed as we speak. Shortly we'll have a very good idea of where Lu, or at least his Bentley, has been over the past few days."

"Bloody hell," I blurted. I got it then. If anyone had that sort of technology, it would have to be Singapore and the CIA perhaps. Imagine it. Load a vehicle's license plates into a supercomputer and simply flash through a billion CCTV traffic images, all time-coded, of course. In a matter of minutes probably, you could track the movement of a lone vehicle—or a fleet of vehicles for that matter —throughout a city, or in this case the whole island.

Most citizens just aren't aware that this sort of technology exists. That's why so many bad guys get themselves caught—they just don't know what's going on behind the blank grey glass walls of the police fortresses. Driving past the police building on Cantonment Road is intimidating if you've got something to hide.

"Incidentally, I have a blueprint of the CCTV coverage with the zones marked. You'll notice we never drive directly to or from any destination."

"I have noticed you seem to be all over the place," I replied, thinking of some of the convoluted routes I'd been taken along on my outings with Sami's people.

"Stanley was very resourceful in his own way, Daniel. Most of our businesses here are totally legitimate, but not all. Stanley's talent was meeting people and, shall we say, through subtle bribery or otherwise, getting them onside. Unfortunately, other elements in his life were not, shall we say, quite as I would have liked." Sami paused. "Well, that's past now. We will continue to take advantage of his good work and let the rest lie." I could picture him sitting there just for a moment. There would be an expression of sadness at what was and what might have been. Then it was back to business. Like my friend, I knew only too well that dwelling on what might have been is fucking pointless.

"Okay," he continued. "My contact in Lu's camp is not privy to everything that goes on, but he did say that one of the South Americans has arrived and that Lu was expecting a shipment. We are, of course, talking cash. The FBI and Interpol have all the major cartels, including my own, under surveillance as far as electronic banking is concerned. They've basically hamstrung us, but cash is always an option." Sami gave me a half grin. "So we are talking about some very big packages weighing tonnes probably."

"Shit!" I muttered.

"No, Daniel, dollars, probably greenbacks. We have to presume that is the money the Colombians have given him to invest on their behalf. My man doesn't know where the shipment is being stored, but you can bet that Lu has been to check on it. He couldn't not go there and gloat over his new-found fortune. We find out where he's been. Once we've got the location of the money, then we really hurt him."

"We go take it off him, huh? How much are we actually talking about here?"

"There has to be a billion for the Colombians' stake in Intella, plus enough to make up Lu's shortfall, say another half billion and the fifty million that was to be Stanley's fee. Say one and a half to two billion."

Nice if you can swing it, I thought. I'd managed to take a little over ten million off the late Sir Bernard Sinclair. That was absolute chicken feed compared to the league these guys were playing in.

"Getting the money off Lu has another purpose, Daniel. We take it and make it appear Lu has pulled a swindle. This will turn his new Colombian friends into his most bitter enemies."

The thought produced some very vivid, very bloody pictures in my overactive brain. I'd heard about the Mendez cartel's methods of showing their displeasure with anyone who crossed them. They didn't do pretty.

"I thought you wanted to kill him yourself?"

"I'm quite happy for them to do it, Daniel. They are renowned for their inventiveness. Anyway, that may be some time away. I'll call you when we have the location of Lu's cash stash."

I chuckled at Sami's rhyming phrase and hung up.

"Cash stash," I repeated aloud. It had a nice ring to it.

It was still early and I'd had a great weekend, but I wasn't yet ready to stay and sulk in my room. I left the hotel and crossed Bras Basah.

Chijmes became one of my favourite Singapore haunts for food and drink on a visit years ago. My first time there was in the mid-1980s, not long after the former convent had been converted into a venue for dozens of restaurants and bars. Everything you want in the way of food, drink and entertainment is there scattered around the courtyards in that one small city block.

I cruised the bars and eventually, when hunger started gnawing, I settled on a prime medium-rare ribeye at China Jump Bar and Grill, another old favourite. As I ate, and later as I sat over a couple of Jacks, I pondered the big question: What the fuck was I doing with Simone? Was I falling in love or had my brain just thrown a shoe?

Thomas Lu's plan depended on two things. One of those was convincing the remaining Mendez brothers that Sami Somsak had killed Raymond and made off with the two billion dollars from the warehouse. The other part of the plan had a split option. He could either succeed in having Somsak killed as a gesture of solidarity with the South Americans, something he would have to ensure happened before either of the remaining brothers and their cohorts flew in to Singapore. Or he could capture Somsak and present him to the Mendez brothers.

Lu pondered his options as he sat in the large spa bath in the spa house on the terrace of his penthouse. He had armed guards, albeit carrying hidden weapons, at every entrance to the building. As well, he had others covering the fire escape, service elevator and the sole passenger elevator that gave access to his lair.

Lu had yet to make the call to Bogota. That would come later, once the warehouse in Jurong was little more than ashes and twisted metal. The body of Raymond Mendez had been removed to a cool room in a meat packing facility Lu owned. It lay in repose amidst pigs, slabs of beef and two other bodies. The three corpses would be returned to the warehouse when everything was set to explode in a fireball. The remains of the madman would eventually be recovered and identified, along with the two expendable members of Lu's staff. People who failed Thomas Lu rarely did it twice.

One of the other victims was the driver who had attempted to run down Sami Somsak and kill him. The man had failed. The other body was that of the motorcyclist who had been assigned to pick up the attempted assassin at East Coast Parkway. The man on the motorcycle had panicked and ridden off, leaving the driver behind. Fleeing on foot, the truck driver had very nearly been captured by the police.

So now there would be three bodies at the warehouse, two of Lu's trusted men and Raymond Mendez, all executed in cold blood seemingly by the Thai gangster. All three men had died from a single gunshot wound to the forehead. The pathologist would recover the remains of the bullets and forensics would confirm that the same weapon had killed all three. Thomas Lu would see that the gun in question, a Ruger .22 automatic with its serial number removed, would be found in Somsak's possession when the appropriate time arrived.

The final touch was the witness. A watchman from a neighbouring warehouse would hear the sound of shouts and shots. He would see a covered truck driving away from the warehouse moments before the fire erupted. He would identify the man in the passenger seat of the vehicle as Sami Somsak. The vehicle would offload its cargo in another of Lu's warehouses close by. The burned-out remains of the stolen truck would be found in Lim Chu Kang in time.

This was the perfect plan, until Lu's secretary came into the spa. He came to the side of the pool and handed Lu a telephone handset. The secretary turned on his heel and, without a word, left the spa house.

The caller was Carlos Mendez. He had been attempting to raise his brother. Somewhere in a meat chiller in Jurong West, the sound of a chainsaw stirred the chilled air. The bizarre ringtone on Raymond Mendez's cellphone was in keeping with the man's mental state.

"He has found a woman who pleases him," Thomas Lu lied yet again to the elder Mendez brother. "He said he was not to be disturbed."

"My brother has a way with women," Carlos responded without the slightest hint of irony in his voice. "When will he be finished?"

"We will be going to the warehouse to await the money at midnight," Lu responded. "Shall I have him call you then?" He held his breath. He was in a most difficult situation and he had delivered yet another lie.

"Wait," Carlos Mendez grunted. He was obviously calculating the time difference between Singapore and Bogota. "That will be eleven our time. We have a lunch meeting. Very important business. Tell Raymond I will call him when the meeting is done. Tell him not to go off whoring again until we have spoken."

"I will, Carlos. Have a good meeting." The relief in Thomas Lu's voice was immense, but the elder Mendez did not seem to notice. The distance drag and faint delay on the line may have disguised it.

"Ciao, my friend."

"Ciao, Carlos." Lu pushed a button to end the call and dropped the phone onto the ledge on the side of the pool. "Yes," he whispered.

"Yes, yes, yes." Soon he would have the Mendez brothers out of his hair and Sami Somsak besides, and he would have two billion dollars to do with as he wished. He would still get part of the Intella pie in time. He had another plan for that. Life, at this moment, was looking exceptionally good for Thomas Lu. He pressed the button on the intercom built into the side of the spa and called for his special friend to join him.

It was after midnight when Sami phoned back. They had mapped out much of Lu's travel. The Bentley had been all around the place, but the trip to The Fullerton, and a day later the Shangri-La and a warehouse complex in Jurong, started filling in the gaps. Staff at The Fullerton told one of Sami's people of the incident with the man they identified as Raymond Mendez and the escorts.

"The man is apparently renowned as a sadist," Sami said. "No wonder Lu is terrified of him. I have people on their way to the warehouse. Jo is in charge."

"Who the hell is watching your back?"

"K and some of my other good people are here and I've had some more of my guys fly in from Thailand. Officially, a social soccer team," Sami chuckled.

"Okay. Speaking of Thailand, how is Tuk Tuk?"

"On his deathbed. One moment, Daniel." I could hear Sami talking with someone on another phone. I couldn't make out the words. After a minute or so, he was back on the line. "Jo called. Lu's warehouse is burning. You can bet that if the money was there, it isn't now. He's pulling a stunt for someone's benefit, the Mendez brothers or mine. Your guess?"

"Burning down your own warehouse is a bit drastic."

"Not if you're trying to cover something up," Sami replied. "I could almost hear the gears in his brain grinding as he searched for an answer. Sami is a devious guy and a master at subterfuge and the counter-strike.

"Lu's trying to cover up the fact he's moved the money again and my bet is the body of Raymond Mendez is in there frying. I think he's setting up a frame and I'm squarely in it."

"Turning the Mendez outfit onto you while he takes the money and runs."

"Yeah," Sami agreed. "If he can convince the crazy Colombians that I took Raymond out and stole the money, he's in the clear. He can finance his share in the project and keep the rest of the pot."

"Yeah. If it sticks you're going to have a whole other bunch of playmates to contend with."

"It won't stick, Daniel. As soon as we finish, I'll have the people on the computers use traffic and security camera data to see if we can find out how and when Lu shifted the cash from the warehouse and where it is stashed now," Sami said. "Incidentally, I'm sending out copies of Stanley's recording now by courier. I need to try and throw him, upset his game somehow. I'll call you in the morning."

"Yo." I folded my phone and lay back against my pillows. Things were moving very, very fast. If Sami could find the money and convince the Mendez brothers that it was Lu and not him who killed Raymond, all very well and good. If not, I suspected that the Colombian drug wars would be moving out of the Americas and headed all the way to staid little Singapore, and that wouldn't be good. Real estate prices might take a hammering, given the Mendez brothers reputation for relocating large buildings in small fiery pieces.

21

"Police confirm that they have recovered the bodies of three men, all bearing evidence of having died from gunshot wounds according to the preliminary reports from the medical examiner's office. A police spokesman said it is too early to speculate, but it is thought that these latest killings may be related to the slaying of the Loh family and their staff and the gun battle that erupted on Sentosa last week. We will bring you further news as it comes to hand."

I switched off the television and debated whether or not to call Sami. It was Tuesday morning and I had another day to kill. I wanted to see my old friend. Okay, the reasons for us not being seen together were more for my protection than his, but working by long-distance remote control has never been the way I've liked to work. I debated heading back to Pulau Ubin and burning off some more energy charging around in the bush. I debated phoning Simone and inviting her to play hooky from work, but I knew that wasn't an option. With Stanley gone, she was effectively Sami's man in Singapore, if you get my drift. At least she was with regard to the many legitimate business ventures Stanley and Sami had been involved in. Then my cellphone rang.

"You want to come and stir up Mr Lu?" Jo and not Sami was the caller.

"You bet," I responded. It seemed I wasn't about to have a totally boring day after all.

"Go to Marina, same as before, 17:00."

"Gottcha," I responded as the connection was broken. Jo wasn't one for idle conversation. It was 09:45. I'd slept late. I went to the pool and did a few half-hearted laps to ease the stiffness from my shoulders and back. After a shower I went for breakfast, or rather brunch, downstairs.

At 12:30 I hit the street dressed as our man from Perth. I had my camera on my belt and a water bottle in my hand. Ed Davidson was on the loose in SIN City. (Well, actually Singapore isn't particularly sinful, but SIN is the airline designation.)

I cabbed it to Little India and then mooched around being a tourist.

I checked out the Tekka market, taking plenty of photographs as I went.

Eventually I worked my way through the area, street by street, until I found my way to the Thieves Market, as the locals call it. The short streets off Jalan Besar, Pitt Road and Weld Road, and the bisecting streets, were crammed with makeshift stalls, many selling junk: household appliances, watches, rings, shoes, near-porn DVDs, used clothing. It was all laid out for sale. The market isn't a tourist attraction, it's mostly for locals, so it doesn't feature in many guide books. Why was I there? Well, it's a great place to pass an hour or so and I thought I might, just might, find something I couldn't live without.

This day, apart from a pocket knife that cost me all of S$3, I didn't find anything I needed. After a late lunch at the food centre washed down with a couple of beers, I caught the Northeast Line back to Dhoby Ghaut. I didn't take the interchange but instead came straight out of the station. It was 15:30. I walked the five blocks back to the hotel in an effort to settle my stomach, which was churning as much from anticipation of what was to come as from the curry I'd eaten for lunch.

Back in my room, I showered away the grime of another sweaty Singapore day and prepared for the evening, dressing in a fresh set of Ed Davidson's typical clothes. The landline rang. It was Simone wanting to know if we could catch up for a meal later. I had to tell her no, something I think disappointed us both. We settled on a lunch on the morrow.

I emerged above ground at Marina right on time. The Mercedes had been traded for a large box-like transit with a windowless back. Jo was waiting by the open rear of the van when I got there. I climbed in and he followed, closing the double door after him. Three other men were in the back. There were no seats, so they were sitting on the floor. Along with the passenger and driver in front, we had a team of seven to create whatever mayhem Jo and Sami intended for Lu.

The van moved away as Jo and I sat. There was a glass partition between the front and the rear compartments so there was enough light for me to check over my fellow passengers.

One of them I recognised from Thailand. The name escaped me, but he had been one of Tuk Tuk's hardmen. He gave me a grin. I returned it. The others, I didn't know. They were all Thai as well. There were nods all round.

"This is Dan," Jo said by way of introduction. "You have never seen him." Jo reached for one of several cartons occupying the rear of the van along with us. From it, he pulled out a sport bag and passed it to me.

"Your new uniform," he said with a grin.

Inside the bag was a one-piece black coverall. I knew it would be my size. Awkwardly, because I was sitting down and the van was swaying more than a little, I managed to strip off my long shorts and shirt and squirm into the overall. There were boots, a pair of canvas, quasi-military combat ones. I pulled them on, again a perfect fit. The final touches were a black full-faced hood with just eye and mouth holes and pair of flash gloves. I pulled on the gloves and jammed the balaclava into my breast pocket.

Jo dragged another box to him. This one was wooden and it was heavy. He reached inside and handed me the first of the goodies. It was, surprise, surprise, a Browning Hi-Power just like the one I'd dropped into the harbour, except this one had a long silencer threaded to its muzzle. As he doled weapons out to the rest of the crew, I checked mine. The automatic appeared to be new. I dropped out the full magazine. The packing grease was gone and the action cycled easily. I tested the trigger pull. The mechanism had been tuned. I reinserted the magazine, jacked a round into the breech and applied the safety.

Jo then handed each of us a pair of spare loaded magazines and a shoulder holster. Because of the silencers, the normally compact pistols were cumbersome. The oversize nylon holsters were designed to accommodate the automatics with the silencers fitted.

"Does Sami buy these by the dozen?" I asked, indicating the Browning as I shrugged my way into the harness and slipped the automatic into the holster. Under my right shoulder was a pouch that accepted the two spare magazines.

"Tonne, Dan, by the tonne," Jo replied. "No shooting unless absolutely necessary," he said to the others. "Understand?"

Everyone understood.

"May I presume that we know where Lu is keeping the money?"

"Yes, Dan. He moved it only maybe a kilometre to another warehouse he owns. Cunning, but not more cunning than the cameras and the computers." Jo smiled at a thought. It was the sort of smile that would make most people very uneasy. "We will be on the same traffic cameras, of course, but in about"—he glanced at the Seiko dive watch on his wrist—"two minutes there will be a computer failure and all the cameras leading in and out of Jurong and covering the entire area will malfunction."

"Clever Sami," I muttered, wondering how much that little malfunction was going to cost.

"We are entering a warehouse compound next to our target." Jo was speaking Thai for the sake of absolute clarity. He well knew my proficiency with the language. "There we will cut the link fence and enter the warehouse. When we have taken it, we will open the gate and a truck with a loader will enter. We will load the contents onto the truck. Daniel and I will go with the truck. The rest of you will return through the fence, get back onboard this van and follow us to another location. Understood?"

Everyone understood. As a Major, Jo had been one of Thailand's top Special Forces officers. He was an immaculate planner and a terribly efficient killing machine. He also had a reputation for getting his people home again, and that was a big thing when you were fighting a dirty war in deep jungle miles outside your own borders. Singapore was just a jungle with concrete trees this late afternoon. The driver turned on his windscreen wipers. It was raining and evening was drawing in. The worse the visibility, the better for us. While we were having a traffic camera outage, the fewer people on the ground who could see what we were up to, the better.

"I am flying in with some of my people." The pronouncement, which was little more than a thinly veiled threat, didn't come as any surprise to Thomas Lu.

"I am sorry, Carlos. Somsak's men took us by total surprise."

"Yet you survived and Raymond didn't?" The accusation in the elder Mendez's voice was not disguised.

"I was using my cellphone. I had to go to the rear of the warehouse because of the bad reception. Raymond and my men were opening the container at the front when the truck burst through the main door. There were at least eight gunmen. They shot Raymond and my men without warning. I hid and escaped from a rear door. I wasn't armed."

Lu's words tumbled over themselves. It was all a lie, of course, but the delivery was all the more convincing because he was a man close to panic, desperate to be believed. His life depended on making Carlos Mendez believe him.

"Sami Somsak?"

"Yes. You have heard of him?"

"Oh yes. Mr Somsak is known to us. Our paths have never crossed until now. The money, of course, didn't burn?"

"No. The truck left before the fire."

"Where were you by then?"

Thomas Lu hesitated.

"I was hiding in the compound," he said, playing the coward to perfection. "I couldn't climb the fence, so I hid until they left. The fire was raging. I left before the police arrived. I called you immediately."

"We will hunt Somsak. Do you know where to find him?"

"I know his offices and his apartment."

"Good. We are flying in a charter jet. We will be landing tomorrow afternoon. I will contact you from the aircraft. Have transportation for five."

"Yes."

"And Thomas?"

"Yes?"

"A secure place to stay and weapons."

"I will arrange it."

"When the authorities release Raymond's body, please arrange for an undertaker to prepare him to be transported back to his home."

The call was terminated before Thomas Lu could reply. Lu leaned back in his chair and sighed. It was done. He didn't care that Carlos Mendez thought him a total abject coward. That had helped Mendez believe him. Now he had placed Sami Somsak firmly in the Colombian's sights he was free, off the hook, and he had two billion dollars.

22

The van slowed and turned into an access way. I could see a heavy steel and mesh gate in front of us. The gate was sliding open as we approached. The driver didn't stop. We were in an industrial compound of some sort. I had glimpses of tall steel and concrete-sided buildings as we threaded our way through them. I could see several large trucks with concrete mixers mounted.

"Cement plant," Jo was saying to me. "When Sami found out Lu owned the warehouse next door, he bought a major stake in this."

"Today?" I blurted out. After all, until just hours ago we had no idea of the location of the money. I knew Sami moved quickly, but this was incredible.

"Today," Jo confirmed, "as soon as we knew where the money was, Sami got on the phone. He knows everyone."

"Yeah, he does," I agreed. "It'll be a very good investment when Intella goes ahead."

"Oh yes," Jo replied with a chuckle.

The van stopped and then backed up. I heard the sound of a heavy door opening and then we were inside a warehouse. The door closed in front of us. Jo stood, then went and opened the transit's rear door. I followed him out.

The warehouse was three-quarters full of bags of what I took to be cement. It was about half the size of a football field and made of steel with corrugated metal cladding. The few lights hanging from the ceiling were huge and dulled by the dust that hung in the air.

Jo led the way down the narrow aisle that ran from the front to the rear of the stacks of cement bags. The door at the rear was just a pedestrian one. Jo signalled me to his side as he opened it. The rain was still falling and the gloom told me that night was coming early.

A few metres beyond the door was a tall mesh fence topped with razor wire. Beyond that was another industrial compound. Three large metal and concrete warehouses were spaced down the centre of the rectangular lot. Several lights on tall poles dotted around the compound fought the rain and the gathering dark.

Jo had a pair of compact binoculars to his eyes. The light-gathering properties of the lenses would turn the gloom back into day.

"Front warehouse is the target. There is a man doing a beat across the rear of that building. No sentry in front, the gatehouse covers that." Jo handed the glasses to me. I waited for several seconds before a lone figure in a rain cape came to the corner of the second warehouse. He glanced down the length of the lot and then retreated back the way he had come. I held up my wrist and waited, counting down the seconds.

"Ninety seconds," I said when the sentry reappeared. He repeated his actions and vanished again. "Dark and wet, he'll have trouble seeing anything."

"Yes. We cut the wire and get into cover behind the second warehouse and make our way to the rear of the target building and take him out. There's a small doorway there, probably alarmed. We send three to the front and go in."

"Why hasn't he got more men outside?" I wondered aloud. The lone sentry wasn't exactly heavy security.

"He's got cameras," Jo replied. "On the four front light towers." I focussed the glasses on the nearest of the four towers and then switched to the other one I could see from our position. He was right. The three light towers in the front third of the compound each had a camera mounted to one side of the light. No doubt the fourth in the far right of the compound was no different. Each of the cameras I could see had a small antenna protruding from its housing. No doubt power was supplied via the light cable. These cameras looked like permanent fixtures. They were small but they weren't as compact as the ones used on Sentosa. It was also obvious that they hadn't been hastily put up on the spur of the moment. The sophisticated mounts and the need to wire them into the light fixtures indicated they hadn't been a hasty duct tape installation just to protect Lu's sudden windfall. This one warehouse might very well be Thomas Lu's personal Fort Knox. I continued to use the glasses. There were no cameras on the remaining towers in the compound.

"No problem dealing with them," Jo was saying. "The only problem is knowing where they are being monitored from."

"Gatehouse," I ventured. Because of the angle we were at, the gatehouse Jo had indicated was situated at the front of the compound was invisible.

"That's what we figured," he agreed.

"So, guessing that they have a couple of guys in there, one with half an eye on the monitors, how many others have they got inside the warehouse?"

"We've had the place under surveillance all afternoon. Our man saw four guys come and go between the warehouse and the gatehouse. At last count there were four inside the warehouse and three assigned to the gatehouse. The gatehouse guys rotate to take an hour on the beat."

So there we had it. Seven of Lu's men, cameras and no doubt an alarmed door or doors into the warehouse and six of us. If the cameras and alarms were monitored from the gatehouse, then we were okay. If they were being monitored in another location, there was a potential problem.

"Don't worry, Dan, we've got it covered." Jo withdrew back into the warehouse. I followed, closing the door after us. He used his cellphone. It was a short conversation. Then he turned to me again and flashed that famous grin of his. "At precisely 20:05, K is going to be here driving a loaded concrete truck that will accidentally go out of control and demolish the gatehouse."

"Brilliant." I glanced at my watch. We had half an hour to wait. I considered lighting a cigarette. I didn't because I'd heard that all sorts of dusts in suspension could make things go bang. Jo sent one of the team back to the van. When he returned, he had the driver in tow. Between them the duo bore a pack of bottled water, a massive pair of bolt cutters and a long metal bar with a flattened end.

Goodbye door, I thought to myself. These long pry bars, when inserted into the gap between door and jamb, could demolish any lock mechanism easily. The leverage delivered to the chisel end was enormous.

We sat and sipped our water. One of the guys went and had a nervous piss in a corner. I resisted the urge to go and squat. My gut was doing its usual pre-op thing.

"Time to go." Jo stood, he held out the bag the water bottles had come in. We all put the plastic bottles inside. The van driver wasn't taking part in the operation. He took the bag and retreated back towards his vehicle. Jo didn't have to explain the DNA thing to the crew. We were leaving nothing behind.

It was ten minutes to 20:00. Outside, the rain still persisted and the night outside of the arcs from the tower lights was almost pitch black.

There was no fear in the dark and rain that the cameras could pick us up so far away, even if they were trained in our direction, which they weren't. They were covering the flanks and front and rear of Lu's Fort Knox. We pulled our balaclavas into place. This was it. My gut had suddenly settled. It always seems to work that way. It's the waiting that gets to me.

The bolt cutters made easy work of the link fence. There was no need to get fancy. Twenty or so links were cut in a vertical line and the fence folded back to create a triangular-shaped doorway. Heavy-duty cable ties were used to secure the wire back.

Despite the distance and the dark, we lay flat along the fence while the sentry came and did his thing again. I presumed that this was a replacement from the guardhouse. I hoped he stuck to the same timing as his predecessor. The moment he vanished, the six of us ran the fifty metres to the rear of the second warehouse. Jo had designated a man for each corner of the building. Lying flat, with binoculars, heads just protruding far enough to see, they watched the sentry go through his next beat. Forty-five seconds from the left front to right front! We had one minute thirty seconds to be waiting for him when he did the full circuit.

The moment the man in the poncho vanished, we started up the flank of warehouse number two. It was only a minute to gate crashing time. Jo was in the lead. I was at his shoulder. We didn't run. This was more of a slow jog. We had time. The moment we reached the corner, we would be on camera. I wondered if Jo was going to kill or just lay the sentry out. That particular question was answered when he removed a set of brass knuckles from an overall pocket and slipped it on his right fist over his glove.

A metre short of the corner we stopped. I raised my Browning. If the sentry came around the corner firing the weapon he undoubtedly had under his poncho, I needed to be ready. In reality, I needn't have bothered.

There was an almighty crash from the front of the compound fifty metres beyond the warehouse we were preparing to storm. The sentry ran into view and stood looking towards the sound, trying to see what was happening. From under his poncho he produced a cut-down pump shotgun. Jo took two paces and his brass knuckles met the man's temple with a sickening sound. The poncho-clad one was out of it and maybe out of life.

I was tempted to pick up the shotgun, but left it lying where it was. We were in semi-silent mode for the moment at least. There were other sounds out front. One of them was the faint rattling thwack of a silenced weapon in use. K was no doubt seeing to any opposition. Jo and I and the guy with the pry bar raced for the door set in the centre of the rear wall of the warehouse, while the other three sprinted for the front of the building. As yet there were no sirens and no alarm bells.

The door gave easily. While it was solid enough, it wasn't reinforced and the two locks exploded as one. We were in and now an alarm bell was ringing.

In front of us was a huge cavernous warehouse. Unlike the one in the next compound, this one was brightly lit and it didn't contain cement. Around the walls were stacked pallets holding boxes and bundles of whatever. In the centre sat half a dozen shipping containers.

The four men guarding Thomas Lu's inner sanctum had all moved to the front of the warehouse drawn by the sounds outside. The pedestrian door beside the huge sliding door set in the front wall was open. They had possibly been going to the assistance of the men in the gatehouse. Now, because we had triggered the intruder alarm, they were turning back towards us, weapons raised.

Whether these guys knew anything about basic military training or had learned all their fighting techniques from bad movies, we'll never know. Whatever, they were standing bunched in the open, aiming a variety of weapons in our direction. The three of us took cover behind the nearest container as the clowns started shooting. One of them was using an Uzi and hot copper jackets were slapping the side of the container and ricocheting off the concrete floor like angry bees.

The noise was deafening. None of these guys were using suppressed weapons. Being inside a large galvanised metal shed while the guns were blazing was like being trapped in a metal drum with half a dozen mad drummers beating on it.

The reason we hadn't opened fire was that the range was long for a handgun under these conditions, almost sixty metres. The other reason was we had guys coming in from the front. Crouched beside my container I could see the door. Our guys arrived fast and low. They came in shooting, fanning out and going to ground as they did so. Above the sound of the unsuppressed weapons came the dull thump of the silenced Brownings. It was over in seconds.

The sudden silence was deafening. I took in a wider view around the edge of the container, my ears ringing from the gunfire. Our three guys plus K were slowly getting back to their feet. Lu's quartet was sprawled on the concrete. They'd not had a chance. I started towards them. Jo and our other man followed, still carrying the pry bar. The four on the ground were very dead, no question about that. Blood was pooling around them. Two of them lay face down, they had been shot in the back. They had never even seen who killed them.

"Amateurs," K said as he checked for any signs of life.

"This must be it." Jo had holstered his gun. He was looking at the markings on the container nearest the front of the warehouse. This had obviously been the last to be off-loaded. There was a big, brand-new padlock fastening the door closed.

"Is it?" I pondered aloud. I went to the second container in the line. It was unmarked and had a shoddy padlock securing it. I waved the guy with the pry bar over. I holstered my own gun, grabbed the bar and in seconds, the padlock disintegrated into scrap. I handed the bar back and Jo and I wrestled with the stubborn door release. It squealed in protest and then the heavy door swung open.

Even given the dim light, I could see that inside the container there were four large hemp and plastic-covered bales and they didn't contain cotton. One of the bales had been split open across the top. It had been crudely resealed but two or three bank notes had caught under the plastic.

"Clever Mr Lu," I said. The first container he had set up as a decoy, perhaps to keep even his own people from helping themselves. Jo and I went into the container. I wasn't convinced that Lu wasn't trying a double double-cross. I used my Gerber folding knife to rip open the re-sealed bale. Jo opened the next bale in line. Inside both were tightly packed, tightly bound bundles of banknotes.

"Good instincts, Dan," Jo admitted. "Here's the truck."

There was the rumble of a heavy engine and the main door was being slid open. A big Isuzu flat-deck with a side loader reversed in. I closed the container door as the deck of the truck slid alongside. The driver leaped down and immediately started working the loading mechanism. There were short heavy chains with hooks attached to the hydraulic loading arms. When the hooks came within reach, Jo, K and I connected them to the rings welded to the container. The moment that was done, the container reared up and away. In a matter of seconds, it was on the flatbed.

"Go, go," Jo was telling his crew. They started away towards the rear of the warehouse and the ruined door, K joining them. The truck driver was climbing back into his cab. Jo and I followed and we were away in a crunch of gears and the snarl of the big diesel.

Out front, little remained of the gatehouse. A concrete truck was sitting in the middle of the ruined building. Incongruously perhaps, the truck's engine was still rumbling and the barrel of the mixer was rotating. The body of one of Lu's men lay beside it.

We were out of the compound and turning onto the deserted secondary road. There were security lights on in many of the buildings lining the road and in the yards, but there were few other lights and absolutely no moving vehicles but for the truck we were in and the transit following a couple of hundred yards back.

Only our driver and Jo knew where we were going. The destination didn't matter to me. We had done what we needed to do and for once, I hadn't had to kill anyone. That was almost a first. I removed the balaclava and Jo did the same. Masked men in a truck would attract a little undue attention.

"We have ten minutes to get where we're going before the cameras come back on. We'll make it."

"How much attention did we get from people on the ground?"

"Industrial area, late at night, continuous noise. Not much I think," Jo replied. He was probably right. I certainly hoped so.

I pulled out my cigarettes. Jo didn't smoke. The driver did. Jo wound down the window and we drove on through the rain. Mr Thomas Lu had just been well and truly shaken and stirred. No doubt about that!

23

The bedside telephone woke Thomas Lu from a deep dreamless sleep. Prior to retiring, he had shared a spa with his lover of the moment and then they had gone to bed for a session of lovemaking that left Lu exhausted. Now, as he reached for the receiver, Michael, his boyfriend, stirred.

"Go back to sleep," Lu commanded gently as he pressed the receiver to his ear. "What?"

Thomas Lu listened to the man at the other end in almost total silence, but for the moan of anguish that escaped his lips. He hung up the receiver and leaned back against his pillows. His face was so pale it glowed in the almost dark.

"What is wrong, Thomas?" Michael was concerned. He sat up in the huge bed and reached out to stroke Lu's forehead.

"Somsak is what is wrong," Lu snarled through clenched teeth. "That fucking Thai gangster is what is wrong. Leave me. Now!"

Fearing he was about to be struck, the younger man recoiled as Lu climbed out of the bed. Michael Yee grabbed up his scattered clothing and rushed from the bedroom as Lu began to pace the room, his ridiculously skinny body a pale shadow as he strode backwards and forwards cursing Sami Somsak and the devils who had brought him to Singapore.

It was later, much later, when Lu made a decision. He used his cellphone again. His orders were terse. Somsak had hurt him. Now he was going to hurt Sami Somsak big time, and he was going to retrieve the money no matter what it took.

"So this is what two billion dollars looks like?" The outer layers of all the bales had been split and the contents of each bale exposed.

The bales had been made up of large individual bundles covered in plastic and fixed with fibrous plastic tape. One of these bundles had been opened. Inside were tightly packed stacks of notes, all 1,000-dollar bills, judging by those I could see. Each pack of notes was held closed by a wide, white paper band, just like notes in a bank. Only these bands didn't bear the insignia of any bank. They bore only the numerals 100000. It appeared then that there were one hundred thousand dollars per stack, one million a bundle and five hundred bundles to a bale. Each bale was worth half a billion dollars. It was almost surreal to me.

"Yes, Daniel," Sami replied. Despite having his left arm in a half plaster and some fading bruising on the right side of his face, Sami looked well. "Friday night is going to be exceptionally interesting, I think."

"What will you do with this?" I waved a hand over the money.

"Put it to good use at some stage," my friend replied. "I may even give it back to the Mendez brothers; after expenses, of course." He picked up a stack of banknotes and tossed it to me. "That's just pocket money. There will be plenty more when we nail Lu's smelly little hide to the wall."

I balanced the 100,000-dollar bundle of notes in my hand for a stunned moment then slipped it into my vest. I was once again Ed from Perth. The quasi-photographer's vest was an essential part of Ed's wardrobe and it had plenty of pockets. Was I tempted to fill them? Of course I was, but that would come later.

We were in yet another warehouse, but this one was more than half an hour's drive from Jurong. We had driven three quarters of the way around the island, I guessed. The warehouse was old, long, low and in need of repair. It appeared to be an abandoned former military facility. The truck headlights had shown a rusted high fence as we turned in. The ground had been tarmac at some stage but was now covered in grass and small trees. There appeared to be taller trees pressing in from beyond the wire perimeter.

Jo told Sami how I'd picked the correct container from the decoy. Sami clapped me on the shoulder and I experienced one of those childish rushes. I'd done good and teacher was acknowledging it. But

I knew what was coming.

"Instincts like yours I want at my side on a full-time basis," Sami said. Yep, once again he was back on his hobby horse, trying to get me to work with him in some sort of partnership. The time wasn't right for me now and hadn't been before, but he would keep trying.

Delivery made, it was now time for Ed Davidson, the tourist from Perth, to go home. It was 02:35. It turned out we were in Pasir Ris, not that that had any particular significance for me. I knew it was close to Changi and that was that. But heck, in Singapore, everything is close to everything compared to just about anywhere else in the world.

Jo dropped me on Bras Basah, a block from the hotel, and I strolled into the foyer playing at being slightly drunk. To the amused staff it appeared Ed from Perth had been out on the town. As I crossed the lobby heading for the elevators, I was loud and vaguely funny and my accent was passable. The only thing that was missing from my pantomime was the smell of booze on my breath. I remedied that in my room by way of a hefty shot of JD. I went to sleep lying on my bed still fully dressed.

24

Simone DeLue was working at her desk. She glanced at the clock on the wall. It was just a few minutes to one. Time to freshen up for her much anticipated lunch date with her man from Perth. She smiled at the thought. Ed from Perth and Daniel Swann had little in common.

As she stood, there came the sound of angry voices from the reception area where Jasminder Kaur reigned supreme. Simone opened her office door to see what the commotion was about.

There were two women standing facing each other in reception. They were both attractive. One was Chinese, while the other looked Malay. They were both shouting. The two men assigned to keep guard on the offices, both members of Sami's Singapore crew, were standing to one side, confused, as was Jasminder Kaur, the receptionist.

"What is going on?"

"They just arrived in the lift. One is accusing the other of stealing her wallet."

"She stole my wallet," the Chinese woman was saying. "Look at my bag, you can see ..."

"Look at my bag. I don't have her wallet," the other yelled. Both women had their bags open, hands groping inside. The guns they produced were levelled first at the men.

"Hands up. Now!" The command came from the taller of the two women. The guards, their own weapons hidden under their jackets, had no choice but to obey. The second woman went to the fire escape door and pushed the door release. Three men came racing in. Two of them carried iron bars. They clubbed the guards to the floor with practised, ruthless efficiency and took the guns from their belts. The third man carried a plastic container.

"You are all coming with us. Now!" One of the intruders shouted as he wiped blood from the iron bar in his hands on the jacket of the guard he had just beaten to within an inch of his life.

"Oh God." Simone swayed, but grabbed the edge of the reception desk to prevent herself from fainting. "What's happening?"

"Why?" Jasminder asked.

"Because Mr Lu says so."

It was after ten in the morning when I awoke. I'd slept like a drugged man. It was the adrenaline hangover that always got me. Despite the fact I personally hadn't had a particularly strenuous outing the previous evening, the adrenaline kicks in when you're in a heightened state. When it leaves, so does most of your energy.

I ordered an omelette and coffee through room service, ate and showered and felt almost human again. Ed from Perth was going to take Simone out for lunch. I dressed up for this one. Casual shirt with sports trousers and actual lace up shoes. This was getting serious.

The plan was that we'd meet at 13:00 hours at Centrepoint on Orchard Road, just a leisurely stroll from Stanley's office, and find ourselves a nice place for lunch at Cuppage Terrace or Peranakan Place. I didn't much care where we ate really. I just wanted to see Simone.

I walked to Orchard and arrived at the designated meeting place on time. However, after fifteen minutes with no Simone, I tried her cellphone. No response. I decided to walk on up to the office to meet her. I had barely reached Lucky Plaza when the first fire engine came screaming down Orchard Road from Tanglin. This was followed by a second and a third. A flock of police cars was weaving in and around the traffic heading the same way. They turned into Scotts Road up ahead of me.

The ice that slashed its way across the back of my neck started me running. I scattered gawking pedestrians. This was one of those moments in life when you know with absolute, cold, dead certainty that your instincts have gone off the scale and are tuned into something far beyond normal comprehension. Supernatural or supernature, who knows? All I did know was that Simone was in trouble.

I turned into Scotts Road; the fire engines had stopped outside the building where Stanley's offices, or should I say Sami's offices, were located. I looked up. I didn't try and count the levels, I knew it was the fifteenth floor. There were no flames, but there was smoke.

Truck ladders were rising into the sky and firemen in breathing apparatus were going inside as people streamed out of the building. Police, also in breathing apparatus, were following them in, while other officers established a safe zone. I anxiously scanned the crowd gathering on the road. Simone wasn't amongst those I could see. Neither was Sami.

I used the cellphone again. No Simone and no reply from Sami—just their cell secretaries! I left messages and stood helplessly watching the controlled chaos unfolding. There was nothing I could do. The firemen had three snorkel units up at the fifteenth level and were streaming water into the building; but still no real flames. Hoses trailed into the downstairs foyer of the building and firemen were coming and going. The flow of evacuees had stopped. Anyone who was getting out under their own power was out, it seemed. It just remained to see who the fire crews managed to retrieve.

The ice that had threatened to sever my neck had settled in my gut. It sat there like a freezing brick. My breakfast omelette had soured and threatened to find it's way to the back of my throat.

I don't think I've ever felt so helpless in my life, just standing there watching, waiting and perhaps praying. I've gotten used to losing people from my life. I care for someone and they're gone. It's a shit equation. I've come so close to losing myself as well. Now it appeared to be happening all over again. Maybe Simone and Sami had got out of the building in time.

What exactly had happened? It had to be Lu, of course. I don't believe in accidents or coincidences in my game, or what used to be my game. Lu was trying to finish the job he had botched with the truck out on the highway. An incendiary of some sort must have been used in the offices. The urgency seemed to have gone, at least as far as the firemen were concerned. Two of the snorkels were already coming back down. Had the fire not taken? What had caused it?

Gasoline? A gas cylinder? Napalm?

Ambulance attendants with their gurneys were now going inside, accompanied by more cops as the firemen exited. There hadn't been any walking wounded coming out. What exactly had gone on up there?

I was now going into professional detachment mode. It's a survival technique. If Sami and Simone had been trapped up there, were they dead? If they had managed to escape, that was, of course, wonderful, but where the hell were they? No matter what their status, I could not change what had happened. All I could do was stay alive and stay invisible and get Thomas Lu. When I did, it would be slow and very painful. Revenge deserves time to be savoured.

"Dan!"

I turned. Jo was standing behind me, his face grim.

"Where are Sami and Simone?"

"I left Sami in the warehouse this morning. I don't know who was in the offices. Perhaps Simone and the other girls who work there and the numbers guy. There were three of Sami's Singapore guys as well."

The other girls were the three additional office staff that Stanley had employed.

"If they were in there, they're dead, they've escaped or Lu's got them," I replied. "Have you told Sami?"

"No. His cellphone appears to be switched off."

"Damn!" I knew Sami switched off his phone when he was out on the dredge barge in the Gulf of Thailand, but why here and now? That's the whole fucking point with cellphones: availability anywhere, anytime—yeah, right!

"No point in standing here, Dan."

"Yeah. Let's go see Sami."

Jo led as we edged our way through the crowd and back towards Orchard. The Mercedes was double-parked down on a side road. We got in. Jo told the driver to head back to Pasir Ris. Jo and I sat in silence as the driver took us on what seemed to be an around-the-island tour. Yes, I knew why, but for once I wanted the direct route and to hell with the CCTV cameras. I needed to find out what had happened to Simone.

I tried her cellphone again and got the damn computer secretary once more.

I pondered exactly what I was going to do to Mr Thomas Lu when I got my hands on him. I imagine Jo was also following that line of thought. Maybe when the time came, we would have to toss a coin to see who got the right to make the man pay.

Thomas Lu smiled at the four women who sat on the chairs in front of him. Two were Chinese, one was Indian and the other, the attractive blonde, was very much of European extraction. The women were gagged with duct tape and their hands were in front of them, also bound with the tape.

They were in the virtually bare penthouse suite at the Silver Sands Hotel, although the women didn't know this. Painters' drop cloths had been used to cover the windows. They had had pillowcases pulled over their heads before they were bundled into the elevator and taken from the office down into the basement car park and the van that was used to transport them to Sentosa. They had no idea where they were.

"We will now see if Mr Somsak values his employees at two billion dollars," Lu purred. The women were staring back at him with wide eyes. They blinked at the amount of money, but they had no idea what this man was talking about. None of them even knew who the man was.

Lu's trio of thugs had disarmed the single guard in the basement car park. The fighting women had distracted the man. The pantomime had been very effective. The man in the garage had not paid any attention to the delivery van. He had been knocked unconscious, bound and gagged and left in a utility cupboard. Lu's men had then disabled the alarm and made their way up the fire escape to the door to the fifteenth floor. On their cue, the fighting women had taken the elevator to the fifteenth floor and distracted the guards. It had worked to perfection.

The women had been easily subdued. A can of gasoline was liberally spread throughout the offices. Lu's men left the unconscious guards where they lay and set the fire. They used the keyed elevator to get back to the basement. High above, the fire erupted as the van left the car park.

Lu was pleased. The whole operation had gone like clockwork. He had Somsak's people. The Thai would return the money and the women would go free. He was sure that Sami Somsak would do it. Already, an emissary was on his way to Somsak's apartment to deliver the ultimatum along with the number of the cheap, prepaid cellphone that sat on Thomas Lu's desk.

The message, computer printed onto a single sheet of paper, was simplicity itself:

> *Give me my money or I will send your women back to you in pieces. You have until seven this evening to contact me.*

A cellphone number was printed in place of a signature.

The only thing that spoilt this moment was the fact that the members of the Intella syndicate had each received a copy of the recording Stanley Loh had made. One of Lu's friends had contacted him to inform him of the fact. He was now on the outside. However, Thomas Lu had a plan to get himself back into the closed circle. First, though, he wanted his money back and Sami Somsak dead.

25

Sami's cellphone had expired. It was as simple an explanation as that. The damn thing had simply run flat. Isn't that always the way with electronics? When you need the fucking things, they die on you.

We returned to the scene. The police were there, of course. I'd stayed well out of things while Sami fronted. No, he didn't know what was going on. No, he had no idea who had attacked his people or why. He, of course, suggested it was linked to the death of his stepbrother. He had come to Singapore to bury his dead and attempt to sort out his brother's affairs. No, he had no idea where his office staff had gone. The accountant had been at a meeting when the intruders arrived. He had arrived back after the fire crews had left.

The guard in the basement had been found seriously dehydrated and suffering severe concussion. Of the other two guards, one was not expected to live. The other, who had received serious head injuries and burns to much of his body, was expected to live. The only favour Lu's men had done Sami was take the weapons that Sami's men had been carrying. At least there were no arms charges on the slate.

The police eventually left. Because there had been no ransom demand for the missing staff members, their hands were tied. Missing person's bulletins would go out and they would mount a full investigation. There was nothing else they could do.

Jo and I answered Sami's call and went into the building and up to the fifteenth floor. The stench of burned plastic, gasoline fumes and water-sodden carpet filled the atmosphere. The air conditioning was on full. There were several broken windows and the others that could be opened gaped wide. The carpet and walls were blackened in places, soot covered everything, but the sprinklers and fire hoses had done the major damage. Everything was soaked. Everything, that is, apart from Stanley's office.

Stanley, it appeared, had been security conscious in one way at least. The office had a heavy fire- and impact-proof door and a serious mortise lock. It had still been locked when the fire crew had smashed their way through the wall beside it. The sprinklers had soaked the room, but apart from that, it was intact.

With kidnap presumably highest on their agenda, Lu's men had hit and run. I assumed that the fire had been more for nuisance value than anything else. Whatever, the office was where K and we three were now congregated. K had arrived from the Cairnhill apartment with the ransom note just moments after the police had left.

It was 15:22. In a little over three hours, Sami had to contact Lu.

"Where is he holding them?" Sami was staring unseeing at the huge satellite photomap of Singapore that was attached to the wall. The map was under a Perspex covering, so it hadn't been damaged by water. Intella Island and the connecting bridge had been added using Photoshop.

"It's a big island when you look at it like that," I said, lighting a Marlboro. I went to stand at Sami's side. I was referring to Singapore as a whole, minus Sami's bolt-on island. Jo was looking out the window behind us. K was sitting on the edge of what had been Stanley's huge desk, seemingly meditating.

"No more warehouses," I replied. "He has to figure you've got him tabbed on that. Given that you cleaned the money out of the last one and he torched another. Just how much real estate can he own?"

"A lot," Sami replied distractedly, "and much of that unofficially so we can't check a register or anything like that."

"Can we try the CCTV cameras again and see what vehicles left the car park just prior to the fire? It had to be a people mover or a van of some sort to shift two or three of Lu's guys and the four women."

"My people are working on it."

"Can we pre-empt him?" It was Jo.

"How?" Sami and I queried simultaneously.

"Figure this," he said. "I would bet that whatever exchange he is going to make, it will be at dawn tomorrow. It needs to take place in a semi-public area, but not right out in the open or in rush hour. Not too obvious, but there will have to be people around. The women will arrive in a van or small bus and there will be an exchange for a truck with the money. Simple swap and enough people around to prevent it all ending in a firefight."

"That sounds about right," I agreed.

"I know where he has the women." It was K. He stood and walked to the map and stabbed a finger at it. "The hotel on Sentosa."

"What makes you think he'll hold them there?" Sami wanted to know.

"He thinks he is very clever. But he has to keep them in an isolated place and that is perfect," K replied. "You said it was deserted but for workmen. Perfect place to house an army or hostages."

"He's just arrogant enough to do that," Sami mused. "It would be just like him to use it again as a private joke against me. He's so sure that because it is so obvious, I'll consider the hotel and discount it."

"Reverse reversed psychology, or whatever," I agreed, "but more than that. On a practical level, K is right. It's logical. It's the ideal place to maintain his people out of sight until needed."

"Then let's look at turning the tables yet again on Mr Lu." Jo had a smile on his face. That was unusual in itself. It was the sort of smile that meant someone was going to get hurt. "I have a plan!"

To work, Jo's plan relied on three things: that the hostages were being held at the Silver Sands Hotel; that Lu would press for a dawn exchange; and that a reconnaissance run be made to check out the hotel. K left to organise that.

Sami used the phone. This call was to the man in charge of the computers. The reply he was seeking came back a few minutes later. They had isolated a van entering Scotts Road from the building's car park at the time of the fire. It was then Sami asked that they cut to the chase. Instead of letting the computers wade through millions of images, he had them concentrate on the Sentosa Bridge footage. Twenty minutes after it left Scotts Road, the van crossed the bridge onto the island.

K reported back half an hour later from the island. There was a transit van parked in the car park at the Silver Sands Hotel. The registration number matched that on the CCTV cameras. He also reported that the relatively isolated car park, with its fringe of tended jungle, was the perfect scenario for what we had in mind. That was, of course, if we were right about the hostages being inside the hotel. If we were wrong, people were going to die.

"I can't seem to stay away from Sentosa," I muttered to no one in particular. Sami heard me.

"At least you won't have to swim this time."

"I hope," I replied, looking round the office, wondering if Stanley's bar was still intact. It was!

It was a few minutes to 19:00 when Sami made the call to Thomas Lu.

Thomas Lu was almost laughing as he set his cellphone down on the shelf protruding from the side of the spa. He had set his trap and now he had received a wonderful piece of news. Bad weather over the Pacific had led to Carlos Mendez postponing the long flight to Sydney to refuel and then carry on to Singapore. Lu not only had another twenty-four or forty-eight hours before the Colombian arrived, but Sami Somsak had agreed to return the money in exchange for the women.

"A soft man at heart," Lu said as he gloated at his good luck. "A soft man to give away two billion dollars for a handful of women."

Lu relaxed in his spa. Michael was in the shower prior to joining him.

The transfer would take place at a location of Lu's selection at dawn. He hadn't told Somsak where this would be. That meant there would be no chance of an ambush. He would direct the whole operation by cellphone.

The truck with the money would be directed on a route he chose, and at the point he chose, the truck would be ordered to stop. He would then verify the money was indeed aboard and then, and only then, he would order the van with the women aboard to the transfer site. The transfer would be made and that would very much be that. Part of him, of course, wanted Sami Somsak dead as part of the exchange. However, there would be witnesses, so Somsak's demise would have to wait a little longer.

In any other situation he would have expected a double-cross, but there simply was no way that the Thai could organise one, short of filling the truck with gunmen, and that would guarantee the death of the women, so it was not going to happen. Thomas Lu took a sip of whisky. There would be no chance of a double-cross. The plan was as near perfect as he could make it.

"I should have done this to get that cursed recorder back," Lu murmured thoughtfully. It would have been so simple. Why had he not thought of it sooner? Now, of course, it was too late. Its damage had been done, but that damage wasn't irreversible. Lu's musings were interrupted as Michael slipped into the spa. The youngster really was beautiful. Lu put down his glass and reached for his lover.

26

Sentosa at pre-dawn. Apart from the cold white of the lights in the various entrances and buildings, there was just a heavy greyness, not pitch black. The moon and the stars, at this transition between night and day, were gone. The air was cool for the moment. There was little noise, just the muted sound of the sparse early-morning traffic coupled with the continual sound of the container port.

Once more it was back to the jungle for K, four others from Jo's old squad and me. Jo was with Sami and the truck bearing the container. And yes, the money was aboard. All of it! If we were wrong in our attempt to pre-empt Lu, then Sami would pay the money over to free the women. Of course, each of the bales in the container had a GPS tracer buried deep in it, but that was little consolation if it all turned to crap and there was blood on the floor.

We were in the jungle fringe surrounding the Silver Sands car park. Each of us was wearing the standard overall plus gloves and a balaclava. Dressing the same meant we knew who was who. It meant observers couldn't identify individuals. The tough, all-encompassing overalls kept everything in, as did the flash gloves. No fibres or DNA could get out. We each carried a silenced weapon. My choice for this exercise was an H&K MP5. The others had a selection of weapons of their choice. The only criteria was that they had to be as quiet as possible and they had to hit their designated targets.

Despite the way they are depicted in movies, silencers, or more correctly suppressers, don't totally muffle the sound of a gunshot. In most cases they reduce it and they change it from a sharp boom-crack to a duller thump. The report then becomes harder to identify. Was it someone dropping something? Was it a backfire? Hell, was it someone farting? Whatever, one problem remained: with a semi-automatic weapon, if the breech isn't locked for single fire, the rattle of the mechanism as the weapon re-cocks is a giveaway to anyone in the know. Nevertheless, to the uninitiated ear of those asleep in the neighbouring hotels, hopefully any gunfire from us would be just an unidentified sound in the gloom.

There were dim lights on in the back of the eight-storey hotel. The only vehicle in the car park was a dark transit. We could see occasional silhouettes against the faint glow of interior lights. There were men on watch at several of the windows. K, possibly the best jungle scout I have ever worked with, did one of his phantom runs to the front of the hotel. Yes, there were men on watch there as well, three of them. Lu was taking no chances that his fortress would be stormed.

We were wired for sound, of course, but the instructions were clear: we shoot to kill and we keep the women alive at all costs. Two of our team, Quong and Sindip, were positioned on the far side of the car park, which appeared to be about the size of two tennis courts. Their task was to take out anyone appearing at the windows overlooking the car park and then lay down suppression fire on the rear face of the building. They both had silenced MP5s and a lot of magazines.

I was situated in the jungle fringe on one side of the sliding glass door that opened into the car park. K was opposite me, hiding in the shadows of the various bins and tanks of the hotel's loading bay. We could trust one not to shoot the other in a crossfire. The remaining pair, Loc and Dnap, were each armed with Sami's ubiquitous silenced Brownings. They were situated ten metres beyond K and me, covering the belly of the car park.

There was movement in the building. Several bright unshaded room lights had come on. There were closed drapes over most of the windows, but with the harsh lights now on, shadows showed plainly. Was this the moment that Lu's people brought the hostages out to the car park and loaded them into the van? What was happening with Sami and the truck?

"You will drive from Changi and down the East Coast Parkway

towards the city and await further instructions."

"We have to go to Changi. It will take us thirty minutes from where we are," Sami lied.

"Do that. Call me when you start on the parkway!"

Thomas Lu closed his cellphone. He was almost gloating, imagining the frustration of Somsak, and imagining his ransom on its way back to him.

Lu was at the wheel of the black Lexus. Although he seldom drove himself, he was proficient enough. Despite the fact that his manpower was stretched thinly, he was confident that all would go well. A second vehicle, an anonymous older model Mazda, was waiting back on the parkway to pick up Somsak's tail. All its occupants were armed. Not that he expected they would need their weapons. Somsak wanted his women back alive. When they parked to make the transfer in the car park beside Siglap Canal, there would be traffic and enough people around to discourage any open aggression on Somsak's part.

"Let's go."

"Okay." Jo Ankar was at the wheel of the truck. Sami was beside him. They had left the warehouse and had been sitting awaiting Lu's call in a side street in Tampines. Now they were rolling. Given the almost non-existent traffic, thirty minutes had been an exaggerated estimate of the time they needed, but Sami hadn't wanted Lu to have any idea where they had been based.

It took a little under ten minutes to get to the East Coast. Jo pulled them over and while they waited out the next fifteen minutes, Sami sat there and wondered what was happening on Sentosa. The moment Daniel confirmed the girls were there and that they were safe, phase two of their plan for Thomas Lu's downfall would go into action. Despite the fact it had been created in just a matter of an hour or two, it was an elaborate plan in that it called for several things to happen in rapid succession.

At the end of it all, Sami Somsak's aim was to have the women back, the money still in his possession, and Thomas Lu as well.

Lu sat in his Lexus and waited for the call from the Thai. Then, once he had confirmation they were moving and there was no tail, he would give them the location of the car park where the exchange would take place. He would only do that when Somsak was well down the parkway. There was no way Somsak could anticipate the meeting spot and set up an ambush.

There was definitely a lot happening inside the Silver Sands. Quong, the senior of our pair at the far end of the car park, obviously had the best vantagepoint. He called in what they were seeing. Lights had come on down the building in what they assumed was the main stairwell. He could see people moving down it through the tinted glass wall. In three rooms there were men stationed at windows looking down into the car park. They had weapons, and they were the first targets. I had to figure that the glass walls of the hotel put them at a huge disadvantage in the coming firefight.

It would, of course, be far better to get the women to safety without a shot being fired, but sometimes it's the old eggs and omelette thing, and I preferred that the armed men's eggs got broken, not ours.

And so we waited.

27

The women had been freed from their duct tape gags and restraints, fed and allowed to use the bathroom during the night. The two men assigned to watch over them throughout the long night had discussed raping them, but in the end they hadn't, fearing what their absent boss might do by way of retribution. Now the four women had once again been gagged and their wrists bound together with duct tape.

The four hostages were led down the stairs towards the ground floor, herded by their two minders.

"Careful of the steps, ladies," one said over his shoulder. Under her gag Simone DeLue snarled, wishing she had an opportunity to get her hands on the man, whoever he was.

The man sensed Simone's outrage and smiled. He was enjoying this game. It would have been interesting to have sex with her. The man with the gun reached out and with his free hand groped the woman's breast. She attempted to kick him. He laughed and pushed her on down the stairs ahead of him. She stumbled but managed to regain her balance.

There were two more armed men waiting at the bottom of the stairs when the group reached the ground floor foyer. There was a third standing beside the main door. He was cradling an AK47.

The leader of the group lit a cigarette and glanced at his watch. Shortly, the boss would call for them to put the women into the van. In the meantime, there was nothing to do but wait. He stared at the blonde woman through his cigarette smoke. He had never had a Caucasian woman before, let alone a blonde. There was a terrible temptation. Should he take her to one of the offices off the foyer and have her? Would Mr Lu ever find out? Would he even care?

Yeo Soon Heng made up his mind in that instant. He would take her and have her. No matter, it would be quick, at least he would be able to say he had tasted this beautiful blonde flesh. Soon Heng tossed his cigarette into a standing sand tray and started towards the woman.

Simone had been watching the leader of the gang of Chinese thugs and she saw his intention immediately. She would fight, of course, but it would do her no good. Even so, she would do her best to hurt him.

"Wait! Look!" one of the other gunmen called. Soon Heng stopped and turned. Headlights, dulled by the growing dawn, showed through the trees as a vehicle turned into the lane that led to the hotel car park. Was this the boss, Thomas Lu, coming or someone else?

"Quickly, out of sight," he ordered. The other gunmen grabbed the hostages and pushed them against a wall to hide them from view through the glassed rear doors.

The vehicle was a police car.

The arrival of the police car came as a shock. I told everyone to freeze, and we waited, lying or crouched in the shadows, to see what the hell was going on.

Two laughing uniformed men got out of their unit car. They produced cigarettes and lit them. One walked a few paces away from the car and proceeded to piss against a refuse drum, unaware that K was on the other side of it, an MP5 in his hands.

We held our positions and waited anxiously for the cops to finish their cigarettes. They took their time, talking and joking as they smoked. It appeared their sergeant was fucking one of the constables. They both thought it was a great joke and that he needed to get his eyes tested.

Then the car radio gave out a call. One of the officers answered it.

It appeared there had been an auto accident by Harbourfront. The pair flicked away their butts, got back into their unit and left the car park under full lights, sirens blaring.

"Damn," I said into my mike. "That must have woken the

neighbourhood."

"Here they come." The voice was Quong's again. I could picture him raising his weapon and covering the first of his targets. We'd had the wake-up call from the police siren. Soon breaking glass and a hell of a lot of dull pops that weren't some kid's breakfast cereal were going to break the morning's peace.

The white Mazda sedan that had fallen in behind the truck with the container onboard confirmed that Sami Somsak and the money were indeed on the ECP and were seemingly travelling alone as instructed. When Thomas Lu received this confirmation, he gave the order for the women to be put into a van and the van also driven to the same location. The van would only drive into the lay-by if the money was there and the driver received the go-ahead from him via cellphone. It was all going according to his plan.

In the Silver Sands Hotel, Soon Heng was ushering the women out into the car park. Any thoughts he'd had of raping the blonde woman had vanished. His reward for the completion of this task was ahead, and it would be in cold hard cash. He would take that cash, go to a high-rent hotel bar and buy a dozen blonde women, women younger and even more beautiful than this one.

Soon Heng led the way to the double glass doors. They hissed open and he stepped through. The designated driver followed at his heel. Behind him came the four women and behind them two more of his men. They moved away from the hotel. The driver was at the van, opening his door.

It was at this moment that Soon Heng knew they were not alone. A figure dressed all in black stepped out of the bushes. The figure was holding a sub-machine gun in front of his face.

I had designated the hits. The first man out of the hotel was mine and I concentrated on him. As I stepped out of the bushes, I gave the order to fire.

My man was turning, raising the automatic he had in his hand. I gave him a three burst and then another for luck. The range was less than ten metres. He was gone. The night was crackling. Glass was falling in a shower from the face of the building above us. I moved to the hostages.

"Down," I yelled and they went to the ground. There was a man with an AK47 coming across the foyer towards us. The glass doors were closed, but just for a moment before they disintegrated under a hail of copper jackets. One of the marksmen across the car park had seen him coming. I finished the job by shooting through the glass-less doorframes. The guy took several hits and fell skidding onto the marble floor.

"All down," K was calling. "Quong, watch the roof. Singdip, cover the windows."

The replies came back from our two guys on the far side. If there were any of Lu's men left alive in the building, we could still have a problem. I anticipated that there were at least two gunmen still unaccounted for. Loc had taken the van driver. The man's body was sprawled under the van's open door. I stepped over him. The keys were in the ignition.

"Everybody in," I called. I was going to be driving. It hadn't been in the original plan to use Lu's van. We had the medium-sized bus, with one of Sami's guys as driver, parked a hundred yards back up the road. The bus was covered in signage. It looked just like the sort of vehicle that tour groups use to get around Singapore. It was innocuous and near invisible. Rather than bring it down, we were going to it.

K was herding the hostages into the back of the van. There wasn't time to get their gags or wrist restraints off.

As yet there were no shouts or screams and no lights coming on in the buildings beyond our narrow fringe of jungle. Maybe the pops and the sound of breaking glass really had been mistaken for breakfast snap, crackle and pop. Whatever, we were out of there.

As I fired the van into life, there was a sudden barrage of pops from behind me and it wasn't the van's exhaust. In front of me a man impacted with the tarmac. I later learned he had been shot off the roof.

"Go!" It was K's call as he threw himself into the passenger seat.

The back of the van was crowded with bodies. Quong and Singdip were crouched side by side at the car park entrance, their guns giving us cover as I pulled a wheel-squeaking turn and sent us their way. I slowed, they scrambled into the back and we were out of there.

At the bus, I stopped and there was a rapid transfer of bodies. We left Lu's van where it was. Aboard the bus it was balaclavas off, gags and bindings off, weapons under the seats, and then the early morning tour began. Simone clung to me and sobbed. Every second word was why?

28

It was daylight. A feeble sun was pushing through the grey dawn as the truck carrying the battered shipping container with its four billion-dollar cargo drove along the east coast. It was close to the Costa Sands Resort and only now had Thomas Lu given Sami Somsak the location for the exchange. Sami quickly passed the information on. They had anticipated this would happen. A hundred metres ahead of the Isuzu with the container was a works truck carrying a squad of gardeners. The works truck slowed as it crossed the Siglap Canal. It turned into the car park. Watching it, Sami smiled. It had been a hellish gamble, but Lu had miscalculated. He had been concerned about a tailing vehicle.

Jo Ankar was slipping into lower gears in preparation for pulling into the lay-by. Traffic was still light. Sami used a small handheld radio. The cellphone was reserved for K and Thomas Lu.

"You catch that, Billy?" Sami asked. Billy Yee, one of his Singapore people, was driving their third vehicle. This was a small unmarked rental van and it was a hundred metres behind, sitting between the Isuzu and the Mazda carrying Lu's thugs. Yee had a vital role to play in what was to come. He'd seen what was happening ahead.

"Confirmed. I'll go down, cross and come back, and park opposite."

"Give us at least five minutes from park-up," Sami instructed. "The signal to get into position will be a double squelch. The signal to go will be a triple."

"Roger!" Two voices responded. Sami Somsak smiled grimly and leaned back into his seat. His guys were professionals. Hopefully, Lu's were just triad street thugs. If they were, it would be no contest.

The light double-cab truck with the covered rear deck had three of his men in it. They were already getting out of their truck. They were dressed as gardeners. The other vehicle, a small Toyota rental van, carried just the driver, Billy Yee. He drove past the car park entrance as Jo Ankar turned in.

"Have you done it, Daniel?" Sami whispered. There were several other vehicles in the car park including a black Lexus wagon. A man was standing beside the Lexus. Sami immediately recognised the tall figure as Thomas Lu. There was no one else in the vehicle or close to Lu.

As Jo made to park the truck close to the Lexus, Sami's phone rang.

"Yes?"

"We have them safe and sound. Do it to him."

"You got it, Daniel!" Relieved, Sami said a silent prayer to his gods. His companion just smiled as he applied the brakes and switched the truck's engine off.

"Playtime," Jo said.

"Indeed," came the response as Sami slipped the small radio into the arm sling he was wearing. He got out of the truck and walked around to the front. He was seemingly unarmed, as instructed. He raised his jacket awkwardly with his free hand and pirouetted to show Thomas Lu there were no weapons, just a cellphone pouched on his belt. Lu pointed to the sling. Sami gripped the radio concealed in the sling and held it in his fist as he pulled the sling over his head and shook it. Lu nodded and Sami awkwardly reversed the process, feigning pain as he did so. Lu nodded. Sami settled the sling back in position. Performance over, he moved forward a few paces and stopped, looking across the intervening empty parking space to where Thomas Lu stood.

"Mr Somsak, I presume?" Lu's voice had a jovial, mocking edge to it.

"Mr Lu!" Sami's voice was flat, emotionless. Anyone who knew Sami Somsak knew that this was Sami at his most dangerous. If the opportunity arose, he would kill Thomas Lu with his bare hands, slowly and with relentless efficiency. Sami was both a Samurai and a very accomplished martial artist. Even at almost seventy years of age, he was lethal. Perhaps Lu realised that as well, because he nervously maintained his distance.

"I believe you have something of mine?"

Sami stared at Lu with an expression that was pure contempt.

"And you have something of mine."

"They will be delivered just as soon as I have possession of the money."

"Then what are we waiting for?"

"Just some friends of mine," Lu replied. "Oh, there they are now."

"This was supposed to be between us," Sami said with just the right amount of indignation in his voice.

"I don't think I can trust you, Mr Somsak," Lu responded as the Mazda sedan carrying four of his men pulled into a park beyond the Lexus. The doors opened and the men got out and moved to stand in a loose group beside the black wagon.

Although no weapons were visible, Sami knew they were there under the hanging shirttails and bulky jackets. He smiled to himself. From the corner of his eye, he saw the gardeners spreading out around the fringes of the car park. Their intention seemed to be to tend the plants on the verge and the plantings beyond the lay-by. One produced a petrol-powered weed eater and fired it into life, concentrating on the narrow strip of grass that ran down the ocean side of the narrow lot. The Singapore garden crews habitually started work early to avoid the human rush, so their presence was of no concern to Thomas Lu or his men. Lu had witnessed their arrival before Sami Somsak and the truck. They were no part of this. His focus was on one thing only. To Lu's minders, the gardeners appeared in the main to be elderly. Most of them were of a small build. They did not represent a threat.

"Let me see the money."

Sami turned and waved to Jo who was still sitting behind the wheel of the truck. Obedient driver that he was, Jo Ankar opened the cab door, slipped from his seat and swung back onto the deck behind the cab. He then walked down to the rear of the container.

Sami walked alongside him. Thomas Lu paralleled them, walking five metres away. His quartet of bodyguards moved with him.

When Lu saw the truck driver reach the rear of the container and start to unfasten the lock, he called out.

"Wait!" Lu quickly gave instructions to his men. One moved to the front of the truck, two stayed where they were. Lu, with the remaining man at his shoulder, moved forward. He was now confident that he had both his back and the car park covered.

The truck driver stood on the truck deck waiting for the instruction to continue to open the container. When Lu and his man arrived at the rear of the vehicle, Lu gave the order. The driver once again started working the locking handle.

The locking bar ground free and the driver moved to one side as he pulled the door open. The man at Lu's side tensed. Under his long jacket, the muzzle of an Uzi was just visible. His right hand was under the jacket. Under his own jacket, Thomas Lu had a silenced stainless steel S&W 459 automatic holstered. He had his hand on its butt. His heart was high in his chest as the container door screeched open.

There was no horde of gunmen waiting inside the container. Lu breathed a sigh of relief. He moved slightly to one side so he could see down the length of the container's interior and counted its contents. There were four bales packed in it in a line, one behind the other, just as they had been when the container had been in his warehouse.

"Wait here and watch them," Lu instructed his bodyguard as he climbed up onto the truck deck. He brushed past the driver and entered the steel box. The bales that had previously been opened had been resealed with tape and plastic sheeting.

Thomas Lu smiled to himself. Was it a trap, a wooden horse? Would men with guns leap out of the bales and take him prisoner? He raised his silenced automatic and calmly walked down the line of bales. As he moved, he fired two rounds into each of them. The sound of the weed eater working away outside was more than enough to cover the sound of the muffled reports. He walked back up the other side of the container and repeated the process. Now he had only two of the fourteen rounds left. He replaced the magazine with another from his jacket pocket. He smiled at Sami Somsak.

"In case you decided to substitute armed men for my money," he said. "In which case they will be very dead. Open it," he commanded pointing at the first bale. The truck driver looked at Sami, who nodded. The man slowly produced a large folding knife from his pocket. He showed it to Lu. Then he began slicing the bindings and the thick plastic outer covering on top of the bale that was a substitute for the hemp that had been cut away previously. Soon the money was exposed.

Lu held out a hand and the driver passed him a block of banknotes.

"Deeper," Lu said as he examined the notes he held. The driver shifted several blocks of notes and buried his arms deep into the centre of the bale.

"Too tightly packed," he grunted in passable English.

"Open that one." Lu pointed to the second bale. The driver moved to it and began using his knife again.

Holding a large packet of banknotes in his hands, Thomas Lu turned to Sami Somsak who was still standing at the rear of the truck, watching the activities in the container. "Is it all here?"

"It is," Sami replied.

"The women are on their way," Lu said as he turned back into the container. The driver had the second bale open and held aloft another large block of notes. Lu pointed to the third.

Sami turned to look back towards the gardener's truck. This game was boring him. It was time to bring it to its conclusion. He cradled his plastered arm with his free hand as if in pain. His fingers found the transmit button on the radio. He depressed it twice. He didn't turn to look, but he knew that the gardeners, who had been noisily positioning themselves, playing their parts with enthusiasm, had begun to move closer.

The man with the petrol-powered weed eater was cutting the grass on the mound behind the truck. One of Lu's men was facing his way, watching him idly, while the other was watching what was going on in the container.

Inside the container, Lu was still fondling the money the driver had been handing him. The driver was preparing to open the fourth bale now. Lu felt that indeed the money was all there. He was smiling.

Sami Somsak glanced around again. The small truck was sitting on the far side of the parkway, almost directly opposite the car park. His other men were all in position and Lu's thugs still had no idea. The weed eater spluttered and died. The man using it cursed. He unfastened the harness and, leaving the machine on the grass, walked off grumbling towards the truck parked twenty metres away. The bodyguard who had been watching him laughed.

"Idiot," he said to his compatriot. "Next time, he will be sure to fill it before he starts."

As the grumbling man walked by, one of his fellow gardeners called to him. "Bring me my lunchbox, I'm hungry."

"It's not even breakfast time, Garbage Guts," came the response. Both men laughed. Sami frowned, hoping they weren't overacting. Lu's watchers standing behind the truck seemed relaxed. They were exchanging words, laughing. Perhaps the comedy show was working.

At the truck the grumbling man retrieved a red and yellow petrol can and a small plastic box and started back towards his weed eater. He tossed the lunchbox to his companion with more insults and carried on.

As he approached his weed eater, he passed the two men standing behind Sami Somsak. He made a show of unscrewing the top of the plastic fuel container. He was still grumbling. Lu's men laughed.

Sami pressed the button on his radio handset three times. A second later, the morning was ripped apart by a massive explosion. The van on the far side of the parkway exploded in a fireball.

Every eye in the lay-by and out on the parkway, with the exception of those who were expecting it, was drawn to the huge fireball that mushroomed into the sky. At precisely the same moment as the van exploded, the gardener with the plastic fuel container dropped it. From under his shirt he produced a silenced Browning automatic. He shot the near pair of Lu's men three times each as they stood only feet away, staring at the spectacle that was taking place across the parkway.

At the same instant that the explosion occurred, the gardener who had called for his lunchbox produced another silenced automatic. He shot the man standing watch beside the front of the truck three times. The man fell to the ground without a sound. Sami Somsak took care of the fourth man who was standing at the rear of the container. Lu's man was caught between watching the activities inside the truck and the noise of the explosion.

The bodyguard's attention was split and for that he died when the blade of the razor sharp stiletto Sami Somsak was carrying secreted in his forearm plaster drove into the man's back, severing his spine. A second knife thrust found his heart.

Thomas Lu heard the explosion and started moving towards the container door. He saw his bodyguard collapse and raised his automatic. Sami Somsak, who was standing over the fallen body, was smiling up at him.

Jo Ankar, the obedient truck driver, pounced on Thomas Lu from behind and drove the long blade of the knife he was holding into Lu's right shoulder. An expert with any blade, Jo twisted the knife viciously and expertly to cause the maximum damage.

The shiny stainless steel automatic fell from Lu's numbed fingers and bounced onto the truck's deck. Ankar caught Lu before he tumbled out of the container and off the back of the truck. He turned the injured man around and threw him back into the container.

"Go, go, go!" Sami called. Jo dogged the container door shut and ran back along the side of the truck's deck for the cab. The gardeners' truck was backing up. The gardeners were dragging the fallen gunmen together. Sami joined them. Like cords of wood, the dead were tossed into the back of the truck. Weapons were collected and tossed in as well, along with the gardening props.

While the explosions out on the parkway continued, the truck bearing the container, followed by the gardeners' truck, started out down the car park. All they left behind were two abandoned vehicles, some bloodstains and spent cartridge cases.

"Total chaos," Sami said as they drove for the exit. The flames from the Toyota were still licking at the sky. Vehicles were stopped on the far side of the parkway and traffic from Changi had slowed. Every eye was still focussed on the blaze. What had or had not happened in the car park would remain something of a mystery that would take the police weeks to unravel. Yes, some people had witnessed what had happened, but they doubted their eyes and their sanity. This was so alien, so surreal, and this was Singapore where nothing ever happened—or so their totally logical brains told them.

"Thank you, Tam Yin Fireworks," Jo said. The occasional spurt of flames still kicked off skyward from the burning truck. He glanced in his mirrors. The gardeners were on their tail as the two vehicles reached the parkway and joined the traffic flow. Because vehicles approaching the burning truck from the direction of Changi had slowed to see what was happening, the parkway ahead was relatively clear, a fact that both trucks took advantage of. Within minutes, they had turned off the parkway and into the maze of side streets that would make them all but invisible to the all-seeing eyes of the CCTV cameras.

29

Two days had passed since the latest shootout. Sami had the money and Thomas Lu. The threat Lu had represented was no more, but that still left the Mendez brothers. According to Sami's inside man, Lu had made no secret that he had put Sami Somsak on the Colombians' radar as the man who had killed their younger brother and stolen their money.

The complete chaos following the latest Sentosa gun battle and the mayhem at the East Coast Parkway had the authorities up in arms. CCTV footage was being scrutinised. Thankfully, Sami's inside information on the coverage blank spots and the absolute red zones had so far been invaluable, allowing our people to be as invisible as possible on the streets.

Sami's crew had been busy. The container truck was stripped down for scrap. The gardeners' truck with its bodies still aboard had been abandoned and still not found. Now it was very much a matter of sitting tight and riding out the storm. There was nothing concrete to connect the latest episodes to the previous ones, but that didn't mean forensics experts weren't trying. All the weapons used in the episode had been melted down in a foundry.

The police had been to see Sami several times. His staff members had been returned unharmed. The kidnappers had been Chinese. They had been masked so the hostages couldn't identify them. They had their heads covered and they had been bound. They had been taken to a warehouse, at least that's what they thought. They had not been harmed. There had been talk of a ransom. Then one of the kidnappers had received a phone call. They'd heard him exclaim "Sentosa". The men seemed to have panicked, the women said. They had their hoods put back on and they were put into a van and driven off. They had been dropped close to MacRitchie Reservoir and it was from there they had phoned Mr Somsak, who'd arranged to pick them up. They had then reported to the police.

The reality was, of course, that Sami, in exchange for a great deal of money and ongoing allowances, had orchestrated their story. None of them would ever have to work again. Their memories and their loyalty were guaranteed. That, of course, should be the end of that story, but it isn't.

One of the great things about saving the life of a beautiful, bountiful woman is the fact that gratitude can know no bounds. Unfortunately, in my case, that gratitude was tempered with tears, fear and recriminations.

The beautiful Simone DeLue thanked me and then asked me to get out of her life forever. She had two children to raise. She had almost left them motherless. She had been terrified. She was involved in things that were horrific and dangerous and illegal. She had witnessed brutal killings. She no longer had a job. She didn't know me. She ... and so the list went on.

Was I surprised by her reaction? No, not at all! Normal people don't get involved in situations that Sami and I do. Normal people don't look at everyone in a room and calculate who is dangerous and plan how to take them out if the need arises. Normal people don't have multiple identities and live in the shadows. Normal people don't ... Oh, what the fuck!

It was 14:30, two days on, and I was half way through my second bottle of JD. Simone had delivered her speech on day one. Sami, Jo and the others had vanished, and only Sami knew where the truck and container and Lu were. I knew Lu had been stabbed but I had no idea how badly, and while I could guess what Sami was doing to the guy, I didn't actually care. Whatever, Lu deserved it.

I booked a flight back to Hong Kong for the following morning. There was no point in me staying now. The meeting at which Thomas Lu was to have been exposed and Sami revealed had been cancelled. There was no need. Sami had been outed as Stanley's brother in several areas of the media following the fire at the office. He'd sent a copy of the digital recording to Intella's consortium members along with a letter of introduction. The tape would no doubt be played, if for no other reason than to leave the soon-to-be-dearly-departed man in a most negative light.

As to the imminent arrival of the Colombians, Sami had his army in place. If the Mendez brothers didn't believe that Lu was the villain of the piece, few Colombians would be flying home again. That much was a promise.

I switched on the television and poured myself a bourbon. The good folks at News Corp and CNN were now in full speculative mode following the latest bloodbaths. Mainland Chinese gang members were being blamed. There was speculation which triad groups the various dead belonged to. The police had recovered many weapons from both crime sites. Crime scene forensic specialists were still analysing the Sentosa hotel and the East Coast lay-by for evidence while the coroner's department got on with their grim task. Just this morning it was reported that several more bodies had been discovered in an abandoned, stolen truck in Simpang. The authorities would bring those involved to justice. Had Singapore suddenly become a haven for Asia's bad guys? There were more security measures in the wind, blah, blah. I turned the television off and at the precise moment my cellphone went.

"Yeah?"

"It's Sami."

"The long-lost Sami Somsak?" I replied sarcastically in my drunken state.

"I'm sorry, old friend. There were a great many things that needed doing and I didn't want you seen or involved. Once again, Daniel, I want to thank you."

"It's what we do, Sami."

"Yes. I suppose that's what we do," he said with a faint chuckle. "The Colombians will be landing tomorrow afternoon. Private jet. I will be meeting them in person. I'd like you there with me. I know you were going to fly out in the morning."

"How did you know that?"

"Contacts, Daniel. But there are some things we need to discuss before you go anyway. Recompense for one."

"Sami, I don't ..."

"Hear me out, Daniel," Sami said, cutting me off at the pass. He knew that I was going to object. "You know I've put Simone and the others on generous allowances. Simone can afford a better apartment and have money to educate her children and travel. She's set for life, so are the others."

"Bribery?" I ventured.

"And loyalty, Daniel. I'm loyal to people who hurt for me."

"I know. Sorry, that was uncalled for," I said, and it was uncalled for. Sami Somsak was one of the most generous people I'd ever met.

"Accepted, Daniel. I know about Simone. I'm sorry about that, but just give her a little time."

"Yeah, we'll see. What about Lu? Did you send him to meet his scaly ancestors?"

"He's alive," Sami replied dryly. "I will present him to the Mendez brothers along with most of the cash. I will deduct significant compensation, somewhere in the region of half a billion dollars."

"They won't like that."

"No, but that is the only hand they have to play. If they don't accept that then they and Thomas Lu are on a fast train to hell. Will you stay?"

"Okay. What time do they fly in?"

"ETA is 13:55. I will have Jo pick you up at the usual spot at 12:30. Wear mourning clothes ..."

"Yeah, and look dangerous," I added. Sami chuckled and the call was over.

I looked at the bottle of JD and put the top back on. I was going to shower, dress and head out. Sitting in my hotel room getting shit faced wasn't going to earn me anything other than a melancholy hangover. The bar I'd discovered up behind Centrepoint, the Cable Car, was a good place to start.

Thomas Lu was in agony. The pain in his shoulder was so bad that he was whimpering. The long blade had sliced and torn its way through his shoulder. It was a deep, wicked wound, inflicted when Somsak's men had dragged him from the container. They had put heavy pads on the wound, strapped it, and now he sat on the cold concrete floor of a storage room, hurting.

Lu's good wrist was handcuffed to a galvanised water pipe. There was a water bottle on the floor beside him but there was no food, no toilet bucket. Lu could stand but with great difficulty, the handcuff sliding up the pipe. He did that now, gasping with pain. He unfastened his flies, unable to hold his penis with his injured hand, and stretching as far as he could, he relieved himself. The acrid smell of urine filled the air.

With difficulty, he managed to close his flies and sat where he had been before. He had no alternative. He moaned in agony, and then felt warm wetness under his buttocks. The floor wasn't level. The urine he had discharged had followed the slope of the floor and found him. Thomas Lu cursed, but he didn't move. There was nowhere to move to.

The pub was a fun place. I was positioned at a table before the regulars rolled in. When they did, they included me in their conversations and banter. They were a mixed bunch of Singapore residents: Chinese, Indian and the inevitable British expats. When they discovered that Ed Davidson was Australian, Oz jokes abounded. I think my accent confused some of them at first; however, I covered it up by saying I'd been born in the UK.

It was after nine when I left the place with invitations to come again ringing in my ears. I wandered down Orchard Road in a state of more or less happy intoxication. As I navigated my way along Bras Basah, I realised I hadn't eaten for far too long. I detoured into Chijmes and found a restaurant where I ordered steak. I didn't need anything more to drink. It had been a long day, and once again, I hadn't actually killed anyone.

30

Carlos Mendez watched as Singapore appeared below the wings of the Global Express 5000 as it started to drop through the clouds. The Mendez brothers had owned the forty-five-million-dollar aircraft for two years, and apart from a brief excursion to Chile, Carlos had never flown in it. He hated flying.

There were only ten seats in the aircraft. The bed at the rear was for Carlos. He had slept fitfully off and on throughout the flight. Because of his fear of flying, every change in engine noise or change of direction had caused him to wake up and lie, eyes wide, anticipating disaster. Only the death of his beloved younger brother had made him undertake the flight half way round the world.

Now Carlos had abandoned the bed and was seated in one of the plush leather recliners that were staggered the length of the aircraft. In addition to the elder Mendez, there were six men seated in the main cabin. Up front was the Express' crew of two.

Mendez had never been to Singapore before. He had heard it was tiny and totally buttoned up. If that were so, he wondered how his brother, who had come from one of the most violent countries in the world, could have met his death here at the hands of the man Thomas Lu had identified as Sami Somsak.

The pilot came over the intercom advising that landing was imminent and advising his passengers to fasten their seatbelts. Carlos did as instructed and prepared himself for the landing, masking his extreme apprehension from his subordinates with a scowl as he gazed out the window.

The tarmac came up fast. The elder Mendez winced and then the tyres bit with a squeal and the small jet was on the ground. The roar of the engines being put into reverse caused the drug boss to feel a moment of near panic, but then the sound faded and the jet slowed and turned off the runway.

As they taxied to the nearest terminal building, Carlos Mendez composed himself. He was now in Singapore. There was business to do. There was revenge to be brought and when that was completed, he would fly back to Bogota with his brother's body.

The Colombians stood out amongst the mainly Asian arrivals at Terminal One. They stood out not because of their swarthy bulk, but because their clothing was flamboyant. Several wore shiny shirts and suits, and were covered in gold rings, neck chains and watches. Large diamonds sparkled in earlobes. Dark glasses topped off all the bling. Watching them as they came through the doors into the main concourse, I couldn't help thinking that they looked exactly like the cold-blooded killers and drug thugs they really were.

Carlos Mendez was easy to identify. He was the man who wasn't carrying anything. All of the others had one bag each. Some carried two and towed suitcases on wheels. The elder Mendez was in the lead. The others came behind in a loose group. Despite the dark glasses, I could sense their eyes were everywhere at once.

We were four to their seven: Sami, Jo, K and me. None of us were armed. Carlos Mendez called a halt in the centre of the concourse. He was obviously looking for Thomas Lu. Sami stepped forward while we three fell in at his shoulder. Sami had asked me to look dangerous. For me that meant taking the black route. Yet again, I had on a pair of black Levi's, black kickass cowboy boots and a black shirt with a light leather jacket over it—black, of course! Like the new arrivals, my costume was completed by the addition of a pair of Ray Bans. As an additional touch, I had put both my wallet and my cellphone in my inside left jacket pocket. The bulge suggested that there was a gun holstered there. That wasn't accidental, of course. We knew that the Mendez crew would be unarmed. Only a complete idiot would have attempted to enter Singapore carrying a weapon.

Mendez's attention was suddenly focussed on Sami, who advanced to within a few feet of the Colombian and stopped. I watched the men behind Mendez stiffen. Bags were lowered to the floor. Jo was standing slightly behind to Sami's left. His right shoulder was towards the Colombians, hiding his left side from their view. K was standing to my left. He was wearing a loose khaki jacket with several bulges. Were we armed? That was the question that was going through the minds of the Colombians. If so, they were at an extreme disadvantage.

"Mr Mendez, Mr Lu is indisposed. I am Sami Somsak. I believe we need to talk."

Carlos Mendez stood motionless. I could feel his X-ray eyes beaming out at us through the dark glasses. Sami, his plastered wrist in a sling again for pure effect, stood waiting for the Colombian's response.

"Is Mr Lu seriously indisposed?" Mendez asked.

"Not at the moment. However, the level of his indisposition I will leave to your discretion once we have had our talk. I invite you and your companions to come with me. I have transportation and I have arranged accommodation for you." Sami paused. "I assure you that this is in no way a set-up. I know you think I killed your brother. I didn't, Lu did, for the money. I will prove it to you, so please follow me."

With that, Sami turned. We, his three minders, did the same and walked slowly across the concourse, headed for the exit. I glanced behind. Mendez was following, as were his thugs. So far, so good!

There were two stretch Mercedes limousines and a van awaiting us when we emerged from the terminal. The van was for the luggage. At Sami's invitation, Mendez and one of his men got into the first Mercedes with him. Jo got in front with the driver, while I got in the rear of the second landship with the other five Colombian thugs. K got in front with the chauffeur.

We pulled away and those of us seated in the lounge-sized cabin of the big limousine looked at each other. I made with the small talk.

"Have any of you been to Singapore before?"

The six looked at each other. One of them, obviously an English speaker, translated. When he had finished, they all shook their heads in unison.

"This is a first time for us," the translator said in thickly accented but clear English. "We have come to take Raymond home," he added.

"It was unfortunate that he met a man he could not trust," I replied. "This man also murdered the family of Mr Somsak."

The translator did his thing for the others. I had the feeling that he was not senior amongst the drug Mafiosi. One individual, a man with an aesthetically thin face and narrow lips, seemed to be the boss here. He looked more Italian than Spanish Colombian. He sported a large diamond in his left ear and had a diamond-encrusted Rolex the size of a dinner plate on his left wrist. The translation was directed mostly at him. He said something in Spanish and the translation came back at me.

"This man Lu, he is still alive?"

"For the moment," I replied. "But I think not for long!"

The words were relayed back to Diamond Ear. He nodded and we sat in silence until we arrived at the Shangri-La Hotel. Sami had figured that the Mendez outfit might as well stay where Carlos's dearly departed brother had stayed, albeit briefly.

When the formalities were over, Sami and Carlos Mendez, along with Jo and the man with the diamond earring, went upstairs to the suite Sami had reserved for the Colombian drug boss. The other five hoods had been allocated rooms on the same corridor as the suite. K and I went up in the elevator with them. The bellhop pushing the loaded baggage trolley had more than an inkling that these guys weren't your average tourists. He nervously showed each man to his room, distributed their luggage and didn't hang about for any tips.

K and I waited outside the double doors of the suite as the Colombians went into their individual rooms. No raised voices sounded from inside Carlos's suite. I opened the door a crack. There was a small foyer inside. Jo and Mr Diamond were both seated in there, waiting. There was no conversation. Jo didn't speak Spanish and the other guy had no Thai or English. I eased the door closed, but not before Jo made eye contact. If the Colombian had noticed the door open, he didn't acknowledge it.

What was happening in the lounge beyond the foyer? Would

Mendez believe Sami? Would he accept the offer Sami was going to make him? Sami wanted half a billion dollars for his loss and inconvenience and for the Colombians to return home and forget Intella. In return, Mendez would get Thomas Lu on a plate and the remaining one and a half billion dollars. Time very much would tell which way this particular cookie crumbled.

Carlos Mendez listened to Sami Somsak's proposition, his face expressionless.

"Through his own greed and pressure from you, Thomas Lu killed my brother, his wife, two children and all his staff. He killed your brother Raymond when they took delivery of the money, which he then shifted before setting the warehouse on fire. He blamed me, of course. We found where he was keeping the money and did take it from him. In retaliation, Mr Lu firebombed my brother's offices and kidnapped the women who worked there, holding them to ransom for the return of the money and a chance to kill me. We turned the tables on him and now we are here." Sami paused and took a sip of mineral water. Mendez followed suit, but his choice of drink was brandy.

"I was going to kill him myself," Sami said. "I was going to cause him so much pain that he would beg me to end it."

"Why did you not do so?"

"I decided that he would be a gift to you, along with one and a half billion dollars of the money you shipped to him. I keep the remaining half a billion for inconvenience and damages and, of course, as a delivery fee for Mr Lu into your hands."

Carlos Mendez spluttered into his drink. The offer the Thai gangster was making was preposterous at first glance. Then the Colombian started to laugh. It was a deep, rumbling laugh that came from way down in his gut.

Outside the door, Jo and the thin-lipped Colombian looked at each other. This was not a sound that they expected to hear in this place at this time.

Sami smiled at Mendez's mirth. The Colombian put down his glass and removed a handkerchief from his pocket. He dropped his glasses onto the table and wiped his eyes.

"Oh, Mr Somsak, I believe your account of events and I admire your business sense. You know, as I do, that in our industry, half a billion dollars is neither here nor there. It is the principle of the thing that matters. Yes, I agree to your terms."

"There is more," Sami said, watching the smile on the Colombian's face freeze. "You do not get a share in Intella."

"But why not?"

"Intella is mine, Singapore is mine and Thailand is mine," Sami replied simply. Carlos Mendez scowled.

"We have difficulty investing in legitimate businesses in the Americas because of the cursed United States. I must invest here. There is nowhere else."

"Yes there is, and I can help you do it."

Mendez sat and stared at Sami Somsak. The man puzzled him terribly. He knew of Sami's reputation; he had researched him well through his underground connections before boarding the flight and coming to confront him. Now Sami was offering to help him.

"Where and why will you help?"

"China," Sami replied. "I will put you in touch with the people who can help you treble your investment in legitimate business in a matter of months. As to why? Maybe I'm growing sentimental in my old age," Sami said in a voice that made a lie of the words. "You lost a brother and I lost a brother to Thomas Lu, and in a perverse way that puts us in the same camp. Also, if you refuse to stay away from Singapore and Thailand, I will have to kill you."

Carlos Mendez blinked. In his world, he was used to making threats and indeed killing or having people killed. However, the Latin temperament often raised the blood level and words and threats were delivered with hot passion. Having this man sitting opposite him deliver an ultimatum and talk of death as if he were simply discussing food items on a menu was totally alien to the Colombian. He could, however, plainly see in the Thai's eyes that his words were a truth and not an idle threat.

Mendez sat and considered the proposition. He knew that in this world, Sami Somsak's world, that the man in front of him was king, very much as he himself was king in his own world. Mendez well knew the entire planet was divided into kingdoms. Each kingdom had its own monarch. Sometimes those kingdoms went to war against each other, but for the most part, they co-operated on business of mutual interest in the quest for greater profits. Unnecessary wars only served to weaken both sides, and often a third player would gain dominance over the distracted and weakened combatants and defeat both.

Carlos Mendez was a realist. He would never wage a war that he couldn't be sure of winning. He made his decision.

"I agree." He had accepted that he and Sami Somsak were both kings and now they were to become allies.

"Good," Sami said simply. He picked up his glass of Evian. Carlos Mendez raised his brandy and the glasses touched.

31

It was the morning of the next day. With Sami and Carlos Mendez now suddenly good buddies, I figured it was time for me to split.

I knew that despite gloves, protective clothing and everything else, there would be something of me somewhere. That's the problem with DNA. The Singapore police and government authorities were pulling out all the stops to find the perpetrators of the crime wave that had suddenly hit the island-state. It would just take one little piece of evidence and the game would be over. You can't continue indefinitely doing what we had been doing in such a confined area without something going seriously wrong. Despite their portrayal in many movies, cops ain't stupid. They have systems and eventually those systems are going to pick up a thread and turn it into a rope with a noose at the end. So Ed Davidson, sans the beautiful Mavis, was going to move back to Hong Kong.

I'd heard that Thomas Lu was still alive in a warehouse in Pasir Ris. Whatever plans Sami and Carlos Mendez had for him, I had no idea and I wasn't particularly concerned. I'd come here and done what Sami had needed me to do. The irony, of course, was that in the end, retrieving the digital recorder from the surrender room had virtually been all for nothing. But hey, that's life; sometimes things just turn out that way.

I was packed and ready to go. There was a 13:50 flight out and I was planning on being on it. There was a knock at the door. I hadn't called to have my luggage, such as it was, picked up. I went to the door and checked through the peephole.

There was no porter waiting at the door. It was Simone! It seemed I was going to miss my flight.

Thomas Lu had been sitting in his own urine for forty-eight hours. He had been given nothing to eat, just warm bottled water. His shoulder was on fire. Infection was beginning to set in.

No one had been to see him, to torture or torment him, or even to re-dress his wound or kill him. His keeper, an unsmiling Chinese man, simply opened the door, shone a torch inside and then shut and locked the door again. Twice the guard had tossed a water bottle at Lu's huddled form but nothing else.

Despite being sick and hurting, Thomas Lu was still thinking coherently and clearly. He had gone beyond the initial shock of both his injury and capture. Now it was time to try and survive. Thinking helped him deal with the pain in his shoulder. People slipped out of handcuffs easily on magic shows and television. He had no illusions that it would be that easy, but could he open the handcuff attached to his good arm? Or rather, could he open the cuff that was attached to the water pipe?

The floor of the room was covered in debris, much of it windblown leaves and grasses pushed through the wide gap under the door. However, there was more. The inner walls of the room had once been lined with wood and many of the planks had rotted and fallen or were hanging. There were nails and nails could be used as lock picks.

Lu used his foot to drag the nearest fallen plank to him. There were nails, several of them. The wood was old and brittle. Using his leg and hip, he forced the plank to within the reach of his tethered hand. He reached for one of the three nails in the end of the plank. The first didn't move, however, on the second, the wood had splintered. The nail came free easily. Lu grunted and examined both the nail and the handcuff. It had to be a simple lock. The only problem was managing to work on it with only one hand. The solution was to use his chin to hold the band of the cuff as far up his arm as he could to hold the chain taut, while he held the nail between his thumb and forefinger and worked on the lock on the other cuff.

Lu started his attempt to open the cuff with wretched determination. He knew that unless he got free, he was dead. It was a simple equation.

Simone apologised for what she'd said to me. It was shock, she said, and I quite believed her. Who the hell wouldn't have been shocked after what she'd been through? We made up. Guilt or whatever produced a passion in her that was far in excess of any of the highly charged lovemaking we had enjoyed together in the past. It was torrid.

Later, spent in the extreme, we lay sprawled on the wrecked bed. I phoned reception and extended my booking indefinitely. All thoughts of returning to Hong Kong were banished, for the time being at least.

We ate an early room-service dinner and divided our evening between the bath with its spa jets and the bed. Her children were both staying with school friends—a treat for them, she said. Now that she had a guaranteed income and no need to work, Simone was relishing her new-found freedom. It was a tremendous evening, right up until my cellphone went.

A voice on the other end told me Thomas Lu had escaped.

32

"He somehow got the handcuff off the pipe. When his guard came to check on him, he was waiting. He'd found a length of metal bar. The guard's brains are spread over the walls."

"Shit!"

"Yes, Daniel. Shit indeed! I've moved the money again and cleaned up the warehouse. I'm making arrangements to shift Carlos's balance to Shanghai. We have people looking for Lu, but I don't know if we'll find him in Singapore. I suspect he'll have gone to KL or Bangkok for surgery. I have people checking. However, I doubt he'll have travelled under his own name or passport."

"What do you want me to do?"

"I'm not sure there is anything you can do," Sami replied, sounding almost dejected. "We'll just have to wait for him to resurface."

"Bugger!"

"Indeed, Daniel. I'll call if I have anything new."

"Okay!" I muttered almost absently as I flipped my phone shut. Should I head home as planned or stay and try and do what I could to help in the search for Thomas Lu? Sami had reasons for keeping Lu alive in the first place, I could understand that, but it ran against the grain with me.

It always had.

As a former sandbagger for Betty Windsor's mob, I always made it a point of doing the business at the first opportunity, no shagging about. To delay could, as it had done in this instant, backfire big time.

"Everything okay?" Simone was asking. I shook my head, then I remembered that she wasn't in the loop—she had no idea Thomas Lu had been held prisoner.

"Thomas Lu has apparently vanished," I replied.

"Oh!" was all she said as she reached for me. Hong Kong could wait a day at least.

Thomas Lu was indeed in KL. The damage to his shoulder was severe. The surgeon needed to first treat him for infection and then do major reconstruction work. He told his patient that once the stitches were removed there would be the need for extensive physiotherapy. Lu was prepared for that. He was also prepared to wait in KL as long as it took for Carlos Mendez to depart for South America. Once Mendez was gone, Lu would then plan his return to Singapore and his revenge on Sami Somsak. In the meantime, wallowing in his post-operative drug high, he wanted company. He wanted his beautiful boy to come and sit by his bedside and comfort him. Thomas Lu made the call.

"He is in a private hospital in KL," Sami said. It was morning. Simone and I were breakfasting in bed. My omelette was getting cold because Sami had my full attention.

"How the hell did you find that out so fast?"

"My insider," Sami replied. I could feel the smile in his voice. "Several months ago I paid a young gay man, a male escort, a fortune to get close to Lu. He has done so. He is Lu's lover."

"Holy shit!" I muttered. My devious friend had done it again.

Sami laughed. "You know how I work, Daniel. Virtually every member of the Intella Island consortium has a mistress, or a male lover, or a confidant who is on my payroll. I've been planning Intella Island for more than three years and I selected my partners, even though they think otherwise. Lu is the only one I hadn't invited to join. Unfortunately, the others did invite him. However, fortunately for us his sexual predilection, not to mention his excessive appetite, has made him the easiest to get someone close to."

"Fortunately," I replied dryly. I didn't mention that lover boy hadn't picked up a hint on what was about to happen to Stanley and his family.

"Daniel, it's insurance. I want to know what those I deal with are thinking and I want to have a little something over them if I need to exert any additional influence."

I didn't reply. There was nothing more to say. I wondered idly what Sami had on me. Then I dismissed the thought. He had everything and nothing on me. That was the way it had always been between us. Total trust. I've spoken of it before, but that is what we have. One word from me and his billion-dollar drug-processing barge out in the Gulf of Thailand would be gone. That sort of information you don't pass on to people who wouldn't die for you. Would I die for Sami Somsak? I probably would. I would rather die for him than die a meaningless death. I have a real fear that one day I'll be taken out in a car accident by some idiot driver. What a stupid way to die.

"I am going to watch him, and when he returns, I'll arrange to have him taken care of," Sami was saying, snapping me back to the moment.

"Why not just set Carlos onto him?" I suggested. "Have it happen up there, not here."

"South American drug thugs running rampant in KL has a certain ring to it, I agree. But no, I'll keep that information to myself for the moment." Sami paused. "We've been lucky so far, Daniel, and that luck can't continue indefinitely. Singapore has too many eyes and we can't stay invisible forever. You go home and I'll call if I need you."

"Okay," I replied. "This time it is ciao."

"And thanks, old friend."

So, there it was. I was going home. Now I just had to figure out how I was going to break the news to Simone. I didn't really have to. She knew and she was reluctantly okay with it. We would spend some time apart. She to regain her equilibrium and give "us"—or the potential of us—some serious thought. As for me, I was going to get back to Hong Kong, sign up to a gym, take up karate and get working on this body of mine. This little excursion had shown me just how totally out of shape I really was. I didn't finish my omelette. Simone and I said a long goodbye.

Hong Kong, one month later

I have spent the past month working out like a fanatic. I have once again become a non-smoker. Perhaps I should say I am a smoker who hasn't touched a cigarette for twenty-nine days and counting. I limit myself to two beers a day and one JD in the evening. Fish, lean steak and salads are on the menu. I joined an Aberdeen karate club, taking up the beginner's white belt for the first week while I learned their protocol. They then jumped me a whole bunch of belts up to brown, explaining that they'll grade me to black in their next grading ceremony. In contact sparring, I have to hold myself back. It's difficult to play-fight when you are trained to kill and maim. Self-control, I guess. When I'm not doing karate, I'm at the gym, the pool, or pounding the pavement.

The only days I didn't train were those that made up the three-day weekend Simone spent with me. And no, there hasn't been another woman in my bed since Simone and I got things together. That's some sort of record for me. When she heard I was back, Mai Ling phoned. I lied to her and told her I was engaged. She wished me luck and genuinely sounded as if she meant it. There had been a wistful quality to her voice. Perhaps she was wishing she were engaged. Not necessarily to me, just engaged.

Was I engaged? It felt like it, I guess. I've never been engaged. My former wife, the stunningly beautiful Doctor Sylvia Dixon, and I had gone from meet, to bed, to marriage in record time. Big mistake! If we'd not tied the knot, we'd possibly still be sharing a bed, occasionally at least.

For the moment though, I am a one-woman guy.

It was Saturday morning. I'd been for a ten-kilometre jog and was cooling down on my patio. I was planning on spending the afternoon in the gym. The phone went. It was Sami, checking in as he did every other day.

"Lu is still in KL. Apparently he has been in constant touch with his people back here, but he's been very careful to ensure Michael doesn't get to overhear his telephone conversations. Michael thinks he's about to make a move of some sort."

"What about Mendez?"

"He's happy with his Chinese investments and left for Colombia yesterday."

"And not one drop of blood was shed."

"Cynicism suits you admirably, Daniel," Sami replied smoothly with a hint of a chuckle in his voice. "You will find your bank account has received a substantial injection of cash. I suggest you look for an investment or two and then come and work with me—just as soon as I take care of Lu, that is."

With that, the phone went dead. I left the patio and went inside. The laptop was more or less a permanent fixture on the bar in the lounge. I fired it up and logged into my Cayman Islands bank account. How Sami had tracked that down, I have no idea, but track it down he had. When I checked the figures, I almost fell through the floor. As it was, I sank onto one of the barstools and tried to focus on the numbers on the computer screen.

There was now US$50 million in my account. That was over and above the two and a bit that had been loitering there, left over from Bernard's loot following my apartment purchase.

"Oh boy!" I muttered. Did the money make any great difference? I really have no idea. The two million and change that had been there would have kept me in luxury until my dotage. Now having a real fortune to play with, what the hell did I want to do with it? Sami was right, of course: invest it. As to going to work for him? Well, I bore easily, and when I'm bored, trouble sort of finds me. Life around Sami Somsak is never boring. Maybe I'll say yes to him.

Half an hour after my conversation with Sami, I was in the apartment complex's pool doing some serious laps. My good intentions were cut short when Nim, the pool girl, appeared holding a towel and a walky phone. I dried a hand and an ear and took the handset. It was Sami, again. There was no preamble.

"Tuk Tuk is dead! I'm on my way to the airport. I'm going home for the funeral."

"Should I come?" Tuk Tuk Song, Sami's uncle, had been both a friend and an enemy to me. I had saved his life and earned his gratitude and friendship. That had survived until I killed his son, Arune. The moment I did that, all bets were off and I was enemy number one.

"I think not, Daniel. You will see Sakura in good time. She has to grieve or be seen to grieve first."

"How did you know about Sakura and me?" I asked, completely dumbstruck. Our final conversation, the one in which she had invited me to come to her on Tuk Tuk's death, had been a whispered one between her and me in the Jeep I'd commandeered from the newly dead Choy Lee.

"Tuk Tuk told me," Sami replied simply. "She told him!"

"That's crazy," I replied. "You don't tell your dying husband that once he has popped his clogs, you'll be seeing the man who was his sworn enemy." Even as I said that, I knew that perhaps it did happen that way. The relationship between the beautiful Sakura and Tuk Tuk was, to say the least, unusual, just as the relationship between Tuk Tuk and me had been. Then, of course, there was the female factor. I have to admit that when it comes to understanding women, I am a complete, abysmal failure.

"Uncle still regarded you as his friend, Daniel. The fact that he was honour-bound to kill you because you killed Arune was something that saddened him greatly. Perhaps he thought that when he was gone and you and Sakura came together, the balance would be restored. He loved her and he greatly respected you. He told me not long ago that he wished you had been his son rather than the idiot he'd bred."

I grunted. My mind was racing, trying to sort out the implications of what the hell Sami was telling me. If I went to Sakura, was I fulfilling Tuk Tuk's dying wish? In reality, would I ever know if it had really been her wish that I go to her, or had it been Tuk Tuk's idea all along? Where the hell was my free will in this whole bloody mess? And what about Simone?

"Are you still there, Daniel?"

"Yeah. I'm just trying to figure out who the fuck is manipulating who here."

Sami laughed. "The workings of the world, Daniel. Just relax and roll with the tide. When the time is right, go to Sakura. If things work out, you can take over some of Tuk Tuk's business interests and we can work as one. If you and Sakura do not work out, Anita is still waiting for you to call."

Anita Somsak, Sami's sister, was a beautiful, intelligent woman and she had made it clear the last time we'd met that she would like it if she and I were to share more than her brother. Why the hell did life have to be so fucking complicated?

"Goodbye, old friend. I'll tell Sakura you'll call on her when Tuk Tuk has been laid to rest for a decent amount of time." Sami was gone again and I hadn't even thanked him for the money. I debated calling him back, but in the end I just started back for the other end of the pool.

33

Thomas Lu was smiling again, despite the continual ache from his injured shoulder. Everything was finally falling into place. He was ready for his return to Singapore. While in exile, he had been busy, very busy. His business interests in Singapore and abroad had been taken care of by trusted lieutenants while he'd been out of the country.

Apart from the fallout of the Intella debacle, where he was definitely *persona non grata* as far as the other members of the syndicate were concerned, he had survived and his other businesses, both legal and illegal, were flourishing. Lu had no criminal charges against him. Officially, no one had pointed a finger at him for the slaughter of Stanley Loh and the others.

While the Intella Island syndicate members well knew Lu had been behind Stanley's killing, they weren't telling the authorities anything. So that particular case, the mysteries surrounding the battles on Sentosa, and the various building and warehouse fires were still unsolved. Chinese mainland gangs and drug wars were still the official explanations. However, for the past month, there had been no more gangland deaths or fires, and Singapore, it appeared, had returned to normal.

In preparation for his return and in order to defend himself against Sami Somsak, Thomas Lu had augmented his seriously depleted force of strong-arm men by calling on reinforcements from the Fang Triad. He had a plan for Somsak, one that would get the Thai drug lord out of his hair once and for all. That plan was already being put into action. He, Thomas Lu, would not even be in Singapore when stage one of it was executed, and no one would be able to connect him to it or anything else. At its conclusion, Sami Somsak and his entourage would be no more.

As for the Colombian threat, here Lu was less sure of himself. Those monitoring the movements of Carlos Mendez and his compatriots had reported that Mendez had left for home. Would he return to Singapore to exact revenge for his brother's death once he knew Lu was back in residence? Or had Mendez entrusted his death to the Thai gang boss? If so, when Somsak was finally dead, would family honour force Mendez to return?

"Michael?" Lu called. He didn't have the answer to these questions. His head was throbbing. He would have his beautiful lover massage his temples for him. They would go to bed together, and in the morning he would awaken to find that stage one of his revenge had been accomplished.

Early morning telephone calls are something that I have never, ever gotten used to. Something I guess most of us dread. When the phone wrenched me from my deep, bone-weary sleep at 04:30 on Sunday morning, I knew in my gut that this was going to be bad. It was Sami.

"Daniel, Simone is dead!"

"What?"

"Simone is dead," Sami repeated, his voice little more than a whisper.

"How?" My head was spinning. If I hadn't been lying down I would have fallen. Total shock hit me like a meteorite.

"She apparently slipped, fell over the railing and down the void space in her apartment building late yesterday afternoon. She was dead when she was found. I found out when I landed."

"Oh!" I whispered. Being killed in a car crash I had always thought was a stupid way to die. This was almost as bad. But the end result was that beautiful, bountiful Simone was dead, stupid accident or not!

"Tuk Tuk's funeral is tomorrow morning. I'll fly back in the afternoon. Simone didn't have any family other than a sister in Cape Town. I'm having my people take care of things. Her sister will be on a flight about now. You coming back?"

"Yes! Of course I'm coming back!"

"I'm sorry, Daniel. I know you two were close."

"Yes we were," I replied, almost absently. I was still trying to fully absorb the fact that Simone was gone from my life. In a flash I was suddenly alone again. Emotionally, I think what had been happening between us was a catharsis for my jaded emotions. I had been changing, no doubt about that. Now she was gone.

I felt a surge of something approaching anger, irrational anger, and it was anger at Simone for leaving my life. Of course it was childish. Of course it was unfair. Of course I was being selfish. From now on, I wasn't going to get close to anyone, I silently promised myself.

I sat there, phone in hand, emotions out of control. Part of me knew I had reverted to being the lost, scared kid. The other part of me simply didn't care that I was, internally at least, acting like a spiteful, snotty-nosed little toe rag.

Whenever I got close, people got hurt. People died. For a moment Simone's face was gone from behind my eyes and in her place was the face of Babs, the beautiful redhead from another time and another place. She and I had gotten close and she'd ended up with her head propped up on my coffee table while her body lay metres away in a pool of blood.

"Sorry, Daniel. I have to go." Sami was dragging me back to the present.

"I'll fly back in the morning."

"I'll see you then. Take care, my friend."

"You too." I hung up and lay there in the dark, staring at the invisible ceiling, wondering how a stupid fucking accident had changed everything. I still don't know if Simone and I would have got together as a normal couple, but things had been heading in that direction. I hadn't strayed once since meeting her, and that was some sort of record. Now it didn't matter. None of it mattered anymore.

"Ain't nuthin'!" I snarled. "Ain't nuthin' at all!" That damn catch phrase from an old war said it all.

I closed my eyes but she was there, and so were Babs and Geezer and a whole bunch of others. People who had been in my life but were there no more, except in my mind. I got up and left the bedroom, flicking on lights as I went. I didn't want the darkness anymore.

There was an almost untouched bottle of Jack Daniels on the shelf behind the bar. I sat on a stool and looked across at the bottle for a long time before I stood and retraced my steps. That was too easy! I pulled on a tracksuit and runners and went out into the night to punish my demons.

Michael Sun, Thomas Lu's lover, retrieved his cellphone from the pocket of a jacket he had hanging in his closet. This phone wasn't his usual one. This was one supplied by Sami Somsak. Sun had overheard Lu using his own phone. They were about to return to Singapore, quietly. Lu's driver was coming to collect them. Instead of the distinctive Bentley, he would be driving a relatively inconspicuous Volvo.

Sami's phone was switched off, so the young man decided to leave a message. It was often this way. He called Sami when he had news. Sami never called him.

"Mr Somsak, it's Michael. We are returning to Singapore in the morning in another car. He is very pleased with himself, but I have no idea why. He's planning something. When I find out, I will call again."

Michael flipped the phone shut and slipped it back into its hiding place. He didn't notice the figure on the patio outside of his room. Lu was standing beside the open sliding door. He had been about to enter the room. He had an expensive gift for Michael and had been wanting to surprise him. Now the realisation that he had been betrayed seared its way into his brain. Lu's breath hissed between his clenched teeth as the red mist of his rage swirled around him.

"Betrayed!" he whispered. Michael had left the room; undoubtedly he would come looking for him. Lu weighed the small package in his hand. The beautiful, gunmetal grey Breightling had cost several thousand dollars. In his rage, Lu turned and hurled the gift-wrapped package away into the night. On the street far below, an old man was about to make a discovery that was worth a king's ransom to him.

"Thomas, where are you?" Michael was calling from the living room of the rented penthouse apartment. Thomas Lu moved along the patio and entered his own room. He suddenly smiled. It was a ghastly smile. He would see that beautiful, young Michael would no longer be able to work his magic on anyone. Certainly not anyone who could see!

"Pretty boy, no more!" Lu whispered. But before he caused that to happen, he would use his lover one more time, and this time he was going to cause Michael Sun pain. But this pain would be nothing compared with what was to come.

34

Changi Airport, again! I entered using a new passport in the name of David Crewe. I was a Hong Kong-based Australian in Singapore on import-export business. A wonderfully ubiquitous occupation. A change of hotel was called for, somewhere low-key. I checked into the Miramar. Old, but comfortable enough. This time I forwent the option of a smoking room.

I still had Sami's original cellphone and I used it, recording a message on it with my new name and location. Tuk Tuk was probably already in the ground and Sami would be saying farewell to Sakura and preparing to fly back. Simone's funeral service was to be at 13:00 the next day, Tuesday. Until then, what was I going to do? It was now a few minutes before noon. One of the rules about appearing in places using different identities is the simple fact that you can't frequent places you have been before. I caught a cab up to Holland Village and found a pub. Cowboy Bar it was called. The motif was of a manic cowboy. The bar staff wore vests, thin bow ties and cowboy boots. It was my kind of bar.

I needed to be around people, but I wasn't out to annihilate myself. I had a late steak lunch and stuck to a few beers, chatting with the few expats who were about. Anything to keep from thinking the sort of thoughts that send people running under trains. I've never been suicidal, but Simone's death was affecting me far more than I guess I expected it would. Of course, there was naturally a deep sadness and a bloody great aching inside. I even felt sorry for myself as well as her, and I felt for the kids. But there was something happening on a much deeper level as well.

"What a stupid fucking way to die."

"What?" The Welshman I was sharing a table with was looking

at me questioningly over his pint.

"Oh. Just thinking aloud," I replied. "Friend fell down a stairwell and died. I'm here for the funeral."

"Lady, right? I read about it in *The Straits Times*. Poor thing."

"Yeah," I replied. I glanced at the clock on the wall. It was almost 16:00. I'd been in the pub for nearly four hours. It was time to go. Then my cell vibrated in my pocket. I fished the phone out and excused myself, heading out onto the terrace. Sami was on a charter flight and an hour away from touchdown. He would come to me.

I decided that I would move into the apartment if I stayed on in Singapore after the funeral. I honestly didn't know if I was going to stay. Regardless, the heat seemed to be off. The gang battles of a month or so before were old news. Yes, there were still a few more restrictions on the books and more CCTV cameras were being installed everywhere, but unlike my previous persona, David Crewe could be visible. I wasn't an assassin or agent provocateur this trip. I was an associate come to bury a friend.

Thomas Lu was also back in town. His penthouse apartment was now a fortress. While he had been in KL, via an agent he had bought the two apartments that made up the floor below. The nucleus of his army was now in residence. One of the apartments had been turned into a control centre and guardroom. The only elevator with access to the top floor had been reprogrammed to stop at the penultimate floor. Armed guards covered the stairs to the fire escape, the basement garage, the main foyer, the foyer on the lower floor and the penthouse foyer itself. CCTV cameras and monitors covered all entrances and exits in minute detail.

Secure in his Nassim Hill citadel, Thomas Lu was a happy man. Michael, his former lover and Sami Somsak's informant, was not. Rather than have him killed, Lu had come up with a punishment he considered even more fitting.

Michael Sun was in hospital in KL. He had been found lying in a ditch on the outskirts of the city. His tongue had been cut out. All of his fingers had been hacked off and as the final touch, battery acid had been poured over his entire body, with specific attention paid to his beautiful face. Michael Sun was no longer beautiful.

Sami hadn't eaten. Neither had I, so we decided on a meal in the hotel restaurant. Neither of us did justice to our food. I damaged a bourbon or two while Sami just sipped at a glass of mineral water.

"This is probably not the time to say this, but Sakura asked that you be reminded of your promise. She suggested that three months from now would be a good time for you to visit."

"We'll see," I replied.

"I believe Thomas Lu is back in town. Michael left me a message. If he's not back yet, he soon will be."

"Are you going after him again?"

"I'm honour-bound to get him," Sami replied. "For Stanley and perversely for Carlos Mendez. If I don't get him, the crazy Colombians will come back and get him. Imagine the collateral damage if they came in guns blazing."

I could see Sami's point. Singapore had been lucky that Sami had managed to put a collar around Carlos's neck. The Colombians were not very subtle when it came to exacting revenge. Big bombs, machine guns and chainsaws were the tools of choice and while we had been causing more than a little mayhem of our own over the past months, it had been controlled, at least to the degree that innocent citizens hadn't been in the firing line. A contradiction, I know, but there was a grain of truth in there.

"I'm going to see Simone," Sami announced suddenly. "Are you coming?"

That startled me. I didn't want to see Simone in death. I would rather remember her as I had last seen her: beautiful, vibrant and so very, very alive. I guess a shrink might say I was in denial, deep denial. Apart from my initial burst of grief and anger when I'd received the fateful call, I'd screwed my emotions right down. Simone was dead. I was alone again. That was it. The fairytale is over, Danny boy. Welcome back to the real world.

Sami was watching me. He could no doubt see the thoughts that flickered across my face. Poker-faced I wasn't at this moment.

"Okay," I agreed, wondering why I had given in. There would

now be one more dead face in my dreams. Until I saw Simone that way she would always be the laughing, beautiful woman I had known.

Simone DeLue looked as beautiful in death as she had in life. Her makeup had been very lovingly applied. There was no trace of the waxy pallor of death on her face or her hands, which were resting crossed on her chest. There was a small white rose lying on her breast and a gold crucifix had its chain threaded through her fingers. Her hair gleamed in the candlelight. Her features were soft in the subdued light. It really was as if she was sleeping and would awaken any moment, turn her head and smile at me. I shook myself. Tears were starting to form.

"She looks absolutely beautiful," I said, trying not to choke.

"I asked that they have the best person in Singapore prepare her," Sami replied. "Fortunately, she didn't suffer facial injuries. Her sister is on her way here now. She will stay to put Simone's estate to rest and take the children back to South Africa with her." Sami touched Simone's hair with gentle fingers. He bowed his head and stood for a moment with his eyes closed, and then he turned away. "I'll leave you two alone." He eased out of the room.

The air conditioning was cold and I felt a shiver run down my spine. What did one do at moments like this? I'd been around death more than most, and I'd caused a lot of it. What I had never really done was spend time celebrating it or celebrating life at funerals or wakes.

I went to stand close to the beautiful lady in the satin-lined casket. The crucifix caught the light. I hadn't known she was Catholic. But then we had never really discussed religion. She had been reluctant to talk much about her past, as I had been, I guess. I think that we had both been looking to the horizon to see if there was any future for us together.

"I'm so sorry," I whispered, and I was sorry. Maybe, just maybe this was the woman I was meant to be with for what remained of my life.

I leaned down and kissed her on the lips. They were like ice. They burned with the cold, but as I straightened I could taste her; the lipstick she wore in death had been the same she had worn in life. My fingers stroked her icy cheek and touched the golden silk of her hair. God, she was beautiful! How long I stood there looking down at her, waiting for her to open her eyes and tell me that this was just a mistake, I don't know. A noise at the door broke the spell. I could hear Sami's hushed voice.

"Goodbye," I whispered and without looking back, I walked to the door and opened it. There were two youngsters standing there. I had met David and Angela only a few times. We'd got on well and had fun. They looked at me. Recognition momentarily overcame the anguish and confusion on their faces. I reached for them collectively and pulled them into a group hug, a hard one. I told them how very sorry I was.

I let the kids go and they reluctantly stepped back. Their eyes were red and their faces pale. Then I noticed the third member of the little group. Standing behind the children was a woman. She was tall and blonde, a slightly older and more weatherworn and travel-weary version of Simone.

"Justine," Sami said, introducing her to me. "This is"—for a moment he hesitated, debating whether or not to use my real name—"Daniel."

Justine looked at me, fighting back tears and jetlag. Her eyes, however, focussed on mine. There was a look of appraisal there, mingled with her sorrow. Obviously her sister had spoken to her about me. She knew exactly who I was and perhaps how much I meant to Simone, or how little, if I were a cynic. I banished that thought as it hit me.

"I'm so sorry for you as well," Justine said to me, the tears finally coming. We hugged. I was close to tears myself. The embrace lasted long enough for me to know that whatever Simone had told her sister about me, cynicism wasn't in the equation.

When Justine and I parted, Sami escorted her and the children into the viewing room while I headed outside. I was contemplating coming off the nicotine wagon and having a cigarette. I didn't have any on me, so I was going to have to find a 7-Eleven or bum one. In the end I did neither. I closed the outer door and just leaned against the wall and breathed in the thick wet air.

Sami's new driver was standing smoking with another man beside the Mercedes parked in the funeral home's small forecourt. There was a golden Lexus parked beside the Merc. I didn't go to either driver for a cigarette. I just stayed where I was. I brushed away the tears and automatically began to analyse the situation. Old habits, huh?

Jo Ankar and three others were in a second car parked across the narrow street. K and several others were in another vehicle a hundred yards further along. With Lu back in town, Sami was not about to take any chances. I sucked in several more deep breaths and composed myself. Simone was dead, the victim of an accident. Now it was time to move on. There would be the funeral tomorrow. Whether I should stay in Singapore to help Sami take Thomas Lu down, or go back to my empty apartment and suddenly empty life in Hong Kong, or quietly head north into Thailand, I didn't know. I'd make that decision when Simone was in the ground.

Sami emerged from the funeral parlour ushering Justine and the children ahead of him. The youngsters were both crying. Their aunt walked between them, her arms around their shoulders. She had dried her tears and was now focussing on the children, whispering first to one and then the other. She lifted her gaze to me, and even in the subdued light I could see the determination there. This was one tough lady. The kids were going to be in good hands. That, at least, was a minor consolation.

The drivers stubbed out their cigarettes. Justine and the children were ushered into the Lexus and it reversed into the street. David, who was sitting in the front passenger seat, gave us something approaching a sad smile and waved as the car purred away.

"The man of the family," I muttered as the boy's pale face receded into the night.

"Yes. Fourteen is too young," Sami said softly. "Will you join me for a late supper?"

I thought about that for a moment but declined. I wanted a walk, a long walk. Sami told me we were in Clementi and it was a long way back to the hotel. "I'll drop you closer," he said. I shook my head.

"I've been averaging fifteen kilometres a day on the road," I said, "and fifty laps of the pool. I think I can handle it."

"If you're sure."

I was. Sami would send someone to pick me up at the hotel at noon the next day. The service was at 13:00 in the Cathedral of the Good Shepherd. The interment was scheduled for 16:00 in the Catholic cemetery at the Choa Chu Kang Cemetery Complex. The reason for the long delay between service and burial was because of a busy schedule at both the cathedral and the cemetery. The mourners would be adjourning to the nearby Carlton for light refreshments before setting off for the cemetery. Obviously, I would not be appearing at the Carlton. Too many staff would remember Ed Davidson from Perth.

I watched Sami and his people drive off and then I dug my street map out of my pocket and set a course for my new temporary home. It was midnight. The traffic was minimal. Singapore, it appeared, had almost gone to sleep.

Walking the pedestrian-deserted streets, I had time to think. Too much time to think. Before I was half way back to the Miramar, I was beginning to wonder if the walk had been a good idea. The demons of the dark were all in my own head. They were congregating there and each shadowy street I walked down added more.

35

I'm not sure how many of the two hundred or so mourners who came to the cathedral were friends of Simone or if Sami had called central casting and had a whole bunch of extras bussed in. No matter, there were a lot of people there. A few I recognised, including the three women who had been kidnapped along with Simone.

The kids, dressed in their best, were in the front row along with Justine. Sami and I were in the second pew. The casket, already in place in front of the altar, was buried under a mass of flowers. A large photograph of Simone sat on an easel at the head of the coffin.

The service was built around favourite hymns, songs everyone knew. The priest who ran the service spoke long and lovingly of Simone, and it seemed he genuinely knew her. He referred to her as a loyal, loving and much respected member of his congregation.

Sami delivered a eulogy. It was a beautiful thing, totally fitting to the lady we were saying farewell to. He spoke of his brother and his affection and respect for Simone who had been his loyal right hand for many years. Sami had obviously given a lot of thought to the moment.

Often I have referred to the many layers that made up my friend the Onion Man. Sami's eulogy revealed even more of his deep and complex personality. There was a philosophical touch to his address and there was humour. He spoke to the children and for them, and then he concluded with a poem, a beautiful thing he had created himself.

The casket was wheeled from the cathedral, with the children and Justine walking beside it. Sami and I came next. I attempted to hang back slightly, but Sami insisted I stay at his side. Once the coffin was loaded into the hearse and driven away, the mingling started.

Gradually, many of the mourners either went back to their places of work or joined the dozens who started across Bras Basah Road to the Carlton, where a function room had been prepared at Sami's request.

I faded out of the crowd and made for Chijmes as the rest of the party continued on to the hotel. I promised Sami I would join him for the drive to the cemetery in an hour and a half. The decision to use the Carlton didn't surprise me as it was close to the cathedral. It was just unfortunate that I couldn't join the others for the reception, but that's life, I guess, and I'm not great at small talk anyway. Especially at funerals! I found a beer at a bar Ed Davidson had never been to. JD was not the drink of choice for the new and improved Daniel Swann—not at the moment anyway.

Thomas Lu was sitting in the heavy leather chair in his home office. He lay with his head back against the padded leather backrest, his eyes closed. The boy who was working his magic on Lu's penis was not as beautiful as the unfortunate Michael Sun had been, and he was being paid by the hour, but Lu didn't mind. Shortly, he would have the world once again at his beck and call, and he would have Intella as well—not yet, but soon. Once he removed Sami Somsak from the scene, the men behind the artificial island development would be in his sights. He would demonstrate to them that he had a right to a share of the pie, a major share. If they did not concede, then he would move on them.

Lu glanced at his watch, and as he did so, the cellphone on the desk in front of him chimed. He retrieved it. The call was short. Without a word, he closed the phone and again lay back against the padded chair. Life was getting better and better for Thomas Lu.

At the appointed hour, I met Sami outside the Carlton. The stretch limousine was not an affectation in this case. Inside were Sami, myself, Justine and the children. Jo Ankar was up front with the chauffeur. The next car in the procession contained five of Jo's men. Several other vehicles with mourners aboard were following. The hearse had returned to the funeral home to wait for us. There, the procession would assemble for the run to the cemetery. Funeral processions were probably frowned upon in Singapore, there were enough traffic problems as it was. However, Sami had planned it, so it would happen.

The hearse was waiting on the street when we arrived outside the Sacred Dream Funeral Parlour. Who comes up with names like that? I thought as we cruised up to it. The hearse pulled away into the lead and the rest of the vehicles came after. From Clementi, it was a relatively short drive to Choa Chu Kang and the cemetery itself.

I'd never been to Choa Chu Kang Cemetery before. I'd never had cause to. It was huge and divided, it seemed, into separate smaller cemeteries for different religious groups. The driver of the hearse seemed to know exactly where he was going, which for everyone was probably a relief.

Angels with wings and awkward pious figures stood with their heads bowed. There were hundreds and hundreds of conventional crosses. It seemed we were in Christian territory, Catholic even. Graves, old and new, filled the immediate horizon. The coarse grass was long. In places, it almost covered tombs and headstones. In other places, it had been cut short.

We stopped. We were here.

"Stanley and his family are buried here," Sami told me. "I have arranged for Simone to be buried beside them." Justine gave him a grateful smile. Jo opened the door and we slowly climbed out. There was rain in the air, but hopefully it would hold off. Petrol-powered grass cutters sounded in the distance. The cemetery custodians, it seemed, were fighting their never-ending battle against overgrown weeds.

The grave was a black gash in the dirt. Squares of artificial lawn had been laid around it and positioned to hide the pile of dirt that had been removed. The undertaker's cradle was positioned above the grave to receive the coffin. Assistants were removing flowers from the hearse and positioning them around the gravesite. It was all very civilised, all very practised and safe.

The other vehicles had arrived and mourners were gathering around the gravesite. I noted the tomb beside the open grave. It was a huge affair. The marble was new. I didn't have to go there to know this was where Stanley and his family lay.

The priest came to the rear of the hearse. Sami gave me an almost imperceptible nod. He turned to the children and whispered to them. Justine was already prepared for what was to come, this, the final physical act she could participate in to lay her sister to rest.

The undertaker and an assistant eased the casket out. Jo took one handle by himself, Justine and Angela shared one, while Sami and I took the other pair. It was only a short distance to the grave, and with the undertaker and his assistant hovering, we made it. The coffin was placed on the cradle and the priest called everyone in closer. Reluctantly, the mourners did as directed. There were now probably fifty or sixty people gathered to bid farewell to Simone DeLue. The rain started and umbrellas appeared like mushrooms.

The priest began with a eulogy of his own. As he talked, my mind started to play the sort of games that used to be a part of my everyday life, the other life, the one I played in the shadows.

Here, in the spectacular coffin lying there in front of us, was a young vibrant woman, the victim of a stupid accident. She had fallen down a stairwell and died. People died in accidents all the time, every day, every hour, every minute, every second probably.

Coincidence in my world is a dirty word. There is no such thing. Things happen for a reason. If you believe in God, then it is God's reason. Everything else happens and I believe the random or fickle finger of fate is a vastly overrated entity. Is anything about life or death truly random? Was it all pre-ordained and written in a big book in a heavenly archive as many maintain?

As the priest continued to speak, I looked up and slowly turned my head to look at all of us gathered there. Sami was beside me. Justine next and then the children. Jo stood to my left and slightly behind me. The others, apart from the three former hostages, I didn't know, but here we all were, gathered in a cluster around the grave.

Then *it,* the nagging thing that had been playing on the edge of my subconscious, found a coherent voice. What if Simone's death hadn't been an accident? What if somehow Thomas Lu had orchestrated it? Lu would have anticipated that Sami, who had gone to great lengths to seek the release of the hostages, would, of course, be in attendance at Simone's funeral. What better opportunity to take Sami Somsak out of the equation with a well-placed round from a sniper's weapon?

Even as that thought crossed my mind, I knew Sami had it covered. He had people scattered throughout the cemetery watching for just that eventuality: mourners with large bunches of flowers, flowers that smelt of gun oil, and eyes that were scanning every inch of the massive cemetery.

The coffin! The thought hit me from out of the blue. In my previous life, moments, nanoseconds even, of understanding had saved my life and the lives of others. Now was such a moment.

Suddenly it made sense, all of it! As I opened my mouth to shout a warning I already knew it was too late. A dull metallic click sounded over the voice of the priest.

"Get down!" I finally managed to scream out as I threw myself sideways. I slammed into Sami, driving him down and away from me as the air exploded around us.

36

Lying there in the rank grass, time seemed to move in slow motion. I was lying prone with most of my torso behind the concrete slab of a low grave. As an automatic reflex, my head was turned away from the direction of the blast. I was looking at the flank of the hearse parked ten metres beyond me and seeing it with the pure clarity of my instant adrenaline overload.

The sound that filled everything around me was a mixture of the sonic whiplash of high explosive and the voice of a million angry wasps. In front of my eyes the hearse, a big, white American tank, rocked on its springs as every scrap of glass disintegrated into sparkling dust. The metal flanks of the wagon rippled and pocked as dozens of holes appeared. The sound of a giant tin opener punching holes in cans underlaid the whine of the metallic wasps that filled the air. The shrill sound of ricochets as metal impacted on the metal and stonework of hundreds of memorials and tombstones created another layer of sound. Then there were the screams and shrieks as the deadly shrapnel found human targets.

As I lay there, I heard the symphony of death and destruction with total clarity. Part of me, the professional me, was analysing the sounds, dividing them into a macabre list.

When a projectile of any sort impacts with a human body, there is always a sound. Hit through the chest, human lungs and the diaphragm often pop like balloons. Meatier slaps tell of hits to the heavier areas of the body, a strike in the head sounds like a leather pillow being struck hard with a baseball bat. All of these sounds and more I heard as the roar of the explosions rolled on over me.

I looked up, and above me the face of an angel appeared silhouetted against the grey sky. I had a glimpse of her bending towards me, her expression more blank than beautiful. Then my world went as black as death itself.

Thomas Lu was waiting for word that his plan had succeeded. The sound of sirens had filled the Singapore evening. News reports speculated that a terrorist bomb had exploded in Choa Chu Kang Cemetery. Police and military units had sealed off the entire area. A stream of ambulances was reported running a shuttle between the cemetery and both the National University Hospital and Singapore General Hospital.

It was mid-morning and Thomas Lu was seated in front of the wide-screen television in his study. He hadn't moved since the explosion. The device used in the cemetery had contained a radio receiver and an electric detonator. Several of his people had been watching from a distance using a high-powered video camera trained on the Christian cemetery. They had waited, as instructed, until the service had begun, and then the bomb had been detonated.

Lu smiled. It was a thin smile, one without any humour whatsoever. The bomb had been more than just a simple device. With several kilograms of C4 explosive at its core, and sandwiched top and bottom with thick steel plates, hundreds of steel ball bearings had been packed around the core. When the device had been detonated, the plates contained the vertical upwards and downwards force of the blast just long enough to send the deadly swarm of the shrapnel blast out of the coffin like a deadly scythe.

The bomb had been the handiwork of one of Lu's newest recruits, an Afghani-born bomb maker, a master of deadly IED booby traps who had perfected his art in decades of conflict in his own country before seeking gainful employment in Asia.

"The authorities have not yet provided us with casualty figures," one of the newsreaders was saying. The young woman was trying to maintain her most professional face, but she was failing. Her male counterpart, a man probably fifteen years her senior, was doing little better. Underlying the makeup, the pair's faces struggled to hide the shock they were both feeling. They had seen live footage of the carnage that had taken place via their own news teams. The general public had not seen those terrible images and probably never would.

"Estimates are that between twenty and twenty-five people have been killed and at least the same number again were injured, many of them seriously. It is not known who detonated the device or for what reason."

Lu sat back in his seat and this time, he did allow himself a smile, a genuine one. There was no way that anyone in the immediate vicinity of the coffin and the graveside could have survived. Sami Somsak and his inner circle must have died. Somsak was human and not a superman, and even if he'd been wearing a bulletproof vest or full body armour, he would have died in the blast.

Lu rang the bell on his desk. It was time to indulge in a little celebration. He would have his secretary make a phone call and summon company. For the rest of this day and long into the evening, he would not celebrate alone.

Call made, Thomas Lu switched channels. The bombing was the lead story on CNN as well. He sat and watched, sipping a glass of expensive whisky.

"... Singapore cemetery. The explosive device is thought to have been an extremely sophisticated one. Singapore military bomb disposal and forensic officers describe it as the sort of improvised bomb widely used in the ongoing conflicts in Afghanistan and Iraq."

"The number of dead has grown to twenty-eight, following the deaths of two seriously injured casualties last night and this morning."

"Officials say that several other survivors are still in a critical condition and are not expected to live."

"More on the fatal Singapore bombing in our special bulletin next."

The two CNN newsreaders tossed the grim facts backwards and forwards like a football, watched by millions of people around the world, including the smiling Thomas Lu.

37

We'd crossed the Mekong in the small hours of the morning three nights before. Now we were in the jungle, staked out on a small ridge. The window we'd cut in the canopy allowed us a view across a narrow valley containing rice fields and gardens. There was a compound on the far side. Tall bamboo fences, earthworks and guard towers contained men with all manner of guns. It was a place where the uninvited were definitely not welcome. We most certainly were not on the invitation list.

"Good to be back in the bush again, Daniel?"

"Fuck off!"

Sami Somsak laughed at my childish response. Jo Ankar, who was ten feet above us, sitting in the crotch of a tree, chuckled. The three of us had played this game before, many times. I used my bandana to wipe away the sweat from my brow and retied it around my head. I did love the bush, it just didn't do to show it. I was more at home here than on the streets of any city.

The jungle, or as we call it "the bush", is pretty much the same in Cambodia as it is on the other side of the river. Same trees. Same bugs. Same snakes and the same stifling heat accompanied by the same unrelenting humidity. It's like living in a sauna stocked with all manner of biting pests. Oh, how I wanted to be riding along in the air-conditioned comfort of the Range Rover I was holding in the sights of the .50 calibre Barrett I was lying behind.

The magnification on the varipower scope was set at x9. It could go up to x20, but long experience had shown me that all the higher magnification did was magnify the motion of my breathing and the slightest movement of my hands. Even the beating of my heart produced a constant repeated quiver at the higher magnification. So I kept the setting under the double digits.

The Range Rover was stationary, sitting in the open gate of the compound. The distance was 700 metres. I knew this for a fact because one of our friendly overhead satellites had measured it most precisely. The centre of the broad but shallow stream that divided the valley was 300 metres away.

"Here he comes." Jo was using a pair of high magnification binoculars. He'd picked out our target as he exited the compound and climbed into the Range Rover. "He appears to have someone with him. I can't make them out. Going in the back seat."

Through the scope, the rear door hid my view. Jo was able to see far more from his vantage point.

"That's unfortunate for someone," I responded, rolling out from behind the huge rifle and standing. We were in no danger of being seen here. Deep under the forest canopy, we were invisible. I stretched and took a few pre-game deep breaths. When the action came down, it would be short, sharp and very brutal.

The Barrett, a semi-automatic heavy hitter, was the ultimate sniper weapon. It fired a big 750-grain phosphorous bronze projectile or any one of half a dozen specialised rounds. These ranged from armour piercing rounds to those with explosive tips. The weapon could wreak havoc on any soft-skinned target. The Range Rover was soft-skinned. As, of course, were the people in it. There was no known body armour capable of stopping the enormous round.

"He's moving," Jo called and that was my cue to get down to business. I pulled off my gloves to push squishy earplugs into my ears. The other two did likewise. We all pulled our gloves back on. They were essential. We weren't leaving anything behind on this job but spent brass.

The earplugs were a necessity because we knew there would soon be a lot of noise. Effectively, Jo was to be my spotter. I had a mixture of projectiles in the eleven-round magazine already in the gun. The rounds included a tracer. A tracer fired into a petrol tank had a very good chance of creating a fireball, and that was most desirable. Sami had a fully loaded spare magazine beside him. There was a round in the breech of the rifle and with two magazines of eleven each; simple math said I had twenty-three rounds to play with to do the job. When they were gone, we would move out fast.

Behind the scope again, I settled and eased the crosshair onto the advancing vehicle. The Range Rover was driving straight towards us. The point where the river and the dirt track bisected was ground zero for me. The scope was calibrated to absolute zero at three hundred metres.

The bugs buzzed and the sweat droplets formed and streaked their way down my cheeks, but I was locked in the zone. My concentration on the job in hand was total.

At four hundred metres, I could plainly see him at the wheel. Dimitri Chekov was his name. He was a Russian bear and he was as big and as mean as one. Chekov was known as "the Headhunter". This former KGB colonel was one of the most vicious killers in the dirty game we all played. Following his KGB and intertwining military career, he turned his talents to crime, big crime. Chekov had been based in Asia for the past five years with a hard-core Russian mafia made up of mostly former Spetsnaz troops and a few local thugs.

Drugs and arms were Chekov's currency. He had become a major player and a major problem for both my people and the Americans, both of whom wanted Chekov taken out with all due prejudice. That was why I was lying there sweating my bollocks off in the godforsaken Cambodian jungle.

"Three hundred and fifty," Jo called from above. I settled my breathing. The first shot would be aimed at Chekov sitting behind the wheel. Sun rays were falling on the windscreen and flaring back at me. I cursed. It didn't matter. Sun flare or not, I knew where the driver was seated. That was where I was aiming.

The Range Rover arrived at the ford and slowly started across. The 300-metre mark was dead centre in the stream.

"Now!" I whispered. I took the trigger pressure and the big rifle kicked and thundered. The Barrett has a real bellow, but the kick and muzzle-rise are negated by a lot of trick modifications, including an enormous muzzle brake. The flame of the first shot was away. A crimson streak sliced through the thick air and terminated in the front left of the vehicle's windscreen. The sun flare vanished, as did the windscreen. I fired the second round to the same spot and then shortened my aim, settling on the front of the vehicle.

The tracer and incendiary rounds that followed all hit home. With an engine that no longer functioned and with flames bursting from under the ruined bonnet, the Range Rover slewed side on and ground to a stop in the middle of the stream. Sami was handing me the full magazine. I changed and went after the fuel tank. Had I got Chekov? I had to believe so.

When the second incendiary from the fresh magazine hit its target, the Rover's fuel tank exploded. In seconds, the vehicle became a complete fireball. I hammered the remainder of the magazine into the driver's compartment. The Barrett wasn't going back across the river with us and when the ammunition was finished, that was it.

"No sign of life," Jo called from above as I stood. It was done. The Range Rover was a gutting mass of flame. Burning fuel was flowing downstream. Reeds and grasses at the water's edge were catching fire. We were out of here.

I pulled out my earplugs and pushed them into my pocket. Long tubes of shiny brass covered the ground around the Barrett. The cartridges had been wiped clean of any fingerprints and had been loaded into the magazines by gloved hands. We were leaving behind a big who-dunnit!

I picked up the rifle and slung it across my shoulder. Jo dropped down out of the tree and the three of us started back the way we had come. Would there be a pursuit? We had to factor that into the equation, but without their leader, would Chekov's mob attempt it? Either way, we had a lot of ground to cover. The principle we always operated on was based on the SAS model: hit hard with overwhelming firepower and get out fast, outrun the opposing force and get far beyond any of the roadblocks they had set up.

I disassembled the Barrett on the run, pieces of it going into streams and simply being tossed away into the jungle as I went. It was a waste in some ways, but the equipment was expendable and we weren't. With the thirty-five-pound weight of rifle gone, I became a hell of a lot lighter on my feet.

Down off the ridge, we hit a dirt road. In the bushes beside the road was the means of our rapid getaway. The battered little Honda motorcycle with the square sidecar attached was probably the number one form of transport throughout much of rural Asia. Sami and Jo, being Thai, were going to play at being locals. Because I was a white guy, I got the sidecar and the wide conical straw hat. With the hat pulled low over my head and by making myself as small as possible, I became the little woman.

We hauled the bike out of the bushes. I got in the sidecar while Jo and Sami debated who was going to drive. Jo ended up at the front. The bike kicked into life and we were away in a cloud of blue smoke. I have no idea what the bike was running on. Probably it was coconut oil. Whatever it was, it went and we started putting kilometres between the kill zone and us.

"Fuck!" Sami shouted and pointed. Above and ahead of us was a helicopter. Not just any helicopter, it was a huge, dust-coloured Russian Hinde. This was the flying version of a damn tank.

The giant bird of prey was nose down and coming at us straight down the road. It was fully armed. There were rocket pods bristling and a heavy machinegun was starting to chatter.

A long line of fountaining dirt swept towards us. Jo was hit. The bike swerved as the first rocket impacted on the road just yards in front of us. The blast lifted the bike and hurled it into the air. I twisted one way, Sami the other, while Jo's body, torn in half by the machinegun fire, was buried by the falling motorcycle.

I hit the ground and tried to get up, but I couldn't. I had no legs and no arms. I was just a torso with a head attached. I screamed, but no sound came. Sami was on his feet. He was staggering and the Hinde was coming towards him, flying lower and lower, its nose almost on the ground. That brought the giant rotors to within centimetres of the road.

Suddenly, Sami was no more. He was lost in a haze of bloody pulp. His upper body was gone. His torso remained standing for a moment as the Hinde settled down to land, and then it fell into the blood-soaked dirt.

The helicopter settled. The cargo door opened and out stepped Dimitri Chekov. He was untouched by bullet or fire. He was laughing.

More than laughing, he was bellowing. His eyes were on me.

"Mr Swann, so pleased to see you again. I have a friend or two of yours here. You could say this is a reunion of sorts. Chekov reached back into the cargo hold and lifted something out. It was a head, a human head. It was the beautiful Babs. She was smiling at me.

"Hi, Dan. Remember me? We had so much fun together."

"Go to your lover. Give him a kiss," Chekov teased. He tossed the head of beautiful Barbara from Bristol into the dirt beside me. She was still smiling at me, her green eyes dancing.

"And another of your friends, Mr Swann." Chekov was holding Geezer's head out to me. Geezer was grimacing. Against the putrid blue-green colour of his flesh, his milky-white eyes found me.

"Dan, you've got to pick your friends better. You've been the death of me."

Chekov tossed Geezer's head towards me. It rolled to stop beside that of Babs.

Death of me. Geezer was right, of course, I had been the death of him, and of Babs and of so many others. The others followed as Chekov lobbed head after head towards me. There was Kim, Sami's beautiful daughter. Her head rolled to join the chorus. Soon the heads of all my dead surrounded me. They formed a circle that was many rows deep. So many dead from my life and they were all talking to me. Talking at me. Some were berating me. Others were laughing and making jokes. Chekov had been right. This was a reunion.

Some of the faces I didn't know, but most I did. I'd killed so many people in my life and so many had died because of me. Was this my hell?

Then I saw Simone and knew it truly was. She was stepping out of the rear of the Hinde. She was wearing a wedding gown, a beautiful creation of flowing silk. There was a long train and two young people followed, tending to it. They were her children. There were flowers in her hands. White roses.

Chekov was no longer wearing the sweaty fatigues of just moments before. He was dressed in a morning suit. With Simone on his arm, he came to where I lay in the blood-drenched dirt.

"Mr Swann, I want to introduce you to my wife. The beautiful woman you killed when you tried to kill me. You are dead and she is mine forever!"

Now I found a voice and the screaming started.

"Daniel, Daniel. It's all right. Everything is all right, my darling."

I opened my eyes. Simone was beside me, holding my hands in hers. I was lying on soft grass. Her hands were warm. There was no ice in them or on the lips that brushed my cheek. She was alive and her smile enveloped me as I lay there dazed, looking up at her. The grey sky was blue and the grass under me was as soft as cloud. This was not the coarse carpet of the cemetery in which I had died.

Simone was wearing the gown she was to have been buried in. It glowed with an inner light, purer than fresh snow. The little gold crucifix that had been entwined in her cold fingers while she lay in her coffin was now around her neck. It sparkled in the sunlight.

"Come with me, my darling." Simone rose to her feet, drawing me effortlessly to mine. We weren't in the cemetery. We were standing in a garden. Hedges defined a pathway that stretched into the distance. Trees towered above us. Flowers filled the air with their sweet perfume. Was this heaven? Had a sinner like me gone to heaven? It must be heaven for Simone to be here with me.

We started walking, she gently leading me after her. It was as if she had walked this way before. Along the avenue of trees we moved, following the pathway to only she and her God knew where.

Then I knew it wasn't heaven. Simone was gone in an instant. Voices were calling a name. It wasn't my name, but I knew it. I had heard it before, somewhere.

A bright light was on my face, my eyelids were being pried open. I fought against it, but failed. There was a face above me. Not one but several and a voice was calling that name again.

"Mr Crewe, can you hear me? Mr Crewe, are you awake?"

I knew Mr Crewe from somewhere, but I wasn't awake. The light vanished and the voice faded. I wanted to find Simone again. I wanted for us to walk hand in hand to eternity or wherever she had been leading me.

But she was gone and I was lost in a black cloud.

38

"Fractured skull and heavily concussed. He's been drifting in and out of consciousness for the last twenty-four hours."

"Do you think he'll be okay?"

"I think so, but it's difficult to say with head injuries like this. He may suffer any number of complaints, temporary or permanent, because of it. Amnesia, for instance."

"That might be a blessing, Doctor," Sami Somsak replied.

"It was a terrible thing that happened."

"Yes it was! Thank you. Please call me if there is any change."

Sami stood and looked down at his friend lying in the hospital bed. Daniel's face was the colour of chalk. There was an oxygen feed running into his nose, but he was breathing unaided. A drip feed was connected to his left wrist. His shaven head was covered in an iodine solution and a mass of staples created jagged patterns across the top of his scalp.

The doctor had told him that they had inserted a small metal plate to replace a shattered piece of skull. There was a drainage shunt fixed to the side of his head. The tube terminated in a bag hanging from the side of his bed. There was another bag beside it. This one was full of dark urine.

"Oh, Daniel," Sami sighed. His friend had saved his life and as fate would have it, he had been smashed on the head by a falling angel scythed from its pedestal by the hail of steel released by the bomb.

The death toll had been horrendous. Jo Ankar, who had been at Sami's side for almost three decades as a brother, minder and friend, had died. Justine, her children, and twenty-five others were dead and many more were in critical condition.

Sami left the room. There were two police officers waiting to interview the injured man. The doctor spoke to them briefly, giving them notice of the patient's condition. The pair departed, following Sami to the elevator.

Sami rode to the ground floor deep in thought. The policemen were talking, discussing the bombing. Sami filtered their conversation out. He had another problem apart from his dead. There was a traitor in his camp and he had no idea who it was. Until he could identify and eliminate that threat, he had to fly solo. With Jo gone, there was only K left who he could trust, but the problem was that K could be that traitor, despite the fact that he had been with Sami as long as Jo had been.

Outside the hospital, Sami got into a taxi. The address he gave the driver was not for the Cairnhill apartment. Until he knew who the traitor was he was not returning there, simply because that person had to be a member of his household and that group included K. Until Daniel was back at his side, he would remain at a secret location, another apartment, a much more modest one than the penthouse, and it was a property that no one knew about. He had maintained it for times such as this. In the meantime, he would continue to do business via cellphone. A rumour that he had returned to Thailand was being circulated. In reality, he would remain in Singapore and plan his revenge on Thomas Lu.

The taxi dropped Sami Somsak close to the apartment block on York Hill. He walked to the building and caught the elevator to the eighteenth floor.

An hour after Sami Somsak had entered the apartment, the door opened and a little old man appeared. He took the elevator back down to the ground floor.

The old man was dressed in the traditional pyjama uniform still favoured by many of the old people. There was a brimless cap on his head. He was wearing a pair of open sandals and held a small cardboard suitcase in one hand.

Out into the muggy afternoon the old man went. He shuffled down to the street and there he waved down a cab. The driver expressed surprise at the address he was given. He would have been even more surprised if he had seen what the old man was carrying in his suitcase. Nestled in the foam rubber cut-out inside the case was an H&K MP5 submachine gun. With it were three magazines and two fragmentation grenades.

Sami Somsak was back on the street in a guise that Daniel Swann would have recognised. This was the same little old man who had saved Swann's life in a Bangkok back street less than a year before.

Being part Thai with Chinese and Japanese in the mix, Sami Somsak could pass as any or all of these nationalities as required. He spoke five languages fluently including Japanese, Mandarin and Cantonese. In his role as the old man, he spoke only Mandarin and Singlish.

"Any improvement?"

"A little, I think. He is opening his eyes, but I'm not sure anyone is home yet."

I could hear the voices. They were coming from a long way off. I tried to speak, to tell them I was home, but nothing came. I could see their faces, a man and a woman. Both were dressed in white. I knew they weren't angels. The angels had gone away forever. This was a doctor and a nurse. I was in a hospital, I knew that much. I tried again to speak, but my eyes closed and I drifted away.

The fact that Sami Somsak survived the bomb blast had driven Thomas Lu into a frenzied rage. He had been in his office when the news channel had released a list of the dead. Somsak's name hadn't appeared on that list nor on the list of the injured that followed an hour later. In his rage, Lu had demolished the television screen by hurling an ornate bronze desk ornament at it.

Now, two days on, Thomas Lu had received word from his spy in the Somsak camp that the Thai gangster had withdrawn back to his Bangkok base. That provided Lu with momentary relief. Somsak had taken a huge hit to his Singapore-based people. Had he retreated only to plot his return? Or had he decided to leave Singapore alone, knowing that the chances of being caught were increasing by the day?

Lu had made sure that he was outside the scope of the police investigation. His bomb maker had fled to Indonesia, along with several of the others in his organisation who knew about the device.

The man he had inserted into the funeral home had gone back to his village in Malaysia considerably richer than when he had left it.

Lu was confident there were no loose ends regarding the police; however, there was one that Sami Somsak could exploit if he put the facts together. Thomas Lu's spy inside the Somsak camp has been a comparatively recent convert and was potentially very exposed.

Lu regretted he hadn't identified and exploited this person's potential much earlier. But then he hadn't known Somsak was involved in the Intella Island project at that time.

"Chance," Lu muttered as he walked from his study through to the lounge of his luxurious penthouse. A chance comment from a lover had resulted in a phone call and subsequent meeting; a connection had been made with the heart of Sami Somsak's inner sanctum. It had been so simple to achieve, and so very fruitful.

The person on the other end of the line was one whose life, loyalty and everything else was governed by the lusts of the flesh and not by power, drugs, money or loyalty. Once the connection had been made, the rest had been easy. Betrayal had been bought with the flesh of a handful of young men and women who were willing to indulge this person's every sexual whim.

Lu poured himself a whisky. "Chance and timing," Thomas Lu philosophised into his glass.

I am drifting in and out of consciousness, but my waking times are getting longer. I know I am in hospital but everything else is fuzzy. There is a mist where my memory used to be. I know my name, Daniel Swann, but where am I?

The police! I knew they were police by their uniforms. They came to see me. But I didn't understand what they were saying. A bomb! People dying. I didn't know and they went away.

There is something in the mist, a part of a memory? I can smell the ocean. I can feel something, but what? It is just out of my reach.

They helped me to the bathroom. That was good. I hated having that tube in me. They have taken the tube from my nose and the one from my head as well. They have told me the wound is healing. What is the wound? What caused it? Who am I really? They call me David, but my name is Daniel? Who is David Crewe?

I want to leave this place. There is somewhere I remember. Somewhere I want to be. There is a telephone. A cellular phone. It is given to me by a nurse. She says someone delivered it for me. It rings.

Sami Somsak? Who is Sami Somsak and why is he speaking to me as if he knows me? I tell him I don't know him. He sounds sad, I think. I flip the phone shut and he goes away.

I want to leave this place and go to the other place. I think I remember how to get there.

The doctors tell me it will be some time before they can release me. The wound in my head is healing well, but my memory isn't. But I am remembering more. I remember the jungle. I am happy in the jungle. I want to go where I am happy. Maybe then my memory will come back to me.

I want to leave this place.

39

"What?"

"I'm sorry, Mr Somsak, he's gone. Some time late last night, he left."

"He discharged himself?"

"Not really, he was in no condition to be discharged. He simply left."

"Is he wearing hospital clothing?" Sami had just the faintest of hopes that if Daniel had left dressed like that, he would be picked up sooner rather than later. This slim hope was immediately dashed.

"He took his clothing from his locker and his wallet."

"He took the cellphone?"

"Yes, apparently."

"Thank God for that," Sami replied. He had sent a new mobile for Daniel because the previous one had been mashed when his friend had smashed him to the ground in the instant when he'd saved his life. At least the phone meant that he had the means of contacting Daniel.

"Thank you, Doctor. If I hear anything I will let you know. You have alerted the police?"

"Of course, Mr Somsak. They are looking for him. If I receive any news I will contact you. The police asked for a photograph of Mr Crewe. Perhaps you have one?"

"I will see if there is one. Thank you." Sami broke the connection.

A photograph of Daniel could be a double-edged sword and do more harm than good, especially if people remembered him as Ed Davidson. Questions would be asked. There would be no photograph.

Sami flicked on his cell and found his address book to get the number of Daniel's new mobile. He hoped that his old friend hadn't yet remembered his evasive skills and that the police would find him before he vanished to wherever he was heading. Would he go back to the Miramar or even the Carlton? Would he remember exactly who he was or would he be lost in a sea of former identities? Loose cannon wasn't a term that Sami Somsak normally used to describe his friend, but in this case it was probably accurate.

"Yes?"

"Daniel. It's Sami. Where are you?"

"I don't know you. Goodbye."

"Daniel?" Sami was speaking to a dead phone. "Oh, Daniel," he sighed. He wouldn't try again. Not now. Tomorrow, perhaps, when hopefully the fog had lifted from his old friend's mind.

Sami stood. He was in his apartment, preparing to assume the identity of the old man yet again. The old man had been busy. He had a plan to get to Thomas Lu. It would just take time for it to be implemented, and he hoped that when that time came, he would have a mended Daniel Swann at his side. He also hoped that K would be there with them and he wouldn't have to execute him for being a traitor.

I like this place! The jungle is my friend. The rain doesn't bother me.

I have found a place that is dry. The house is old but it has a roof.

I made a snare and I caught a pig. Then I made a fire to cook it over. It tastes good. I like pig. There is fruit and there are coconuts. I found a big knife and I can open the coconuts with that.

I saw a man on the road when I came back here with my pig. He walked away quickly. There is a place where the river flows in and beside it a boat sits on the shore. There is a net in the boat. When I've eaten the pig, I will catch fish. I know I have never been hungry in the jungle, but I don't know how I know this. The jungle is my friend. It is my new home.

The man called Sami has used the cellular phone again. He tells me he is my friend and we have known each other for many years. I don't know him. I was going to throw the phone away, but I will keep it. If he is my friend, as he says, perhaps soon I will know him again.

My mind is becoming clearer, I think. I can remember a lady. I think she is my wife. Her name is Sylvia. I can also remember a man, an old man. I don't think he is my friend because I think I have put a knife in his throat.

I can hear voices, many voices. There are men in uniform in the jungle below me. I don't know these men. They have guns on their hips. I must hide from them.

"They have found him, or rather found his location."

"Where is that, Doctor?"

"An island. Pulau Ubin, the Granite Island. It is a few kilometres off Changi."

"How do they know he's there?"

"A worker on the island saw a man carrying a dead pig along a pathway in the jungle. The man was big and European. He had a shaved head and was dressed in a suit with no shirt and no shoes. The worker reported what he had seen to the island police. They spoke to the men who run the bumboats from Changi and they remembered him. One of them said he appeared to be acting very strangely. He also commented on the man's lack of a shirt and that he had a bandage on his head. The search for him has begun. Police and the army are combing the island."

"Good luck," Sami muttered. He knew that if Daniel remembered even a fraction of his jungle skills, they would need shoulder-to-shoulder sweeps to find him, and even then there was no guarantee that they would. "Thank you, Doctor."

Sami Somsak hung up and sat in the shadows. Across the road from him there was a construction site. Two lots down was the condominium complex that housed Thomas Lu's penthouse. Soon he would be confronting Lu there and it would be over once and for all.

"Daniel?" Sami whispered. He wanted his old friend back.

He wanted him at his side when Lu went down. But here he was, a fugitive, albeit a sick one, hiding on a tiny island. He hoped that those hunting Daniel weren't armed. If they were, there could be a killing, and the chances are it wouldn't be Daniel Swann who was killed. Not initially anyway.

These men are not very skilled in the jungle. I think I can slip past them easily. They are calling for this Mr Crewe. I don't know who he is. Do they think I am him?

They have gone past me. It was easy to hide from them. I just lay on the roof of the house while they searched through it. Now they are in the jungle behind me. I have another place to hide when they come back. They will come back. I know this somehow. I think I will go and catch some fish while they search the jungle. They have the remains of my pig and now they know where I was living I can't stay there anymore.

There are more men coming along the road. I can see them. They are marching. These men are dressed as soldiers, but they are not carrying guns. That is good. If they have guns, they might get killed. This is something else I know. I think I am good at killing people. It is just a feeling that I have. I know I know things, many things, but I don't know how I know them.

The boat is still on the bank of the river. I will take it and go and catch fish. They won't look for me out on the water. They think I am in the jungle.

The boat isn't big. It has oars and I am rowing out into the mouth of the river. There are rafts all around out here. Fish farms, I think. The cellular phone is ringing again.

"Daniel?"

"I am Daniel."

"I am your friend, Sami. We are best friends. You have had a terrible accident and your memory has been damaged. You must let me help you."

"I am busy, Mr Sami. I have to catch fish."

I switched the cellular phone off. I don't remember a lot about these phones, if I ever knew anything at all, but they run on batteries and batteries don't last forever. How do I know that?

I can see some of the men on one of the fish rafts looking my way. Perhaps it was not a good idea to come out this far to fish? I row back to the mouth of the stream. There is a current pushing me deeper into the stream. The current is called the tide. I know this. The tide will carry me along while I fish.

And there are fish in the water. Many of them! I can see them all around me. The net rolled into the front of the boat is very big. Too big. But there is a smaller net, one with a handle.

I sit in the boat as the tide pushes me along. The small net is now in the water. A fish, a long skinny fish swims past. It is very close to the boat. I lift the net and I have the fish. I do this again and again and again until I have four of the long green and silver fish flapping in the bottom of the boat. I know these fish but I can't remember what they are called. That doesn't matter. I do know they can be eaten. I have eaten them before, I think. I will eat these.

The stream has become small and the bottom of the boat is touching the mud. I will get out now, take my fish and go to that other place to sleep. This is a place where the men in the uniforms will not find me. It is a place I found when I was here before.

"Where the hell is he?" Colonel Arthur Soon, co-ordinator of the Singapore Search and Rescue Division, was standing looking at a large-scale satellite map of Pulau Ubin.

"We've searched virtually the whole island, Colonel. He's vanished. They found the boat and some footprints, but that's it. Have we got a photograph yet?"

"Negative. The doctor said he had asked Mr Somsak for one. Maybe you can follow that up, Louis?"

"I'll do that, sir." Major Louis Yap left the office of his superior and went into his own. The fugitive from the hospital, a man suffering serious head injuries, was making them all appear to be fools. If the man really was so mentally damaged as the reports suggested, just how was he managing to stay hidden?

"I have to give them a photograph." Sami Somsak had just received a call from a major of the SSRD. It had been shunted through a Bangkok switchboard and back to him.

They wanted a photograph of David Crewe. The problem Sami faced was obvious. Any photograph of David Crewe was also a photograph of Ed Davidson and Daniel Swann and any one of the half a dozen aliases that his friend had used in Singapore in the past few years. It would be posted on all the media channels. What to do?

Then he had an idea and made a phone call. He would provide the searchers with a photograph of David Crewe, but it wouldn't be Daniel. It would be of someone who looked vaguely like him. It would be of a man with a full head of hair. Not a man with a shaven head. Perhaps, just perhaps, they would get away with it. Just about all the people who would know the photo wasn't David Crewe, or indeed Daniel Swann, were dead.

When he completed the call, Sami made another, but the phone he was calling was switched off.

It was evening. Anyone watching the little old man shuffling down Nassim Hill Road would have taken pity on him. There was an air of dejection about him. It clung to his body like a blanket.

High above the street Thomas Lu was standing at the railing of his wide terrace. He was wearing a dressing gown and held a tumbler of whisky in his good hand. Soon he would get into the spa bath and a young man he had never met before would join him. He was very much looking forward to meeting this fresh new boy from the agency.

From Lu's vantage point twenty levels above the street, the small figure walking down the road below was tiny, but even from where he was standing, Lu could see and feel the dejection drifting up towards him like a scent on the wind.

"Go home and die, old man. Your time is done!" Lu smiled and turned towards the spa. It was time to meet his lover of the evening.

40

They have all gone for the night. I am almost alone in the jungle. The place I have come to sleep is a small cave. It has been used as a place to sleep by others. There is a bedframe and a fire pit, but I will not use fire tonight. They would probably smell it if there were people on watch. The fish is fresh. I have a sharp knife. I took it from the boat when I caught my fish.

I clean the fish and slice off the meat. It is sweet. I have picked more fruit. I eat all the fish, every scrap. I am hungry. Now it is time for me to sleep.

Earlier, I took clothes from a house. Some were hanging on nails. They were the dry ones. Other clothes were lying tangled on the floor, wet and rotting. I am now wearing a shirt and a pair of rubber boots that fit. I left my shoes in the first house when the people in uniform came. Now I am warm, and I am tired. My head doesn't hurt as much as it did. Soon I will have to take out the metal things that are fixed to my scalp.

I lie on the bedframe. It is comfortable enough. I can hear the night creatures. There is the sound of insects and there are rustlings in the leaves. A pig squeals in the distance. I will catch more pigs when the searchers have gone.

My eyes are wet. I am crying, but I don't know why. Was I sad before I hurt my head? How did I hurt my head? I lie in my little cave in the jungle, crying. Is Sami really my best friend? Should I ask him why I am crying?

But then I go to sleep. Sleep comes easily to me.

"He's skilled in jungle craft. He must be."

"Either that or he is just lucky." Major Louis Yap stood staring down at the A4-sized photograph that had arrived from Sami Somsak. The photograph showed a fair-haired man with a moustache. He was thirty-five or forty years old. His hair was medium length. The face was soft. The man looked as if he could have a weight problem. This did not look like the face of a jungle specialist.

"He's deranged enough to fear us. Have the searchers not call out his name. Tell them to remain as quiet as they can. They might have more luck."

"Yes, Colonel, and we are putting another one hundred people on the island. We must find him soon."

"One would think so, Louis. One would think so." The Colonel came to his subordinate's side and stood staring at the photograph, trying to see beyond the bland image. "Where are you, Mr Crewe?"

I wake suddenly. I can hear movement in the jungle outside the cave. There are people out there, but they are not calling out as they did before. They are trying to move silently, but they are not succeeding.

It is morning. Late morning, I think. I have slept for a long time. My headache is almost gone. Am I getting better?

I crawl to the front of the cave and stay in the shadows. A pair of boots attached to legs in jungle camouflage trousers walk past. They have not seen the cave entrance because I cut bushes and pushed them into the holes I made in the earth. To them it looks as if there is nothing behind the bushes but the steep bluff that rises above it. How did I know to do this? There are just so many things I know. If only I could remember why I know.

There is another figure further away down the slope. I can see that he is not carrying a gun. Instead, he has a bush knife. He is slashing at the bushes as he moves forward.

I wait for some time until the sounds pass on into the jungle and then I leave the cave. I could stay here all day, but I want to walk in the jungle and enjoy its smells and its sounds. I want to pick fruit. I want to feel myself alive.

It is easy to see where the searchers have been. There are scuffs in the leaf mulch on the jungle floor. There are broken and cut branches. They are clumsy. Very clumsy!

There is a road below me. A narrow road. Parked on it is a utility truck. There is no one around. I squat and wait in the undergrowth to see if this is a trap, but it isn't. There is no one here. On the tray at the back of the truck, there are two large plastic containers. This must be food and water for the people in the jungle.

I drop down to the road and go to the truck. Yes, the first container is filled with plastic water bottles. I take two. They are cold. In the second container, there is food. There are packets of cooked rice, sauces and fruit. I take some of each and fill my pockets. It is good of the people searching for me to provide me with food. Why are they searching for me? Have I done something bad? Do they want to punish me?

I move on down the road a little, and as I hear another vehicle approaching, I moved back into the jungle. A utility loaded with more people in uniform goes past.

"Why are they searching for me?" I ask the question aloud, and the sound of my own voice startles me. I think this is the first I have spoken aloud since I spoke to Sami Somsak on the telephone.

"Sami Somsak?" I repeat the name aloud. "I know Sami Somsak!" I have a picture of the man in my mind. Yes, I know him, and yes, he is my friend. My good friend. My very good friend.

I sit and drink some water. The fog in my head is slowly clearing. I see other faces, and with some of them come their names. There is the beautiful lady, Simone. Something happened to her. Something bad. I can't remember what it is. Not yet!

I eat some rice and drink more water. Sylvia! I was married to her. Am I married to her now? Simone? Am I married to her? The fog around her is thick. I can see her face and I have her name, but that is all. Jo Ankar! This name arrives out of nowhere. I can see his face. He is Thai, a handsome man with silver flecks in his short hair. He is a friend, a good friend and he is dead.

The realisation that Jo is dead unlocks the confusion in my brain. Suddenly everything pours back. Simone. She is dead. Jo is dead. So are many others. I remember the coffin and then the angel bending down to kiss me. Then nothing until I woke up in the hospital when I lay there hearing the doctor and the nurse talking about me, and me being unable to answer them.

"Dead," I whisper. "All dead." Now I start crying uncontrollably. These are silent tears, but my whole body is shaking as the images of my dead pass behind my eyes. This is my waking nightmare. The tears flow like a river. They burn a course down my cheeks. There is salt in my mouth. I am back in the land of the living again, and I'm not sure that I want to be here. So I cry on. I'm sad. It goes so deep, right to the very core of me. It aches. I am sad for me. Sad for everyone who is dead. Sad for everyone who is alive. Sad for the world!

After a while, I stopped crying. The tears had purged me. The front of my shirt was soaking. There was a breeze from the ocean. The shirt was cold against my chest. I wondered just how many tears a human being has in them.

I took the cellphone from my pocket, turned it on and tapped out the number printed on an adhesive strip and stuck to the side of the phone. My call was answered immediately.

"Daniel?"

"Yeah, Sami. I'm back!"

"Thank God. Are you okay?"

"I will be. I'll go and be found."

"They'll take you back to the hospital, but it sounds as if you're okay."

"I'll go back. There's some annoying metalwork on my head I want removed."

"Can you remember everything?"

"Most of it, I think. The bomb. The angel kissing me."

"Some kiss. It damn near killed you."

"Lu had Simone killed to get us together in the cemetery. I want to kill him very badly, Sami."

"Soon, Daniel. I have a plan." Sami's voice was soft. "Go and get yourself found, Daniel, and then we will take care of Mr Lu. I'll see you at the hospital in a couple of hours. And thank you, old friend."

"For what?"

"For saving my life again."

"That's what we do, Sami." We both signed off and I stood and retraced my steps to the utility. It was unlocked. I climbed into the passenger seat and drank some more water. It was twenty minutes before someone came. Then they all came.

41

I was back in Singapore General for the night and this time I didn't mind. The search and rescue crew flew me back by helicopter. They were delighted to find me in one piece. There was good PR in it all for them and I didn't begrudge them that. Sami arrived a few minutes after I'd showered and been tucked up in my bed in the same room I'd escaped from. They didn't put a guard on the door.

Sami came in smiling, bearing gifts in the form of clothes. He had arranged for my bag to be retrieved from the Miramar and was now carrying it. We embraced as old friends do. Then he sat on the edge of the bed and we talked.

First we talked about the dead before he thanked me yet again, which made me uncomfortable.

"Your instincts are remarkable."

"Not remarkable enough," I replied bitterly. "If only I'd realised sooner, we could have saved everyone."

"You know in life that's not the way it works, Daniel."

"Yeah, I know. On the island, I cried a million tears." I stopped when I realised what I had said. "Jesus, I sound like a fucking love song, but I've never really cried in my life before and I just couldn't stop."

"Grief," Sami replied softly. "You needed to grieve for Simone."

"Not just Simone. I had a dream, a hallucination maybe. All my dead were there speaking to me. Maybe I needed to grieve for them all. Maybe they needed to see me cry."

"Maybe."

"What about Lu? Have you figured out the how and the when?"

"Yes," came the reply. "He thinks I've withdrawn back to Thailand. Remember my little old street peddler in Bangkok?"

"I'll never forget him."

"Well, he's back. Slight change of costume, but it's him all over again. He's been sitting watching Lu's place and planning, and that plan is very nearly ready to be put into action. Before we get to that though, the police will want to question you. They have been questioning all the survivors, as you would expect. They are waiting for Sami Somsak to return to Singapore. They are apparently not at all happy that he left so suddenly." Sami gave me a tired smile.

"I'll just play the amnesia game," I replied. "I think after the past three days, they'll buy that."

Sami chuckled at that and nodded. "Yes, I think you're right. Your background checks out. I had to provide a photograph, it was a close likeness, but it was not you."

"Okay. I'm David Crewe. I thought I recognised the name they were calling out to me, but I didn't know it was me," I admitted. So, all I had to remember was my fake name. I could do that now, but yesterday, I wouldn't have had a chance.

Thanks to my years with The Firm, Mr Crewe, along with all of my purloined passports and identities, had a history and everything that went with it. I'd become an expert at this over the years. David Crewe had an apartment and a business address in Hong Kong and the import-export company he worked for, Kavac International Ltd, actually existed. On computer records at least. An answer service meant someone always responded when the company telephone number was activated. A quick electronic shunt and David Crewe could answer from anywhere in the world. Incidentally, that guy also lived in my apartment, which was actually quite cramped, considering about twelve other identities lived there as well.

"Remember they're not stupid, Daniel. They're just lost in the mist," Sami said softly. The warning was clear. "The enormity of the bomb on top of everything else that's happened over the past few weeks has them very agitated. Play it safe, my friend. Amnesia is good. You did business with Stanley. You developed a relationship with his assistant Simone. You came back for the funeral. Got it?"

"Absolutely," I replied. "So what about Lu?"

"They put out the full media list of the dead and injured two days ago. I'm not on it. So he finally knows I'm alive. He's holed up in his palace."

"Damn," I muttered. It would have been perfect if Sami had managed to swing things so he appeared to be dead.

"I spread the word that I've gone back to Thailand to recuperate and bury Jo," he added. "I had his body shipped back to his family." It obviously hurt Sami that he wasn't there for his friend's funeral. I could see the effort it required to move on. "I have a plan and I'll tell you about it in time."

"One question: Simone ... was she in that coffin?" I asked. That had been uppermost in my mind since I'd got it back in working order. I couldn't stand the thought of her having being blown to pulp in the blast. Sami was shaking his head.

"The police found her in her original coffin in the warehouse the undertakers use as a transit depot to store their coffins and equipment. The coffin containing the bomb was an exact duplicate. The undertaker's assistant and the driver didn't notice the difference when they reloaded it back into the hearse."

"Transit depot?" I was struggling to keep up with Sami's words. My brain was understandably still sluggish and the painkillers didn't help.

"When they have several funerals scheduled throughout the day and are busy, they don't go back to their parlour which, as you know, is quite small," Sami patiently explained. "Like a lot of funeral parlours, they have a warehouse they use as a way station. Because of the prior bookings at the cathedral, we had to have the service early while the burial had to be scheduled later, for the same reason. They needed the hearse in between times, so after the service, they stopped off and unloaded Simone and the flowers and went back to the parlour for another pickup. After that funeral, they returned to warehouse, reloaded the coffin with the bomb in it, and drove to wait for us outside the parlour in Clementi. Apparently, this sort of thing happens all the time."

"Someone must have been on the inside to switch the coffins."

"Obviously," Sami replied grimly, "and we have a traitor on our team."

To me, even lying there trying to get my brain back into full working order, I realised what he was getting at. "You were in Thailand when you heard the news of Simone's death. Did you specify which funeral home to use?"

"No. I left that to my people back here."

"Lu can't have people in all the funeral homes in Singapore, but he either had someone on his payroll in one already, or he managed to get someone into that home at short notice. Right?"

"Right! Remember that it wasn't the home itself, but their transit warehouse. So it was probably a labourer who made the switch and not one of the morticians."

"So it appears that someone on Lu's payroll and on your team selected the funeral parlour." I wasn't surprised really. To me, the huge money on permanent offer in Sami's world meant there would always be a traitor.

"I haven't been to the apartment since the bombing. My own people think I'm back in Thailand. I've been routing my calls through Bangkok. I've told them you are coming, so you go there when you're released in the morning. K will be there. Go in through the front entrance, but later when you want to get in and out unseen, there's a basement service tunnel that links three of the buildings in the complex. Access is through the parking garages via this key." Sami handed it to me. "I suggest you use the tunnels when you want to be invisible. Just in case Lu has anyone watching, which he probably does. Be very careful and trust no one, not even K." There was a deep sadness in Sami's voice.

"You suspect he's the rat?"

"I honestly don't know, Daniel. There were six people in the apartment when I called from Bangkok: K and five others. One was Stanley's former in-house accountant, Paul Wang. Paul was out at a meeting when the office was attacked. That in itself raises suspicion. There were two house staff there and two others from Jo's crew when I called. I haven't had the time to play detective. I'd hate to think it was K."

"So would I." We all went way back. To have to kill a man you once called friend was the pits.

"I'll be in touch, Daniel! By the way," he paused, "on the subject of spies. Michael, my man in Lu's camp, has been severely tortured and is in intensive care in KL. Obviously, his cover was well and truly blown." Sami's expression was grim. "Another score to be settled, Daniel. We'll bury Simone and the others when Lu is gone. It will be more fitting then. Take care, my old friend." Sami patted me on the arm and walked out of the room without a backward look.

Shortly after Sami's departure, the detectives arrived.

To the police officers, David Crewe was an injured man with blank eyes and very little memory. I could see they were frustrated by my act, but I was convincing. Given I'd spent the past three days hiding in the jungle on Pulau Ubin helped give credence to the amnesiac angle. That and the nurse who was hovering in the background like an anxious mother.

Eventually, after asking questions that drew only the vaguest of confused responses, the interview or interrogation or whatever it was came to an end.

"I don't think he has anything for us," one of the detectives said to the other.

"No. He checks out with Hong Kong, no problem."

The two of them were still standing at the foot of my bed. They were speaking Mandarin. I didn't let on I knew what they were saying, I just stared blankly up at them.

"Thank you, Mr Crewe. We will be in touch if there is anything else we may need. Here is my card." The conversation was now in English again. The more senior of the pair put his card on my side table and they turned for the door.

"If I remember anything at all, I will contact you," I called after them as the door swung shut. I could have added a big fat "Not!" to the end of the sentence, but didn't.

Soon I would be out of this place.

42

They took the staples out of my head and washed off the iodine. The scars are vivid, but they will fade or vanish under my hair when it grows back. However, I made a decision about my appearance. The photo of the man Sami told the police was David Crewe had been all over the newspapers and on television. I needed to make myself as dissimilar to that photo as I could.

A nurse brought a razor. She carefully shaved my head, and then I shaved off my moustache. It was the first time in two decades I actually saw my upper lip. It came as a shock, but suddenly I looked nothing like the man in the media.

My good doctor Dr Chang was on his way to give me a final assessment. I was hoping to be released before lunch. I needed to get out. There were things I had to do. People I had to kill—just joking!

Dr Chang did give me the all clear with the instructions I was to contact him directly at the first sign of any problems. There was a stark white bandage turban on my head. I had some painkillers and sleeping pills. He wanted to see me in a week's time. That, of course, was supposing I was still alive.

I thanked the doctor and was escorted down to a waiting taxi by a pretty young attendant. I gave the driver the Cairnhill Circle address Sami had given me and sat and undid my bandages as we travelled. I looked stupid in a turban. I would get a tanning agent to hide the vivid paleness of my scalp. It would glow in the dark the way it was.

We pulled up at the entrance to the condominium complex. It was imposing. There was a uniformed doorman. He made a call and K appeared in less than a minute and greeted me with a big grin as he took my bag and led me to one of the elevators. I noted that he pressed the button for "Penthouse Only". It was key controlled. I wondered if Sami owned the apartment building. I suspected he probably did.

Sami's domain was magnificent in every way. The rooms were large and airy, the furnishings expensive. There was much wood, but that was to be expected; Sami Somsak loved wood and used it extensively in all of his homes that I had seen. There were several of them I knew about but doubtless he had many more.

K showed me into a bedroom; or rather, into a suite, a large suite. The bedroom itself was the size of a normal lounge, plus there was a sitting room with a bar and a small kitchen off to one side. The bathroom had an enormous spa bath and double shower. It was magnificent.

The first thing I needed to do was meet the other residents. K gathered them in the main lounge. Apart from K, there was the accountant, Paul Wang. Following the firebombing, he had been relocated to the apartment. He had known Simone, so why hadn't he been at the funeral? I couldn't remember seeing him there, and what about his absence from the office when it had been attacked? These were things about Mr Paul Wang I would need to find out about.

That's the thing about not trusting people. Everyone is a suspect. Everyone can be a traitor. That's a great way to judge people.

Then there was Kaylin, the apartment's housekeeper. She was a short, attractive Chinese woman in her mid-thirties. She was all smiles and helpfulness. There were two Thai minders, Quong and Dep. I'd met Quong before, of course. Dep, however, was new to me. He was a young guy, maybe thirty, handsome, with a physique that suggested a lot of hard gym work. He was potentially a real lady-killer. Regardless, he was too young to be one of Jo's original core group of Special Ops people, so he had to be a new recruit. Maybe he was the traitor?

The last of the group was a young Singapore Chinese named George Hu. He was the live-in chef. A considerable waistline showed he loved his food. He was another who smiled easily. That's the problem with smiles, of course; they are an easy shield and can hide a multitude of sins.

These, then, were the six people who had been in the apartment when Sami had phoned following the news of Simone's death. He told me Kaylin had answered the phone and taken down his instructions, but had she personally made the funeral arrangements? I would be asking her that question when the opportunity arose.

I couldn't help but think that because the arrangements that our Judas had made with Lu had been aimed specifically at killing Sami Somsak, he or she would assume there would be no follow-up. If the plot had succeeded in killing Sami, as intended, there would certainly have been no follow-up. In fact, there would have been no one left to investigate the "how" of it all.

On that basis, I figured that the insider wouldn't necessarily have bothered with an elaborate scheme to cover up the plot. Time would surely tell on that one. My arrival here would probably shock the traitor, more so if he or she knew the real reason for my presence.

The fact that I looked like something from a horror movie hopefully would lull the Judas into thinking I was simply here to recuperate.

Introductions over, I settled into my room. I had only been in my luxurious suite for a few minutes when there was a knock at the door. It was K. He handed me a Browning Hi-Power, a shoulder holster, two extra loaded magazines and a silencer.

"A welcome gift," he said with a grin as he went out, closing the door behind him. I balanced the automatic in my hand and checked it. The weapon was clean and any excess oil had been wiped off. The magazine was fully charged and there was a round in the breech. The safety was on. No doubt K had prepared it. Only a pro left a round under the hammer and he only did that when he presented a weapon to another pro.

I genuinely liked K, and until events of the last few days, I had trusted him completely. I certainly hoped it wouldn't be him that I had to kill, perhaps with the very weapon he had just given me. I unloaded the piece and stripped it down. The firing pin hadn't been removed or filed down. That's the oldest trick in the book of dirty tricks. Everything looks absolutely fine until one goes to use the weapon and finds it has no teeth.

I used the shower. There was a full cabinet of every type of toiletry known to mankind, including a tanning agent, or rather a type of staining lotion. I used thin strips of plaster to cover my wounds and applied the solution as directed.

Ten minutes later, my glow-in-the-dark head was an almost match for my real tan. I wiped some of the solution across my upper lip. The result wasn't perfect, but it would do. I now didn't look like a freshly bald man who had just shaved off his moustache. I certainly didn't look like David Crewe, and that was fine.

I was just finishing my makeup session when I noticed that the bathroom had two telephones. There was one beside the twin vanity and another between the toilet and the bidet. Overkill perhaps, but it started a train of thought. It was something I should have worked out sooner, but I was still a little slow in the brain department.

Obviously, most modern digital telephone systems retain call records as a matter of course, and that was the initial key to finding out who the traitor was. I quickly dressed and went hunting for Sami's office. I had complete access to the joint. Sami had made that perfectly clear to everyone. K was stationed in the foyer watching a CCTV monitor. The images flicked between garage, elevator and fire escape. There was an MP5 sitting on the table beside the monitor. I asked where Sami's study was. K pointed to a set of double doors set off to one side. I went and opened them and stepped into Sami-land.

Sami's obsession with wood is one thing. His other passion is artwork, and stepping into his magnificent study was like walking into an art gallery. There were paintings on the wall I had seen in books and magazines; paintings that, in any other situation, I would have said were copies. There were pieces of sculpture in marble, bronze, maybe silver and gold even, and in various woods. They stood on pedestals and several of the larger ones were free-standing on the highly polished wooden floor. I wasn't up on sculpture, but these looked impressive.

More impressive was the Samurai warrior that stood to the right of the massive mahogany desk. I'd seen its twin in Sami's Bangkok mansion. It was a very scary, lifelike figure. The lacquered wood and leather armour was black and gold, as was the full-face helmet. The gauntlets of both hands were around the long handle of a magnificent katana. The shimmering blade of the sword formed an arc above and behind the warrior. The Samurai was poised for the killer stroke, the blow that would form a cleft in his unfortunate target from shoulder to hip, angled through the body. Sami was an expert with the beautiful, deadly sword. He was Samurai by heritage, through his father. He adhered to the best of that ancient culture and wove it through his Chinese and Thai backgrounds. That perhaps explained, in part at least, some of my friend's complexities.

I suppressed a shudder as I stepped past the warrior and sat at the desk. The figure was so powerful and so very lifelike that I had to force myself to rationalise that it was just a mannequin, like those in Fort Siloso—but this one was much more realistic.

Half an hour later, I left Sami's office none the wiser. His phone records showed normal traffic. Business calls to and from our accountant friend. There were calls from the housekeeper and chef ordering in goods and a variety of incoming calls from several different sources. The call from Sami was also logged, but there was no record of anyone—through the time leading up to or following that call—phoning any number not already logged in the system.

The one thing I did note, however, was that following the call from Sami, there had been a long delay of almost two hours before the call had been made to the Sacred Dream Funeral Home. Why had Kaylin waited so long before making it?

Of course, cellphones threw the whole equation sideways. Everyone in Singapore has a mobile. Short of gathering everyone's personal cell and searching their individual records, how was I going to identify who had been talking to Thomas Lu or one of his crew?

I wasn't prepared to point the finger at anyone just yet, but the two Ks (K and Kaylin), along with Paul Wong, were high on my list. What had Kaylin done during the two hours between Sami's call and her phoning the funeral parlour? Had she used her cell to call Lu? Had he called her prior to Sami's call. Had he ordered her to use the Sacred Dream Funeral Home where he had a man or men in waiting? Did he, in fact, own a share of the business itself? That was something that would be difficult to confirm either way.

I found a baseball cap to cover my scalp wound. It had a Levi's 501 logo on it. I would have preferred something a little less distinctive, but my BMW one hadn't made this trip with me and the 501 cap was the only other available. It would have to do. K gave me an elevator key. I put it on the ring already containing the key for the service tunnel doors as I travelled the twenty or so floors down to the basement car park. I unlocked the heavy steel door into the service tunnel and went through the garage of the neighbouring building and on to the next. The garages were all identical and so, I guessed, were the buildings above.

I made my way up the ramp to street level. The man in the cubbyhole at the top nodded to me and wished me a good day without blinking an eye. I returned the greeting and stepped out into the Singapore evening. Incidentally, I had left the Browning behind, but the borrowed Fairbain Sykes look-alike was in the sheath stitched into the lining of my left boot. Being totally unarmed was something I rarely did. A blade in my boot was more a talisman than anything else, although it had saved my life in Phuket just a few months before.

"He must have gone back to Bangkok as he said he was doing. We have not seen him in days, but his friend is here."

"Friend?"

"The man called Crewe, he was injured in the bomb blast. The man they were looking for on Pulau Ubin. He is staying in the apartment."

Thomas Lu grunted. He didn't know anything about this man Crewe other than what he had seen in the media. Had he been one of those who had captured him on Sentosa? Had he perhaps been the man who had raided the fort and made off with the recorder? Was it in his interests to capture or kill Crewe? He decided it wasn't, not yet anyway. If Somsak stayed in the north and kept out of Singapore, he would let the status quo reign, at least until he could devise a means of getting rid of the Thai gang boss once and for all.

"Keep me informed."

"I will. And Mr Lu?"

"Yes?"

"I will be calling on my friends tonight. Is everything arranged?"

"It is arranged."

"Thank you!"

"Goodbye." Lu hung up. He had a substantial libido of his own and he exercised it frequently, but the appetite of his spy in the Somsak camp amazed him. "If only we had made contact earlier," he mused, not for the first time. A chance comment from one of his male escorts had opened the lines of communication. It appeared that his spy and he shared the same exclusive escort agent. "If only," Lu repeated as he again reached for the telephone. His appetite had been whetted by the thought of what the previous caller had planned for the evening. He would now see to his own growing needs.

43

The building on Nassim Hill Road was tall and the penthouse atop it was no doubt one of the most expensive pieces of real estate in the city, if not the whole island. Thomas Lu lived the high life in more ways than one.

Everyone wants to live in a penthouse, I thought. I did live in one myself, but it was a comparatively modest one, despite the hefty price tag of eight million dollars. I knew that like Sami's place, Thomas Lu's lair would be worth millions and millions.

My cellphone rang.

"A rich address, Daniel."

"Absolutely, old man. I feel your eyes, but I can't see you." Sami chuckled at that and then I saw a movement in the shadows further up the street opposite a construction site.

"Have you any thoughts on the Judas in our midst, Daniel?"

"Not yet, but I am working on it."

"I hope it is not K."

"So do I, old friend, so do I," I replied and I meant it. With Jo gone, apart from me, K was now the last of the original inner circle.

"Any advance on your plan to get to Lu?"

"Oh yes," Sami replied. "Things are almost in place. Let us meet tomorrow lunchtime, the hawker centre on Smith Street, twelve-thirty. You can buy an old man fish head curry. Okay?"

"Okay!"

With that, the shadows reclaimed my old friend. I flipped my phone shut and turned to retrace my steps back towards Orchard Road. I was just another tourist out for a stroll. I wasn't far from Cuppage Terrace and the pub I'd enjoyed so much on my first visit. Dare I go back there? In the end, I decided it was too much of a risk.

Ed Davidson and David Crewe should never be in the same place at the same time. Of course I didn't look much like either at the moment, but I didn't want to risk it.

I found another pub close by. It was on a steep little street set in an old shophouse. It was crowded, noisy and the beer was cold. I allowed myself a couple of pints and stayed out of trouble. Drinking alone is not a problem. In fact, when planning a strategy to uncover a traitor, it can be beneficial as the alcohol and the atmosphere assist the brain. It didn't work this night. I left the pub without a plan.

Sitting on the edge of a concrete planter in the shadows, Sami Somsak was almost invisible to any passers-by. To anyone who saw him, he was just a harmless old man taking his ease and watching the activities on the construction site. This was a huge project as yet another small apartment building had been torn down to make way for a larger one. Already, the new structure had clawed its way fifteen storeys into the Singapore sky.

Sami was dressed in the traditional pyjama-like smock and trousers favoured by the old. He wore a brimless cap on his head and sandals on his feet. The small battered suitcase sat at his feet.

As he sat watching, waiting, a large tractor and trailer unit came slowly up the street. Under the harsh white lights of the building site, the lone watchman opened the gates to allow the truck entry. A second vehicle came grinding up after the first. When Sami saw what was on the heavily laden trailer, he smiled to himself. In a day or two, he would be ready to say farewell to Thomas Lu once and for all. With a grunt of satisfaction, he stood.

It was almost midnight, time for an old man to be home in his bed. Shuffling his feet, the small, hunched figure began to walk away down the street. The bowed legs and rounded back gave any watcher the impression that the old man caught in the lights of the passing traffic was an ancient creature.

A passing police car slowed and stopped by the kerb. Sami stopped walking and turned towards the car as the officer in the passenger seat called to him. He wanted to know if "Uncle" was okay. Did he need a ride home? Sami gruffly thanked the policeman and told him he was fine. The policeman waved as the unit pulled away and Sami Somsak breathed a big sigh of relief. If the policemen had had any idea of what he was carrying in his suitcase, he would have been on a fast train to Changi Prison.

At some stage during the night, my nightmare about Simone and the bomb was dashed into the razor fragments of a painful memory. I woke with a start. I had no idea what had awoken me, but here I was, wide awake. At least when my mind had been lost in the fog, sleep had come often and deeply.

I lit a cigarette and flicked on the television to see what CNN's version of world events was this day. It was 02:30. I was in time to see the latest fiery airliner crash. Suspected terrorist missile. Iran and Israel were once again trading verbal barrages. Some rising movie star had driven into a semi-trailer and was being likened to James Dean.

Then, as the tale of world woe continued, I made the decision as to how I was going to smoke out our spook. It was going to be face-to-face and direct. I stubbed out the first butt and lit another. Yeah, I know! My ration of five a day was in for a hammering.

As a last resort, I decided I would commandeer every mobile phone in the apartment and see who had called whom in that vital two-hour period between Sami's call and Kaylin's call to the funeral home. But first, I was going to conduct my own inquisition.

It would be gentle, but my antennae would be on full BS scan. The only bullshit that got past me was generally my own, but I was good at catching out liars. At times, back in the other world, that had been another skill that had made the difference between life and death. Would my skills at detecting who was and was not lying be as sharp now as they had been prior to my angel's kiss? I guess I was about to find out.

Perhaps it was the simple fact that I had decided how I was going to proceed that did it, but I managed to drift back to sleep and this time it was dreamless.

It was a few minutes to 09:00. I'd showered and shaved and was dressed in my gear designed to scare the shit out of everyone. Wearing all black is one thing, but for this occasion, I added the shoulder holster under the lightweight leather jacket. The butt of the Browning showed clearly. I left my suite ready to go hunting bear.

Quong was in the apartment foyer. He was sitting at the desk. As always, an MP5 rested on the desk. Sami, it appeared, bought these by the tonne as well as the Brownings. We exchanged greetings in Thai and I entered Sami's office.

That damn Samurai warrior statue, as with its twin back in Bangkok, made my heart lurch. It really was so fucking realistic. I skirted around the other end of the desk, keeping as far away from it as I could. Logic told me to treat it as some sort of oversized transformer or game piece.

That really didn't work. Something about that ancient blade with its razor edge negated that theory. Any kid's toy with that damn thing attached was a weapon of war in any language. Seated behind the desk, I ran through my options. Who should I summon first? My initial thought was that I had to start at the beginning. Kaylin had taken Sami's call and delayed for two hours before acting on it. Or at least appearing to act upon it.

There was an intercom consul in the drawer to the right of the desk. Various locations were named, as were individuals. I pressed the button bearing the label "Kaylin", presuming it was connected to her room. There was a long delay before a sleepy voice answered. I glanced at my watch. It was 09:05. I told her I needed to see her in Sami's office and hung up.

Five minutes after the call, the housekeeper appeared. She was dishevelled. Her hair was a hairdresser's nightmare. She was wearing a bathrobe and slippers. Her face was puffy. It looked as if she had slept in her makeup. She didn't look so great this morning.

"Sorry to wake you," I said cheerfully as she came up to the desk. "Please sit down." She sat with a flash of shapely legs. Was she working me before she even knew what I wanted?

"It's okay. Today is my day off."

"I'm sorry. I didn't realise."

"You weren't to know. What did you want to see me about?"

I smiled my meat-eating smile and gave her the stare. It generally worked on people, but on her, I don't think so. She matched me stare for stare.

"When Mr Somsak phoned you from Thailand when Simone died, you waited almost two hours before phoning the funeral home. Why so long?" Now the housekeeper blinked and I saw a flash of fear or panic cross her features.

"I was shocked. I went and was sick," she said. "I was upset, very upset. I knew Simone well. She was a friend."

"Okay," I conceded. "How did you choose the funeral home? Mr Somsak didn't tell you to use Sacred Dream."

"I didn't choose the funeral home. I was so upset, I asked Paul to do as Mr Somsak asked. He phoned the funeral people, not me." Kaylin started crying. There was a box of tissues on a side table. I reached over and retrieved it, placing it on the desk in front of her. The cynic in me well recognised that tears are a woman's number-two defence after attack. Kaylin had gone straight there, side-stepping the former. Maybe she was telling the truth.

"I'm sorry," I said softly. "I have to ask the questions because there are too many unanswered ones out there. Go and enjoy the rest of your day off." I know it sounded absurd, but what else could I say?

Kaylin stood, her face buried in tissues. Again there was a flash of legs and then she was gone. She used her legs well. The movement had been far from accidental. Despite seeming to be so upset, she was in control.

"That went fucking well," I muttered sarcastically to myself as I selected the button on the intercom for Paul. If Kaylin was telling the truth, Paul was very much in the hot seat. He was at the office door within a matter of seconds. Dressed in a pair of dark trousers, white shirt and tie, he looked every inch the accountant he was, and nothing like the traitor he might indeed be. Again, I didn't beat about the proverbial bush.

"Were you at Simone's funeral?" I asked. Above all else, I wanted to know the answer to that question.

"I was at the cathedral service," he replied, "but Mr Somsak asked me to stay here rather than go to the cemetery. There was an important call he was expecting and he asked that I be here for that."

That sounded perfectly logical and, of course, it would be easy to verify, so I moved on. I could see Paul's eyes moving between my face and the butt of the automatic under my arm. He was used to taking people down with a balance sheet and not a gun, I guess.

"The night Sami phoned with the news of Simone's death, Kaylin took the call. What happened then?"

"She went off to her room in tears. I asked if there was anything I could do, if there were any instructions from Mr Somsak, but she just rushed into her room. She didn't come out for maybe an hour and a half. I knocked several times but she didn't open the door."

"When she did come out, what happened?"

"She gave me a piece of paper with the phone number for the funeral parlour on it and asked me to contact them. She said that Mr Somsak had asked that we use these people. She said she would make arrangements for Simone's sister to fly in if I would make the funeral arrangements."

"So you phoned Sacred Dream Funeral Home?"

"Yes; and they did the rest."

"Thank you, Paul," I said standing. Now I knew exactly who the traitor was. I quickly left the office with the bewildered accountant trailing in my wake.

"Don't let Kaylin leave," I snapped at Quong as I hit the foyer.

"She's just gone!"

"Shit!" I fished out my key and stabbed the elevator button. I pulled the Browning out of the shoulder holster and lobbed it to Quong.

"How long ago?"

"Two minutes."

"Has she got a car?" I directed the question at Paul, who was standing there like a spare prick at a wedding.

"No," he replied, "she can't drive."

"Small mercies," I snarled, launching myself into the lift, fitting the key and sending the car down to the ground foyer.

Kaylin was running for her life and she knew it. She had double-crossed Sami Somsak and now his killer friend was on her tail. She crossed the apartment foyer at a run. All she carried was one small bag. A tracksuit had replaced her dressing gown and her slippers had been traded for sneakers, but her hair was still a wild mess.

"My mother is ill," she called, sobbing to Quong who was watching her from his desk. "She may die." Kaylin entered the elevator with her key and feverishly fumbled to insert it. Eventually her trembling fingers guided it home. She stabbed the button for the foyer and breathed a long sigh of relief as the car started towards the ground.

The doorman barely had time to open the large double doors before the housekeeper was through and out onto the street. She started running down the footpath, frantically looking for a cab. Rush hour was over, but the traffic was still heavy.

Nothing was supposed to have gone this way. Sami Somsak and his immediate people were supposed to be dead. She, they, had never anticipated that the plot on his life would fail or that someone would come looking for answers. Thomas Lu had insisted she remain at Somsak's apartment and she had agreed because the rewards were great. That had been a huge mistake.

There was a cab. She waved, but it pulled up short and another woman got in. Kaylin screamed in anguish. She looked back up the street and then she saw the figure in black arrive on the footpath. He turned first the other way and now towards her, and he started running.

Another taxi pulled up. The housekeeper threw herself into it. "Changi Village," she gasped. It was the first thing that came to mind, probably because it was as far away from here as she could get. The taxi pulled away from the kerb and swept past the running man, who partially stepped onto the road to block it. The driver swerved and cursed, but carried on.

Kaylin turned in her seat. The last thing she saw was the man in black holding out one hand, the index finger extended pointing directly at her face, his thumb raised for a moment and then it snapped down.

“Oh my God,” she whimpered. She knew that if she and the man in black ever met again, she was dead.

44

I arrived back in the penthouse like a tornado. I was fuming. I should have instructed Quong not to let anyone leave. Of course, the traitor could have been him in the first place, and that would have alerted him—a semi-automatic pistol is no match for an MP5.

I retrieved my Browning and holstered it as I carried on into the apartment. The staff rooms were to the left of the main corridor. I stormed down the side passage. It wasn't hard to spot Kaylin's room. The door was wide open. One of her slippers was on the floor in the doorway.

Inside, her room looked as if a hurricane had blown it apart. I was in a force ten mood. So close, yet so damned far!

There were clothes scattered all around the room, but worse still were the pictures on the wall—they would have made a madam blush. Hard-core, total hard-core, large photographs of men on men, women on women and everything in between. There was a big flat screen television with DVD player and sound system. There was an image on the screen, but the sound had been turned off.

As I watched, I saw Kaylin's image fill the screen, all of her, every inch, in full living colour. She and her three playmates. Two males and another female were indulging themselves in a good old-fashioned orgy.

I ignored the moving pictures and started looking for any paperwork, a cellphone, anything that could help track her down when she landed, wherever she landed. It appeared Kaylin had a fetish, or maybe several. Drawers revealed a range of sexual appliances that could have stocked a full-fledged sex supermarket. I had absolutely no idea what the hell some of them were used for.

There was no diary, no address book, no cellphone, nothing but hundreds of DVDs and sexual playthings. The big walk-in wardrobe was full of clothes, shoes, boots and costumes. From Heidi to Catwoman with crotchless latex trousers, they were all there along with whips and restraints and every other bell and whistle you could think of.

I searched the bedroom from top to bottom, lifting carpets, looking for a safe and any other hiding places. I did the same in the bathroom. Nothing! The housekeeper had grabbed what she knew I would come looking for and made a run for it.

The room's locks were many. Obviously, being the keeper of the royal household, Kaylin had ensured that no one could ever enter her little corner of paradise uninvited. I didn't bother locking the door when I left.

I went into Sami's office and tapped out his number. The only good thing about this situation was that K was not the one who had turned traitor. Lunch with Sami was still on.

"And what do you expect me to do about it?"

"Help me!"

"We had an agreement. You do as I ask and I make sure that your wildest fantasies are realised. Is that not what we agreed?"

"Yes, Mr Lu. I still want that, but now the man, this Mr Crewe, knows I helped with the bomb. He will kill me when he finds me."

"Then don't let him find you," Thomas Lu replied, smiling his humourless smile. "Run, rabbit, run!" He hung up.

"The man in black," he mused. "Mr Crewe. Perhaps it's time I found out a little more about you." Lu reached for his phone again.

"She had been in my household for three years," Sami said. He paused and contemplated his next words for a moment. Then he sighed. "I have to tell you about Stanley's other life for it to all make sense."

"Other life?" I replied. Then I remembered he had hinted that there were some things about his stepbrother that troubled him.

"Other life," Sami repeated. "On the surface, Stanley was a straight-laced family man with a loving wife, and he did love Helen. He loved his kids. He was a good businessman. Very talented, but he had what one could consider a problem."

"Which was?"

"He was a sex maniac," Sami said simply. I sat there stunned. "He had a whole other life beyond his office and home in Goodwood Hill."

"Did his wife...did Helen know?"

"Most of it, yes. She tolerated his indiscretions providing they remained private. She loved him and he loved her, but Stanley just had to have constant sex." Sami's eyes met mine. Could I see myself reflected there and in his words? He didn't dwell on it. "I own the penthouse but I have, until the last few weeks, never lived there. In fact, I had never even been inside it."

"What?" I was absolutely stunned by his revelation.

"Previously when I came to Singapore, I used my secret apartment. Or if on business which involved Stanley, I stayed at his home. I bought the penthouse, but I let Stanley set it up. His furnishings, except for the study. He installed his people, including his frequent mistress."

"Kaylin," I added.

"Yes, Kaylin. She could do what she wanted on her own time, but she was at his beck and call. She hosted his private business dinners and gatherings." Sami paused again and took a mouthful of his food.

"Fucking hell," I muttered. I could see it all now.

"Until I walked into the penthouse and announced who I was, Kaylin had no idea I was Stanley's brother. She had no idea."

"That must have stunned her."

"The fact Stanley had a brother stunned everyone, Lu included. But thinking back on Stanley's last days and the situation with Lu, I wonder if at that point Kaylin was working with Lu against Stanley."

"But she had everything," I blurted out. "A beautiful apartment, a rich sponsor."

"Sex," Sami replied. "That appears to be what she wanted. You told me about the photographs and videos. She and Stanley had a lot of playmates. I'm not suggesting Lu was involved physically, certainly not with Stanley, but someone amongst the playmates was involved with Lu and Kaylin. Whatever Lu offered her, it possibly wasn't money. Stanley was very generous when it came to money. Perhaps Lu offered her more sex?"

"Perhaps Kaylin was involved with Lu?"

"No. Lu is one hundred percent gay. But maybe a bi-lover, who knows? Even here, or maybe particularly here, these things flourish and it is a very closed, underground society. The male escorts are flouting the law. Getting caught is not a good option. They all know each other. Someone like Kaylin who, judging from what you said, swings both ways and is as hungry as she appears to be, would no doubt be very well known in those circles."

So much was clearer. It didn't matter now; what had happened had happened. All we had to do was bring things to a close. We concentrated back on our food, for the moment at least. Sitting there in his makeup and garb, Sami looking as though he was in his eighties. He concentrated on working on a fish head. I've eaten them often, but they have never been quite the same delicacy for me that they are for many Asians. I had settled for a simple pork curry washed down with a Tiger beer. I had a bigger thing for pork now than I ever had. I stabbed at a piece of the tender meat and Sami and I sat chewing our respective meals in thoughtful silence for several minutes. Sami finally spoke.

"Sex worked both ways," he suddenly said around a mouthful of food. "When I knew Lu had his damned foot in the Intella door, I decided to use his homosexuality to get an advantage. I found Michael through a gay friend. Michael joined the same agency that Lu obtains his treats from at my instigation, and through the agent, I manipulated things. Michael soon became Lu's favourite and eventually his live-in lover. However, Lu has a prodigious libido, according to Michael, and often he would invite another boy or two from the agency to join them in a romp. So perhaps Kaylin was a member of the same agency or a client of the agency. Not that it matters damn now."

"I guess." I took a swig of my beer. "I imagine, and I'm not joking here, that the playmates get to know each other pretty well, and not in the obvious sense. They talk and gossip and connections other than the carnal ones are made."

"Just like in real life," Sami agreed. "Anyway, traitor identified;

we have solved one problem and I have the solution to the other."

"When do we go?"

"Saturday night."

I did a mental check. It was Thursday. One full day to kill and then we could pay Mr Thomas Lu a visit. I decided to play devil's advocate, a role that comes naturally to me.

"He has a not-so-small army covering his place. How do we—and I presume we're talking you, me and probably K—get through them to Lu?"

"We don't go through them," Sami replied, chuckling. Given that it was in his old man voice, it sounded more like a cackle. He stood, leaving me sitting alone at a table covered in fish bones. "Thank you for inviting an old man to share a meal with you," he said in Mandarin.

"My pleasure, Uncle," I replied in the same tongue. Several of the old people sitting at a table next to ours looked at me with something approaching respect or puzzlement that I, an Anglo, spoke their old language so fluently.

I finished my beer as I watched Sami slowly wander off. He really was a most accomplished actor. As for my acting abilities? I guess as some director said of Clint Eastwood in his cowboy days: "He has two expressions, hat on and hat off." That's me. I've either got my scare face on or I haven't. There's not a lot in between, apart from my amnesiac episode, I guess.

I stood and made my way back out onto Smith Street and turned down New Bridge Road. I needed a walk. It had been a crazy day and it wasn't over yet.

Thomas Lu was confused and more than a little concerned. He had well-paid people in a great many places. The name David Crewe pointed to an expatriate Australian living in Hong Kong. He was a businessman, import-export, involved with security systems. The company existed. Something, however, didn't sit right for Lu. From what the housekeeper had said, this man did not appear to be a harmless businessman. He had been injured in the bomb blast, concussed and wandered off to Ubin in a daze. But he had survived there three days with an army looking for him. Then he had gone to them in the end.

Kaylin said he had been wearing a gun. Even in Thomas Lu's murky world, legitimate businessmen did not wear guns.

Lu tapped a button on the computer keyboard in front of him. A face came into focus. It was an image taken by one of his people in the cemetery. It showed the dead woman's mourners carrying the coffin from the hearse to the graveside. Lu used the mouse to isolate the figure of the tall man and enlarge it.

Although the image was grainy, the head and shoulders filled the screen. Thomas Lu sat and studied it. This was not the man the media said was David Crewe. This was another man altogether.

The man onscreen had his face to the camera. He was of indeterminable age. He could have been late twenties or he could have been fifty. He had medium-length fair hair, and a thick moustache of the same colour that extended to just below the corners of the hard-looking mouth. The chin was square and shaven. It was the eyes, however, that held Lu's attention. They were cold and blue and they appeared to meet the camera with an unflinching directness that distance could not disguise. The eyes spelt "danger" in every way.

"Killer, not businessman," Lu blurted. "You're an assassin and you're here because of the girl and because of me." Thomas Lu fell back into his seat. This was the man who had saved Somsak's life and almost caught the woman Kaylin. This man was exceptionally dangerous and he was smart, that much had already been proven. No matter what his real name was, the man called David Crewe would be looking for him.

"I need to find you first," Lu said. Decision made, he again reached for his phone.

45

It was the morning of the next day. I was walking down Cairnhill Road and had decided to kill time by taking a constitutional the length of Orchard Road before meeting up with Sami.

We had—or rather I had—one day to kill before Thomas Lu met his maker. Perhaps his soul, if he had one, had come straight out of hell via FedEx the moment he was born. Maybe he had been doomed to stoke the devil's furnace all his living days. Either way, I frankly couldn't wait to do whatever Sami had in mind. The moment that was accomplished, I would be away—Thailand, Hong Kong, anywhere.

When you are being watched, you can feel the eyes. Sometimes they just stroke your senses and drift on. Those are the eyes of a professional; they don't focus for more than a nano second, and unless your senses are particularly acute or you are trained in martial arts, you may not notice them. When you are being watched by an amateur or someone consumed with a passion, whether it be love, hate or anything in between, the eyes fix and literally burn holes in the air and your psyche.

It was the latter that I felt. It wasn't the caress of a passing gaze. This was intense. I knew that I had a tail.

It was a few minutes to 09:30. There were a lot of people around and plenty of traffic. I had no idea where the watcher was. He or she could be in a building, on the footpath or in a vehicle. Probably not a vehicle, given the difficulty of trying to match a pedestrian's pace while on wheels in heavy traffic. Anyone kerb crawling was going to get a going over from the traffic. Singapore drivers don't take prisoners.

I was walking for the sake of it. Later, I would be meeting Sami for lunch. This time, we were going to eat at the Newton Circus Food hawker centre. If the tail stayed with me I would beg off the lunch and attempt to draw the watcher into a position where I could identify him and do whatever I needed to.

The point here, of course, is that I could be under observation from someone other than Lu's people. I could have a bunch of special police or security types on my tail, or maybe someone from the old days. I had a lot of enemies in Asia, people who would happily dice me with a blunt knife and feed me to the sharks piece by piece.

How to draw the watcher out? On Orchard, I swung left. The locals and tourists were both out in force along the platinum retail mile. I slowed and made a pretence of window shopping, but decided that was too obvious. I just didn't look like a shopper. Then I had an idea. It was 09:40, time for breakfast. I cut into the first café I saw. I quickly walked as deeply into it as I could and grabbed a seat.

Okay, it's the oldest trick in the spy handbook, but it generally works. For a tail, losing sight of his or her quarry produces an often uncharacteristic knee-jerk moment of panic.

My tail was Asian, surprise, surprise! Tall, with long hair pulled back into a ponytail. She was wearing a crisp white blouse under a well-cut navy trouser suit. She looked every inch the businesswoman. It was the perfect cover. If a guy hadn't chosen that exact same moment to pull the door of the café open, framing her in the doorway, she might have managed to remain anonymous.

I was sitting low in my seat with my cap and Ray Bans off. The menu covered most of my face. There was a waitress hovering at the next table that was positioned between the door and me. I had cover, while Miss Corporate Singapore stood there exposed in the open doorway. For a moment she stayed frozen, her eyes darting, trying for a fix. Had I slipped through the café and out the back? Was I inside, innocent, unaware and simply ordering breakfast? Or was I fully aware of her presence and watching?

I don't think she saw me. The door closed and she moved on. I waited until she had passed across the front window, then I quickly stood and made my way back towards the toilets. I went past them and into the kitchen. There I found controlled chaos, as was normal in most restaurants at peak times. Startled waitresses and cooking staff looked at me as I entered.

"Back door?" I asked. One of the chefs pointed. I thanked him and went to the door he'd indicated. It opened into a narrow alleyway that ran parallel to Orchard Road. The alley was filled with crates, boxes and gas bottles. I let the door close and went to where the alley joined a wider service lane that cut back to the street. Peering around the corner, I met my shadow. She was actually standing at the end of the service way where it joined the footpath to Orchard. She was using her cellphone. Her back was to me. I waited.

The call was short, very short. The woman flipped her phone and slipped it into the black bag she had slung over her shoulder. Judging by her body language, she was agitated. Had she reported to Lu that she had lost me, or had she been speaking to some other entity? My bet was she'd been talking to Thomas Lu; however, I needed to know one way or the other. The woman waited a few more minutes, standing watching the passing throng, then she made a decision and started back up Orchard, back the way she had come.

I ran to the corner. I was just in time to see a flash of blue entering the café I had just left. I gave her time to do a quick circuit and prepared to sprint back to my cover if she came back out and turned my way. She came out, but turned in the opposite direction and continued on up Orchard.

Now I had to do some big-time guesswork. Was she going back to her base, wherever that was? Was she going home? Was she going to throw herself under a bus? If I could just get her alone, I could find out who she was working for. If it was a government tail, I was busted and I'd be on the first flight out of the country, or more likely a fishing boat up the Straits. If she was working for Lu, maybe I could use her to my advantage. Either way, I needed to know who she was working for.

Miss Blue continued on ahead of me. Now with my jacket over my arm, my cap and glasses in my pocket, I was just a clean-shaven Anglo guy with a shaved head wearing a pair of Levi's, battered cowboy boots and a white T-shirt bearing a Nike logo. Nothing obvious. I certainly didn't look like the black-jacketed guy wearing dark glasses and a 501 baseball cap on his head that she had previously been following.

I had to take a chance. The MRT. Was she going to cross Orchard and go down the MRT? If so, was she going north or south? The pedestrian lights fifty metres up ahead changed and a flood of humanity started across the road. I did likewise. I lost sight of Miss Blue, but walked quickly at a pace just short of a jog. I sliced through the slower traffic, doing a good imitation of a knife through butter. I wanted to get in front of her if I could. Tailing someone from in front is a tough ask, but to the experts, it's often the best way to do it. If you're good enough! Thing was, I hadn't done this for a long time. Was I still capable of pulling it off?

I turned into Orchard MRT station and slowed, letting the natural movement of the human flood carry me along. I hit the escalator and was soon in the bowels of the station. I stepped to one side and stopped in the main concourse as the continuous stream of people chose a turnstile and slapped down their entry cards before going even deeper into the complex.

After three minutes of loitering, I thought I'd misjudged Miss Blue's intentions. I was about to give up and move on when I saw her approaching. Because she was relatively tall, she stood out above those around her. She was thirty metres away, fished her wallet out of her shoulder bag and pressed her ez-link card to the turnstile.

Moving quickly, I swiped my card too, went through the nearest gate and carried on down to the platforms below. Would she head north or south? I found a pillar and leaned against it, pulling out my cellphone and pretending to talk. A dozen people around me were also chatting on their phones.

Miss Blue arrived at the bottom of the escalator and turned for the left platform. She was heading back down the line. Would she get off at Somerset or stay onboard and maybe change at Dhoby Ghaut? The train was pulling in. I moved closer and waited. She went into the rear of the train. I went into the next section. A seat was vacant. I dropped into it ahead of an old Chinese lady. To her equally old friend, she scolded me in Mandarin. I let it slide. I was just a dumb, bad-mannered Anglo. Despite that, she said that the scars on my head looked bad. Thank you, Auntie, I thought as the train pulled away.

Over the top of the other passengers, I could just make out the top of Miss Blue's head in the next carriage. She was standing. A minute or two later, we slowed to a stop at Somerset. Would she get off? For a moment, as the doors opened, I thought she was going to. I stood. No, instead she took a vacant seat. I went to sit down again, but the auntie who had scolded me had slipped behind me and was now sitting in that seat. I almost sat on her lap. She looked up at me and cackled. Her friend, who was still standing, congratulated her in Mandarin. This horse's behind was too slow, it seemed!

I bent my knees slightly and merged with the standing crowd. Again, I could just see Miss Blue's head. If she got off at the Dhoby Ghaut interchange, where to next? Would she take the green line and head east or west? Or take the purple line. The choices were all there. Of course, she might just stay on the train.

When we reached Dhoby Ghaut, she stood and got off the train. I followed. There was little chance of getting in front of her, and she had so many options of where to go that it was impossible for me to outguess her. The only alternative was to stay on her tail and hope that she didn't realise she was being followed. Judging by her lack of expertise to date, I didn't think that was likely. I hoped I was right.

Purple line! She was either going to Harbourfront or Punggol or anywhere in between. I followed and yes, she was heading west. Now that she had lost her subject, Miss Blue was no longer scanning the crowd. The fact that I might have turned the tables on her had obviously not entered her mind. Amateur!

Again I hugged a pillar and pantomimed with my cellphone as we waited for the next unit, all the time keeping watch on my former spook out of the corner of my eye. I avoided staring directly at her. Even if she weren't practised at shadowing, I didn't want to risk her picking up eye-burn as I had. Given that she was quite an attractive woman, I imagined she was used to receiving a fair bit of attention from appreciative males, and another passing glance wouldn't alert her.

The train pulled in and I did as I had done before. There were fewer people getting on, so I stayed at a discreet distance and slumped into a seat, pretending to text on my mobile. From where I was sitting I could see Miss Blue's crossed legs in a seat not too far from me. She had nice legs, but her shoes, with semi-high heels, were not exactly ideal for a shadow. That added to my conclusion that she wasn't a complete professional. A real pro would have had on walking shoes of some sort.

At Outram Park, Miss Blue stood and made her way out onto the platform. I did likewise, but hung back. My former watcher was making a call on her mobile. This call wasn't as difficult as the first, it appeared. She actually laughed before slipping the phone back into her bag. I followed, just close enough to see which one of the dozens of alternative exits she used. She chose the Cantonment exit. I'd been here before. This was the exit that came up directly under the police complex. Shit! Was she a cop after all? I quickly slipped my cap back on to cover the scars and let the cap's oversize brim and my dark glasses cover as much of my face as possible. I knew there was CCTV aplenty in the MRT station, but assumed there would be even more cameras near the police precinct.

I stayed on Miss Blue's tail. If she were a cop, I would be leaving Singapore just as soon as it could be arranged. I had no illusions that if the authorities were interested in me, I would be in great danger, and life in Changi Prison was not something I was eager to experience.

We emerged on the ground-level concourse in the police building, but rather than turning to the right and entering the precinct itself, Miss Blue carried on, exited the foyer and walked on up the side of the building. There was a gap in the hedge at the top. She stepped through and waited to cross the road in front of her. I hung back in the shadows under the building's overhang. I found a cigarette and made a play of lighting it. Hell, this was my first of the day. I had so far almost stuck to my limit of five a day. My lungs were beginning to thank me for my restraint.

Miss Blue crossed the road and headed to a large housing estate directly in front of her. I let her get into the grounds before I tossed my cigarette away and judged my run to make it across the road without being flattened.

Miss Blue had gone beyond the first line of buildings and was moving deeper into the cluster of apartment blocks. I stayed on her tail. She paused at one stage to talk to an elderly woman. I lit another cigarette for cover and sat at one of the seats dotted around the open park space.

Eventually the pair separated and Miss Blue moved on. She turned into the entrance of one of the towers. I slowed. This was going to be the tricky bit. Then I noticed the post boxes. I tried to make myself invisible by pressing my body into the wall outside the open entrance. I watched. Who doesn't check for mail mid-morning? Miss Blue kept my faith in humanity. She produced a key from her shoulder bag and opened a box. I was too far away to read the numbers, but I counted. Three down, four from the end.

My quarry closed and relocked the box, then moved towards the bank of two elevators, sorting her mail as she went. A lift arrived and three people exited. Miss Blue stepped in and was gone. I waited for the foyer to clear and went to the bank of post boxes. Three down and four across was box number 09-04. A sticker on the letterbox read:"Lucy Pang Hooi Ming—NO junk mail, thank you".

I went to the elevators. The television monitor mounted on the wall above each of the lifts showed its interior. Miss Lucy Pang, if that was her name, was standing, head down, reading a postcard. She was nodding her head. I guessed she was laughing. When the elevator stopped, she got out without looking up at the camera. Like people who were around them a lot, she had probably forgotten it was there.

I glanced at the floor counter mounted above the door. Level nine.

Shrugging on my jacket, I got in the next lift to arrive. Like Miss Blue, I avoided looking up at the monitor just in case it was being taped. I pushed the button for her floor. I had no idea just what I was going to do when I got to unit 09-04. What if Miss Blue was not alone in the apartment? That was something I'd just have to take a chance on.

I arrived at level nine. The open landing had four doors off it. Two of them were closed behind their wrought-iron security screens. One door was open, with just the security screen closed and padlocked, letting the humid air circulate while keeping out any stray burglars. The security screen to Miss Blue's apartment had been left half-open; however, the door behind it was closed. Was it locked? Was Miss Blue expecting someone to call? Was there anyone else in the apartment? Her aged father, perhaps? Or a rambunctious young brother, boyfriend or husband who would want to deal with any intruder?

I never go anywhere without gloves of some sort in my pocket. The ones in my inside jacket pocket were latex, a thicker version of the standard surgical model. I pulled them on and shut down my imagination. The door was unlocked! I didn't need to try and pick the lock mechanism.

Taking a deep breath, I pushed the door open and stepped inside.

46

Sami Somsak, still in the guise of the little old Chinaman, was pleased, very pleased. Everything was neatly falling into place. The old man was sitting on the edge of a concrete planter taking his leisure as he had done for several days. As always, his small battered suitcase sat at his feet. Across from where he was sitting, construction on the new apartment building was going well, but his eyes weren't on the construction site. He was watching the front of the towering building two down on the same side, waiting for a sighting of the man he would soon kill.

Almost on cue, the gold Bentley swept out of the underground car park and onto Nassim Road. Lu was out of his fortress and on one of his rare expeditions since the cemetery bombing. Following the luxury sedan came a black Range Rover, no doubt filled with Lu's bodyguards.

"When the time comes, they will do you no good whatsoever," the old man chuckled to himself. "No good whatsoever."

I was in a small foyer. To my right was an open-plan living room and I could see two doors opening off it. To my left were three doors. Somewhere to my right a door slammed. Back on my left what I took to be washing machine whirred. I stood motionless, trying to interpret the sounds. I moved into the entrance to the living room. There was a kitchen on the left with a servery and breakfast bar opening into the living room. There was music playing softly, the sound emanating from the speakers of a home theatre set-up. A large television screen dominated one wall of the room. A toilet flushed. There was a bathroom, beyond the kitchen but it was out of my line of vision.

I heard the sounds of a shower being turned on. Miss Blue, it appeared, was about to wash away the results of her exertions. I drifted back to the main door and closed it. I slid the intruder chain across and pressed the locking knob on the door handle to set it. While Miss Blue was occupied in the shower, I quickly went from room to room checking for any other occupants. There were four bedrooms, all of them empty.

Miss Blue's bedroom was the largest. It had two doors, one to the living area, and one that either opened into an *en suite* or at the least allowed her access to the bathroom area.

I knew it was her room because her blue suit was spread across the bed. Shoes were lying on the floor along with a bra and panties. It appeared Miss Blue hadn't wasted any time at all getting into the shower. From the amount of splashing, she was having quite a time of it in there.

The bedroom had its own television. There was a sound system. Nice prints and maybe a couple of original paintings were on the wall. The curtains were open and the light flooded in. I went and drew the curtains. Whatever happened, I didn't want some voyeur with a camera or a telescope watching. I wanted a restraint for our Miss Blue when she emerged from her ablutions. Dressing gown cords are good, as are belts.

There was no belt on her skirt and no dressing gown in sight. I crossed to the large built-in wardrobe and pulled the double-doors open.

"Shit!"

There were at least five police uniforms sitting neatly on hangers along with neatly racked shirts. There were several pairs of highly polished practical shoes stacked neatly in the bottom of the wardrobe. Three uniform caps sat on a high shelf. Miss Blue was not only neat, she was a fucking cop! The shower had been turned off. She was about to walk back into the bedroom.

I had no choice but to play this thing out to whatever end we came to. I cursed at my dumb luck, and grabbed a scarf from a rack of several hanging on one leaf of the wardrobe door. I quickly crossed the bedroom to stand with my back pressing against the wall beside the *en suite* door. The door opened and Miss Blue came into the room. She was naked, which of course was to be expected. She was drying her hair with a towel which obscured her face as she moved. She stopped momentarily and realised that the curtains had been drawn. She lowered the towel and started to turn.

I came off the wall and went for her. It wasn't pretty, but it was quick. I grabbed a handful of hair and drove Miss Blue forward towards her bed, clipping her feet out from under her as I did so. She fell full length onto the bed. I straddled her, letting my ninety-five kilos drive her into the bedding as I held her face into the bedcovers. I didn't want a shout or a scream.

She was trying to fight. Her legs were scissoring wildly. Her heels were hitting me on the back but with no real force. She was trying to reach back and fight me with her hands. There were fingernails. I slapped her hands away with my free hand. She wasn't giving up easily. Miss Blue planted her hands flat on the bed and tried to force herself upwards. I just leaned on her, using my weight to keep her face buried in the soft counterpane.

The suddenness of the attack and the fact she couldn't get breath into her lungs was now starting to take the fight out of my cop. Now she was panicking, simply trying to get some air into her oxygen-starved body.

"Listen," I said softly. "I just want to talk. I'll let you breathe but you scream or you fight and you die. That's a promise, got it?" There was an explosion of sound from deep in the bed and her legs stopped thrashing around. I lifted her head and she gulped in air. I released her hair. "Hands behind your back."

She started to object, so I grabbed hair and pushed her face back into the bedding. Her hands came back instantly. I let go of the hair once more and used the scarf to tie her wrists together. Only then did I get off her and stand at the foot of the bed. I rolled Miss Blue onto her back, touching my finger to my lips as I did so. Her eyes were huge. Her mouth was opening and closing silently like a guppy in a fish tank.

I sat on the edge of the bed and removed my fighting knife from my boot. I held it casually in my hand with the blade just touching her thigh. Her eyes widened even further and she tried to squirm away. I grabbed her shoulder with my free hand and anchored her where she was.

I don't even think at that moment she was aware of her nakedness; the sight of the blade and perhaps the guy holding it had her full attention. The big dark eyes switched between my face and the razor-sharp blade of the knife. I pulled my Ray Bans off and slipped them into the pocket of my jacket. Some people say I have very cold eyes, at least when I want to use them that way. I did now.

"Here's the thing," I said softly. "You were tailing me. As you have discovered, two can play at that game. I know you're a cop, but are you working for the police on this or Thomas Lu?"

If Miss Blue's eyes were wide before, now they were positively huge. Her lips had stopped moving and just for one magic moment, I could read her thoughts. She was going to say that this was a police gig. No one in their right mind was going to mess with the boys and girls in Singapore blue. That was her theory and she was wrong.

I reached out and grabbed her pert right nipple with my left hand and laid the blade of the knife on the swell of her breast beside it.

"Before you say a word, consider this," I paused and touched the edge of the blade to the edge of her nipple. Yes, it was cruel and sexist and all that shit, but I needed the correct answer and fast. Would I have cut her? I don't think so, but there must always be a first, I guess. "I will know if you lie and if you do, you will lose a nipple. If you lie again you will lose your life."

It was then I knew for a fact that she wasn't going to lie as the acrid smell of urine filled the bedroom.

"Thomas Lu," she blurted. "I did this for Mr Lu."

"He pays you to work for him?"

"Yes, little things. Sometimes...like today he has me follow people."

"He obviously gave you a good description to work with."

"Yes!"

I had to figure that Kaylin had described me to Lu in some detail and he had given Miss Blue that description.

"You told him you lost me?"

"Yes. He was very angry."

"Your police bosses would be very interested to know of your relationship with Mr Lu," I suggested. I released her nipple and removed the knife from her breast, slipping it back into the sheath built into my boot. I made a show of pulling down the cuff of my jeans. The pantomime was simply to reinforce the fact that we were done. I now had the power. I didn't need a weapon. I literally and figuratively had her career and maybe her life in my hands at this instant in time.

"Please." Miss Blue's huge eyes blinked in terror. "That would mean prison. Being a policewoman in prison would be my death."

"Perhaps we can come to an understanding," I said as I stood and looked down at her. Bondage has never been my thing. I rolled Miss Blue onto her side and undid the knot in the scarf. It was too pretty to be cut. That done, I handed her the towel. "Dry yourself off, find some clothes and we'll put you back in Mr Lu's good books and get me out of his sights."

Thomas Lu flipped shut his cellphone and settled back into the Bentley's luxurious leather seats. Things were getting better. First the girl had lost the man David Crewe. Then she had found him again. He had been coming out of the Singapore Airlines office on Orchard. Going inside, she had used her warrant card as leverage. Lucy Pang had discovered that David Crewe was booked on a late afternoon flight to Sydney the following day.

"Mr Crewe," Thomas Lu murmured, "I think you have just saved your own life." With the man booked to leave Singapore, he, Thomas Lu, had no more to fear from Sami Somsak's assassin. Now he could concentrate on getting a share of the Intella Island project for himself, and he had plans for that. There was nothing like the threat of scandal to bring reluctant colleagues on side, and he had the means of creating considerable scandal. Thomas Lu flipped open his cellphone again and selected a number from his address book. The phone range twice before it was answered.

"Mr Lu!'

"Yes, Kaylin. I'm sorry, my dear, I was a little hasty during our last conversation. How would you like to come and work for me, in my home? I have a feeling that there is much we could do for each other."

"Yes, Mr Lu, yes!"

"Good. You know the address. Please come as soon as you can, we have things to discuss."

"I will be there within the hour."

"Thank you, Kaylin."

For the second time in a matter of minutes, Thomas Lu hung up his phone. He was smiling. He had a plan. He would use the woman's insatiable appetite to his own advantage. He had no interest in the female of the species in any sexual manner. However, to use her and her eager body to help him achieve his ends, that was another matter. He would arrange it so that she had every partner she could handle and more, including the chairman of the Intella syndicate, Morris Boon Meng. Lu well knew that Meng, on the surface at least, was a long-married, straight-laced pillar of the community. Behind the façade, however, Lu had proof that the chairman had a soft spot or, Lu chuckled, a hard rod for a particular type of woman. That woman was epitomised by Kaylin, who would enjoy playing totally uninhibited sex games with other women and any number of men while he watched and eventually joined in.

The young policewoman and I had parted company as co-conspirators and almost friends. To sweeten the pot, I gave her a hundred dollars and told her to buy a new bed cover. She had made coffee for us and told me what little she actually knew about Thomas Lu. It was apparent that she had no idea of the extent of his villainy. She had just been asked, through another cop, if she were interested in doing a little moonlighting, basically as a private eye for a wealthy businessman. Always in need of extra cash, she had agreed, and until this very day she had done nothing that could even be remotely termed as illegal, other than accepting cash for trailing people and reporting back to Lu or his people.

Of course, moonlighting is an absolute no-no as far as her employers were concerned. To be caught out doing it, especially for someone like Thomas Lu, would be instant dismissal at least and perhaps a prison term. I assured Miss Blue that this was the end of it. I also suggested that she forget all about Thomas Lu. She took that on board and saw me to the lift. I caught a cab down on Cantonment Road and headed for the Newton Circus hawker centre.

I was late for my lunch with Sami, but that didn't matter in the scheme of things. Over our meal, I told him of my eventful morning. He approved of what I had done. I gave him Lucy Pang's mobile number. There would maybe come a time when he would need her services himself.

"We are on schedule," Sami said as he demolished yet another fish head curry. He had a thing for them, no doubt. I stuck with Soon Wah's fishball noodles and a side dish of cockles and sausage. I was hungry! Somewhere along the way, I had missed out on breakfast.

"Any sign of that bitch Kaylin?"

"No. I've got eyes out and about, but no one has found anything out. She's gone to ground," Sami replied, sipping at his water. I had the inevitable bottle of Tiger. I joined him in a silent toast. Somewhere, some day, Kaylin would put her head above the parapet and Sami or I or one of ours would be waiting to take it off.

After lunch, Sami went on his solitary way, a little old man lugging along his battered little suitcase. He told me he was going back to Nassim Hill. I realised that I hadn't even asked him exactly where his bolthole was and he hadn't offered to tell me. That was the way he worked. As I watched him go out of sight, I decided that he really deserved an Oscar for his performance.

I decided to walk to the apartment. I felt confident that Lu had called off his hounds. Why risk another incident when I was scheduled to get out of his patch in a day's time?

On the way back, I came across a mock Irish pub in a shopping block. I sat on the terrace over a beer and a cigarette and watched the traffic roll on by for a while before heading on down to Cairnhill Rise.

I didn't bother doing the subterfuge number of going underground when I arrived at the complex. I think I was a little too relaxed or I would have seen it coming. I was about fifty metres from the entrance to the apartment complex when a large white sedan swept into the kerb beside me and stopped sharply with a squeal of rubber. I was totally out in the open. The nearest cover was metres away. Lost in a fucking daydream, I was toast if this was one of Lu's moves.

47

"Mr Swann, a word?'

The voice was smooth but strong. The fact that this guy knew my real name was enough to anchor me to the spot. I turned towards the white sedan. It was a medium-sized Mercedes. The tyres needed blackening and the wheel trims deserved a polish. Funny the inconsequential things you notice when your life is potentially on the line. The speaker was in the rear seat, the tinted window was down but no gun was pointed my way yet. Okay, I was still alive, and the speaker wasn't Lu. Was this the moment the Singapore police department got their man? Or was I about to die here on the streets of one of Singapore's most illustrious enclaves at the hands of an old adversary?

The man leaned forward so his face was framed in the car window. There was still no weapon pointing at me. He held both of his hands up for me to see. They were empty. I stepped closer to the car. The front passenger door began to open. I put the sole of my boot on it and forced it shut.

"Everyone stays inside the car!"

"As he says. Stay inside," the speaker ordered, then he turned back to me. I knew the man although I had never met him. There was a wicked scar across his forehead. He was smiling at me, a pearly white smile against his swarthy complexion.

"Mr Marco Mendez?" I ventured. The man in the car removed his sunglasses as he nodded.

"Yes, Mr Swann. Would you agree to sit with me for a moment or two? I have something to discuss with you."

I checked out the rest of the car. There was a man in front, the guy who had started to get out, doubtless to frisk me or for some other purpose. Beside the minder was the driver, a nervous-looking local. Marco Mendez was alone in the rear seat. I nodded and reached for the door handle. Marco moved across. "Go around a large block, driver," he said. "We need ten minutes to talk."

Given the Mendez brothers' reputation for violence, I hitched the cuff of my left leg as I sat, just in case I had to pull my blade in a hurry. The car cruised away from the kerb.

"You know my name." I stated.

"We have done some research," Marco responded. "We looked closely at Mr Somsak and his friends."

"Sizing up the opposition?" I suggested. Marco Mendez laughed.

"Exactly, and that was before we decided that to go up against Mr Somsak, especially on his own territory, would be extremely stupid and doomed to failure. Just as Mr Somsak coming up against us in our own country would be equally foolhardy." Marco paused, his hand slid into his jacket. I tensed, mentally planning to block the hand with my right, while driving the edge of my left into his Adam's apple. The Colombian shook his head, reading my thoughts.

"Cigars, Mr Swann, Quai D'Orsay from Cuba. I favour their panatellas. Do join me." Mendez took a leather cigar case from his inside pocket. He removed the end of the case and slid two long, thin cigars part way out. I took one and peeled off the wrapping. Marco did likewise and lit up for the both of us using a diamond-encrusted lighter. He then leaned back in his seat, intent no doubt on enjoying his cigar. I did likewise. What the hell, a good cigar is a good cigar, no matter who gives it to you.

"Delicious, don't you think?" Marco blew out a stream of the sweet smoke as I savoured my first hit. There was no doubt the Colombian drug lord had taste, at least when it came to cigars. "You are a very dangerous and resourceful man, Mr Swann. I congratulate you on having stayed alive for so long in a very dangerous occupation."

"I'm retired now," I said taking another larger bite of the expensive smoke. "I agree, delicious!"

"Yes, Mr Swann, it is a premium cigar." Mendez chuckled. "But as for your retirement, that makes me smile. You will never retire, as

I will never retire. That is the sort of people we are."

"Maybe," I replied noncommittally. "Why are you here?"

"We heard about the bomb, naturally. We know that Mr Somsak has left Singapore and that Thomas Lu is still alive. I have come here to take care of the man who killed my brother." Marco sent another plume of smoke into the air. "We need him dead. It is a matter of family honour."

I sat in silence for a moment. Marco was looking at me. I made a decision and removed my cell from my pocket. I tapped out Sami's number. He answered within seconds. It wasn't the old man's voice.

"Yes, Daniel?"

"I am in a car with Marco Mendez. He and Carlos are concerned that you are not in Singapore and that Lu is still alive. Perhaps you would like to reassure him that everything is proceeding as it should." I handed the phone to the Colombian drug lord.

The conversation was a long one and one-sided, with Sami doing all of the talking. When the call reached its conclusion, Marco handed the phone back. He was smiling and nodding.

"Mr Somsak is a very clever operator. I look forward to witnessing tomorrow night's performance."

I had no idea exactly what "performance" that was. At this moment in time, Marco Mendez obviously knew more than I did about what was going to take place. I glanced outside the car. We had completed the long block and were pulling up back outside the apartment.

"Just one word of caution for Mr Somsak, please. It is not a threat, Mr Swann." Mendez used his cigar as a pointer to emphasize his point. "Lu must die tomorrow night as planned. If he doesn't, we will immediately take whatever measures necessary to kill him. The bomb at your cemetery will perhaps be a firecracker compared to what we are prepared to do to remove him if Mr Somsak fails."

I opened the door and sat for a moment. "I have heard that some of your, shall we say, terminations, have been quite spectacular. Not subtle to be sure, but definitely spectacular."

Marco Mendez laughed. It was a big laugh. "Yes, Mr Swann, we do it big to send a clear message to our enemies. Our messages usually get through, in most cases anyway. Your Mr Somsak likes to be a little more, as you said, subtle. Each to his own."

"Indeed, Mr Mendez. Each to his own! Enjoy the show," I added, stabbing right out there into the dark as I got out of the car.

"We'll be waiting," came the response through the closing door.

With that, Marco Mendez disappeared into the evening traffic and I went up to the penthouse to ponder the day's happenings and try and guess what Sami had in mind for the following night. The fact was plain enough: if we screwed up, Singapore was going to see the biggest bang since WW2, and that would not be pretty.

"Welcome, Kaylin. I am so sorry about the little misunderstanding we had." Thomas Lu was all smiles. Kaylin was also happy. Happy she had the protection of Thomas Lu against her former employer, happy that the promise from Lu would accomplish all that she dreamed of and more as far as serving her particular addiction went.

Lu personally showed her to her quarters. She was not just staying in a room with a bed and a bathroom; this was a mini apartment. There was a bedroom with a huge bed, plus a spacious *en suite*. The apartment was completed by a lounge with a small kitchen attached.

"I think you will be very comfortable here," Lu said. "I would ask you not to bring guests back here unless by prior arrangement with myself," he added. "Security, my dear."

"Of course, Mr Lu." That did disappoint her, but having Lu's protection meant more.

"We will, however, bring some entertainment in and you will certainly be able to indulge and participate if you want to, of course."

Kaylin wanted that very much and she told her new master so. Thomas Lu smiled at her eagerness. The next few days are going to be very interesting, Lu thought as he made to leave his new houseguest's suite.

"By the way," he paused in the doorway, "I believe you left virtually all of your possessions behind at Somsak's apartment."

"Yes, I left in a great hurry."

"Tomorrow we will arrange a shopping expedition for you. I'm sure we can obtain most of what you lost. At my expense, of course."

Lu departed, leaving Kaylin wondering if all her Christmases had come at once. As a Christian, she believed in Christmas. However, something about Thomas Lu sent a shiver down her spine. She knew deep down that he didn't believe in anything but Thomas Lu.

"I had no idea that they were back."

"Slipped in quietly through some back door perhaps. He didn't mention if Carlos was here with him."

"No, but Marco has brought a team with him it appears. The chaos of the past weeks has distracted me," Sami said. Even through my cell, he sounded tired.

"You lost a lot of people," I countered. "You can't be everywhere."

"You are right as usual, Daniel. But still, I do not like it when something like this happens. I need the Mendez brothers to stay away from Singapore. If they detonate this bomb that Marco hinted that they have with them, this place will lock down so tight that the Intella Island project will stall. I can't have that, Daniel. It is too important to me."

"Then we had better make sure that tomorrow night's little soirée doesn't fail. When are you going to explain what the hell is going to happen and who will be involved? Lu has a fucking army in the building; we're going to need our own army."

"No, Daniel. There will just be the three of us. You, me and K, that's all we'll need. I'll come to the penthouse mid-morning and I'll explain it all then." The phone went dead. I closed my handset and pondered what to do with the evening that was falling outside. I was twitchy, unsettled. I needed to do something, anything, and I wasn't in the mood for a run.

In the end I showered, dressed and headed down to Orchard. I had a meal in a restaurant in Peranakan Place and then followed that with a couple of beers at a pub before I headed on up the street to Orchard Towers. I'd heard about the infamous "Four Floors of

Whores" and figured it was time I paid the place a visit. I wasn't looking for a pick-up, but curiosity has always been a big factor in my makeup.

I know most of the fleshpots of Thailand well. I'd spent a lot of time working in the underbelly of the place over some fifteen years based in Bangkok. The Towers experience was pretty much the same as many of the Thai meat streets and clubs. Wall-to-wall pussy. There was a bit more clothing evident than in many of the Thai bars and clubs, but the faces were the same. There were Thai girls by the score, Chinese, Filipina, Malaysian, even Japanese and more than a few Europeans. I didn't know whether to be elated or depressed by the abundance of willing flesh, albeit available for a price. I guess you pay one way or another anyway. Who is to say that a cash transaction for sex is any less honest than a shitty marriage with its constant bartering, bribes and bullshit?

I left the Towers alone. Despite the hundreds of distractions that had thrown themselves my way, there was only one woman on my mind and she was sealed in a coffin waiting for the time she was finally laid to rest. Yes, I was depressed. I stopped at a pub and had a beer and then another. There was a bottle of Jack Daniels calling me from the shelf. I ignored it and walked home. I was sober and sour. Not a good combination in Daniel Swann!

48

The day of Thomas Lu's impending death dawned with a clear sky. I felt as flat as I had when I'd gone to bed. I'd tried to put thoughts of Simone and what had been and might have been away into a deep place in my brain. It hadn't worked. As a result, I'd had a more or less sleepless night. Nightmare explosions and flying tombstones shattered what sleep I did manage to get.

I showered and dressed. I felt gritty and tired. Breakfast didn't hold any appeal, so I collected a pot of coffee from the kitchen and went through to Sami's study. There, I fired up the computer that had been cunningly built into the desk. The keyboard was on a sliding shelf that came out and then folded back over the edge of the desk. One touch of a key and the wide screen rose up vertically on the far side of the desk. It was a very sophisticated set-up and a very powerful computer.

I'm not a great one for emails; however, I keyed into my account and it was full of messages. I canned most. Annoying how, despite the number of SPAM filters in use, the shit still gets through. Two mails in particular, however, gained my undivided attention. One was from the beautiful Dr Sylvia Dixon, my former wife. She was getting married again. The mail was a week old. I replied that I was glad for her and clicked the send button. Was I pleased for her? I guess in a way I was. Sylvia was beautiful, smart and she deserved all the good things in life. We had been good together, but not good for each other.

The second email was from Sakura. She was asking how I was. What could I say? That I had lost the woman I maybe loved. That half the world wanted to kill me while the other half didn't care if I lived or died.

"Oh crap!" I snarled aloud at myself. "Stop feeling sorry for yourself, you sad fuck!" My cellphone went a moment or two later. It was Sami.

"Yes, Daniel," he said. "Stop feeling sorry for yourself!"

"You what?"

"I agree with you. Stop feeling sorry for yourself. Sylvia is getting married again. Sakura is calling to see how you are. As you have often said to me, life goes on, my friend."

"How do you know this?" The answer was obvious, Sami had bugged the office and wherever he was calling from, he had a monitoring system. He laughed.

"Go to my Samurai, Daniel. Lift off his helmet."

I did as Sami told me. I stepped around the figure to the rear. The fucking thing still gave me the shivers. I didn't want the arm that held that damned sword to suddenly come to life. I lifted off the ornate, full-face mask. There, in place of the mannequin's head, was a camera on a swivel mechanism. As I stood looking up at it, the camera moved without a sound. The lens turned 180 degrees and stared down at me. I moved past the warrior and put the helmet down on the desk. The camera followed me. I picked up the mobile and put it back to my ear.

"You look like shit."

"Thank you, Doctor," I replied. "I guess the microphone is in the armour."

"On his belt, actually. It's amazing what my Samurai sees. Our friend Kaylin indulged herself in here several times with a variety of playmates; including my brother, unfortunately."

"I didn't know you were into voyeurism," I said sarcastically.

"Only when my security is threatened," Sami responded smoothly.

"Sorry, my old friend, I'm a bit shitty-livered today!"

"It's called grief, Daniel. I'm feeling it too, but let us put Lu away, say farewell to the Mendez mob and bury our dead. Then we'll grieve properly."

"You're right," I replied. "Absolutely right. When are you coming in?"

"I'll be there in fifteen minutes."

"Roger that!"

I replaced the Samurai's mask and sat back down at the computer. I wrote to Sakura asking her how she was doing and told her I was fine. I ended by saying that I would come and see her in a few weeks. I sent the mail and then flicked into my bank account.

I had US$52 million plus change sitting warming itself in the Caribbean. There was some comfort in that, I guess. I poured another coffee, lit a cigarette and waited for Sami. Nicotine and caffeine, the diet of kings and killers!

I've always had a problem killing time leading up to an operation, and this day was no different. Sami came. We talked and he outlined his plan. It was simple. It was, dare I say it, brilliant. Now I knew what he meant when he said that just three of us could storm Thomas Lu's fortress in the sky and take it. If all went well, Thomas Lu's death would appear to be a suicide. Failing that, it could be seen to be the final act in the gang war that the media and police still maintained had caused the dozens of deaths and injuries in Singapore in the past few months.

However, if things went totally out of control and we failed to kill Lu, the magnificent condo block in which Thomas Lu lived would be reduced to rubble in seconds. The Mendez brothers always kept their promises, according to their legend anyway. Now was not the time to check the veracity of that legend.

Their cartel had blown up the main prison in Bogota in 2003 in a controlled blast. While it had freed dozens of their own men, who obviously knew it was coming, it had also killed two hundred other inmates, many of whom were members of rival drug gangs. Fifty police and prison guards also died in the blast.

The cartel was also blamed for an explosion that completely destroyed the mansion of a legislator from La Palma, chairman of the anti-drug wing of the government in neighbouring Panama. Thirty people died in the blast, all because the official had aligned himself firmly with the Americans and introduced an anti-smuggling regime that seriously hindered the Mendez cartel's movement of drugs across that border and into vessels bound for the US and Europe.

There had been other bombings attributed to the cartel, many of them, so both Sami and I knew full well that Marco's threats were far from idle.

"It will work, Daniel, and it will appear as a suicide. I can see the headlines: 'Financial woes lead Singapore businessman to suicide!' It has a nice ring to it, doesn't it?" Those had been Sami's last words on the coming night's activities. He vanished, or should I say the little old man vanished, and I was left waiting. It was thirty-five degrees outside with a humidity rating in the high nineties, so naturally I went for a run.

Thomas Lu had someone watching the entrance to Sami Somsak's building. The watcher wasn't the policewoman. He had phoned her and asked her to do it, but she'd told him she was on shift, so he used another watcher, a former cop with a serious alcohol problem. He worked in return for whisky.

The watcher reported that Crewe had run out of the complex dressed in a tracksuit at a few minutes to noon. Lu wondered briefly at that. Supposedly David Crewe was flying out to Australia this day, in just a few hours. What was he doing out running? Then Lu shrugged. No matter what he did in the meantime. As long as this man, Somsak's hired killer, was gone by day's end, he could forget him.

Lu opened a drawer on his desk and flicked a switch on the panel inside. The flat screen television mounted on the wall opposite his desk flared into life. A basketball game was on. Lu liked watching athletes at play. The sound was off. He pressed another button and the image changed. Now he was in the bedroom of Kaylin's suite. The woman was there. She was trying on clothes, of which there were many, both in bags on the floor and lying across her bed.

Undressing, she pulled a dress over her head. But for a pair of high-heeled shoes, she was naked. Despite his preference for men, Lu could still appreciate the female form, albeit from a purely aesthetic perspective. He could see why men such as Chairman Meng would be attracted to the likes of her.

He watched as Kaylin lifted a bag from the floor and spread its contents onto the bed. There was black leather, silver studs and chains. This was the type of costume that he had seen Kaylin wearing in the photographs he had seen of her at play. She selected a pair of leather shorts and wriggled into them, parading in front of the full-mirrored wall beside the walk-in wardrobe. The shorts had a full-length zip that ran from the waistband at the front to the band at the back. The woman undid the zip and the crotch on the shorts parted. Kaylin's hands went between her legs. Watching her reflection, she stood there with her legs wide apart. She began to pleasure herself.

Fascinated by the pure wanton display on the screen in front of him, Thomas Lu found he was experiencing the beginnings of an erection. This was a first. Never before had a woman had that effect on him. He reached for the zip on his trousers and opened it, groping to free his penis. Perhaps, just perhaps, he would ask this woman to try and work her magic on him? Perhaps even this very evening!

49

It was time to move. Sami had planned everything to happen at midnight. At 11.30pm Sami, myself and K got into the plain white four-door utility that had appeared in the underground car park late in the afternoon. K was driving.

Sami sat up front with him, while I was in the back. All three of us were dressed in dark overalls. We were workers going on a late shift or coming off shift, even though our overalls were perhaps too clean for that scenario.

The guns and our other equipment were in a bag on the seat beside me. We weren't going prepared for a big firefight. There was a Browning each, silenced and with a shoulder holster and spare magazines, and each of us had a handheld stun gun. These were the torch-like devices, not the taser version that fired hooked darts with wires attached. These weapons had two metal prongs protruding from the front. The prongs were held against the unfortunate subject and the button on the body of the device pressed, sending 50,000 volts into the victim.

I'd been hit with tasers and stun guns several times over the years. It had been highly unpleasant, totally immobilising, and definitely something I did not want to experience again.

In addition to the automatics and stun guns were the inevitable gloves, along with restraints in the form of nylon cable ties. There was also a glasscutter, a small jemmy bar and other assorted bits and pieces. We also had balaclavas, not so much to hide our faces from Lu but to hide from any casual observers.

K obviously knew Singapore better than I did. Apart from my short hundred-yard dash on Sentosa, I'd never driven here at all. When on a mission in a strange country, I never wanted to drive.

Local talent was the best option. A skilled local driver, paid a great deal of cash and given a vehicle other than his own, usually led to him doing a great deal of inventive and often spectacular driving, especially when the proverbial shit hit the fan and a fast getaway was called for.

K wove a confusing trail around a network of streets. I was totally lost and said so.

"Keeping away from the obvious as always, Daniel," Sami said by way of response. K made another turn and there we were on Nassim Hill Road. We drove past Lu's tower and I noted a late model Rolls Royce parked in the forecourt. A chauffeur was rubbing a cloth over it. Poor arsehole! Midnight and you're waiting for some rich prick to stop shagging his mistress and let you take him home. Something like that anyway. Years ago, before I joined The Firm, I'd been a chauffeur for the diplomatic corps. Apart from the offensive and defensive driving courses, it had been a crap job.

My silent history lesson was interrupted as K turned us into our destination. It was the construction site Sami had been so interested in when he had been playing his little old man role. The gate rolled shut behind us. We were expected, it seemed.

Lights burned everywhere, both at ground level and in the lattice of beams rising above us. There was no one around but for the man who had opened the gate. Sami told me that because of noise restrictions, no construction was carried out at night.

We drove to the rear of the lot and parked behind the portable site office. It was time to cover up. I handed out the masks and the heavy rubber gloves we would wear instead of flash gloves. This was partially in deference to the stun guns. We pulled on the balaclavas and gloves before getting out of the utility. I hefted the sports bag as I slid out. Our next mode of transportation was waiting. The only other man on the building site was many, many metres above us, invisible against the black sky.

I couldn't verify it in the dark but I knew, from what Sami had told me, that the giant crane that stood on the site had grown considerably higher since I had seen it several days ago. Sami had hatched his plot well. There had been time enough to add another four sections to the crane's stem to raise it high enough to accomplish what he had in mind.

We were going to visit Thomas Lu, but we weren't going to have to fight our way up to him past his army of thugs. We were going to drop in from above. One of the disadvantages of living in a penthouse was about to be illustrated to the man; hopefully, that demonstration would take place in the most final and complete way possible.

The basket, a three-metre square, open-topped box constructed of heavy piping and steel mesh, was sitting on the ground waiting for us. The side gate was open. I went in first and laid our bag of goodies down on the wooden deck. The others followed. There was a handheld radio in a bracket on the top rail of the basket. K, the last one to climb in, pulled the gate shut and slid the retaining bolt across. Sami picked up the radio handset.

"We are ready. Take it away!"

No sooner had he uttered the instruction than we were airborne, silently gliding upwards, passing the lights on the floors of the skeleton building in rapid succession. Looking up, I still couldn't even see the boom of the crane against the black sky.

Now we were high above the site, still climbing and swinging through an arc as the crane driver somewhere above us manoeuvred us to our target. The lights of Singapore were laid out below us. Even at midnight, cars streamed on the streets. The city was wide awake.

We continue climbing. We were now above the crane operator. I could see his head and shoulders in the dim lights as he sat inside his tiny cab as we wound our way upward. Up where we were beyond the light haze from the buildings, the black night was crowded with stars. It would have been almost romantic in another setting. I could imagine lying on a hilltop on a rug with Simone and simply counting stars on a night like this.

"Fuck it!" I snapped. I could feel Sami and K both looking at me, although they were just shadowy outlines against the lights of the city. "Sorry," I muttered. "Just a bad memory."

"We all have those," Sami replied.

We were now sweeping over the apartment complex that separated the construction site from Lu's building. This was obviously the reason Sami had ordered the extensions fitted to the crane, to get it high enough to get over the intervening structure. I hadn't asked him how he'd organised that. Did he own the construction site? Had he simply bribed the right person or people? The fact was that somehow he had got it done.

Sami was now working the radio as we started to drop down towards our target. The crane operator was now flying blind. It was up to a combination of Sami's precise instructions and the driver's skills. K and I pulled on our shoulder holsters and quickly checked our weapons in the half-light. They had been checked before, several times, but old habits die hard. I put a stun gun into one pocket and a bundle of cable ties in another. I hitched the jemmy bar through the belt on my overall. I was ready for whatever came next.

Below, Lu's lair was rapidly coming up at us. The penthouse roof covered much of the actual area below us. There were, however, two large patios. One, the largest, was on the street side, while the second, adjoining one was on the side from which we were approaching. Looking down, I could see deck furniture on both patios. There was a covered pergola on the smaller one and a closed octagonal structure on the larger one.

"Spa," Sami said as he came to my side, pulling on his shoulder harness. "My bet is that Lu will be in there right about now. Michael said he is a real night owl and always has a late night spa before going to bed. Let's hope he's right or we'll have to go into the penthouse after him."

Sami started talking to the crane guy again. He slowed us down and moved our cage slightly to the right. Our landing zone was the smaller patio and we had to avoid the pergola.

The apartment building we were sliding by as we came down didn't have balconies facing us but there were windows. Would anyone be looking out of them? Would they actually see the basket? Would they see what was about to happened on the terraces below? Too much speculation is bad for one. I stopped asking, "What if?" and concentrated on what I could control.

"We won't touch down, too much chance of noise. We'll hover and jump."

"Done," I agreed. There was no wind, so the cage could just hang there while we did what we had to. I held my Browning at the ready. I couldn't see any of Lu's people on either of the terraces, but it was possible there was a man on watch inside the building. Unless Lu was an exhibitionist, it was doubtful he would have anyone close enough to watch or overhear him and his playmates at bathtime. I didn't know the guy, but I was hoping I was right in my assumption.

We crept down to a metre off the patio deck when Sami gave the word to stop. The basket jerked to a halt. K eased the bolt on the gate out of its cleat and carefully swung it open. He used a cable tie to fasten it so it couldn't swing and make any noise. There was little noise up here, other than the whisper of the wind and the hum of the traffic far below. These sounds were punctuated by the occasional aircraft passing overhead. The night outside the subdued patio lighting was as black as velvet. It was studded with stars. A perfect night in Singapore and a perfect night to kill Thomas Lu.

K was the first down, Sami next. I brought up the rear. The windows and the one sliding door on the wall facing us were all closed, as well as the drapes. That was a bonus. K led the way to the corner of the penthouse. The bathhouse was fifteen metres away, half way along the second side of the penthouse. There were uncovered windows and light spilled out from inside the penthouse itself. Dim lights glowed through the darkened glass of the spa.

If Lu were inside the spa, would he see us coming across the face of the penthouse and sound the alarm? We eased back from the corner. The only logical approach was to pull back and move around the edge of the patio and come in from the street side where there was little light. The door to the spa house was nearest to the wide, uncovered double doors leading into the penthouse. Anyone inside the penthouse would probably be able to see us as we came around the front. Was there anyone inside?

There was a sound from the spa. A woman laughed and there was the unintelligible response from someone else, a male. Using hand signs, it was decided that K and I would take the circuitous route while Sami would stay at the corner of the building and give us what cover he could.

I pressed close to the glass. How many people were in the spa? I could hear the voices clearly now. Lu, no doubt, but the woman, who was she? He was gay, so what was happening? Was there another silent partner in there as well? I listened for a moment longer. Lu was obviously enjoying whatever was going on.

"You are surprised?" the woman was saying. She was laughing, her voice teasing.

"Very. You are very good," the man I had to assume was Lu replied.

"I know," the woman chuckled. "Now lie back and imagine I am your favourite boy."

That was the end of the conversation for the moment. Who was the woman? Her presence meant that we now had to deal with two people. We had factored in the likelihood that Lu might have a boy with him, but what if there were three in the spa? A double-suicide yes, but a triple? That could get messy.

So my attempt at deciphering what was going on inside the spa and the number of bodies involved was inconclusive. We had a minimum of two and a maximum of I had no idea how many. Whatever, we were going in. K and I split and one of us came around each side of the spa house. We were on our bellies, keeping below the tall black glass windows. Sami, meanwhile, was crouched at the corner of the main building with his Browning held in both hands, the long silencer pointing across the face of the building. I could see directly through the double patio doors. There was no one in the lounge beyond the doors and no sign of anyone in the lighted rooms on my side of the spa. Hopefully it was the same for K on his side.

There were more human sounds from inside the spa above that of the pumping equipment. I moved to the front of the spa house. K was waiting. I signalled for him to get the outward-opening door while I did the bust-in. I had the Browning in my right hand. I transferred it to my left. Yes, I am ambidextrous when it comes to guns. I put the stun gun in my right. I had a plan for that. Electricity and water are great playmates.

I nodded to K. He pulled the door open and I went through.

50

The interior of the spa was surprisingly large. The pool itself was maybe built for eight or ten people. There were only two in it. Thomas Lu, who was lying back against the spa surround, had one arm on the edge. The other, the one attached to his injured shoulder, was crossed over his chest and held by a strap. Lu's long legs were stretched out in front of him, resting on the bath's central seating core. On Lu's left side, a woman was kneeling in water up to her shoulders. Her mouth and right hand were working diligently on Lu's erect penis. The woman was Kaylin.

Thomas Lu's eyes snapped open as I arrived at the edge of the bath.

"Greetings, Mr Lu, and you too, Kaylin. So pleased to find you both here and enjoying yourself."

"Thomas, I never knew you had it in you." Sami was at my shoulder, the muzzle of his Browning aimed directly at Lu's open mouth.

Kaylin had stopped pleasuring Lu and was staring at us, her face going the colour of chalk under the glow from the spa. She looked as if she were building to scream. I pushed the head of my stun gun into the water and pressed the go button.

The stun gun crackled and buzzed. The static tableaux in the water suddenly became very mobile. One could even say the motion was frenzied. Kaylin's body jerked and fell backwards into the rolling water, while Lu's long frame contracted into a fetal position and rolled off the seat into the water.

"That works," I said to Sami.

"Very effective," he agreed. "K has the watch!"

"Leave her in the water. She accidentally drowns and remorseful

Thomas Lu commits suicide. Another take to be considered," I suggested. Lu's face came above the surface of the water. He gasped in air. Kaylin was also gaining some control of her limbs. She heaved herself upwards like a breaching whale to stand swaying, waist deep in the water. She coughed out water and then pulled in a deep breath. I put the head of my stun gun back into the water and pressed the button. Both of them vanished back under the water, limbs thrashing.

"I could get to enjoy this."

"Yes, Daniel. But let's get it over with."

"You're right, of course!" I carefully wiped the stun gun dry on my overall and pocketed it for the moment. I didn't want to experience any reverse blast if I got my glove wet.

Was I a sadist? Perhaps I was, at least I was as far as seeking revenge for my dead Simone, and for Jo, and all those who'd died at the cemetery. The kids especially. I was enjoying bringing the pain and the understanding that death was just around the corner to Lu and to the cold-hearted bitch in the spa with him.

Sami holstered his gun, as did I. They weren't needed at the moment. Lu was back on the surface of the bath and breathing heavily. The good thing about mullet-style haircuts is that they provide a very good handle in a fight, or in this case as a lever to get Lu out of the spa. I grabbed a handful of hair and simply pulled him out of the bath and over the edge, letting him go when he hit the rubberised mat on the floor.

There he was in the ugly, naked flesh. The man who had killed Simone and all the others. He lay on the floor gasping for breath, terrified, his eyes bulging out of his head. He was skinny, almost a stick insect, and he was as pale as a corpse. His penis had wilted. That was understandable—50,000 volts will do that to you every time. Lu opened his mouth, whether to beg or shout I had no idea. Sami leaned down and pushed his stun gun into Lu's groin. Thomas Lu would have screamed his agony if he had been able.

"You're sinking to my level," I told him.

"Sometimes one just can't help oneself, Daniel."

I looked into the spa. Kaylin had come to the surface. She lay there, face up, her eyes wide, her mouth working on words and breath. The plea was coming and I didn't want to hear it. I didn't want her to have another breath.

"Excuse me for a moment," I said to Sami as I put my gloved hand over the woman's face and pushed her head under the water. Her hands grabbed at my wrists and her legs kicked wildly, but I held on, and on, and on, and finally there was a big burst of bubbles and her struggles ceased. The hands fell from my wrists, but I continued to hold Kaylin under the water until I was sure she was dead.

Meanwhile, Sami had called K. There was still no sign of life inside the penthouse. No doubt there were people in the foyer on the other side of the building and we knew about all the other troops. However, Lu's desire for total privacy in his impenetrable luxury nest was leading to his downfall.

Satisfied that Kaylin was no longer in the land of the living, I helped Sami and K get Thomas Lu into one of the plastic pool chairs that were arrayed around the inside of the spa house. We all knew the rest of the plan. It's easier to carry an unconscious or incapacitated person in a chair than by trying to manoeuvre them manually, especially a slippery, gangly, naked body such as the one we were dealing with.

In deference to Sami's still-mending wrist, K and I each took a side of the chair while Sami went ahead of us to check that none of Lu's heavies had miraculously appeared. They hadn't. We were almost at the edge of the terrace when Lu started to stir. Sami easily remedied that. K and I put down the chair and he pressed his stun gun against the back of Lu's neck. Any pleas or resistance he might have offered were gone in a violent spasm that unfortunately threw him out of the chair.

K and I retrieved the stricken man. However, because we were only a metre or two from our destination, we left the chair where it was and half-walked and half-carried Lu to the railing. We leaned him there, giving him a moment or two to see his fate.

In the street below, across from the complex's entrance, a white car was parked. It was a Mercedes. Despite the acute angle, I could see a faint red spark in the open rear window. Marco Mendez was sitting enjoying one of his Quai D'Orsay panatellas while he waited for the very final curtain to come down on Thomas Lu.

Lu was making gurgling noises in the back of his throat. His last pleas, which even if we had heard and understood them, were falling on the deafest of ears. He started urinating. Hell, I would have been doing that as well, standing there contemplating the long drop ahead of me.

"You killed Stanley and too many innocent people, Thomas. Time to go to hell. Goodbye!" Sami delivered his eulogy.

K and I picked Lu up, one of us on each elbow. He moaned in agony as I grabbed his strapped arm. K nodded to me. We drew Lu back from the edge. Then K and I stooped simultaneously. We each grabbed one of Thomas Lu's skinny ankles, stepped forward and heaved upwards and outwards, releasing our grips at the apex of the arc. Thomas Lu cleared the balcony by a metre as he soared out into space.

"I guess you could say that's a perfect Singapore Sling Shot," I said to no one in particular.

"Bad pun, Daniel," Sami replied.

We watched as Lu hit the forecourt below, inches from the parked Rolls Royce. The chauffeur had just finished wiping it down and got back into the car. The owner of the limousine was lucky. I doubted his insurance company would have met any damage caused by this act of God. Of course, there would be a few bloodstains to be removed from the side of the car.

Thomas Lu's blood was pooling against the white marble paving stones on the forecourt. Across the road, a car horn sounded once and the white Mercedes pulled away. Ruby sparks exploded momentarily on the road beside it. The colours of the sparks matched the flare of the car's tail lights as it disappeared down the road. One day soon, I was going to look at getting some Quai D'Orsay panatellas. I'd enjoyed the one I had smoked with Marco.

"Goodbye, Marco," Sami said. "Let's go!" We started back towards the side patio. I detoured slightly, just to check.

Kaylin was floating face down in the spa. Satisfied, I joined the others and we were whisked away into the night sky. Job done!

We were high above the penthouse and just starting our arc back towards the construction site when K pointed down at the front of the apartment building. The uniformed chauffeur and several other people were clustered around Lu's body. Lights were coming on in the lower levels of the building. However, what had attracted K's attention were the two furniture removal vans that had appeared from the condominium block's underground garage. The two vans drove out of the complex nose to tail and vanished away down Nassim Hill Road.

"Jesus," I muttered. "He wasn't joking."

"No," Sami replied. "I don't think humour is one of Marco's strong points."

"You know, you could honestly say that by killing Thomas Lu, we have saved Singapore from an absolute disaster."

"Yes, Daniel. You could say that, but I don't think we'll say it out loud," my friend replied with a faint chuckle. "Now we have to bury our people and get on with our lives."

"Yeah," I agreed, but I was wondering about life beyond this moment, beyond Simone's funeral. What lay ahead for Daniel Swann?

Maybe I would try to get a real job, one that didn't involve death and destruction. Problem was my CV was both very specific and very much out of date.

Epilogue

We buried Simone and the others. Sami used considerable influence and money to purchase a huge number of adjoining plots in the cemetery. One of the ironies of this, of course, was that after fifteen years the bodies would be dug up and the bones reburied in smaller plots or cremated. I wondered if I would be there to collect Simone's bones.

As I was leaving Singapore, Thomas Lu's suicide had been replaced as the headline of the day by the discovery in Sembawang of two trucks loaded with nitro-based fertiliser. This was the same stuff that was the explosive of choice for terrorists around the world. The detonating mechanisms were in place, but not connected.

It was suspected that religious or political extremists had perhaps spirited it in from Malaysia and were waiting for the moment to position it and take out whatever targets they had selected. Relations between the two countries deteriorated considerably once that viewpoint was made public.

As I was making my way to the KrisFlyer lounge in Terminal Three, prior to boarding my flight, I had a moment of near panic. Two police officers were standing on the concourse. One was male, the other female. They were both armed with the standard issue sidearm. I'd never had a close look, at them but they appeared to be S&W model 64s in .38 special or something similar. They were more effective than a brick—just!

However, standing further along the concourse was another group of three policemen. These were wearing combat overalls and were all armed with submachine guns. Okay, armed anti-terrorist types were a common enough sight in airports worldwide. Were they looking for me? Or someone like me? They seemed to be paying particular attention to European males.

With my shaven head encased in a cap and without my moustache, I didn't look like David Crewe. I was using another passport and another alias just in case Crewe had appeared on the police radar.

To have turned and walked away would have been too obvious. The policewoman was looking directly at me. It was now that I realised I knew her. This was Miss Blue, Lucy Pang Hooi Ming. She turned and said something to her companion and then came towards me. What had she said?

Behind the advancing policewoman, her male companion was speaking on his radio. Was the alarm going out? Miss Blue came to a halt in front of me. She put out a hand.

"Shake," she breathed. I took her hand and we shook hands. She was smiling. "They are looking for David Crewe."

"I'm not him," I replied under my breath, faking a laugh. "I have another identity."

"Good. You don't look like the image we have." It was then I saw the computer-generated snapshot she was holding. It was a variation on the one Sami had prepared, but this time it was closer to the way I used to look. "I don't think Mr Crewe should come back to Singapore, ever!"

"He won't. Thank you!"

"We are even."

"Yes we are."

With that, she waved to me and went to rejoin her companion. He lowered his radio handpiece and spoke urgently to her. Suddenly they were on the move away down the concourse. I breathed out and carried on towards the lounge. The heavily armed trio didn't even look my way.

"Thank you, Officer," I whispered as I moved on to the lounge. So they had a profile, but as yet, not a name. If and when I came back, I would have to be someone completely different in every way.

So now, in the guise of Donald Wrathe, sales manager for Kervon Security Systems Inc, I am sitting in an air-conditioned metal tube thirty-five thousand feet above the South China Sea, sipping at a Jack

Daniels. I am flying home to Hong Kong. In a few weeks, I will go to the white palace at Phetchaburi and meet with Sakura.

Sami still wants me to join him. Maybe I will, maybe I won't. My world at this moment in time is full of maybes. By the way, I received an invitation to Sylvia's wedding. I am considering going to it. Why not?

I don't think, however, I'll be asked to be best man or give the bride away—I did that years ago and it still hurts.

ANOTHER DANIEL SWANN THRILLER!

DEATH IN THE KINGDOM

Andrew Grant

British agent Daniel Swann fled Thailand after murdering the son of the Kingdom's top underworld boss. Now he is back, ordered by his government to recover a small black box from the bottom of the Andaman Sea. Business as usual, he doesn't ask questions. But as his friends are beheaded one by one and he is pursued by CIA agents, Swann realises his mission has become personal. Someone wants him dead.

Trying to stay alive on the streets of Bangkok, Swann engages in a deadly game of cat and mouse. When he finally discovers the contents of the black box, he is caught up in a government-level conspiracy. But with his enemy always one step ahead, Swann knows he is being betrayed. So he turns to the only people he can trust—the underworld.

Praise for *Death in the Kingdom*

> "This book really is a cracking yarn ... If you have spent some time in the military, the accurate description of the weaponry will lend much weight to the plot ... *Death in the Kingdom* will have all those who enjoy a good thriller asking for more. According to the publishers, Andrew Grant is already writing the next Daniel Swann epic. Look for it, but read this one first!" *Pattaya Mail*

ISBN: 978-981-05-8492-4
(www.monsoonbooks.com.sg/bookpage_0584924.html)